Praise for
Dave Wolverton

"Wolverton . . . is moving through the science fiction galaxy at warp speed."—*Portland Oregonian* on *Beyond the Gate*

"When you want to slap a character for her naive arrogance on one page and comfort her on the next, you know you've found a writer with a gift for characterization. Dave Wolverton has that gift. He also writes a neatly plotted novel that combines swashbuckling action with hi-tech SF. . . . This is an enjoyable story. Recommended."—*Starlog* on *The Golden Queen*

"A rainbow mixture of technology and mythology, filled with vibrant colors, larger-than-life heroes, and thunderous action. A grand quest across a kaleidoscope of parallel worlds."—Kevin J. Anderson, author *Star Wars: The Jedi Academy Trilogy* on *The Golden Queen*

"As rip-snorting an adventure as one could hope to find."—Orson Scott Card on *Path of the Hero*

"No one who has read much of Wolverton doubts that he is a major talent."—Algis Budrys

BEYOND THE GATE

DAVE WOLVERTON

A TOM DOHERTY ASSOCIATES BOOK
NEW YORK

This is a work of fiction. All the characters and events portrayed in this book are either fictitious or are used fictitiously.

BEYOND THE GATE

Copyright © 1995 by Dave Wolverton

Cover art by Tim White
Edited by David G. Hartwell

A Tor Book
Published by Tom Doherty Associates, Inc.
175 Fifth Avenue
New York, NY 10010

Tor Books on the World Wide Web:
http://www.tor.com

Tor® is a registered trademark of Tom Doherty Associates, Inc.

ISBN: 0-812-55031-5
Library of Congress Card Catalog Number: 95-6320

First edition: August 1995
First mass market edition: July 1996

Printed in the United States of America

0 9 8 7 6 5 4 3 2 1

For Paul Toups, the master
of Froghollow Farm, who once said,
"You should write a book!"
Now look what you've got me into.

One

___

After his recent adventures with Gallen and Maggie, risking his hide on half a dozen planets, Orick felt that his life was somehow charmed. A few weeks ago, he couldn't have imagined sitting here, a hairsbreadth from winning the title of Primal Bear.

Along the banks of Obhiann Fiain the bears had gathered by the hundreds for the annual Salmon Fest. The icy waters of Obhiann Fiain thundered through a gorge, and many a cub was perched on the large rocks, waiting to swipe at any salmon that tried to leap past.

The older bears had gathered near the dark pines that morning. Fires burned low along the hillside, and salmon skewered on stakes were cooking slowly so that smoke crept along the ground.

But Orick the bear did not have his mind on fish. After over a week of athletic competitions and feasting, Orick felt as sated as he'd been in his life—or at least as far as his gustatory appetites were concerned.

But now came the final athletic event of the Salmon Fest—

the much-anticipated pig toss. After all the contests—the tree-climbing, the wrestling matches, the log pull, and the salmon-catch—Orick lacked only five points to take the lead in the competitions. The pig toss would make or break him.

Orick's nerves were frayed. He watched dozens of younger bears toss the "pigs"—burlap bags filled with forty pounds of rock. Legend said that in the old days, bears had actually tossed live piglets, but Orick couldn't imagine his ancestors engaging in such brutish activities.

Anxiously Orick waited for the toss of old Mangan, an aging bear with an especially large snout and a blaze of white on his chest. For five years—since before Orick was even born—Mangan had held the title of Primal Bear for the twin counties, an honor which allowed him the privilege of selecting ten or twelve mates a year. Orick had matched him in nearly every competition.

The competitions proceeded. Each bear snagged a pig and then took it to the tossing ring—a small circle of stones. The bears in the crowd would cheer and jeer in their deep voices.

Orick watched the first few throws, his heart pounding. He wanted to win, could taste victory. He looked out over the crowd, scanning for the females he'd most admired during the past weeks. He particularly liked one big she-bear, one with a thick, glossy coat, long, shiny claws, and large teeth. Certainly there were some fine specimens in estrus, and their scent left Orick dizzy, reeling.

He met the eyes of one young she-bear, but the undisguised lust in her glances left him feeling empty, hollow. Am I nothing more to her than a breeder? he wondered. The boar that might sire her cubs?

And he knew it was true. She-bears did not form strong attachments. God had so fashioned them that they desired but one thing from a male, and after their sexual appetites were sated, they would become irritable, chase him away.

Even now, many females huddled around Mangan, the favorite to win the games. They tempted him with their scent, gazed imploringly with their deep brown eyes.

And Orick, watching those she-bears, suddenly felt empty, desolate.

If he won this contest, what would he win? A few nights of frolicking with she-bears who would hold him in contempt a week later? It seemed an empty prize. For months now, Orick had considered entering the priesthood, giving himself into the service of God and mankind. It seemed a noble thing to his mind, yet here he had let his gonads bring him to this Salmon Fest to engage in these bestial contests.

If he bred widely, he would perhaps gain some form of immortality through his offspring. But if I give myself into the service of God, he told himself, wouldn't I gain a more sure form of immortality?

And so Orick was at war with himself, disconsolate. Before he knew it, old Mangan marched up to the circle with a burlap "pig" in his teeth. The she-bears in the audience called out, "Hurl that pig! Make it fly, Mangan!" Many she-bears cast him demure glances. Some stood on all fours and arched their backs, raising their tails seductively.

Old Mangan turned to Orick, a calculated gleam of malice in his eyes. "Looks like you'll be taking second pick this year," he shouted.

Mangan stood on his hind legs. He was tall, over six and a half feet at the shoulders. This gave him a real advantage in the toss, for he could swing with a long arc. And he had a great deal of muscle in those shoulders.

The old bear reached down with a contemptuous swipe and snagged the pig. Then he stood majestically, a sudden gust of wind rippling through his fur. He swayed back and forth, swinging the pig in long arcs, then with a snort that was almost a roar he swung one last arc and tossed the pig high. It sailed over the playing field, far past the longest mark from the younger bears, and slammed into the gray trunk of a pine tree. The burlap bag split on impact, spilling red clay dirt down the side of the tree.

Around Orick, bears hooted and cheered, shouting Mangan's name. But Mangan looked at where his bag had landed, and his upper lip curled into a snarl. Obviously, he had not counted on hitting the tree.

The other real contenders for the title of Primal Bear hung back, waiting to see who they would have to best. But Orick was suddenly tired of the games.

He rushed forward, looked at the "pigs" in their pile. He doubted that he could toss a burlap pig as far as Mangan had. Throwing was never his strong point.

So he would have to gamble. He found a bag that was halfway torn open, giving it a little more length so that it could be swung in a wider arc and would come free without snagging into his claws. Still, the bag could also rip halfway through the toss, losing mass so that ultimately Orick might not get as long a throw as he hoped.

Orick bit the thing in a fit of frustration and carried it up to the circle in his teeth. He was dimly aware of the cheers from the females in the camp behind him, and he looked out over the field. He needed five points. He would have to beat Mangan's toss by more than five feet in order to win the title, and even then Orick would have to wait to see if the other contenders would best his own mark.

He had never tried throwing a bag underhand the way that Mangan had just done. The only advantage Orick might really have was that he was younger and stronger than Mangan. But Mangan, having a long reach, had thrown his pig in a long arc that Orick could not match. Which meant that he would need to hurl that pig with a sidewise toss.

Orick took his well-ripped bag back to its pile, found one that was still new. He carried it to the circle, closed his eyes, twisted a three-quarter turn, and roared in frustration as he threw with his might.

The pig sailed toward the same tree Mangan had hit, and for one moment Orick thought he would repeat the older bear's performance, but the bag missed the tree trunk, lofted past it a few feet and tangled in the branches, then fell to the deeper grass beyond. Orick could not tell how far the pig had gone.

A dozen cubs rushed up with the measuring rods in their

teeth, and a moment later they announced that Orick had beat Mangan's mark by twelve feet. For the moment, Orick was leader in the race for Primal Bear, and roars of delight came up from all around, from males and she-bears alike, for now it marked the end of Mangan's reign. This year, there would be a new Primal Bear.

Still, at least two other bears could possibly beat Orick, and as he walked back to the crowd, he listened to the deep cheers, and for one moment, just one moment, he wished that Gallen and Maggie could be here to see what he'd accomplished. But they were off in Clere, planning their wedding.

He looked over the crowd at old Mangan, who scowled at the ground, defeated, and Orick suddenly felt no victory.

He sniffed the delicious scent of the females in estrus, looked at their lustrous fur and the shining eyes that watched, and suddenly he knew, he knew what he had to do.

Orick turned his back on them all and walked away.

Perhaps he would win the title of Primal Bear, and perhaps he wouldn't. In either case, he wasn't going to stick around the Salmon Fest to find out.

He marched past the crowd, into the woods. Perhaps the others thought he went into the woods only to relieve himself, but Orick trekked on up a trail through the sheltering pines where the salmon sat cooking on their skewers.

Ahead, at the top of the hill, the trail forked. One branch led north to Freeman, the other led southeast to An Cochan and beyond that to Clere where Orick's best friend, Gallen, would soon wed. All through this past week, Orick had imagined that after the contests he would sate his lust upon at least one female before heading home.

But suddenly he thought of Gallen's wedding, and a longing came over him that was too painful to name. If he dirtied himself by breaking his vows of chastity—for he had taken those vows in his heart, though he never had spoken them to God or man—he wouldn't return home with any sense of real victory.

So Orick went to the fire pits, stood in the blue-gray wood

smoke, and began pulling salmon off their skewers, swallowing them hot from the fire. A full stomach was all he would take from these contests, he decided.

Farther up the hill, a feminine voice called to him. "Are you leaving already? Aren't you going to wait to see if you've won?"

Orick looked up. A young she-bear lay sprawled under a tree, and before her was a large, leather-bound book. Orick realized with a start that she'd been sitting here reading while all of the others watched the game. This in itself marked her as an unusual kind of bear. Furthermore, she did not ask the question with the batting of eyes and coyness he would have expected. Instead, she asked with a tone of apathy, as if she were intrigued by his answer, but it wasn't especially important to her.

"No, I'm not waiting. I've done my best, and that is all I wanted to do." Orick studied the young thing. Her eyes looked bright, alert. He guessed that she was perhaps four years old, but rather small for her age. He hadn't met her before, didn't know her name.

"What about the she-bears in heat?" she asked. "They're all drooling for you. I've seen the looks they give you. And 'a she-bear in heat is the best kind to meet,' or so I hear."

"I'm not interested," Orick said. He pulled another bit of salmon from a stick and swallowed, savoring its smoky flavor with bits of ash on it.

The she-bear pricked up her ears, sniffed the air as if testing for his scent. Orick sniffed back, wondering if she was in estrus. She wasn't. So perhaps her questions were not the byproduct of some sexually induced intrigue, but were rather guided by a sense of curiosity. The she-bear was not particularly attractive. She had a dull coat of black hair with brownish tips. Her nose was petite, her paws rather overly large. Finally, she asked, "I don't get it. You could mate with any she-bear down there. Why don't you?"

Out of curiosity, Orick sauntered over to the she-bear. She was reading from a book on how to rig sailing ships—perhaps the most useless topic a bear could study.

"I don't know," Orick answered honestly. "I guess I want more from she-bears than they're willing to offer."

She studied his eyes. "You're that bear that runs with Gallen O'Day, aren't you? So what is it you are after—fidelity?"

Orick hesitated to answer, afraid that she would laugh at him, but something about her demeanor said that she wouldn't. "Yes."

She nodded. "I've heard of some males who want things like that," she said. "It's the cub in you. You still want someone to care for you, even after your mother chases you off. You'll grow out of it."

"Perhaps I want someone to care for—as much as I want someone to take care of me," Orick said. "Perhaps I have something to offer."

"Perhaps." She nodded. "So where are you going?"

"To Clere. My human friends, Gallen and Maggie, are getting married."

"Hmmm . . ." she said. "I was heading that way myself. Do you mind if I come along?"

"Only under one condition."

"What?"

"If you tell me your name . . ."

"Grits," she answered.

Orick wrinkled his nose in distaste. "That's not much of a name," he said, perhaps too honestly.

"I'm not much of a bear," she answered. She flipped her book shut with her paw, then gingerly picked it up in her teeth and carried it to a red leather pack under the tree. She nuzzled the book into the pack, then stood and slipped the pack straps over her head. Within moments the pack was on, two leather containers dangling at her side when she walked on all fours, as if she were some pack mule carrying its burden.

Then they padded off up the worn trail. By late afternoon they reached Reilly Road, which led south along the coast to Clere. As they flitted beneath trees, the sun shone warmly on them, almost as if summer had returned. And each time the road crossed a stream, Orick was obliged to stop and slake his thirst. His mouth was made dry by more than the constant exercise, for he talked long with Grits about many things—about his interest in religion and her interest in the ways that ships were constructed. They talked of far lands, and of the strange rumors they'd heard of heavenly and hellish creatures walking alive and in the daylight down in County Morgan.

Orick didn't tell Grits about his part in such matters, how he'd just returned from a journey with Gallen O'Day and learned of the vast universe beyond their small world. Although all the rumors said that Gallen O'Day was up to his neck in affairs with creatures from another world, and though Orick was Gallen's best friend, Orick preferred to feign complete ignorance of the matter, hoping that Grits wouldn't press him with questions. The poor she-bear just wouldn't be able to comprehend such talk, and, if it frightened her, he feared that she might blather the news about willy-nilly.

So it was that they climbed down out of the tall hills and into the green rounded hills of the drumlins. By dusk they reached the village of Mack's Landing, beside a long gray lake where geese and swans gathered out on the flat waters. Jagged clouds hung on the horizon, curtains of rain falling from them. The town itself was nothing more than a grove of old oak house-trees that sprawled at the bottom of the green slope of a long hill. The house-trees' rust-colored leaves flapped in a small wind.

The wood smoke from the cooking fires left a pall over the glade, and two large flocks of black sheep had come down to huddle for shelter under the trees. Orick hurried his pace, hoping that he and Grits might be able to earn a meal before dusk. Yet as they neared the town, he got an odd, uneasy feeling at the pit of his stomach. He slowed.

There were travelers in town—four dozen sturdy mountain horses, so many men that some were forced to camp outside the only inn. The men wore brown leather body armor over green tunics, carried long swords and spears. He knew they were sheriffs from the northern towns, but he'd never seen so many gathered together. It could mean only one of two things: either they were chasing a huge company of bandits, or they had gathered for war.

Orick stopped, raised on his hind legs and sniffed the air. The scent told him little. He could smell leather saddles, horses, well-oiled weapons, the common odors of a camp.

"What do you think they're up to?" Grits asked.

And Orick suddenly had a sinking feeling. "With all the stories we've heard in the last week of angels and demons warring openly in County Morgan, I fear that we've attracted some defenders." Orick licked his lips. "Do me a favor, Grits. I'm a known companion to Gallen O'Day, but I don't want *them* to know it. Call me what name you will, as long as it isn't Orick."

"Of course, my dear Boaz," she whispered.

They plodded silently along the dirt road, Orick with his nose down, until they reached the camp under the trees. These were not grim soldiers, worn with experience. Most of them were younger men out for an adventure, strong and limber. One played a lute, and several of the fellows sat beside a campfire, singing drunkenly a rousing old tavern song,

> *"My lady fair, my lady fair,*
> *was drunk as a duck and fat as a bear.*
> *And if you saw her prancing there,*
> *You'd lose your heart to my lady fair."*

There was merriment in the sheriffs' twinkling eyes, and they laughed and boasted as they gambled at dice and drank themselves silly with beer, hardly noting the presence of two bears wandering into town. One young man with long brown hair and a thin vee of a beard spotted Orick and shouted at him, "Och, why, we have strangers in our camp. Would you like to work your jaws a bit on something to eat? We've just boiled up a pot of stray lamb stew."

"Stray lamb stew" was another way of saying "stolen lamb stew." By law, a traveler could claim a stray lamb if it wasn't with a flock and its ragged appearance made it look as if it were lost. In practice, if men traveled in a pack of more than six, they tended to butcher any lamb they came across, figuring that they could intimidate the rightful owners.

Orick sniffed at the stew from outside the circle of the campfire. It was well seasoned with rosemary and wine. Bears were notorious for begging food from travelers, and were therefore not often so welcomed to camp. "Why, I thank you, good sirs," Orick said in genuine surprise at the offer.

The lad got up from the rock where he sat, staggering from too much beer, went to the stew pot and made up two heaping bowls. He came and bent over, set the steaming bowls before Orick and Grits—then pulled them back.

"Ha!" he laughed, seeing how the bears' mouths watered at the stew. "Not just yet. You have to earn it."

"And how would I go about that?" Grits asked.

"With a tale," the lad laughed. "You've likely heard more news out of County Morgan than we have. What tale have you? What rumor of demons? And make it straight for me!"

Orick was in no mood to humor the lads. Sheriffs or not, this was a dangerous company of men, rowdy and full of themselves. "I'll give you no *rumor* of demons," Orick grumbled in his loudest, most belligerent voice, "for I've seen them, and what I have to tell isn't the kind of idle gossip you've likely heard up north!"

Suddenly, the lutist stopped and over two dozen heads turned Orick's way.

One old sheriff with a slash under his left cheek looked up and sneered, "Out with it, then. What did you see?" His tone of voice said he was demanding an answer, not requesting it.

Orick looked at the sheriffs. They were weary from the road, and they weren't in the mood for any slow tales. Orick licked his lips, remembering. "Two weeks ago yesterday night," Orick said, "I was in the city of Clere, on my way north for the Salmon Fest, when the first of the sidhe appeared. It was a man and woman who came into town, late of the night, in the middle of a storm. I was begging scraps at the tables of John Mahoney, the innkeeper at Clere, when the sidhe opened the door and stepped out of that damnable rain.

"The woman was a princess of the Otherworld, more beautiful and powerful and fair than any woman who walks this earth. Oh, she had a face that an angel would envy." Orick recalled Everynne's face, and he let the memory of her beauty carry in his voice. Some of the men grunted in surprise at the sound, for it was obvious that Orick loved her, and the sheriffs seemed amazed that a bear would love a fairy woman, so they leaned closer. Orick decided to stretch the tale a bit, try to fill these men with the proper sense of awe. "Beside her was her guardian, an old bearded man who was stronger than any three men I've ever met, and swift as a bobcat. He guarded her jealously, with two swords that glowed magically. And though the rain was pelting the inn like a waterfall, neither of the two had a drop on them."

Orick stopped a minute, gauging his audience to see if they believed that last bit about people walking dry through the rain. Some of the rough lads had their eyes popping out at his tale, and they gaped with open mouths.

"I've heard rumors of the sidhe coming to town, but I've never heard report of these two," the old scar-faced sheriff said.

"That's because you never heard the tale proper, from someone who was there," Orick continued. "At first, no one quite believed what they saw. The princess sought dinner and a room for the night, and she asked to hire someone local to take her into the woods, to Geata na Chruinne, the Gate of the World."

The sheriffs hunched nearer, and one of the younger ones muttered, "That's where the demons were headed, too."

"Aye," Orick said. "Gallen O'Day, who legend says is the best of you good lawmen, happened to be in the room, and when the princess turned her eyes on him, he must have fallen under her spell—as we all did—for he agreed to guide her, never dreaming the consequences."

At this point, Orick licked his lips. The sheriffs listened with rapt attention. He had begun to hear rumors of late, nasty tales where Gallen was named a conspirator with the sidhe. Orick couldn't come right out and say that such tales were lies, couldn't tell men that the Lady Everynne was no more a magical creature than any one of them, that she was just some woman from another world, trying to defeat the swarms of alien Dronon that were sweeping across the galaxy. What did it matter if she carried weapons that could demolish worlds? She was still only something akin to human, and even though she had no magical abilities, she was still more marvelous and powerful than these men could comprehend. And Gallen had done right in becoming her servant and protector. But Orick could never convince these men of the truth, so he bent the tale, making it seem that Gallen had been a slave who couldn't control himself, and maybe that wasn't far from the truth, for even Orick had fallen under the spell of the Lady Everynne.

"So it was that the princess sought rest and refreshment that night, for she had been running long and hard, trying to escape monsters straight out of hell."

"You saw them?" one of the young sheriffs asked, leaning nearer and spilling a wooden cup of wine in the process. His hands were shaking.

"Aye, I saw them up close, I did," Orick said. "And I'll never sleep deeply again. Some of them were giants, and the biggest of you would hardly stand above their bellies. Their skin was green, and they had large orange eyes as big as plates. They were strong creatures. When they walked into town, I saw one of them kick a wood fence just in passing, and it splintered into kindling. Others had the same green skin and walked like giant dogs, on all fours, sniffing for the scent of the princess and her bodyguard. And with them was a major devil. A creature with wings the color of ale and a skin blacker than night. It had great clusters of eyes both on the front and on the back of its head, and it had feelers like a catfish's under its jaw, and when you saw him, you knew his name: Beelzebub, the Lord of the Flies.

"The demons walked into Clere just after dawn, and Father Heany confronted their master. Now Father Heany, there was a man of God. He had no fear for himself, only for his parishioners, and he rushed to block the path of the demons. And Beelzebub raised a magic wand, and a bolt of lightning flew out of it, striking Father Heany dead right there in the street, right in front of every woman and child in Clere. And when that lightning hit him, it melted the man. The flesh stripped from his bones and melted in a black puddle as if it were pudding.

"Then the demons marched on to Mahoney's Inn and asked after the princess and her guard, but the princess must have slipped out in the night. When the demons learned that she was gone, Beelzebub flew into the air and bit John Mahoney, ripping his head off."

Orick fell silent, and the eyes and ears of every sheriff were upon him.

"What happened next?" Grits asked.

"I can't be sure," Orick answered. "At that moment, I turned and ran from Clere for my life. It was in the first dawnlight of the morning when I took off, and I didn't stop running until the moon set that night, and even then, I hid. I went to the Salmon Fest, and from there I've heard stories the same as you—about how Gallen O'Day came back that day at dusk, with the sidhe warriors at his back, and the Angel of Death himself walking at his side, and then hunted the demons until nightfall. Some say that the sidhe chased the demons back to hell. Others say that the two sides are still fighting in Coille Sidhe. All that is sure is that no one has seen any sign of the demons, or of the sidhe, but Gallen O'Day rests easy in the village of Clere and is making plans for his wedding day."

"And other folks say that it's Gallen O'Day who opened the door to the Otherworld in the first place, at Geata na Chruinne," the scar-faced sheriff said. "They say that in order to save his own life, he prayed to demons in Coille Sidhe and opened the doors to the netherworld."

Orick considered the threat implied by that story. If these men believed Gallen was consorting with demons, they'd put him to death. Orick wondered if he might be able to turn these men from their course. "I wouldn't believe such talk," Orick said, hoping to calm them.

"It's true enough," Scarface said. He nodded toward a small fat man that Orick hadn't noticed before. "Tell him."

The fat man looked uneasy, bit his lip. "A-aye," the fat man stammered. He had a bowl of stew in his hands, and he tried to set it down out of sight, as if he'd just been caught pilfering it. "It's true. Me and my friends were planning to rob Gallen O'Day's client, but he—Gallen—put four of us down before we could defend ourselves. It was only a lucky blow from one of us that felled him, and then that Gallen, he began praying long and low to the devil in a wicked voice. That's when the sidhe appeared.

"I—I know it was wrong to try to rob a man, but if we'd known a priest would die from our wickedness. . . . Now, now I just want to wash my hands of it."

Orick looked at the greasy little man and imagined sinking his teeth into the rolls of fat at the man's chinless throat. The robber was glancing about, as if daring someone to name him a liar. Orick would have shouted the man down if he dared, but he knew that now was not the time.

Scarface said, "We intend to arrest Mister O'Day and put him on trial. Bishop Mackey signed a warrant"—he nodded toward the town's inn—"and the Lord Inquisitor himself has come with us, along with two other witnesses who will swear that Gallen O'Day prayed to the Prince of Darkness. Aye, this O'Day is guilty of foul deeds, all right. And we'll not let any *southern* priests conduct the questioning—not with their soft ways. We'll wring the truth from him, if we have to skin him alive and salt his wounds."

Orick raised a brow at this, then licked his snout. A full Bishop's Inquisition would involve days of torture and scourging. They might even nail Gallen to the inverted cross. And though Gallen had a lot of heart in him, even he couldn't endure such punishment. The lad would have no recourse but to fight these men for his life.

"Are you sure there's enough of you to take Gallen O'Day?" Orick asked. "They say he's a dangerous man himself. He's killed more than a score of highwaymen and bandits. And if the Angel of Death *is* on his side, you'll need more than thirty men to take him—even if you have the Lord Inquisitor to back you."

Some of the younger men looked about to the faces of those around them. Fighting against Gallen O'Day was foolhardy enough. But no one would want to be found fighting against God.

"Hmmm . . ." Scarface muttered, squatting on the ground to think. "Things to consider. Things to consider." He got a wineskin from his pack, filled a bowl, then looked up at Orick darkly, his thick brows pulled together, and said, "You've earned yourself more than a little supper. Sit with us tonight. Drink and eat hearty, Mister . . ."

Orick did not like his probing look.

"Boaz," Grits answered quickly. "And I'm his friend, Grits."

"Keep those bowls filled," Scarface ordered his men, and he offered the wine to Orick.

Orick thanked him and began lapping at his bowl of stray lamb stew. He intended to eat his fill. He'd need the energy later tonight, when he ran to Clere to warn Gallen of the danger.

TWO

"Maggie," a man's voice called. "Maggie Flynn? Are you in there?" His voice trailed to a garbled string of words Maggie couldn't make out. She knew everyone in town, and whoever was hollering for her was a stranger.

Maggie looked up from sewing ivory buttons onto the back of her wedding dress, stared up toward the door of the inn, expecting the stranger to enter at any moment. It was a bitter cold day in early fall, with a sharp wind—sharp enough so that the fishermen of Clere had dragged their boats high onto the beach. A dozen of them were lounging about the fire, drinking hot rum.

Danny Teague, a stable boy who had shaggy hair and a fair-sized goiter, opened the door and looked out. A horse cart had drawn up outside the door. Its driver was a stranger in a gray leather greatcoat, a sprawling battered leather hat pulled low over his face. He had piercing gray eyes and a neatly trimmed sandy beard going gray. Still, at first glance, Maggie knew that it was his moustache, waxed so that the ends twirled in loops, that she'd remember when he was gone.

"I'm calling after Maggie Flynn!" the stranger shouted at

Danny. "You don't answer to that name, do you, man? What's the matter with you—did your father marry his sister or something?"

Danny closed the door and sort of stumbled back under the weight of this verbal insult, and Maggie shoved her wedding dress up on the table.

"It's all right, Danny," she said with obvious annoyance. "I'll have a word with Mr. Rudeness out there!"

Already, several fishermen had got up from their seats by the fire and were rather sidling toward the door. If the stranger had hoped for an audience—and folks who stood in the street and hollered usually did want an audience—well, he had one. And whatever Maggie said to him now was likely to be talked about in every house tonight—as if the town didn't have enough to gossip about after the past few weeks: with demons and angels and fairies battling in the forests outside of town, the priest and innkeeper murdered.

Maggie got up, straightened her green wool dress and a white apron so that she looked the part of a matron who kept an inn—albeit a very young matron. Her long dark red hair was tied back.

She went and opened the door, gazed into the biting wind that smelled of ocean rime. The man's wagon was old and battered, and it was drawn by a bony horse that looked as if it hoped to die before it had to plod another step. The blacksmith's hammer had quit ringing across the street, and he stood squinting from the door of his shop. Elsewhere, an unusual number of people suddenly seemed to have business on the streets.

The stranger set the brake on his wagon and greeted her. "Damn it, Maggie, you look too damned much like your mother."

She studied him. Since he spoke so familiarly, she thought she should know him, but she'd never seen his likeness before. "I'll thank you to speak more reverently of the departed, Mr. . . . ?"

"Thomas Flynn. Your uncle."

Maggie glared at him, trying to consider what to say. Her

mother had been dead for three years. Her father and brothers had all drowned a year and a half before that. And in all of that time she'd not seen so much as a whisker of Thomas Flynn's beard nor got a single message expressing his sympathy.

"That's right," Thomas said, "your only kin has come to call. You can close your mouth now."

From across the street, the blacksmith cracked a huge smile that barely showed through his bushy black beard. "Will you be giving us a song, Thomas?" he called.

In answer, Thomas reached behind him and pulled out the rosewood case for his lute, stood and shook it over his head. "I'll give you many songs in the days to come!" he shouted, and his coat opened. Beneath it, Maggie could see a beautiful plum-colored shirt tied with a gold belt, pants that were forest green. His outfit was slightly festive, slightly dignified, and slightly absurd—as befitting a minstrel. Indeed, she realized now that he had been striving to draw a crowd by shouting for her from the streets. He was a man of wide repute, a satirist with some reputation for having a quick wit and, as they say in County Morgan, "a tongue sharp enough to slice through bones."

Such folk were always good for songs and tales of faraway lands, mixed with a fair amount of political commentary so burning hot that you could use it to scald the hair off a pig.

Maggie said, "We've heard of you—even in this little backwater. Everyone knows Thomas Flynn, who goes about aping the great men of the world."

"Aping great men? Oh, heaven forbid! I'd never ape a truly *great* man." Thomas grinned, removing his hat to show a full head of close-cropped hair. "They're too strange and fine a thing. But, now, for those who call themselves 'great,' but who are in fact deceivers—those men I will not spare. For through my aping I can sometimes prove that those who call themselves 'great' are nothing more than great apes."

"So why have you favored us with your presence, Uncle Thomas?" Maggie said in a tone that flatly admitted she wanted to be rid of him quickly.

"Oh, it's worried about you that I am, darlin'. Rumors. I've been hearing disconcerting things, Maggie. Rumor says you plan to marry a man named Gallen O'Day, even after he prayed to the devil and got your village priest murdered."

"Och, and what would you know of it?" Maggie asked. There was far more to the story than she ever planned to tell her uncle—or to anyone else.

"I'm only repeating the tales that I've heard on the road," Thomas answered, "tales everyone is telling nowadays.

"Some say that Gallen called upon the devils, unleashing them on the town, and others say that the demons came of their own accord and that Gallen struggled against them until God's angels came to fight beside him. In the last two weeks, every person in twelve counties has worn out their jaws yapping about it."

"Sure, and I suppose you don't believe such stories?" Maggie challenged, unwilling to so much as venture an opinion about the recent happenings. "So you've come to write a song to mock the good folks of Clere—and my beau Gallen, too, I imagine."

"Ah," Thomas said, looking around at the folks in town. "I've seen no proof that the accounts are anything more than fables. Why, I just drove forty miles from Baille Sean, and I spotted nothing more menacing than an old red fox that was slinking from pine to pine, hunting partridges. If there be green-skinned demons about, I've had no sight of them. And as for the tales of angels or fairy folk with flaming arrows, I've seen no flames at all—except in my own campfire. If I were called to write a song right now, I'm afraid that I'd have to damn you all as liars."

"I'm not surprised that you saw nothing in the woods," Maggie said. "The militia says the roads are clear."

"And I'm not surprised that I saw nothing, neither. Little surprises me anymore. In fact, the only thing that surprises me more than the human facility for prevarication is some people's nearly equal facility for staring a known liar in the face and believing every fantastic word he utters. That's a fair *part* of why I had to come—to see if there's any truth to this gossip about demons and angels and fairy folks in the woods."

Maggie half closed her right eye, stared up at him. Out

behind the inn, a sheep bleated. The same damned sheep she'd had penned out back for two weeks, waiting for slaughter. But since word of the goings-on in Clere had spread, no one had dared the roads, and the inn had remained empty, except for locals who came to drink and exchange theories on what had happened.

Maggie smiled faintly. "There's some truth in those tales, Uncle Thomas. Satan himself came marching up that road not two weeks ago, parading at the head of a band of demons. And they heartlessly murdered Father Heany and John Mahoney— but those demons were never conjured by Gallen O'Day." She watched his face for reaction. "And angels came that snowy night and drove the demons from town, and one of them fought at Gallen's side—the angel Gabriel—that part is true.

"But now Gallen's enemies—cutthroats and thieves all— have been telling tales on him, naming him a consort of the devil, hoping to discredit him."

Thomas scratched behind his ear, and Maggie tried to imagine what he was thinking. Maggie knew that he wasn't a simple man. He'd never heard a tale that featured demons walking in broad daylight, or angels fighting with magic arrows. But everyone within fifty miles swore that it happened, and the tales were stranger than any lies these unimaginative folks could conjure.

He looked about at the crowd that had gathered. "Well," he said. "I suppose that there's more than one song in such a tale, so I'll have to stay a couple of days at the least. You wouldn't mind preparing a good room for an old man, and maybe heating up a mug of rum for me to wrap my cold fingers around."

"I'd like to see the color of your money first," Maggie said, giving him no quarter.

Thomas raised an eyebrow, fumbled under his coat and muttered, "Och, so you're a frugal lass, are you? Generous as a tax collector. Well, I like that in a woman, so long as she's my niece." Thomas pulled out a rather large purse and jingled it. Maggie could hear heavy coins—gold maybe—in that purse. Only a fool would display so much money in public, Maggie thought. So her uncle was ostentatious as well as cantankerous.

And with so much of a purse, she wouldn't be able to toss him out on the streets any time soon.

Thomas grabbed his lute and climbed down from the wagon, and Danny the stable boy was forced to suffer the indignity of tending the horse of a man who'd abused him.

Thomas stumped into the common room of the inn, looked about. The inn was built inside an ancient house-pine that had a girth of some sixty feet. The rooms rose up through three stories. Like all house-pines, over the years this one had grown a bit musty, and the walls creaked as the wind blew in the pine's upper branches. The smell of pipe smoke and hard liquor filled the air. The windows were large and open, covered with new white curtains that Maggie had made the week before. The common room featured six small tables, and chairs set in a circle around a fireplace. A small bar separated the kitchen door from the common room. The bar had two barrels on tap—one of beer and one of rum. The ale, whiskey, and wine were stored in back this time of year.

"A fine place you have here, Maggie," Thomas muttered.

"Oh, it's not mine," Maggie returned. "It belonged to John Mahoney. I'm just running the place till one of his kin comes to claim it."

"Nope, nope." Thomas sighed heavily. "It's yours, now. Or it will be when you reach your majority. Mahoney sent me a copy of his will two years ago, and I stopped in Baille Sean and had the deed transferred into your name."

Maggie was rather dumbfounded by all of this. John Mahoney had never bragged much on his family. He'd once mentioned an older brother who lived "down south," and he'd posted letters once in a while, so Maggie had assumed the brother would come to take possession of the inn.

"I don't understand," Maggie said, a bit breathless. "Why would he give it to me? I mean . . . I don't understand this. I've never much liked working here, and I'm not even sure I want the damned place."

"Well, now," Thomas said, "for a frugal woman, you don't sound overjoyed with your new fortune. I'll tell you what. Why don't you and I go find a quiet corner, and let's talk about it."

Maggie led Thomas to the corner table where she'd been working on her wedding dress. He stopped at the taps and took a large tin beer mug, then filled it up with rum and set it on the grate at the edge of the fire. "A man who has been driving a cart all day in the cold needs something warm to wrap his hands around," Thomas chided her. "You should know that." Maggie looked at the full mug. It seemed her uncle planned to be drunk in an hour.

Then he came and sat across from her, folded his hands, and looked her in the eyes. She knew that he was no more than fifty-five, but he looked older. His face had grown leathery from years on the road, and his stomach was going to fat.

"Well, Maggie," Thomas said. "I've been driving for over a week to reach you, and—och—to tell the truth, I'm not sure you're going to like what I have to say. So it's begging you that I am, to not take it too hard." Thomas reached into his shirt, pulled out a yellowed envelope. "This here is a paper that your mother made out on her deathbed. She was always harping on me to take more responsibility for the family, sending me letters and whatnot. So she wrote out her will and had John Mahoney witness it, then had it sent by post. By the time the letter found me, it was months after your dear mother's death. But in this letter, she acknowledged me as your only living kin, and made me your legal guardian. So . . . the burden of seeing that you're properly cared for falls to me, don't you know?"

She sat back as suddenly as if he'd dealt her a physical blow. She gaped at him, then the words tumbled from her mouth. "Mother has been dead for years—and in all of this time, I've not had so much as a letter from you!" But now I have an inn, she thought, so you've come to make yourself my legal guardian.

Thomas held up his hands, as if to ward away the accusation in her voice. "I know, I know . . . and I'm dreadful sorry. But I've lived the life of a wandering man, don't you know, and I couldn't have cared for you properly on the road."

Maggie looked over her shoulder. Several townsfolk had slipped into the inn, and all of them had listening ears. They were gathering at nearby tables like a flock of geese to a fistful of grain.

"Anyway," Thomas said, "your mother appointed me to be your legal guardian until the age of eighteen. It's all signed by the bailiff, proper and legal." He held the paper out for her inspection.

Maggie gaped at him, astonished. "Now don't take it so hard, darlin'," Thomas offered. "It's true that I didn't split my britches running to your side after your mother's death, but you were fourteen, old enough to work, and there's nothing that will build character in a person faster than having to look after one's self. Besides, did you ever know a teenager who wanted an obnoxious old man like me hovering over her shoulder? Oh, I've worried long nights about you, worried that you might make wrong decisions or worried that you might take sick, and I exchanged letters with your old employer, John Mahoney, on the subject. But I knew you were in the hands of a good, saintly person, and you didn't need me to meddle in your affairs. But now things are different."

Maggie wondered what he meant, when he said that now things were "different." Were things different because she was wealthy, or was he planning to meddle in her affairs? Or maybe both.

Thomas leaned back, smiled a charming smile, as if considering what to say next. "By God, you're a beautiful young woman, Maggie," Thomas said, condescending, and she remembered an old saying: compliments are so cheap to give that only a fool would hold one precious. "I can tell that John Mahoney cared for you well. He said in his will that you were a special kind of person, one who doesn't let life just happen to her, but one who would likely go out and make a good life in spite of what happens. He had faith in you." More compliments, she mused.

He glanced at the wedding dress spread out on the table. "So, when are you planning to marry?"

"Our wedding is set for Saturday," Maggie said, not sure what else to answer.

Thomas frowned. "And when did this Gallen O'Day propose to you?"

"Two weeks ago."

"The day John Mahoney died?" Thomas looked skeptical.

Maggie nodded.

Thomas gazed at his hands, cleared his throat. "It seems that he decided to fall in love with you at a very convenient time—just when you were ready to come into a nice, juicy inheritance."

Maggie said nothing at first, couldn't quite think of what she should say for there was too much to be said all in one breath. Neither she nor Gallen could have known anything about the inheritance, and there were so many things that Thomas didn't know. She'd spent time on other worlds, risked her life fighting the Dronon to save rascals like her uncle.

"It's not like that at all!" Maggie said. "You—and you don't care about anything but my money! In all these years, you've never so much as written me a letter—but now that I have an inheritance you come banging on my door! I should sic the sheriff on you, you nasty old lecherous thief!" She threatened him with the law, suspecting that she couldn't legally get rid of him, but willing to give it a jolly try. Still, she wanted to frighten him.

She saw a flicker in Thomas's gray eyes, a slight flaring of the nostrils as he drew breath. She knew she'd struck him right. "You plan on moving in here, don't you?" Maggie said. "You plan on coming to the inn to lord it over me until I'm old enough to toss you out on your ass."

"That's not a fair assessment," Thomas said calmly. "I'm well-known as a minstrel. Many a satirist my age takes up a winter residence in a hostel, and we enrich the landlords with our talents. I'll earn more for you than my keep."

"So you admit it: you plan to live here—for free—while you lord it over me? My mother wouldn't have made you my guardian. You must have forged that letter."

Thomas licked his lips, stared at her angrily. Obviously, he had not expected her to see through his ruse, and he hated having it discussed openly, here in front of everyone. He called himself a "satirist," but he was a professional backbiter. He was used to bullying others, pouncing from behind like a wolf. He'd tried to put her on the defensive, keep her mind occupied. Now she was turning to attack. "I'll thank you, Uncle Thomas," Maggie said, struggling to sound calm, "to take your wagon and ride out of my life forever!"

"I don't begrudge you your hard feelings," Thomas said. "If you were a filly that I'd left in the pasture for three years, I expect that I would have to use a strong hand to break you. And, alas, that is what I intend to do now."

"Maggie, darlin'," he said, "whether these magnificent stories told on your beau are true or not, your name—our family name—is mixed up in this scandal. I've heard you spoken ill of fifty miles away. You're running about, making mad resolutions that will most likely ruin your life, and I have to step in. I'm afraid I can't allow you to marry this Gallen O'Day."

Thomas pulled at the wedding dress on the table, as if he'd take it, and Maggie grabbed it from his hands.

"There will be no wedding," Thomas said, slamming his fist on the table. "How could there be? What kind of priest would perform a marriage for a girl so young?" His tone made it sound as if he were naming her a dreamer or a liar. It was true that she was young to marry.

"Gallen's cousin—Father Brian of An Cochan!" Maggie said, feeling a thrill of victory by being able to name such a priest.

"Father Brian, eh? Not without my permission, I'll wager." Thomas glared at her coldly, and Maggie realized he'd just tricked her into telling the priest's name.

He reached into his purse, and tossed a shilling to a boy of fourteen. "You're a bright-looking lad. You look as if you know where the cat's hid its kittens. I want you to carry a message for me: run to An Cochan and tell Father Brian that Maggie's wedding will have to be called off for the time being. Tell him I'll arrange a suitable donation to the church in order to . . . compensate him for his trouble."

"Don't do this," Maggie said.

Thomas stiffened at the dangerous tone in her voice, and his own voice took on a hard edge. "I didn't come all this way just to acquiesce to your wishes, child. And I'll not haggle about it. The wedding is off!"

"You can't," Maggie cried. "Gallen's a fine man. I love him!"

"This isn't about love!" Thomas shouted. "This is about *judgment.* Judgment—a damned fine quality that you're too young to have in abundance. So the wedding is off! Your mother gave me the right and the moral obligation to use my judgment in raising you, and I'll exercise that right now. And quit giving me the evil eye!"

"I'll not let you do this—" Maggie hissed. She shook with rage, and her jaw was set. She thought of the big carving knives in the kitchen. She could hardly believe that a stranger would walk into her life intent on causing so much trouble. It was like getting mugged, only Thomas was doing it legally. She wondered if she should get that letter from Thomas, try to prove that the will was a forgery; but she suspected that it was real, that in a moment of despair her mother really had sent the letter to Thomas, asking his help. And if that were the case, Maggie would be stuck in the boiling pot, certain.

The butcher Muldoon came in through the front door— apparently having heard that Thomas Flynn was in town. Both Maggie and Thomas had lapsed into silence, and Muldoon called, "Give us a song, Thomas!"

Thomas got up, went to his mug of rum that had warmed on the fire, and he took a few stiff drinks, then got his lute out of its case and began plucking strings.

Maggie sat numbly, wondering about her options. She could stay here and put up with this man, which seemed impossible. Or she could get a knife and stab him—which right now felt like a desirable thing to do, though she didn't like the thought of getting hanged afterward. Or she could try to talk Gallen into running away with her, and she wished that right now Gallen was here instead of being off in the woods.

Maggie's attention was suddenly caught as Thomas began his song. In his youth, Thomas had had a famous voice. Maggie had a handbill that she kept in a box upstairs, advertising one of Thomas's performances. On it, another bard said that Thomas's voice was like a mountain river, all watery and rippling light on the surface but with deep currents that could sweep you away, and beneath it all was a rich and abrasive gravel that could cut a listener to the bone.

And so in a moment, Thomas sang to the local fishermen an old ballad called "Green," the tale of Claire Tighearnaigh in her green days of love, raising daisies and sweet red roses on the hillsides to sell in the gray streets of Finglas. Thomas had the finest voice that Maggie had ever heard, and she tried to shut it out, but he sang the ballad with warmth and richness, so that she could almost feel the sticky flower stems in her hand and bask in the scent of bloody-colored flowers.

And when he sang of Ian Phelan, who loved a good fight as much as he loved his young fiancée, Thomas let his melody wend its way around the hearts of his listeners, sucking them down into a turbulent morass where their bodies were constantly spinning in the eddies and whirlpools, torn between the worlds of water and sky.

And when Thomas sang of how Ian Phelan was brutally stabbed at the hands of a jealous suitor, Thomas let his voice become gravel, so that his listeners could see how Ian's corpse had been left on the rocky hillsides above Finglas, his lifeblood leeching into the green flower beds of Claire's youth, the reds and greens tumbling together like lovers rolling down a hill, caught forever in a place where pain and beauty fuse into one.

When he finished, every rugged fisherman was weeping into his drink, and someone cooed, "Ah, now *that* was worth missing a day's work for." Several folks called loudly for another song, but Thomas refused, saying, "Come back tonight, and I promise you'll tire of listening to this old voice croak out its songs."

And Maggie saw that despite her personal problems with Thomas, he was already winning over the hearts of the townsfolk. Sure, and many of them would agree with Thomas, that Maggie was just too young to marry. They'd take his side.

He asked Maggie to escort him to his room. She led him upstairs to a cozy room above the fire, and opened the door for him.

"I'll expect you to behave as any other guest, Thomas Flynn," she said. "No sleeping on my clean sheets with your boots on."

Thomas went to the edge of his bed, set his lute on it, and looked up at her. "Well, Maggie," he said conspiratorially, "how do you think they liked our performance?"

"Our performance?" she asked.

"Aye. We gave them a good fight, and a grand song. I swear, the inn will be full tonight. You've never seen such drinking and carousing as you'll see tonight. I'll make you a fortune, sure."

"What?" Maggie asked, taking a deep breath. "You mean that was all an act?"

"I know about love," Thomas said, and from the way he had sung, Maggie knew it was true, and she wondered if he secretly intended to let her marry Gallen after all, but his next words dashed that hope. "But it's for your own good that I'm keeping you from your beau."

"For *your* profit, you mean," Maggie grumbled.

"That, too," Thomas said honestly. He watched her for a reaction, but she didn't give him the pleasure. "Maggie dear, if you live long enough, you're going to find that sometimes you have to play the villain in another person's life. It's just the way of things, that sometimes our goals cross. You'll have to spoil someone's plans, ruin their day—maybe even stick a dagger in someone's back. Just remember this: when that day comes, make no apologies for what you're doing. If you must play the part of the villain, play it with gusto. It's one of the sweetest sensations in life." He held his breath a moment, then said, "At least, that's how I intend to play it."

Then he lay down on the bed, put his dirty boots on the blanket. "Now there are rules in this world that tell us how to get along in polite society. I didn't make those rules, but we have to live by them. One of those rules is that we don't go marrying children. So, you'll wait to get married, till you're the proper age. That's final."

"What if Gallen and I don't follow your rules?" Maggie said. "What if we marry, and run away?"

"Think about what you would be giving up, woman: your young beau has won himself a reputation as the finest body-guard in seven counties. Rumor says that he's killed as many as forty highwaymen. It's a grand reputation, a romantic reputation.

"And as if his reputation as a fighter weren't enough, now folks are saying that angels—the Angel of Death himself, by God—have come down from heaven to help Gallen O'Day drive Satan from the village of Clere.

"Why, with such talk, Gallen could find himself sitting in the seat of the Lord Sheriff of Tihrglas in a year, and in five years he might be Lord Mayor of the whole land.

"But on the bad side, Gallen has also been accused of consorting with devils, and for that he could be hanged.

"Now, I doubt both stories. But, as they say in the south, 'You could spin the wool from a whole flock of sheep and never come up with such a marvelous yarn.'"

Thomas sat up, leaned closer. "In any case, the wedding must be canceled for now. If things go ill for Gallen, then your good name won't be besmirched. There's not a man or woman alive who didn't fall in love at your age, and they'll forgive you for your wrongheadedness. On the other hand, if things go well, then Gallen will need to wait to marry you, if only to enhance his political career, and in another year you can marry the man you love, and someday you'll find yourself living in one of the finest houses in the land! Oh, oh, oh, wouldn't that be grand?"

Thomas smiled and shook his head. "Och, I think you've got a future, darlin'. I can hardly wait to meet this Gallen O'Day."

Three

━━━━━━

That afternoon in a forest glen high above Clere, Gallen O'Day practiced fighting alone with his knives. He wore some attire he'd earned while fighting off-world to save the Lady Everynne: a robe woven of thread that held small nanotech machines that could change colors to fit with any background, and others that could mask his scent; tall black boots and gloves that had a selenium matrix worked into various parts of the toe, heel, palm, and fingers so that his blows carried more punch. And most importantly, he wore his mantle, a personal intelligence made of small black metallic rings, strung with silver knowledge disks.

As Gallen practiced, the mantle fed him images that he could distinguish from reality only because the mantle fed him no audio: five swordsmen with sabers and small shields swirled around him in a fevered dance. They wore white robes that swished silently as they leapt over the forest floor, kicking up humus, grimacing and sweating with every slash and thrust.

Gallen leapt and ducked, weaving between them, seeking to block or avoid their blows as much as possible, slice them with his own daggers. When he scored a hit, his blade would mark them with blood, so that after hours of practice, the swordsmen now appeared as gory apparitions.

Yet they were extraordinary swordsmen, each man fighting in a different style, using his own tactics. One was a whirling madman whose sword blurred in continuous motion; another stood back and studied Gallen, seeking to strike only at the most opportune moment, then jab with deadly precision. Another used the cutting edge of his shield as much as he did his sword, while the other two seemed to change fighting styles to suit their needs.

Gallen was struggling for air, sweat pouring from his body. Yet his enemies showed no sign of slowing due to fatigue. Gallen had wanted to stop for nearly an hour, but he was trying to build his endurance, so he kept up the gory battle. Time and again, his foes stabbed him, and each time, the mantle sent him a searing phantom pain at the point of impact.

When Gallen's arms were impossibly heavy from fatigue, his mantle suddenly dispersed the image of the fighters, and Gallen stood panting.

"Why did you stop?" he whispered.

"You have an incoming message from the Lady Everynne," the mantle whispered. "Are you ready to receive it?"

Finally she sends word, Gallen thought, after two weeks. "Yes," he answered, and Gallen sat down in the shade on a rock encrusted with yellow lichens. He closed his eyes, stilled his breathing, waited for Everynne's image to appear.

Instead, the sky darkened, as if it were covered with a curtain, and he heard the rumbling of thunder in the distance. His heart pounded in terror, and he found himself in a strange city on a cobbled street, leaning against a stone wall in an alley.

What's this? he wondered, willing his head to turn and look about. But the view did not change. Instead, he only saw the view as if he were staring ahead, and Gallen realized that this vision of another world must be a part of Everynne's message.

He looked about, watching the narrow streets to his right, the smooth stone buildings with enormous doors and huge windows set high off the ground. He was in a business district of a large city, and all the shops were closed for the night. The black cobblestones gleamed wetly. Through the thick storm clouds, he could make out the muted light of three separate moons, and dim lights shone from a few windows down the street. But the alley behind him was dark and sheltering. He looked farther down the street to his left, hoping for more darkness, but there was a tavern there with a lantern burning from a hook outside its doors. He couldn't run that way. The light would show him up.

Not again, not again! he thought, and his lips emitted a high whimper. Yet Gallen knew it was not his own thoughts or words, but the words of someone else. The fingers that clutched the edge of the stone wall were slender, on pale feminine hands, and Gallen felt the unfamiliar weight of a woman's breasts on his body, and wondered at it.

"I am feeding you the memories of a dead woman. This is Everynne's message to you," his mantle whispered.

Off in the near hills, light flashed in the clouds, then thunder snarled and echoed, washing away all sound. He waited breathlessly, listening for sounds beneath that booming echo. Down the stone street, around a corner, he heard booted feet thudding against stone, saw three men rush into the square. Their sabers were drawn, and they silently moved into the shadows, scanning ahead.

Gallen—or the woman whose memories Gallen was reliving—moved farther back into the alley, suddenly looking about for safety. There were no windows, and the lip of the roof was ten feet above her head. Her only hope lay behind a heavy oak door.

She went to it, tested it. The door was securely locked from the inside. Its brass handle was too heavy for her to break. Lightning flashed overhead, and thunder boomed. She rattled the door as loudly as she could under the cover of that noise, not knowing even what type of business this was, hoping desperately that the shopkeeper slept at the back of the shop, that he would hear her and come to her rescue.

She thought she heard the heavy thump of a foot on wood floors behind the door.

"Is someone in there . . . ?" she whispered fiercely. No answer. She couldn't wait again. "Help me!" she whimpered, hoping that the person behind the door was human, that he would taste the pheromones of her Tharrin body and be forced to respond to her plea. "Please, open the door," she begged. "The Inhuman is coming!"

She rattled the door again, this time without the covering echo of thunder. Perspiration beaded on her forehead, and she wiped it away just as a thin drizzle began falling. From behind the door, a woman's voice whispered. "Go away! I have children in here to care for. Don't bring trouble down on this house!"

And with those words, the Tharrin whimpered, knew that she had just heard her death sentence. By her very nature she was forbidden to harm anyone. She could not endanger this family. She lurched back from the door as if it burned her, and a new steadiness came over her. She whispered to the woman inside, "Stay in with your children, then. There is only enslavement out here."

She wondered if there was a place to hide, but as she glanced back at the mouth of the alley, she saw a swordsman standing in the open, looking at her. The wind was growing wild as it will before a storm, and his shadowy cape twisted and fluttered behind him. He whistled softly, and with his free hand motioned to his companions. Presently, they joined him, and the three proceeded toward her abreast. A heavy, steady rain began sweeping toward her in a curtain. The alley filled with the hiss of rain slapping against stone.

The Tharrin sniffed the air, smelling rotting food and dust from a trash bin behind her, then let out a bloodcurdling cry, something that might have come from the throat of a child, Gallen decided, for it did not sound like the voice of a woman, and suddenly he understood that this was no woman's body he was in, but the voice of a girl barely into her teens.

The three men rushed toward her, one of them pulling a heavy bag out from behind his back. "Shush, child," he hissed. "We do not want to harm you! We only want you to join us!"

The young woman went rigid. She had a knife sheathed at her hip for just such an emergency, a knife tipped with deadly poison. But she was a Tharrin. She could not harm another sentient being, and the men before her were not evil, only the victims of evil, hosts to the Inhuman.

She pulled out her knife, waved it before her, hoping that the threat would hinder them. "Stay back!" she warned. Then she shouted once again, "Help me! Help!", hoping that perhaps someone at the tavern down the way might hear her.

One of the men laughed. "You won't use that," he said with certainty, and the young woman strained her ears, hoping desperately to hear the sound of running footsteps, of rescuers. But she only heard the steady rain, and realized that it must have covered the sound of her cries.

The servants of the Inhuman marched toward her warily. They were almost upon her. Lightning flashed above them, gleaming off their swords.

They think I can't use the knife, she considered, and she stood up straight and tall, knowing what she must do. She reached up quickly and slashed her own throat from ear to ear.

The searing pain was exquisite, shocking, and she felt the hairs on her head stand on end in reaction. Her heart thumped wildly, kicking in her chest, and hot blood spattered down between her breasts, a seeming river pouring out of her. She staggered back against the wall, felt the poison doing its work, numbing her jaw and neck. She tried to remain standing for a moment, but the knife slipped from her hands, and she slid down the wall.

Suddenly the three servants of the Inhuman were upon her, and one of them, a man with a dark red moustache and crazed eyes, grabbed her by the head and shouted in her face. His voice was a roaring watery echo in her ears, the voice of a waterfall or a storm rushing through trees. "You think you can escape us so easily? You think you can hide in a temporary death? When you next take a body, we will hunt you again! We will not give up so easily!"

And then he let her hair go, and she was falling, falling into pain and darkness, and the cold rain sizzling on the stones was the only sound as she silently gulped, crying as she died.

* * *

A woman's voice, Everynne's voice, rang in Gallen's ears, but he did not see her image, only a gray light in the distance. "Gallen, these are the memories taken from Ceravanne, a Tharrin who somehow managed to stay alive on Tremonthin for the past sixty years. When last I saw you, I told you that I would call upon you again for service. Her clone has been infused with all her memories but the last. I charge you to go to Tremonthin and protect her. I charge you with becoming Lord Protector of the planet for now, and as part of that charge, you must seek out and destroy the Inhuman."

The gray light faded, and Gallen stood up in the glen, looked about at the bright sun sprinkling on the dark green leaves of the pines, splashing upon the yellowing leaves of the alders. He smelled the fresh scent of earth.

This glade, this world, felt so welcome and open, so refreshing, and he suddenly realized that he did not want to go to the dank, smelly world of Tremonthin.

Gallen wished that he had an ansible, some way to talk to Everynne, find out when he had to leave.

His wedding was scheduled for Saturday, yet he had felt such a sense of urgency that he wondered if he could afford to wait.

Overhead, high white clouds were washing over the blue. He could already feel a chill as the sweat dried from his body. He took off his mantle, boots, and cloak, packed them away tightly in a sack, and with a heavy heart headed home to Clere, where sweet Maggie would be waiting.

Four

Thomas Flynn bolted the worn wooden latch to his room at Mahoney's Inn, then sat on the plump feather bolster, tasting the scent of a cold room that had been closed too long. It was a simple room—a chest of drawers with a small brass oil lamp on it, along with a white ceramic basin and pitcher of water should he want to wash off the dust from the road. He looked out the window with its old wavy glass, past the few small house-trees and sheds to the mountains beyond.

Everything in Clere seemed so normal, so restful. Yet he was the only guest at the inn this night—the only person brave enough to have stayed here in the past two weeks, so rumor said.

But Thomas Flynn knew a bit about people. Rumors of demons might keep folks away, but a demon itself wouldn't—not if it was safely stored in a jar of brine. Thomas had seen oddities displayed that way—a cat with two heads, a midget child. And he wondered if he might be able to preserve something as large as one of these demons in such a fashion.

Thomas could imagine how the sign out front might read: Thomas Flynn's Curious Inn. Aye, people were afraid to come around now, but in a couple weeks, he might have them pounding the doors to get in.

Thomas had never believed in demons or angels, but something had frightened these people, and if a battle had been waged, then there would be corpses about.

It was early afternoon, but he had several good hours of daylight. He rested on the bed for a while, feeling his brain swim around in his skull from too much rum, then went downstairs to the common room. It had begun to fill up nicely. A good thirty men lounged about.

He managed to warm himself another bit of rum without falling into the fire, then drank it and clattered the empty cup against the bricks of the fireplace to get attention. "Good afternoon, gentlemen. I'm after finding myself the corpse of a demon. I imagine they should be in the woods about, and I'm offering a bounty. I'll pay twenty pounds to the first man who brings me one!"

One customer had been drinking, and he began coughing his beer up through his nostrils. Another had been leaning in his chair, and he barely saved himself from falling over backward.

"Uh," one lanky woodsman said, "talk to Gallen. He's the only one who goes about these days. He's in the woods now. Some say he's still hunting the last of the demons down!"

"Hunting demons, is he, eh?" Thomas shook his head.

Thomas looked out over the crowd. There were some stout men in the group, but none of them were eager to take him up on the offer. They stood drinking, studiously ignoring him.

"All right, fifty pounds, then!" Thomas said.

No one stirred, and frankly, he could go no higher.

"Man, you don't have to kill the buggers, mind you!" Thomas said. "If I understand right, they should already be dead." But no one budged.

"Och, there must be a trapper hereabouts, someone with the need and gumption to hike the woods?"

Several men shook their heads, and Thomas was a bit amazed at their lack of spine. "Then come outside and point the way to Geata na Chruinne for me. I'll go myself!"

A couple of men led Thomas outside, pointed down to the

ridge of a nearby mountain. "At the foot of the ridge is the gate. If you wander around enough, you'll find it in a dark hollow there. It's about four miles by foot, and no man in his right mind would get caught off the road there after dark. The wights are thick in Coille Sidhe."

Several onlookers stopped to see what Thomas was up to, and Thomas said loudly, "Oh, sure I'll be back by sundown. I plan to have a word with the man that wants to marry my Maggie."

Thomas went to his wagon, got out his walking stick and half a skin of stale water. His joints felt loose, and his head was a bit foggy. And he found himself watching the gray woods, wishing that Gallen was here now. The men of town were spooked, sure enough, and he convinced himself that that was good news, for it meant that perhaps there was something for him to find out in those woods. Perhaps he'd find more than he could handle.

He headed north, walking to the edge of the forest, and a shout went up from some of the boys. Soon there were forty people walking behind him, children and women, curious folk, but most of them stopped at the edge of the wood, frightened to go in.

Thomas turned and addressed them. "If any of you older boys have a mind to come with me, I've a mind to go and collect some artifacts. I'll be looking for the skulls of demons or angels, any of their clothing or weapons. I'll pay a pound for each boy that comes with me to pack the bounty out."

Many of the boys looked around a bit as if trying to think what business they might have elsewhere, but one young lad stepped forward on shaky legs, a tough-looking boy with a broad chest and intelligent eyes. "I'll help, for five pounds."

"Five pounds then, if we find anything," Thomas said.

The boy nodded in agreement.

"Good lad," Thomas said, and he turned, leading the way. The boy rushed across the street, grabbed a hatchet from the doorstep of a house-tree where someone had been chopping kindling, then hurried up, walking right at Thomas's heel, gripping the hatchet in white fingers.

They walked under the pines for a hundred yards, until the

limbs of the tall trees began to block the sun. The humus was thick and held a print, and in no time at all, they came upon a trail that held stunningly odd prints: some of the tracks came from booted feet that couldn't have been less than eighteen inches long and ten wide. Other tracks were handprints of some creature with a span of twenty inches, but the monster had only four fingers.

Thomas stopped and surveyed the prints for a long time, found his breath coming ragged, and his mouth felt dry. He took a swig of his stale water.

"Those are demon tracks, certain," the boy said. "The ones that look like handprints are from the creature that walked on all fours."

"By all that's holy!" Thomas mouthed. "To tell you true, I wasn't certain we'd find anything."

"What do you plan to do if we get a demon skull?" the boy asked.

"I'll mount the damned thing on a wall in the inn," Thomas said, perhaps being too forthright.

"Aye," the boy breathed, "that would be something! I'll tell you, the reason I came is I want some of this stuff, too. A demon head maybe, or something from an angel. When the angels came through town, I climbed the steeple of the church and looked out over the woods. That night, there was smoke and fire coming from the forest, flashes of lightning. I reckon there was a fearsome battle, and I prayed to God and the saints something fierce. But what happened out here, no one knows— only Gallen O'Day. He came out to battle with an angel at his side, and he's not breathed a word about what happened. But no angels came back, and no demons, either. I figure Gallen bested them all."

Thomas glanced up at the boy, saw that his face was pale, frightened. "What's your name, boy?"

"Chance," the boy answered.

"Well, Chance, if we find a demon skull, it's mine and I'll pay you the five pounds I promised. But if we find two, the second is yours. Beyond that, if we find the mother lode, I'll give you some of the booty."

Chance smiled at that, and they took a pee, then hurried down the trail.

Thin high clouds were coming in, making it darker and cool, promising rain. Thomas hurried, and the forest went silent. No birds sang, no squirrels leapt in the trees. It was a strange, ominous quiet. Even the trees seemed to refrain from creaking in the small wind.

Thomas had been in the woods plenty of times when the forest was just as quiet, but this silence got his heart beating. He kept stopping, looking behind him. He felt as if he were being watched.

"Sure this is an unholy silence," Chance breathed at one point, loosening his collar.

And Thomas stopped, his heart was beating too hard. He kept thinking of that nice warm inn, with its mugs of beer, and he wished he was back there.

But they followed the tracks over a long hill, up a ridge, and back down to a creek. There the trees opened up, letting in more light. Still, the deathly silence reigned in the forest.

Chance began slowing, and to hurry him, Thomas said, "Pick up your pace, you old cow—it's not as if you're pulling a plow!"

The boy picked up his pace, and ten yards farther he grabbed a stick and walloped Thomas in the back of the head.

Thomas turned so fast that he fell on his butt. The boy was so mad he was in tears. "I'll not have you talkin' down to me, like I was some cur. My name is Chance O'Dell, and you'll address me proper, or you'll find yourself in trouble with me and my clan! I'm *Mister* O'Dell to you!" The boy shook his stick in Thomas's face, and Thomas took a moment, trying to think how he'd offended the boy. His mind was still foggy from too much rum, and it took a few seconds for understanding to burn through the haze.

"I'm sorry if my rudeness wounded you, young Mister O'Dell," Thomas said. "I meant nothing by it. I say such things by force of habit. And if you think me evil for it, think on this: what is in another man a vice, is in me a virtue. As a satirist, I walk behind the proud men of the world, making rude noises.

And the louder and ruder I get, the more good folks like you pay me. So, it's true that I've got no common sense when it comes to addressing decent, honorable folk like yourself."

"Well," Chance growled. "If you make more rude noises about me, I'll pay you fair, all right. I'll pay you with a stick!" He shook the stick in Thomas's face, then threw it aside.

Thomas laughed. "Well, next time I want a good spanking, I know who to come to. Come now, friend, help me up, and let's go find us something grand!"

The boy gave him a hand up, and they hurried along, and the boy seemed to calm down quickly. In minutes the whole incident was perhaps forgotten by the boy, but Thomas filed it away in his brain. A boy who was that brutal and quick to take offense likely came from a family with a strong sense of honor, and it wouldn't be wise to ever cross one of them O'Dells again, or else Thomas would end up in a blood feud. And with only two Flynns left in the world, it would be a short feud.

At the foot of a mountain, in the shadow of a glade, they came upon some booted footprints that were more proportioned to the size of a man.

"See," Chance muttered. "This is where the angels came on their track. It looks like there were four, maybe five of them, and they came stalking the demons."

"Some say that it was the sidhe who came, not angels," Thomas ventured.

"Angels, I think," Chance whispered. "You've never seen people so beautiful, so regal. And Gallen said it was the Angel of Death that walked at his side."

Thomas just grunted. He had a hard time imagining angels that wore boots—slippers maybe—but he didn't want to argue. Besides, he wondered, would an angel even need to walk? Didn't they have wings? He thought it more likely that they would just flap about like giant white crows.

They followed the trail along the creek, both of them stalking warily, looking about. Suddenly the brush exploded just before them, and Thomas's heart nearly stopped. A stag leapt off through the forest, but Thomas had to stop to let his pounding heart rest.

He looked back, and poor Chance had a face whiter than sea foam. "Come on," Thomas said. "Let's look just a bit farther."

A hundred yards on, they smelled the scent of burnt brush and left their trail to find a large circle of scorched earth. There, in the center of the burn, lay a huge pile of bones from some manlike thing that would have stood nearly nine feet tall. Its flesh had melted into the bones, and for all the world it looked as if it had been struck by lightning.

Thomas walked around the thing, afraid to touch it. The giant was sprawled out flat on his belly, arms wide. He held a long black rod in one hand. Bits of metal were fused into his bones in some spots, as if necklaces and bracelets had melted into him.

"So, this was a demon?" Thomas asked, circling the thing.

"Aye, that was one."

Thomas went to the head, kicked it off, then rolled it over to look at its face. The skull was covered with a black tarry substance from the melted flesh, and the eyes had burned out of their sockets. The eye sockets were large enough so that Thomas could easily fit his thick fists into them. But it was the massive jaws and teeth that attracted him. Those teeth were big enough for a stallion, and twice as yellow.

"They had orange eyes," Chance said, "and skin as green-gray as a frog's."

Thomas just knelt there, shaking his head in wonder. "Who'd have thought?-Who'd have thought?" He sighed. "Well, here's one oddity for my inn."

He tried to lift the head, but there was still a brain inside, and the thing was as heavy as a good-sized boulder. They rolled it over to the edge of the creek, onto a worn path, and determined to leave it while they searched ahead.

They hiked along for an hour heading up Bald Mountain, finding nothing more, and Thomas began to feel doubtful, and he began to rest more easily. They'd been out for hours and seen nothing horrific. He hoped, he'd hoped for the mother lode, but all he had to show for his day's work was one misshapen skull.

They finally climbed up past the road to An Cochan, and

near the mountaintop they came to an old burn where there were no trees. The air was cold up here, and chunks of ice lay in the ground. Even now, it felt as if it might snow. It was beginning to get late, and Thomas was thinking of heading back, but they climbed up onto a log, looked up over a little valley where a fire had burned off the larger trees years earlier. Many great logs lay fallen, and ferns had grown chest-high in them. Here and there were clumps of snow from the two storms that had swept over the countryside in as many weeks. Thomas looked for any blackening in the ferns, any sign of a recent fire.

They stood, heaving from effort, looking up the little valley to the mountain beyond, and a few pigeons began cooing from their roosting tree at the edge of the forest.

It was silent, peaceful. A cool wind played with Thomas's hair, and his breath came out and blew away in a fog from his mouth.

Then for no discernible reason except to ease his stress, Chance let out a long howl, as if he were a wolf. In the center of the clearing below them the ferns erupted and a jaybird flapped into the sky, chattering angrily, searching for the source of the howls.

Thomas and Chance looked at each other, both of them realizing at the same time that the jaybird had been feeding, and as one they jumped into the deep ferns below them, raced tripping and fumbling until they climbed on a wind-fallen tree and looked down. Chance hooted for joy, for there in the ferns lay a dead demon with one massive hand wrapped around the throat of the most beautiful woman Thomas had ever seen.

She had golden hair that she wore in tiny braids, and over her hair she'd worn a net of silver with teardrop-shaped disks of gold. Even now, a blue jewel glowed in the net just above her eyes. She wore a cloak that was colored the green and yellow of ferns, and beneath it was some kind of armor made of a material that Thomas imagined to be some sort of exotic spun metal, like silver maybe. Her face was regal, and her arms were strong, with sensitive hands.

For her part, she had thrust a magic sword through the heart of the demon before she died, and even now, the sword shimmered and its blade looked as if it were liquid quicksilver in motion, baffling the eye.

Behind the demon lay its severed right hand and its magic rod, just where it must have fallen when the angel lopped it off.

The bodies were well hidden from the sun. The icy ground had preserved them remarkably well. The jaybird had been having a go at the face of the demon, scoring on its huge eyes, which were glassy yellow-brown in death.

Thomas caressed the flawless skin of the woman's face, and she looked as if she were sleeping, her mouth in a tiny frown as if she had just had a disturbing dream. Her skin was stiff from cold, and the wind blew through her delicate eyelashes. Thomas saw that as he touched her, his own hand was shaking, and he sat and considered just how he felt right now.

For years he had lived on the road, plying his trade as a minstrel and satirist, and though he had seen many beautiful women in the far corners of the world, he had never before seen anything quite so exquisite and wondrous as what he beheld right now.

Thomas had always been a cautious man, unable to trust others. He'd never much believed in God. The imperfections of the world had always seemed ample evidence that there could not be a powerful and compassionate god. Yet now he quivered inside as he touched the dead angel, and he felt somehow transformed, holy.

It was as if a great light welled up within him, burning away years of doubt and cynicism that he had carried as some burden, almost unaware, and he dared not look up at Chance, lest the boy see the tears forming in his eyes. This is as close to heaven as I may ever get, Thomas thought. And he wondered if this was the true reason he'd come back to Clere. In part he'd wanted to take care of his niece Maggie and spend a profitable winter away from the cold, but deep in his heart, he'd hoped to see this wonder, to see an angel and be certain.

So, God, he thought. You've played a good joke on me, letting me go on in my doubts for all these years. And yet he wondered, he wondered what kinds of creatures these were— demons and angels as mortal as men. Perhaps their own immortal powers had somehow canceled each other out, so that they could kill one another. No doubt the priests would find some explanation. Yet here he was, caressing the cheek of a fallen angel, daring to hope that she would come back to life under his touch.

"Let's get into town," Thomas whispered to Chance roughly, his voice tight from emotion. "We'll hire some men and bring my wagon. She died to save us. I can't let her sit here through another night."

Five

Just after dusk, Maggie served in the common room at Mahoney's Inn. The place had filled up with fishermen who knew how to draw their own rum from the tap and could be trusted to leave the proper coins on the table.

They were a nervous lot, wondering aloud how soon Thomas might come in from the woods, speculating as to whether it would be wights—a very common threat in this neck of the woods—or demons who got him.

And of course there were many there who wished him well, for they'd come to hear him sing.

Thus it was that Maggie's uncle came bustling in a fluster, smelling of the road, with an odd expression—something between exultation and manic joy. Thomas just stood in the doorway for a moment, grinning.

"I found them—" he said softly to the crowd. "A dead demon and an angel with it, and they'll both be on display in the stable in an hour!"

For one moment, no one spoke, then suddenly everyone was talking.

Thomas hurried Maggie into the kitchens, and began pulling

sacks of flour and sugar out onto the mixing table. He said urgently, "Old John Mahoney must have had someone who helped out during his busy season. You'll need to round up those folks—anyone who's handy at cooking and serving. Then you had better go to the butcher and buy a pig and a goose and get them roasting. We'll need dinner for a hundred tonight."

"A hundred?" Maggie said in astonishment.

"Aye," Thomas said with a wink. "At the very least. I know you resent me, but I promise you, Maggie, I'll make you a fortune at this inn. Between my singing, and heavenly hosts on display—this place will be a madhouse within a fortnight!"

And Maggie said in frustration, "The larder is empty and I don't have coin to buy so much food. The shops are closed or closing for the night—"

Thomas reached to his belt and pulled out his purse, heavy with coins. "Hurry, then, and buy what you can for tonight and tomorrow."

Then he rushed into the night, out the back door. Maggie grabbed her shawl and ran to the butcher's and the miller's. She saw Thomas and four men go rumbling off into the dark in a wagon moments later, and half wished that the wights would take them all.

In an hour the town was bustling and the inn was deluged. Whole families who had never set foot in the inn were too flustered to fix dinner for themselves, and they pounded on the tables. Maggie muscled a hundred-pound pig onto the spit, planning to carve off the meat as fast as it roasted. Ann Dilley came in of her own accord and began cooking potatoes and loaves of bread, while Ann's daughters waited tables.

Gallen came in just after dark, and he took Maggie's hand, went into the kitchen with her, and stood beside the woodbox. "What is this I hear? You've got an uncle who has called off our marriage—and brought the bodies of a Vanquisher and one of Everynne's guards into town, all in the same afternoon?"

"Aye," Maggie said angrily. "The jolly old bugger. He's paid Father Brian to call off the marriage!"

Ann Dilley rushed into the room at that moment, hurried past them. "You might as well bring the ale and wine out front and save us some trips," she said, grabbing a small keg of whiskey, then she hurried out.

"I'll have a word with your uncle," Gallen said.

"Don't stab him!" Maggie said, suddenly fearful at the note of anger in his voice.

Gallen looked at her askance. "Stab him? What do you take me for?"

Maggie realized it had been an unwarranted thought, but tried to explain. "You never know." She shook her head. "He's the damnedest man I've ever had the misfortune of meeting. *I've* thought of stabbing him today—more than once!"

"Well, don't!" Gallen laughed. Ann Dilley plodded back into the room, frowned at Maggie as she got a flagon of wine and pulled some rolls from the oven. "Look, I can tell you're busy," Gallen said. "Let's talk tonight, after you close up. It's important."

Gallen left.

Maggie was grateful when the wagon rolled into town moments later, and for a while nearly everyone cleared out while Thomas displayed the corpses in the stable. That gave time for the meat to cook. And yet, it was only the beginning of the night. Soon the tables began to fill with villagers from An Cochan, three miles away. They were coming as fast as they heard the news, walking over the mountain road by lantern light, the wights be damned, bringing whole families by wagon.

Thomas raised the price on his rooms and food and liquor and stabling, and by eleven he was selling sleeping space on the floor of the common room, and he'd rented out the lawn to campers.

The amount of work to be done piled up like snow before an avalanche, ready to topple at any moment. There was more work than twenty people could do. Maggie was forced to just grit her teeth and bear it. She cooked and served dinner, took money, cleaned the cooking pots, churned the butter, and prepared the ingredients for breakfast. By twelve-thirty the common room was more crowded than she'd ever seen it, and Gallen came to help her wash dishes, while every other person who'd ever lent a hand during the traveling season helped prepare food for the morrow.

Maggie could sense that Gallen wanted to speak to her as he worked, but with a dozen people bustling in and out of the room, he didn't dare. There was a certain tenseness in his movements, and twice she put her wet arms around him to hug him, give him comfort, wondering what was on his mind.

By two in the morning, the place was a madhouse—folks had come from twelve miles away, and Maggie wondered at how they were all making the trip so fast, on such a dark night.

They closed the common room then, with four dozen folks asleep on the floor, and every bed in the house taken. Thomas came to the kitchens. "Leave the rest of those dishes until morning, darlin'," Thomas said. "I'd like you to lock up the stable. I don't want folks mucking about there in the middle of the night."

"And what will you be doing, your lordship?" Maggie asked.

Thomas hefted a bag of coins—more money than Maggie had ever seen in one spot. "I'll be tallying receipts."

"Uncle Thomas," Maggie said angrily, "what will you be doing with all that money? It's a shame before God for a man to make so much in one day! Why, it would serve you right if someone knocked you in the head and danced off with your purse!"

Thomas laughed. "As the good Lord said, 'The poor you have with you always'—and might I add, they're always red-faced indignant when someone else falls into a bit of money. So don't go getting all self-righteous on me, Maggie Flynn. After all: you own this inn. I'm just helping you run it, until you're eighteen. I'll take a cut for showing the demon, but the vast majority of this fortune is yours!"

"And you can have it all, for all that I care!" Maggie said. "And the inn with it!" For I'm going away, and plan never to return, she wanted to say.

Thomas grinned. "Oh, you're speaking out of your anger and weariness. Get some sleep, and your head will be clearer in the morning."

Thomas looked at Gallen as if he'd just seen him. "This purse would make a *fine* start for a dowry, don't you think, Mr. O'Day?"

"Aye." Gallen nodded. "A start."

"I meant to have a talk with you, Mr. O'Day, about your intentions toward my niece——"

"Let's talk, then." Gallen pulled a worn chair away from the cutting table. The cooking fire was nearly out, and the oil lamp above the sinks was burning low so that Gallen was just a shadow moving in the dark.

"I know you're in a hurry, young man. In a hurry to talk, in a hurry to marry my niece. But it would be unpolitic to hurry the marriage, and as for the talk—I'm afraid I'm all stove in for the night," Thomas said. "Besides, it wouldn't be proper to discuss the matter in front of her . . . you know." He nodded toward Maggie.

"I'm not some heifer that you'll be bartering over," Maggie said. "I should have a say in any deals you go making. It's my money you'll be spending for the dowry!"

"I didn't say you were some heifer," Thomas growled. "But you're young. You're just too damned young, and your mind isn't as fully developed as"—he waved vaguely toward her breasts—"the *rest* of your body. So I'd like to have a delicate talk with Gallen, man-to-man, and I don't need your meddling!"

Maggie stared hard at him, and she could feel her face burning. She wanted to scream or shove him into the big baking oven in the corner till his skin turned black, but she only glared at him.

Thomas said to Gallen, "It's time for you to go, young sir. I suspect you're an honorable man, but it wouldn't be proper for you to be skulking around here so late of the night without an escort."

Thomas turned and disappeared into the common room through the swinging doors, giving them one last moment alone. Maggie was so mad she wanted to follow Thomas out and shout to his back as he walked up the stairs to count the money, but there were too many folks camped out on the floor of the common room, and she didn't want to make a scene. So she just stood with her fists clenched until she realized that she still held a wet washrag and she had squeezed water from it onto her foot.

She spun and tossed the rag into the sink. "Well, how do you like *him?*"

Gallen chuckled at Thomas's back. "I see what you meant about wanting to stab him. 'Skulking around' he calls it. The nerve of him! Well, he's a nuisance, all right. But don't judge him too harshly. He thinks he's making you rich, and you can't fault him for that. And if your mother or father were alive, they wouldn't be talking to you much different. They'd be against you marrying so young, too."

"Oh, don't take his side. He's just a big tick trying to suck the blood from me, and he wants me to feel fine about it."

"Any sixteen-year-old woman," Gallen whispered, "who can steal a key to the Gate of the World, make her way across half a dozen planets, pilot a hovercar under a nuclear mushroom cloud, and face up to the Dronon Lords of the Swarm is surely a match for one dried-up old crooked uncle," Gallen whispered. "I'm sure you can handle him."

Maggie smiled, still angry, but subdued by weariness. "Sure, I'd gut him in a second if he wasn't my only kin," she teased. She buried her head in his chest, just resting her eyes, swaying gently. "Gallen, we've got to get out of here. I won't stay here and be his slave, working in this place for another year!"

"Of course not," Gallen said. He wrapped his strong arms around her and just held her. She could feel his heart beating strong and steady in his chest, smelled the clean scent of his cotton tunic. He didn't speak for a long time. The cooking fire crackled as a log shifted.

"Let's go lock up the stables," he whispered. "We can talk in there."

Maggie went to the cabinet where John Mahoney had kept his locks, took out the big iron lock that he used for the stables when he bothered to lock them at all. Gallen went to a peg by the back door, took down Maggie's shawl and put it over her shoulders, and they hurried out under the boughs of the house-pine.

A blustery wind was blowing, and all under the tree that formed the inn there were tents pitched, and up on the hill north of town, Maggie could hear whinnying. She looked up, and spaced along the mountain road were lanterns as people wended their way down the road.

"This is madness," Gallen whispered, watching the lanterns. "I've never seen the likes."

They picked their way carefully around the side of the inn, went to the stable. A lamp burned inside, and a couple of young boys were staring into the wagon at the corpses. Gallen shooed them out.

In the stable, the horses were backed into their stalls, staring out with tired eyes. Gallen pulled the door tight, locked it with a cross-beam.

As soon as they were alone Maggie tumbled into Gallen's arms and kissed him, a sweet, slow kiss. She'd been craving his touch all day, and now they just held each other, satisfying that urge. She shook as she held him, and Maggie found her eyes tearing, and Gallen whispered, "Oh, my sweet Maggie, what's wrong?"

"Thomas," she said. "He's mucked it all up for us."

"He can't muck it _all_ up, so long as we still love each other," Gallen whispered. He pulled back, held her hand, and looked steadily into her eyes. "Maggie, we don't really have to get married here. You and I could go to any world your heart fancies, and the marriage would be just as valid."

Maggie's heart skipped. "I know," she said. Yet she felt cheated. Clere was her home. By tradition, a proper woman wouldn't marry outside her own hometown, even if the groom came from another country. It was a matter of propriety. Only a girl who had come down with a child would marry in a far county, and if Maggie were to run off now, everyone would suspect her. And even though through her travels Maggie had learned that she no longer wanted to live on this world, she was saddened by what her friends and neighbors would think.

"Yes, I've always wanted to get married here," she said. "I wanted to marry in my own hometown, dressed in white, with a priest."

"I'll talk to your uncle, tomorrow," Gallen said, "press him for an early marriage. Maybe he'll listen." She looked up into his blue eyes, and with her fingers combed a wisp of his long hair back from his face.

Gallen pulled away from her, walked over to the wagon, looked down at the corpses of a green-skinned Vanquisher and one of Everynne's personal guard, a beautiful female soldier. The night air was chill, and Gallen's breath steamed from his mouth.

Maggie could tell that he had some distressing news to tell.

"What's wrong?" she asked.

"Maggie, I got a message from Everynne. She wants me to go to a planet called Tremonthin to protect someone, a Tharrin named Ceravanne. It's important that I go soon."

"Protect her from what?" Maggie asked. "The Dronon?" She shivered involuntarily as she imagined the huge insectlike alien that the townsfolk had mistaken two weeks ago for Beelzebub, Lord of the Flies.

Gallen had defeated the Dronon Lords in single combat, winning the title of Lords of the Swarm for himself and Maggie, and as the new queen of the Dronon Swarm, Maggie had banished the Dronon from the human-occupied worlds before she returned home to Tihrglas for her wedding.

Still, she imagined that some Dronon would cause trouble. They didn't think like humans at all. Certainly, when the next Dronon hive queen matured, she would bring her Lord Escort to battle Gallen and Maggie, hoping to win back the title of Lords of the Swarm, believing that the title gave them the right to control ten thousand human-occupied worlds.

So Maggie's return to Tihrglas served a purpose beyond allowing her wedding, for it kept her hidden from enemy Dronon.

"No, it's not the Dronon," Gallen said. "There is something called 'the Inhuman' on Tremonthin. I'm not sure what it is—a

secret society, perhaps. A group of people seeking control."
Gallen's jaw was set, rigid. Maggie knew that look. He was
ready for a fight, and God forgive anyone who stood up to him.

"The Lady Semmaritte warned me of Tremonthin before she
died," Maggie said. "She wanted us to go there, and she said
that your skills as a warrior would be sorely tested."

In the past two weeks, Gallen had been preparing for battle
in ways that Maggie had never seen before. With this mantle of
a Lord Protector that he wore during practice, this artificial
intelligence that stored more information than a thousand
libraries could hold, Gallen was learning secrets of combat that
he'd never imagined. He said that he wanted to be more
prepared when next he met the Dronon, and Maggie suspected
that he would be up for the test on Tremonthin. But the Lady
Semmaritte hadn't seemed so sure.

Gallen seemed preoccupied as he looked at the corpses.
Thomas had put the weapons from the dead Vanquisher and
Everynne's warrior atop the bodies. Gallen picked up the
Vanquisher's incendiary rifle. "We shouldn't leave these weapons functional," he said. "Some kid might pull the trigger and
put the town to fire." He cracked the rifle at the stock, pulled
out its power pack and projectiles, then laid it back down.

Maggie stood beside him, picked up the vibro-blade from the
dead woman's hand, pulled out its power pack. The dead
woman had a bag at her side, and Maggie pulled it open. Inside
were rations, a couple of Black Fog grenades, a microwave
bomb, a light globe that flashed blindingly when she squeezed
it.

Gallen stuffed the items into his pockets, then pulled some
weapons from the green Vanquisher's munitions belt.

Once he'd secreted anything that might prove dangerous,
Gallen stood for a moment, then took Maggie's hand, let out an
uneasy breath.

"I have to go to Tremonthin soon. A week or two at the
longest. I'll try to finish the job quickly. But Maggie, darling, I
think you should stay here."

"I won't have you leave me behind," Maggie said. "You could
get hurt or killed or lose your key to the Gate of the World, and

I'd never see you again." She didn't speak her greatest fear: that the Dronon were hunting them, and without Gallen, Maggie would have no protection from the creatures.

"But if you come away with me, you'll be exposing yourself to more danger," Gallen said. "I'd rather have you safe, here, planning our wedding."

Maggie folded her arms, looked down at the ground, thinking. Gallen wanted her to stay. It might well be that he had her best interests at heart, but she couldn't bear the thought of remaining here in Clere. What if he lost his key to the Gate of the World and never came back? She could never be happy on a backward planet like Tihrglas, not when there were worlds with starships and immortals out there. And she couldn't be happy without Gallen near.

And suddenly she knew why Gallen was so distant. "You're not ready to leave Clere yet, are you?"

"Sure, I'm not happy to be going. I came home imagining how I'd snatch some rest, thinking about going fishing one last time. But we've been home two weeks, and I've thought of nothing but the Dronon—how I'll handle them when next we meet.

"One day of rest—that's all I want," Gallen said. "I'll go fishing tomorrow, and we can pretend that nothing horrible ever happened to us. Come with me, okay? We can make a picnic."

Maggie squinted, wondering what Thomas would say about her leaving a hundred guests unfed at the inn. But it was her inn, and she could walk away from it if she wanted to.

"I'm coming with you, Gallen," Maggie said, taking both of his hands in hers, looking into his face. "I won't feel safer without you, and I certainly couldn't be happy without you. I'll go anywhere you want to go—fishing tomorrow, if you want— Tremonthin the day after. I'll be your wife. You know that I'd jump into pits of hell with you on a moment's notice."

"Oh, that's what I'm worried about," Gallen said solemnly. Now that that was settled, he looked around, talking as he thought. "I'll need to hire someone to watch my mother while I'm gone. I'll tell her I've got work on a merchant ship sailing to Greenland. With the wild rumors flying around about me, she'll think I'm just leaving till the furor dies. And we'll have to send word to Orick, discover if he wants to come with us."

Maggie found herself trembling with anticipation at the thought of getting back on the road. "He'll come."

There were a million things to take care of, Maggie knew. They'd have to leave town—escape Thomas—without drawing undue attention.

Gallen kissed her one last time for the night. Then he took her hand and they slipped out of the stable.

Six

Night came with darkening clouds at Mack's Landing, and Orick sat with Grits and the sheriffs on the strand under the shade of the oaks, warming by the campfire.

He'd finished his third bowl of wine and sixth bowl of stew, and he felt more than a bit dizzy. When he'd first come into camp, Orick had been tense as a reed. But the warm wine had performed miracles. He felt drowsy, ready to sleep.

It was late, and the sheriffs had gone to telling unlikely stories. One boy told of the village of Droichead Bo far in the north, where a young witch named Cara Bullinger learned the banshee's song and sang it upon a hill, slaying every person, horse, cat, and cockroach within the sound of her voice. He said that after they took care of Gallen O'Day, they should go after this Bullinger woman. Another man agreed, saying that he too had heard of strange deaths up there—livestock and whatnot—and most likely it was this woman causing trouble.

While some younger sheriffs looked about the campfire with frightened, pasty faces, Orick just guffawed and said, "Why, where'd you ever hear such a concoction?"

"I have a cousin who swears it's true," the boy sheriff said. "He heard her singing the banshee's song."

"He can't have heard any such thing! If he had, he'd be dead, too!" Orick grumbled, not wanting to listen to such foolishness. He'd given them a real tale about how Gallen had gotten involved with otherworldly beings. Not some lie.

Across the fire, the scar-faced sheriff, who'd given his name as Sully, poured another bottle of wine into a bowl for Orick, and handed it to him. "Ah, don't get angry at the lad, Orick. He's just trying to keep the men entertained. No harm in that."

"But it's a flawed tale—" Orick began to say, and Sheriff Sully looked up at him with glistening, malevolent eyes, and suddenly Orick remembered that he'd been going under the name Boaz, and he hadn't wanted these lawmen to know his real name, for they planned to kill Gallen O'Day.

Sheriff Sully grabbed for his sword, growling, "I'll have a few words with you. I'd like to discover your part in this whole affair!"

Orick spun away from the campfire, but a young man had come up behind him, sword drawn. Orick was trapped between the two. Grits grumbled into his ear. "You told him your real name! Is there anything else you want to tell them?"

More sheriffs leapt up and pulled their swords, surrounding them.

Orick couldn't think straight, his head was spinning so badly. He worried about blades slicing his pelt, but remembered Lady Everynne's gift. The nanodocs flowing through his veins were marvelous at healing wounds.

Orick spun and lunged, pushing past one young sheriff. The sheriff's sword whipped through the air, slicing deeply into Orick's shoulder.

Orick roared at the pain, but continued running on three legs past a tree where the horses were tethered to a line. He roared again, spooking the horses so that their lines snapped as they reared and kicked. A couple of hounds rushed out from under a tree, yelping and snapping. Orick slashed one with his paw, knocking it into the ground, and the other yelped and leapt back, then Orick was running beside the lake under heavy cloud cover.

Orick could run faster than any human over short distances, so he sped out over the mud, turned toward the mountains and the highway beyond, and kept running until he was out of bowshot. Then he turned and stood. He was bleeding profusely, and he looked back toward the sheriffs. Their camp was in an uproar. Men were rushing for their horses, breaking camp. Grits stood beside the campfire on all fours, her back arched, growling as sheriffs ringed her about with swords.

Orick whined, then sniffed the air ahead toward a row of dark hills. He was nine miles from An Cochan, twelve miles from Clere. Normally it would be a casual day-long ride for the sheriffs, but they could make it in hours under a forced march.

He licked at his wound, and pain lanced through him. He got on all fours, then hobbled along as fast as he could. He'd have to reach Gallen soon.

Seven

———

Orick shouted, "Man, get your legs into your pants—or it's your life!" Orick shoved his snout into Gallen's ribs, and Gallen roused himself enough to sit up in bed.

Orick smelled of damp fur and the woods, with the metallic tang of blood. The bedroom door was open, and embers smoldered in the fire in the living room, enough so that Gallen could see dimly.

"What is it?" Gallen cried, trying to clear the cobwebs from his head. He'd been up half the night, and it was not yet dawn.

"There's an army of sheriffs and their deputies coming!" Orick panted. "Some northern bishop served a warrant. And they've brought the Lord Inquisitor. Some ruffians swear you prayed to the devil," he panted, "that killed Father Heany. They're coming, and they're not far behind me!"

Blood matted the fur of Orick's right shoulder. "Are you all right?" Gallen asked.

"I'll not die from this scratch. Run, man!"

Gallen leapt from bed, hair prickling on the back of his neck. He pulled on his tunic and britches.

A heavy pounding came at the door, and someone shouted, "Gallen O'Day, rouse yourself—in the name of the law!"

"By God, they're here!" Orick cried. "Run!"

Gallen sighed, knowing it was too late to run. "Don't excite yourself, Orick. You never run from the law. If those sheriffs have got their bows strung, they could shoot me in the back, and they'd be in the right."

"Come out, now!" a sheriff roared. "Or we'll break the door in!"

"Coming!" Gallen called. He felt awake now, awake enough to know he was in mortal danger, sleepy enough to be unsure what to do.

If I was the fastest talker in the world, he wondered, what would I say to these sheriffs right now? He closed his eyes a moment, wondering.

Gallen's mother had gotten out of bed. She went to the fireplace in her nightcap and robe. She called in a frightened voice, "Gallen? What is it?"

"Open the door, Mother," Gallen said. "Tell them I'm dressing." He pulled on his soft leather boots.

"Coming," Gallen's mother shouted.

The front door crashed open, and a scar-faced sheriff rushed in, shoved Gallen's mother to the floor. She cried out, and the sheriff stood over her, backed by two rough-looking men with drawn swords. Behind them, in the shadows, stood a tall man with a narrow face, wearing the crimson robes with the white cross of the Lord Inquisitor. Gallen's mother put her hand up to protect her face, lest the sheriff beat her.

"Come out here!" Scarface ordered.

Gallen slowly strapped his knives over the outside of his tunic, and the sheriff simply raised one dark eyebrow and watched him, licked his lips, and studied Orick.

"You have a warrant?" Gallen asked.

"I do." Scarface answered just a bit too slowly. "You're to be taken north to Battlefield, where you'll be tried for witchcraft."

Gallen looked into the man's dark eyes, and saw that he was frightened.

"If you've got a warrant," Gallen said, "let me see it."

The sheriff hesitated. "You'll have time enough to study it on the road north."

"I'll study it now," Gallen said. "And we'll have a talk with the local sheriffs. You had better show just cause for breaking down my mother's door, and you've no right to hit an old woman in any case," Gallen said. "I'm going to make you pay dear for that!" Gallen tried to keep the deadly tone from his voice. He'd never killed a sheriff, but just at this moment, anger blossomed in him, and he was fighting the urge.

Scarface studied Gallen. "Are you threatening me?"

Gallen looked up at the Inquisitor standing behind Scarface. The churchman had glittering, calculating blue eyes. He was waiting for Gallen to give him the slightest pretext for an arrest. "I wouldn't think of threatening you," Gallen said calmly. "But I'll swear out a complaint on you for battering my mother— now, show me your warrant."

"Just come peaceful," Scarface said, "and we'll take it easy on you." He stood straighter, widened his stance, and put one hand on his own short sword.

"You know who I am," Gallen said softly. "I'm a lawman, just like you—a licensed guard with my oath-bond posted at Baille Sean. You're fifty miles out of your jurisdiction. Now, the law says you can arrest me if you've got a warrant," Gallen said softly. "But if you don't have it, I can defend myself from wrongful arrest, *if need be*."

Scarface signaled to a man behind him, and the fellow produced a wooden scroll case, painted in thick lacquer.

"Here it is." The Inquisitor spoke from behind Scarface, taking the tube in his own hand. Gallen was surprised at the softness of his voice. He sounded like some gentle monastic brother who tended lambs, not the fearsome torturer he was reputed to be.

"There should be no need for all of this posing, for hiding behind legal technicalities," the Inquisitor told Gallen softly. "Sir, you have grievous charges leveled against you. A priest has died, and this is a matter of deep concern to the clergy. I should think that you would welcome the opportunity to clear your name. After all, if it were commonly believed that you were guilty of witchcraft, your family's reputation would be stained. . . ." He looked meaningfully to Gallen's mother. Gallen was not fooled by such soft words. This man was hinting at retribution against Gallen's whole family.

"If there are charges against me," Gallen said, "then they're leveled by false witnesses, and I'll fight those charges as best I can. I'll have a look at your warrant." Gallen stepped forward and took it from the torturer's hand, carried the paper over to the wan firelight. His mother got up and looked over his shoulder with Orick. The Inquisitor and his men shifted uneasily.

"This paper isn't legal," Gallen realized. "You can't take me north without the signature from the Lord Sheriff at Baille Sean."

Scarface said forcefully, "We were on our way to Baille Sean for the signature when we met that bear friend of yours! He came to warn you. We couldn't just let you go running off into the night!"

Gallen shrugged, handed the paper to Scarface. "I'm afraid you'll have to go to Baille Sean and talk to Lord Sheriff Carnaghan. And say hello to him for me. He's a good friend. I once saved his son from some highwaymen."

Scarface shook his head angrily, growling from the back of his throat. "Damned southerners! How am I supposed to execute a warrant against you?"

"Legally—" Gallen said, "or not at all." He rested his hands on his knives. If the man was going to attack, now would be the time.

Scarface studied Gallen, eyeing the knives that he wore. Gallen almost hoped that he'd make his move. But the Lord Inquisitor backed up a step, told the men, "Surround the house. I'll go to Baille Sean and speak with Lord Sheriff Carnaghan personally."

He backed out slowly, and Scarface closed the ruined door. Gallen let them go. Gallen's mother shoved the door tight, bolted it. "That sheriff is a blackguard, sure," she said. "The nerve, breaking into an old woman's house and knocking her off her feet!" She looked at Gallen disapprovingly, as if he should have come to her rescue.

Orick hurried to Gallen's side. "Gallen, you're not going to let them get away with this, are you?"

Gallen looked from his mother to Orick. There was little that he could do. A moment later, Thomas Flynn pushed his way through the door, followed by Gallen's cousin, Father Brian from An Cochan. The sheriffs were so thick around the house-tree that the two men could hardly get through.

Thomas Flynn seemed unperturbed by the whole affair, but Father Brian looked about with wide eyes. The young priest had obviously rushed to get out the door at his own house. He had on his black frock, but without the white collar. His face was red from the night air.

"They've got Maggie," Thomas said to Gallen. "They say they're taking her north as a witness against you. They're already filling out a subpoena."

"Those . . . rascals!" Father Brian said. "They're low, dirty rascals, that's all I can say of them! The thought of it—holding the girl hostage!"

"They only took her to keep Gallen from running," Thomas said. "And she gave one of them a bloody nose for it. I like that."

Gallen clenched his fists, looked about. There was nothing he could do to stop them from taking Maggie. They couldn't arrest Gallen without a warrant signed by the Lord Sheriff, but they could subpoena a witness, and they could hold her in prison for questioning for weeks.

"It's that damned Patrick O'Connor," Father Brian said. "He's been telling everyone false tales about you! I should have had you kill him!"

"Patrick O'Connor?" Thomas asked.

Gallen was deep in thought, so Father Brian offered, "He's the son of a sheep farmer, Seamus O'Connor, from An Cochan. Two weeks ago, Seamus hired Gallen to escort him home, and they were set upon by robbers. Gallen fought them, but the robbers had him down and would have slit his throat, when the Angel of Death came and rescued Gallen and Seamus, too.

The next day, Gallen and I caught that blackguard Patrick with soot on his face and blood on his shoes. We discovered that the boy had set the robbers on his *own father*, hoping for a cut of the money! I thought to have Gallen kill the boy, but Gallen is a merciful sort, so we outlawed him from County Morgan. But now Patrick is mucking about the countryside, telling stories on Gallen, causing trouble!"

"It wasn't just Patrick who caused the trouble," Gallen said, grateful that the priest was willing to bolster Gallen's good name by claiming that it was his idea to show some mercy to the lad. In truth, neither of them had thought of killing the boy. "He's down south telling his tales. But some other robbers from up north escaped. They must have heard of Patrick's efforts to smear my name. Now Orick says that they've put a story together and plan to testify against me."

"Like as not," Orick grumbled, "some of those sheriffs out there are relatives to the robbers!"

"Granted, I'll give you that," Father Brian said. "Some of those northerners are an inbred lot, but a man can't choose his kin." He thought a moment, pacing nervously, and said, "I could raise the town in your behalf, Gallen! Most everyone is awake already, circling the house. We'll show these *northern* sheriffs!"

"If you do," Gallen said, "there will be bloodshed. We don't want that. I can't think of a man in town who I want to see dead. Besides, even if you won, you'd find yourself on trial."

Gallen's mother sat heavily on the sofa before the fireplace. She wrapped her arms around herself protectively. Gallen wondered at how small she'd become in the past few years. When he was young, she'd seemed beautiful and tall and strong. But over the past few months, since the death of Gallen's father, she'd gone into decline in a terrible way. Now she was a mere potato, a lumpy, frail woman with graying hair.

Her jaw trembled. "You'd better get out of here, son," she said, as if the words were bitter on her tongue. "You can fight your way past these sheriffs, I'll wager."

"I won't do that," Gallen said, wondering. His prowess with weapons seemed to be growing to legendary heights if even his own mother thought he could fight his way past dozens of well-armed opponents. The really frightening thing was, Gallen was tempted to give it a try. "I won't play the outlaw. I couldn't make a run for it without a fight first, and I'd have to kill some of them. And even if I won through, Maggie would still end up in their prison, and there's no telling what the Inquisitor might do."

"If the girl loves you, nothing would make her happier than to help you, whatever way she can," Gallen's mother protested.

"No," Gallen said. "I won't play their game. We have to fight them legally."

He looked up, saw that Maggie's uncle was watching him, measuring him with his eyes, and he wore a look of respect. Thomas was an odd one, in Gallen's book. He'd been around the world, probably been in his share of scrapes. He'd come to lord it over his niece, stop her from marrying in order to line his own pockets, and that showed a bit of larceny in his heart. And he had a commanding way about him. While others here were all floundering about for solutions, Thomas seemed unperturbed, as if he knew how Gallen could get out of this spot, but just wasn't saying. Gallen decided to ask him bluntly.

"You've been around, Thomas. Have you got any ideas?"

"If you let them take you north, you're a dead man, sure," Thomas grumbled. He went over to the rocking chair by the fireplace, pulled a pipe from his pocket, and began tamping it full of tobacco. "They don't like southerners much, and they're a close-knit lot. Inbred, some of them. You've killed their kin, and even if you got off with a whipping, some of them are likely to lie in wait for you and slit your throat on the road home. You need to stay here, fight them on your own ground. Take this thing to trial here. That's your legal right. And make sure your friends and cousins are all sitting in the jury."

"That's correct, a man has a right to be tried in his own town!" Father Brian said.

"Not in his own town, but in the jurisdiction where the crime was committed," Thomas corrected. "Which is one and the same, in this case. But to tell you straight, I'm worried that these sheriffs will go carting Gallen and Maggie off, in spite of the law. There's not much here to stop them."

Father Brian frowned. "Then there's only one thing to do. I'll go to Baille Sean and talk to Lord Sheriff Carnaghan. I'll raise an army of sheriffs and deputies to make sure that Gallen gets an open trial here in town. That way, these damned northerners won't be able to torment him in secret, and they won't table a jury stacked with his enemies."

Thomas nodded, and Father Brian got up, went outside into the darkness, shoving past the sheriffs and grumbling, "Out of my way! Get out—or I'll excommunicate the lot of you!" Outside the door, the sky had lightened a crack. Dawn was approaching.

Moments later, Gallen heard a horse race by on the road south, and Gallen was surprised that Father Brian would ride with such daring in so little light. Silently, Gallen prayed that Father Brian's horse would race surefooted over the mountains.

Orick nuzzled up to Gallen, putting his face against Gallen's ribs, and Gallen stroked his nose absently. He could see no easy way out of this.

His mother got up from the couch. "It's going to be a long day, what with everyone running off to see the Lord Sheriff. At least we don't have to wait on an empty stomach."

"Aye, what a day," Thomas said. "Between the trial and my oddities, the inn will be bustling. We might as well put a tent over the whole town. Why, all we lack for a circus is a few dancing horses and a singing dog—the clowns and ringmasters are already in attendance."

In the kitchen, Gallen's mother began mixing dough and banging pots.

Orick lay at Gallen's feet. The bloody wound to his shoulder was all scabbed over, and the poor bear lay for a bit, licking himself.

When Thomas was sure that Gallen's mother was occupied, Thomas leaned forward. "Lad," he said, "I'm afraid that this trial might go bad for you. It's said that the angels have come to your aid before. Is there a chance that they'll come now?"

"I'm afraid not," Gallen said.

Thomas licked his lips. "Then they're gone now, to whatever world they hail from?"

Thomas looked into Gallen's eyes quizzically, and Gallen wondered how much he knew—or had guessed. "Yes, they're gone, and I don't think they'll be back."

Thomas leaned forward conspiratorially, and whispered, "You've talked to an angel? Wha—what did the creature say, man?"

Gallen found his heart hammering. He was torn between the desire to speak the truth, and the desire to keep his secrets. "There are many worlds beyond Geata na Chruinne," Gallen said, "and people there are not so different than they are here. Some of them are far more beautiful than anything you dream. Some of them are wise. Some of them live forever. In many ways, life is easier there than it is here, but there are also greater perils."

Thomas sat back, stunned, his face a mask of hope and confusion. "Well, I'll be . . . I wonder . . . I wish I could see . . . I wish I could have talked to an angel."

Gallen could see Thomas's secret desire written plain on his face. The man wanted to see what lay beyond Geata na Chruinne, and Gallen had promised Maggie that he'd talk to Thomas about a quick date for the wedding. He wondered if he told Thomas the truth, if Thomas could understand how important it was for Maggie to marry soon.

"Maggie and I have both been beyond the gate with the folk that you call angels," Gallen said. "And now that Maggie's been there, she won't rest easy until she washes the dust of this world from off her feet once and for all."

Orick had quit licking his wounds, and now he looked up. "Well, if you're going to say that much, you might as well tell him the whole truth, Gallen." Orick turned to Thomas. "Gallen and Maggie are people of some import out there now. They have to return. The fate of ten thousand worlds rests on their shoulders."

Thomas sat back, as if expecting Gallen to sprout horns from his head or wings from his back. It was an utterly fantastic tale that Gallen was telling, yet the dead "demon" and "angel" in

Thomas's shed gave some proof of it. Thomas must have believed him, for the old minstrel began to weep. "People there can live forever?" Thomas asked. "And all you have to do is walk through Geata na Chruinne?"

"You need a key to the gate," Orick said.

"And have you got one?"

Gallen nodded.

"Can I see it?" Thomas begged, making little grasping motions with one hand.

Gallen checked to make certain that his mother wasn't watching, then he went to his room, came back with the key—a glowing crystal globe with golden wiring inside.

Thomas stared in awe, held it in both hands. "This is not of this world, that's sure," Thomas said. "But I don't know if it's a thing of God, or of the devil."

"Neither," Gallen said. "It was made by the Tharrin, a race of good people who rule the heavens."

Thomas licked his lips, handed the key back to Gallen, who scooted it into his pocket. Thomas said, "So why haven't you gone already? Is it those green-skinned devils?"

"Something like that," Gallen said. "Maggie and I have enemies who will begin hunting us soon, and this is a good place to hide. Maggie wants to get married here, before we leave. And to tell the truth, I wanted to say goodbye to my friends."

"So that's why Maggie is so hot to marry you now," Thomas said. "She doesn't care about your political future, because your future lies elsewhere."

Gallen nodded.

Thomas folded his hands, stared at them thoughtfully for a long time. "And if you don't like it out there, you can always come back here, I suppose?"

"Aye," Gallen said. "We could."

Thomas leaned back in his chair, studied Gallen a moment, his gray eyes measuring the boy. His beard and moustache were impeccably trimmed. His body was leathery, but he had a gut growing on him. He was at that stage of life where he was still tough, but somewhat worn. And in his bright purple pants and a peach-colored shirt, he looked as if he should be out juggling or singing in the streets. "I want to go with you," Thomas admitted at last.

"Are you sure?" Gallen asked. "It's a big place, stranger than I have time to tell."

"Hmmm . . ." Thomas eyed the boy thoughtfully, almost grudgingly. "I've never put much faith in God and heaven, or any rewards in the afterlife. But dammit, boy, *I want to live forever!*"

"And if I were to take you with me," Gallen mused, "what could you pay?" He said it as a joke, but Thomas didn't see it as one.

"How much do you want?" Thomas asked, licking his lips.

And Gallen realized that there was only one answer. Nothing that Thomas took with him would be of any value out there. "Everything you own," Gallen said. He watched the old man smile weakly, thinking he would balk at the price. "All of it. You'll give it all to my mother, and go into the next world as broke as a babe."

Thomas watched him calculatingly. "I'll need my lute and my mandolin and flutes."

"You can keep those," Gallen said.

"A fitting price," Thomas agreed. "I'll make out the papers this morning."

"And one more thing: I want consent to marry your niece."

"No, no," Orick said. "You can't barter for her like that, Gallen. It's not proper."

Thomas smiled greedily, and he scratched his beard, thinking.

"Maggie won't care. We'll all get what we want," Gallen said. "What does it matter what price Thomas and I agree on?"

"It's a deal," Thomas said, and he reached out his hand. The two men shook. "I'll go tell her. She's got her dress made, so you can marry as soon as the priest gets back."

Thomas got up, swaggered to the door, opened it and looked out at the sheriffs all gathered around out there. "Oh, it's going to be the damnedest long day you ever saw," Thomas bellowed, and he was out the door.

After Thomas left, Gallen's mother fixed a huge breakfast of ham and eggs with sweet rolls, and in the early morning dawn, Gallen, his mother, and Orick sat down to eat, watching the sheriffs outside through the windows, who all stared in at the banquet with envy.

All through the morning, there was nothing to do but sit, and Gallen waited with a heavy heart, considered routes of escape. But escape was out of the question. Orick tried to go outside, for the sheriffs had one of his bear friends, a female named Grits, in custody, but the sheriffs would not let him past.

And so they sat. In a couple of hours, Thomas came back and sang to the sheriffs a bit, sat with them and drank, laughing, as if they were all as thick as thieves. He came in for a minute, warned Gallen to lock all the doors and windows, and keep his weapons handy. "There's some sentiment for a lynching out there among those boys. They've come a long way to get you, and they don't want to go back empty-handed. But I think I can cool their heads," Thomas whispered, then he was back out the door.

In the early afternoon, the scar-faced sheriff came back to Gallen's door, offering him a bargain. "If you come with us now," the sheriff said, droplets of nervous perspiration on his brow, "I'm prepared to set your fiancée free. No harm will come to her."

"And if I don't come with you?" Gallen asked, wondering why the sheriff wanted a bargain, what had spooked him.

"Who knows?" the sheriff said. "We'll take her north for questioning. It's a dangerous road. Prisoners have been known to get killed while trying to escape. And the interrogations can get brutal. Even if your girl does make it through all of this, she'll have a long walk home, over lonely roads, where robbers sometimes would rather take a woman's virtue than her purse."

"You wouldn't dare," Gallen said. There was some shouting outside, townsmen arguing with sheriffs, and Gallen suddenly knew why the sheriff was getting nervous. The crowd was growing, becoming unmanageable.

"With fifty men to back me?" the sheriff said. "Oh, I'd dare."

Just then, Thomas came up to the door behind the sheriff. "Say, Gallen," Thomas chortled. "It looks as if you're getting pretty thick with Sheriff Sully here. He's the leader of this band of merry lawmakers, you know."

He pushed past the sheriff, carrying his lute in its case of rosewood, leaving the door wide open. He sat on the couch, pulled out the lute.

"Why don't you invite Sheriff Sully in, Gallen?" Thomas said. "I've been working on ballads about this meeting—the meeting of Gallen O'Day and Sheriff Sully—and I'd like you to hear them. They may be sung all over the world for many years, so I'd like your opinion."

He began fingering his lute, then apologized. "This is an early draft of the song, as you'll gather. It's a bit simple, a bit crude, but I always think a song should reflect its subject matter, don't you?"

Gallen looked to Sully, and he shrugged.

"Now, there is one point I want to be clear on," Thomas said. "You've got a nasty scar on your face, Sheriff Sully, and with a man in your line of work, one might imagine that you got it fighting some notorious outlaw. But that's not how you got the scar, is it?"

"No," Sully said.

"As I understand from your townsmen out there, it came about through a whittling mishap?"

Sully squinted and nodded.

Thomas plucked a few notes on his lute, then sang sweetly,

"Come near and listen girls and listen boys,
Whether you be virtuous or bullies
Learn good from bad while you're still young
Don't let your name be Sullied."

Sheriff Sully stiffened, reached for the haft of his sword, a sneer spreading across his face.

"Och, now!" Thomas stopped, looked up. "Do you know the penalty for drawing a blade against a minstrel?" Thomas said.

"We carry a license for this work from the Lord Mayor, you know."

"You can't sing songs about me, unless a judge approves them!" Sully cried.

"I can't sing songs *in public*," Thomas said. "But I can compose them in private. I'm sure I can clear the song through the review process before going public. It contains nothing slanderous, only the facts. Here's how it goes . . ." His hands strummed, and he continued in a sweet voice,

> *"Now, when Sheriff Sully was a lad of ten,*
> *he slept in his own piddle.*
> *He drowned young rats in his grandma's well*
> *And sliced his face up when he whittled."*

When Thomas sang the word "whittled," he hit a sour note on his lute, smiled up at the two of them. "That's the first verse. Sheriff Sully was a bed wetter, Gallen. Did you know that?" Sully's face had turned a bright red, and he stood there mortified. Several other sheriffs were standing outside the door, and Thomas had sung loud enough for them to hear. Their guffaws reverberated through the room, and they pressed closer. "Anyway," Thomas said, "here's my idea for the chorus!" His voice took on a gravelly note as he pounded the strings of his lute and snarled,

> *"But who knew,*
> *that when his body grew,*
> *his mind would stay so damned little?*
> *Yes, he wounds himself when he whittles!*
> *And you never know where he'll piddle!"*

Thomas got up and strolled the room as he sang through the next two verses. And Sully's eyes became more and more wild, more desperate and full of rage.

> *"Sully matured into a fearsome lad,*
> *He turned his knife on others.*

And as sheriffs go, he wasn't bad,
at poking the wife of his own brother!

But who knew,
that when his body grew,
his soul would stay so damned little?
Yes, he wounds himself when he whittles!
And you never know where he'll piddle!
And with his sister-in-law he diddles!

Now Sheriff Sully knew he was brave,
And he vowed to stamp out sin!
So he hunted that worthy Gallen O'Day
backed by only a hundred well-armed men!

But who knew
that when his body grew
his heart would stay so damned little?
Yes, he wounds himself when he whittles!
And you never know where he'll piddle!
And with his sister-in-law he diddles!
And what he calls 'valor' is a riddle!"

"Enough!" Sheriff Sully screamed, reaching for his sword. But one of his men, who had been inching in through the open door, grabbed his arm and wrestled it behind his back.

"Oh, I don't think it's nearly enough." Thomas grinned. "I've got several more verses."

"I challenge you to a duel . . . you," Sully roared. "You knave!"

"Oh, a duel, is it?" Thomas said. "Well, if you're going to abuse me with language like that, then I accept."

Gallen looked back and forth between the men for a moment. Sully was younger, bigger, and stronger than Thomas, and in any match, the minstrel was sure to lose.

"I accept your challenge," Thomas said, "and since you've offered the duel, I shall choose the weapons!"

He walked over to the sheriff, who suddenly was glancing about worriedly, wondering what trick the minstrel was playing. Thomas glanced meaningfully at Gallen's knives, looked over the swords of a couple of Sully's men. "It shall be a duel . . . of tongues," Thomas said. "You and I shall stand and hurl insults at each other for an evening, and we'll find out who wilts first under the weight of a good tongue-lashing."

"You . . . you bombastic, overdressed . . ." The sheriff could not think what next to say.

"Ah, how right you are!" Thomas said, looking down at his own peach-colored shirt and purple trousers. "You wound me with your foulmouthed invectives, sir—mortally!"

Thomas plucked at his lute, a tune that was now becoming familiar, and Sully let out a scream of frustration. He shouted at his own men, herding them outside, and rushed from the house, slamming the door behind him. Gallen could hear Sully's own men guffawing as he passed.

"You shouldn't have done that," Gallen said. "You've only infuriated him."

"No," Thomas said, putting the lute away. "I've done right. Every man who abuses power as he does will come under scrutiny in time. He wants to be your judge and executioner, but his deeds here will be judged by others for years to come. My song only reminds him of this fact."

"He might kill you for what you just did," Gallen said.

"Very likely," Thomas agreed. "And if I died tonight, every minstrel in the land would come to sing of it, and Sully's fate would be far worse than he fears. Mere mortals cannot withstand the muse."

Gallen stared at the door a moment. "I find it odd that this Mister Sully should hate me so much. As far as I know, I've never harmed him or his kin."

"You're a great lawman, Gallen," Thomas said. "And he's not much of anything. You wound his pride just by being alive. You'll find that he's much like small men everywhere."

Gallen studied Thomas, and found that he felt a new respect for the man. He'd just sliced Sheriff Sully to the core as easily as Gallen would gut a highwayman. There was no remorse, no fear of recourse, and now Gallen saw why Thomas carried himself with a lordly demeanor.

"I don't mean to sound critical," Gallen said. "But that wasn't much of a song you sang. I mean, it was a nice ditty, a catchy tune, but I think it needs some work."

Thomas looked up at Gallen with disinterested eyes. "You're a critic, eh? Don't fear. That bit of bawdy wasn't meant to immortalize Sully, only intimidate him. In the business we call it a 'driver,' for it is meant only to drive a man away from his hometown. The real ballad will have to be much longer, with entire stanzas devoted to Sully's bed-wetting, and whole movements devoted to exposing his acts of incest. I feel sorry for the man. Few men's lives can bear such close scrutiny." Thomas sighed. "And now that my day's work is done, I think I'll take a nap."

He yawned, made his way back outside. The sheriffs hooted and cheered as he passed.

In the early evening, Father Brian rode back on a winded horse with a writ from Lord Sheriff Carnaghan deputizing every man in Clere to make sure that Gallen wasn't taken from the city, and he forbade the prosecution from securing testimony by torture, and ordered Maggie Flynn to be freed. Because of the fear that open warfare might break out between the northern sheriffs and the locals, the city of Baille Sean was sending a judge in great haste.

Gallen had hardly heard this news from one of the local fishermen, when Father Brian came banging on the door, calling, "Out with you, man. Get on your finest duds, and out of the house with you!"

"What's happening?" Gallen asked, opening the door enough to see the sheriffs all crowded about, with Father Brian standing there, looking a bit worn.

"Today is to be your wedding day," Father Brian said. "It seems that Thomas Flynn has taken a sudden fondness to you, and he says that if you so desire, he wants you to marry his niece before nightfall!"

Eight

Gallen and Maggie's wedding was perhaps the strangest that ever took place in the village of Clere. By dusk, nearly everyone from as far as fifteen miles away was in the village, so that tents and wagons filled every field within half a mile of town. And over two hundred men came north from Baille Sean, driving hard, hoping to see what all of the hoopla was about.

Between having a minstrel in town, along with a display of a demon from hell and an angel from heaven, and an occupying army of northern sheriffs who'd come down to hang the local hero, an impending trial on witchcraft, and the marriage of Gallen O'Day—it was all too much for anyone to miss. The poor old church couldn't have held a tenth of the number of people who wanted to view the wedding; and, as Orick grumbled, there was a grand lot of speculation as to the cause of the sudden marriage.

The most evil-minded folks figured that Maggie had come down with a child, and this was all an effort to make it right.

But many a bedazzled maid believed that Maggie loved Gallen, and so she wanted to make him her husband all in one grand gesture before he got hung.

But some old deacon remembered an obscure verse in the Tome of Law, where it pointed out that it was illegal to hang a man within a month of his wedding day, for to do so would not only deny him his life, it would deny him the chance of having posterity.

This last bit of news thoroughly enraged some of the northern sheriffs, who saw this all as some grand scheme to keep Gallen alive for another month, even if they could convict him, ensuring him greater chances of escape.

But the northern sheriffs didn't cause much of an uproar, for to tell the truth, the majority of them began to join in the festive attitude. While the rest of the sheriffs, seeing how with every wagon that pulled into town they were more and more outnumbered, decided to remain quiet. So the sheriffs paid their shillings to go see Thomas's angel and demon, and one sheriff, after seeing the demon, said, "Well, if Gallen O'Day fought those monsters, he's a better man than I am." And he rode off toward home to much applause.

And so the wedding was held in an open field, just before sundown, Maggie in a white dress that made her look radiant, and Gallen dressed in his finest blue tunic with gray hose.

Gallen's cousin, Father Brian of An Cochan, wedded the two, administering the oaths.

Orick the bear played the part of Gallen's "best man," and that caused many a stare. Thomas sang, with the church choir joining him, and never had so sweet a music been heard over the city.

Folks from all over Counties Morgan, Obhiann, and Daugherty tried to outdo one another on wedding gifts—trying to show those northern sheriffs how much they admired Gallen. Seamus O'Connor gave Gallen a nice carriage, while a friend of Gallen's father gave the couple a brace of white stallions. Silver teapots took all of one table, while blankets and coats and saddles and all other manner of finery filled up others.

Someone brought out a whiskey keg, and those folks who had nothing else to give began filling it with money, and more than one gold coin was seen therein. Over the past years, Gallen had saved more than a dozen locals from highwaymen, and the roads around Clere were notoriously safe—all because of Gallen O'Day. So folks let their money flow freely in gratitude.

It was just an hour before dusk, and the dancing was in full swing, when the Lord Inquisitor rode into town in a hired coach, his face clenched and frustrated.

Obviously, the terms of the trial were not to his liking. "We'll begin jury selection tonight!" he announced to his men, and they rounded up Gallen and his young wife and herded him back to Gallen's home.

Gallen selected Deacon Green to be his defender in the case, and within the hour the townspeople drew lots for jury duty. All of the northern sheriffs put their lots in, and to Gallen's great dismay, four of them won seats on the jury, along with two men and a woman from nearby. Even in his own village, the jury was stacked against him.

Gallen was given copies of the affidavits sworn against him, and he and Maggie and Orick and Deacon Green studied them for a bit. Three men out of County Obhiann told how they had planned the robbery two weeks ago, how they had taken Seamus O'Connor down, then Gallen, and were beating the men, planning to rob them (they omitted the fact that they were planning to cut Gallen's throat), when they swore that Gallen uttered his prayer and hell itself disgorged one of its minions, a magical man with wicked swords and a face that glowed like starlight. Later, as they ran away, they claimed that they looked back over the hills and saw a strange light, as if the very bowels of hell had opened.

Technically, their case had some weaknesses. In many places their sworn testimony had been copied verbatim from one document to the next, so it would be easy enough to prove that they had been in collusion. Second, they were all felons— robbers who nevertheless swore that murder had never entered their minds that night.

And there were some holes in their testimony. None of them had actually witnessed the bowels of hell open, and they did not claim to have seen any other sign of the demons that troubled the area the next morning.

Yet as Deacon Green, a tall, balding man with round

spectacles, studied the testimony, he muttered under his breath. "Och, Gallen. You're in a tight spot, sure, lad. I don't see a way out of this. You'll do prison time, at the very least."

"How can that be?" Maggie said, sitting on the sofa, holding Gallen's hand. "Why would anyone believe those robbers, instead of Gallen?"

"The Bible says that out of the mouths of two or three witnesses, every word shall be established," Deacon Green said. "And so according to law, if three witnesses testify against a man in a capital case, then that man will . . . well, he'll hang—unless we can shake the accusers."

"What about Seamus O'Connor's testimony?" Maggie asked, biting her lower lip. "We can put him on the stand."

"But what can the man swear to? He was so drunk he had to hire Gallen to keep him from falling off his horse, and then he got a knock in the head halfway through the battle and didn't wake up for four days. He says that he's willing to swear that the men who tried to rob him were murderous bastards, and he hopes they all go to hell. But I'm afraid people can only laugh at any testimony he has to give."

"But we can prove that the witnesses here have something against me," Gallen contended. "Mason and Argent Flaherty both had a brother and a cousin killed in the attack that night. They have a blood debt against me."

"But both of them swear that they came forward to the law out of remorse," the good deacon said. "Both of them are to be whipped with forty lashes for their crime, once they testify against you. If they only wanted revenge, they could have lain in wait for you of a dark night and cut your throat. Now, I know that you feel they have something against you, but the fact is that their remorse seems genuine, and this could sway the jury."

Gallen shook his head, wondering. "Could they have worked out a deal with that Bishop Mackey? Perhaps they'll get a commuted sentence for testifying against me."

"All three men claim that they sought such a bargain, but that Bishop Mackey never spoke a promise in return."

"And what of the reward?" Maggie asked. "Isn't there money

for proving witchcraft against a man? These men are robbers, so why wouldn't they be willing to lie for some money?"

"Fifty pounds." Deacon Green sighed. "Not enough to risk your life for."

Gallen wondered. There is always someone who holds life cheap. All three of these men were desperate. To some degree, they had all risked their lives in trying to rob Seamus O'Connor of fifty pounds, but then it had been nine men against two—and the robbers had never expected Gallen O'Day to be among those two. They'd hoped to get five pounds per man then.

Would they go to so much trouble for a share of fifty pounds split three ways? Not likely, not when you considered that they could be whipped within an inch of their lives, in the bargain.

No, there had to be some other reason for them to bring false charges against Gallen.

So Gallen sat with his head bent low, wondering why these strangers would come like this and try to bring so much trouble down on him.

He wondered if it simply might be a matter of conceit. If they got away with this, these three robbers would be revered among outlaws all across the land as the men who had killed Gallen O'Day. And the very irony that they had taken a lawman and had him executed by the law would be a great jest.

Deacon Green made studious notes, probing for weaknesses in the transcripts, hunting for avenues to pursue. Gallen studied with him for a bit, but his eyes ached from lack of sleep, so he and Maggie went to his room to rest. Maggie just sat on the edge of the bed, holding him for a while, as Gallen considered.

If I were the greatest counselor in the world, Gallen asked himself, what would I do? He rested in Maggie's arms for a long moment, waiting for some insight to fill him, to send knowledge coursing through his body until it seemed that understanding flowed from his fingertips. So often in the past, this technique had served Gallen well. But Gallen waited long, yet no insight came.

Finally, Gallen realized that the deacon's expertise in such matters was far beyond his, so he closed the door to his bedroom, leaving Deacon Green to study and Orick to sit out on the couch talking with Gallen's mother about the injustices committed by the northern sheriffs who were holding Orick's good friend, a she-bear named Grits.

The house began to feel stuffy—with that wet, earthy smell that fills a house-tree in the evening—so he opened his window a crack, looked out. Twenty sheriffs surrounded the house, and Gallen's opening of the window was the most exciting move he had made in hours. Four of them drew in closer, backlit by their campfires.

Gallen sat on his bed, and Sheriff Sully stuck his dark face through the windows. "Needing a bit of fresh air, are you?" he leered. "A bit winded, are you, from doing your business with that juicy little wife of yours? Well, I've got a bit of fresh news for you: guess what? I got on your jury. Isn't that worthy of a laugh?"

"Every juror has to swear that he has nothing against me," Gallen said, surprised at the undisguised malice in the sheriff's voice.

"Oh, and I'll swear it," the sheriff said. "I've got nothing personal against you. It's not your fault that you're so good at what you do. Why, whenever a highwayman strikes, there's always a bit of a bustle, folks wagging their tongues. 'Why can't *our* sheriffs protect us?' they ask. 'Why do we pay these louts three pounds a month, when for just a bit more, we could get Gallen O'Day up here to do the job proper?'

"And when one of us lads goes to a dance and asks an ugly young woman onto the floor, like as not she'll say, 'And who do you think you are that I should dance with you—Gallen O'Day?' So you understand, Gallen, that it's nothing personal, but after the trial, I for one shall be glad to be rid of you!"

Behind Sully, several other sheriffs laughed, as if this were all just part of some great meaningless hoax. They'd come for entertainment, and they didn't care if they were cheering Sully on, or Thomas, or Gallen. It was all just fun.

But there is a look that a man gives you just before he seriously tries to kill you. It is a fixed stare with constricted pupils and a face that is set and determined. It's a look that is both relaxed and calculating, and Gallen saw that look now in the eyes of Sheriff Sully. The man was jealous of him, so jealous that he thought it a small thing to kill Gallen.

The sheriffs turned away, walked back to their campfire. Gallen stood at the window, watching them.

Gallen could smell the scent of fires. "That croaking old frog," Maggie whispered. "I'd like to gouge out his eyes and use them for earrings."

"That isn't a ladylike thing to say," Gallen whispered. A cold pain shot up the back of his spine and through his heart. Never had he felt so weak, so unable to defend himself.

So this is the way it ends for me, he wondered. He had done his job as a bodyguard, perhaps done it too well. Now, highwaymen with blood debts against him would stand as witnesses in his trial, and jealous lawmen would cast their jury ballots against him. And there was no way that he could win.

All of this time, Gallen had believed that others respected him, believed that by fighting so hard against the evils of the world he had won their favor. But now he saw that some of them only feared and hated him for what he'd done.

He laughed under his breath. He'd come home to Tihrglas after his adventures on far worlds, come home with the hope of going salmon fishing in the river, of resting and tasting the scent of the clean air under the pines. He had done it so often in his youth, casting his yellow wet-water flies out into the flood and jigging through the rippled stream until a salmon struck, bending his old hickory pole to the snapping point.

But he hadn't been fishing now in years. Sometime a couple of years ago, he'd put the rod away, and now it looked as if he'd never have the chance to take it up again. Sometime, while trying to win honor and right the wrongs of the world, he'd given up the things he'd enjoyed most.

Gallen glanced into the living room. Deacon Green sat on the sofa, still studying the testimonies of the felons. The creases in his brow and the singular concentration with which he studied showed just how worried he'd become.

It was getting late, and Gallen looked out the window. People were still pouring into town to see the demon and angel in Thomas Flynn's stable.

The trial of Gallen O'Day would be an added sideshow that few would want to miss. Even now, the sheriffs had a fire beside the road, not twenty feet from the door, and they sat together with their three witnesses. Perhaps two hundred observers had gathered around the house to listen while the false witnesses drunkenly railed against Gallen O'Day, telling how he'd summoned demons from hell, and how he'd laughed about it after.

Gallen studied the faces of the men. The two Flaherty brothers were difficult to miss. Mason was a tall man, hard and strong, and Gallen couldn't even recall having seen him in the battle on the night that Seamus was attacked. The younger Flaherty, Argent, was one that Gallen recalled well. He had put a knife to the boy's throat, tried to hold him hostage so that the robbers would back off, let Gallen and Seamus go free. Now, Gallen wished that he had killed the boy in cold blood when he'd had the chance. He doubted that he would be able to get either of the Flahertys to change their testimony.

The third man, though—he interested Gallen. His name was Christian Bean. He was a small man, fat and soft, with a rounded face accentuated by a thin beard. He kept more to himself, seemed almost afraid to talk. Gallen remembered him from the battle, too, but only dimly. The man was a coward who had hung back during the robbery.

Gallen looked up at the stars, thought for a moment of the planet Tremonthin and the young Tharrin woman whose whole world was in jeopardy. Gallen licked his lips, enjoying the way his pulse quickened. Gallen always felt most alive in battle, when the threat of death was imminent. Gallen smiled, for at the moment he felt the thrill.

The spectators at the front of the house began plying Christian Bean with liquor, and he railed against Gallen. Gallen could see the man's face only by firelight—little piggy eyes that glanced worriedly, hunting the shadows around the house as he described the demon he'd seen, its face glowing like a blue star, the swords in its hand.

"It's a shame you don't have another witness in your behalf," Maggie muttered absently from the bed.

With a start, Gallen realized that there *had* been another witness to the attack: the very demon that these men accused Gallen of summoning. Little did anyone realize that the demon was Gallen O'Day himself, in disguise. Everynne had sent him back in time after his journey, so that he would return from his long foray to other worlds before he'd even left his home.

And with a second shock, Gallen realized that Christian Bean didn't fear Gallen or fear that his testimony would be controverted and shown to be a lie. He feared the fairy folk of Coille Sidhe who might yet come to Gallen's aid. With that recognition, Gallen laughed aloud and rushed to Maggie's side and kissed her. He knew what he had to do.

The wind came in blustery just after midnight, and the limbs of the house-tree swayed and cracked. Gallen wore his silver mantle, and his robe of changing colors had taken on a deep black to match the night. He wore his black boots and black fighting gloves, carried a single sword, and in his pockets he had the mask of Fale, a mask of palest silver-blue that shone like starlight.

"Are you sure you should be going out there?" Maggie whispered, as she tied the hood of his robe over his mantle.

"It's the only way I know to shake the witnesses," Gallen said. "If I can scare them into admitting the truth, there will never be a trial."

Maggie gave him a kiss for luck, then sent him on his way.

Under cover of darkness, and with the sound of the wind and the chattering of voices and the singing accompanied by lutes in the distance, Gallen climbed to the attic of the house-tree and slid open the service door. Slowly, and ever so quietly, he crept out on a limb, then reached back and closed the door behind.

There were people everywhere below him. There could not be less than a hundred just under the bough he was on. Some were sheriffs, but many were just curious onlookers.

Gallen closed his eyes and let the sensors on his mantle show him the scene in infrared. He climbed from limb to limb, until he was nearly over the little knot of sheriffs who sat beside the fire.

Taking a small Dronon translator from his pocket, he clipped it to his lapel, then flipped off the translator so that its microphone would simply amplify his voice.

All night long, travelers had been forcing rum and beer onto the sheriffs and the witnesses, and Gallen sat listening to them talk, until at last Christian Bean began raging in a loud whiny voice. "Aye, that Gallen O'Day is half a devil himself. He's more than a murderer. Mark my words: if he can pray to the devil once and raise hell itself, surely he can do it again—so none of you are safe!"

With those remarks, Gallen grabbed the mask of Fale from his pocket and quickly pushed the rubbery thing over his face. The nanotech devices within the mask immediately flowed into position, conforming to his face, and pulled energy from his body heat, releasing it as photons.

Gallen leapt from limb to ground, so that suddenly he stood in the midst of the crowd. With a roar, he drew his shimmering vibro-blade and pointed it at Christian Bean.

"Behold, a liar and murderer who shall himself soon be a denizen of hell!" Gallen shouted.

There were screams, and all about him, the people fled. The sheriffs were a swirl of motion as they stood, drawing arms. One of them clutched at his sword and stumbled backward, falling into the fire.

Christian Bean just sat, his face lit by the twisting flames of the campfire, his mouth opened wide, clutching a bottle of wine in one hand, a goblet in the other. He was shaking, and Gallen watched in dismay as he soiled his pants.

There was a great uproar, and people from all over town began rushing toward Gallen.

"I warned you," Gallen said loudly, pointing his sword toward all three of the robbers, "that those who commit murder in Coille Sidhe would have to answer to me." His voice carried over the town and reverberated off the walls of the stable. No one on this small world had ever heard such a shout. "Yet now you have returned, and you seek to bring death to a man through your false witness!"

The sheriffs faded back a few steps, leaving the robbers alone beside the fire. All around Gallen, the curious onlookers were quietly retreating, leaving a larger and larger circle.

Gallen moved toward the robbers, and the young Argent Flaherty stood, tried to back away. Gallen commanded him to stop with a roar, and the boy froze, knees shaking.

Gallen moved to within a dozen feet of the men, and suddenly the Lord Inquisitor rushed forward with Sully at his side, and the two put themselves between Gallen and the witnesses. The Lord Inquisitor looked up at Gallen with his piercing blue eyes, and of all the people in town, he did not seem frightened.

"What are you?" the Lord Inquisitor asked, raising a hand as if to stop Gallen.

And at that moment, Gallen realized that he felt odd. Wearing his mantle and the clothing of a Lord Protector, he somehow felt as if he had been endowed with power. Surely, the artificial intelligence within the mantle did give him knowledge beyond the understanding of men, and Gallen felt that he was no longer a common man.

"I am more than a man, less than God," Gallen said.

"And I am Brother Shayne," the Lord Inquisitor said softly. He seemed to be wary, and he looked about, trying to see in the distance behind Gallen. Gallen wondered if the Lord Inquisitor wasn't signaling with his eyes for one of the sheriffs to rush him from behind, but the sensors on his mantle assured Gallen that none were so foolhardy. "You are an angel, then?"

Gallen did not consider. "I am the Lord Protector of this land. I come to protect the righteous, and to bring evil men to judgment."

Gallen did not want to answer more questions, so he thrust his hand into a fold of his robes and pulled out the light globe he had taken from the corpses in Thomas Flynn's stable the night before. He raised the globe aloft and squeezed so that a piercingly brilliant light burst over the town, and he stood as if in sunlight while all around him the townsfolk gasped and groaned, shielding their eyes.

"Behold the light of truth," Gallen shouted. "No mere mortal can look upon it and lie, for he who lies shall be consumed in holy fire!

"You—" Gallen waved his sword toward Christian Bean. "You seek to kill a man by bearing false witness. You have admitted to church authorities that you are a robber. What boon were you granted for bearing false testimony?"

Christian Bean half stood, and the poor man began gasping in fear. Though it was a cool night, he was sweating profusely, and he stammered, "M-m-money. B-Bishop Mackey said he prayed, and God told him that Gallen was responsible for Father Heany's death. He offered us each a hundred pounds to testify!"

Young Argent Flaherty was nodding his head hugely in agreement, and Gallen stepped closer. "Yet you are under the penalty of a whipping. How do you hope to live through such a beating?"

Christian Bean's eyes opened wide, and he began wheezing heavily. He dropped his brown bottle of wine and his goblet, and he stumbled backward, moaning incoherently. Gallen advanced on young Argent Flaherty and pointed his sword. "Answer me, Argent Flaherty!"

"H-he promised to commute our sentences after the trial!"

"Yet you have sworn in your affidavits that you asked this boon, and that Bishop Mackey denied it?"

"We said that he 'never spoke a promise to us'—and he never did! He wrote the promise in a note, then told us to word our testimony this way so that we wouldn't be lying."

"Keep silent!" Mason Flaherty shouted at his younger brother, grabbing the boy's arm. "If you answer no questions, you'll speak no lies!"

"Och, you child of a serpent!" Gallen sneered at Mason. "Hardly shall you escape the wrath of hell! What does it matter if you worded a portion of your testimony with half-truths, when the brunt of your tale is a lie? I was never summoned by the prayers of Gallen O'Day or any other man, nor have I opened the gates of hell. What of this tale you tell?"

Gallen pointed his sword at Christian Bean, who was writhing on the ground. He was so terrified that Gallen was sure he could get the man to speak, to admit to perjury, but Christian Bean looked up through slitted eyes, gulped at the air loudly, and suddenly grabbed his chest. He began shaking uncontrollably, muscles spasming in his legs, his eyes rolling back in his head. A deep rattling noise came from his throat, and Gallen suddenly realized that the man had just died of fright.

Young Argent Flaherty stared at Christian and gasped, lurched away, rushed toward the crowd. He tried to beat his way through, but several townspeople caught him. The boy pulled his knife and took a swing, and some worthy drew his own blade and plunged it in the lad's ribs. He gave out a startled cry and sank to the ground.

Gallen went to Mason Flaherty, looked down at him steadily. The man was shaking, but stood his ground and met Gallen's eyes. Gallen had never seen such controlled hatred in a man's eyes.

"And you," Gallen said. "You alone are left to bear witness. Tell us now: was your testimony false?"

Mason gritted his teeth, spat his words. "I'll-Not-Speak-Of-It! You cannot force me to talk! Gallen O'Day killed my brother and my cousin, and I've got nothing to say to you!"

Gallen looked at this man and wished that Mason would give him some other choice. He couldn't leave the man alive. The man had tried to kill him on the road, and he'd tried to do it in court. To let such a stubborn and evil man live would only bring trouble later on.

Gallen looked up at Sully. The sheriff stood beside the Lord Inquisitor, shaking. "Do with him what you will," Gallen told the sheriff, and he turned and walked away.

As Gallen passed the front door of his home, he clenched his fist over the glow globe so that there was a bright flash, then he quit squeezing his glow globe so that the light suddenly failed, and he ripped off his mask and headed into the woods.

At his back, he heard Mason Flaherty's sudden scream and the sickening sound of a sword slashing through flesh, snicking through bone. Once, twice, and the head was off. Sully had done a poor job of it.

Gallen reached the edge of the woods, and there he stood panting. Hot, bitter tears were streaming down his face, and he found himself breathing heavily, gasping. He hadn't cried in ages, not since that first time he'd been forced to kill a highwayman three years before. Then, he'd cried because he'd felt that somehow he'd been robbed of his innocence, but with every killing since then, he'd felt justified.

Now, more than ever, he could feel that his innocence had been stripped away. He'd just killed three men, and though they were highwaymen and would have used their testimony to nail him to the inverted cross, still they had not held any weapons, and because of their ignorance, they had been powerless against him.

Gallen rushed up the hillside, under the shelter of an old apple grove. There he fell to his knees and began praying sincerely for the first time in years, begging God for forgiveness.

And as he prayed with his eyes closed, the amplified words hissing from his microphone, he suddenly saw a weak light before him.

He opened his eyes. A pale-blue glowing figure stood before him, leaning against the tree. A wight.

Two weeks ago, the sight would have frozen his heart. But now he knew that it was only a creature formed from luminescent nanotech devices, like the glowing mask he wore from Fale. Yet this creature had the thoughts and memories of a long-dead human inhabiting it. It was a heavyset man with lambchop sideburns.

"I don't know who you are," the wight said, in a deep voice, "but this is an interdicted planet. By charter, you cannot be carrying the kinds of weapons you have on you."

"Then why don't you take them from me?" Gallen said. He didn't need a sword. His mantle whispered that it could incapacitate the creature with a burst of radio waves at any time.

"Och, there's not much that *I* can do against the likes of you," the wight answered. "But I can raise the hue and cry against you. I'll call you a demon. At my word, every townsman in a thousand miles would come marching to war against you. Sooner or later, we'd get you."

"You would let that many people die—just to rid this world of one man?" Gallen whispered.

The wight didn't answer. "We've chosen how we will live here on Tihrglas."

"Eighteen thousand years ago you chose how you will live. But you're dead, and this isn't your world anymore," Gallen said.

"It is filled with our children. If they wish to change the planetary charter, they may do so."

"Yet you don't even let them know that there are worlds beyond this. How can they choose?"

The wight sat down a few feet from Gallen, folded his hands into a steeple and stared at them thoughtfully. "You know of the worlds beyond this, of the wars and horrors found in the universe. Of what value is such knowledge? Our people lead simple lives, free of care. It is a commodity that cannot be purchased."

Things had changed much in the past eighteen thousand years. New subraces of humanity had been engineered. The Tharrin had been created and given leadership of most planets, ending the petty conflicts and wars that the galaxy had endured under the corporate governors so long before. Gallen did not know much about how the galaxy had been run millennia ago, and he wondered how much the wights understood about how it functioned now.

"I fear," Gallen said, "that much has changed in eighteen thousand years. When you built this world, if I remember my history right, corporate wars raged between planets, but mankind has come far toward making peace with itself."

The wight smiled wryly. "From your words, I guess that mankind has not managed to bring about perfect peace?"

"As long as men are free to do evil, and have the power to do so, there will be evil," Gallen answered. "But the evils of today are perpetrated on a smaller scale than in the past."

"In other words, you've cut the balls off the bigger predators. You've taken away their power."

Gallen considered a moment. He'd seen how heavily modified the Tharrin were, and in a sense they were no longer even human. Yes, mankind had stripped their leaders of the capacity to do evil. "We've modified mankind to some extent. Most people do not have the same level of desire to do evil that your people had in your time."

"Aye, we knew it would be done. It was such a seductive solution to the problem, that we knew others would not resist the temptation. You can place evil men in jail, or you can make the flesh a prison in itself where evil cannot enter. There's not much difference. But you're still restricting people's freedom."

So you created bars of ignorance, Gallen thought, and imprisoned them anyway. "The point is," Gallen said, "that the universe is not so dangerous now as it was in your day. Perhaps it is time for your children to join it."

"Mark my words—" the wight said, suddenly angry, "if our feral children go into the universe, in two generations they'll pose such a threat that none of your peaceful planets would want them!"

Gallen studied the wight, and realized that he had a point. Gallen had just seen the face of evil on his own world, and if highwaymen like the Flahertys were given power, they would take their criminal ways out into the larger galaxy. He envisioned pirating fleets and judges who had been purchased.

In the greater universe, others had chosen to reengineer their children, rid them of the desire to dominate and oppress others. On some worlds, he knew, huge police forces had been created to handle the problem. No matter how you looked at it, bars had been created, and Gallen's ancestors had chosen to control their children by giving them an inheritance of ignorance. Perhaps they had been right to retreat from the future.

Yet Gallen and Maggie had both seen the larger universe, and they had grown from it. Gallen had come home only to find that there was nothing left for him here. He had few friends. And something inside him had changed. He'd outgrown this place, and he felt free to leave now.

He thought of the Tharrin woman, Ceravanne, whom Everynne had shown him on Tremonthin, and he was suddenly eager to be off.

Gallen sighed, looked at the wight. He was an older man who had graying hairs among his sideburns, someone who looked as if the heavy burdens of life had bent him low. "If the only other worlds out there were inhabited only by humans," Gallen said, "then perhaps I would be content to admit that this world should stay as it is. But there is a race of beings called the Dronon, and they will come here. Perhaps, someday, they will come to war against this world. If they do, your people will need to grow up, or they will be destroyed."

The wight gave Gallen a calculating look. "We saw one of your Dronon not two weeks ago, and wondered how it came to be. I'll take this bit of news to Conclave. Perhaps we must reconsider how this world is run." He stood up.

"And I," Gallen said, rising, "will leave this world with all possible haste, without alerting anyone else here of the universe beyond."

"Not just like that," the wight said, shaking his head. "I'll not let you go at your own pace. We'll escort you, if you please. Just tell us where your ship is."

Suddenly, there was an uproar in town. Gallen looked back down over the small seaport. Hundreds of glowing wights were striding through the edge of town, past the fires and tent cities. The townsfolk were terrified. The wights only came to town if a priest tied someone to a tree for breaking the laws found in the Tome. And a person taken for such an offense never returned.

"My mother lives down there," Gallen sighed, realizing that the wight must have had a built-in transmitter. It must have called its companions. "I'll go down to say goodbye."

"I wish you wouldn't," the wight said with just a hint of force.

"You can't stop me," Gallen replied.

"You wear the mantle of a Lord Protector," the wight said. "If you would protect those people below, then you will leave now. It is against the law to wear such mantles on this world. You know that. And things have already gotten out of hand—what with off-worlders coming through the gates. But things aren't too bad. For now, we will clean up the evidence of off-world intruders, and in a generation these shenanigans will all be forgotten, the stuff of legend. But if you go back to town and pollute those folks down there with more knowledge, we will be forced to eradicate them."

Gallen studied the wight's face. The old creature was not bluffing. Gallen pulled out the glowing mask of Fale, considered putting it back on his face, but decided against it, and then walked unmasked down through the apple grove in long easy strides.

As he passed the china shop, he looked into its windows and thought, I shall never see this place again. And as he passed the quay with its little boats pulled up onto the pebbled beach, he inhaled the sea air. He moved like a wraith through the streets, and all ahead of him, people stepped aside, and the wights drifted in behind him.

He stopped at his own home, and his mother stood outside the door of the little pine house-tree, looking more haggard and world-weary than he'd ever seen her. He hugged her briefly. "I don't know if I'll ever be back," he whispered into her ear as he stooped to hug her, and she reached up and managed to hug him around the ribs.

"Where will you go?" she demanded in a tone of disbelief.

"To another world, to dance with the fairy folk and fight demons."

She squeezed him tight. "Be good," was all she managed to say between sobs. Gallen reached into his pocket and pulled out his coin purse, gave it to her. "The money, wedding gifts, the inn—they're all yours," he said.

Then he went into the house, retrieved his sword, daggers, and the incendiary rifle he'd brought home from his previous trip. Maggie had already gone to fetch her own things.

When Gallen got out of the house, Sheriff Sully came out of the crowd, and growled in a bitter voice. "You—you made me kill a man," he said, rubbing his hands on his shirt as if they'd been soiled.

"Not I," Gallen said. "I told you only to do with Mason Flaherty 'what you will.' You came here with murder on your mind, and murder is what you've accomplished."

Gallen pushed him away, and some of Sully's own men grabbed him, placed him under arrest.

Orick rushed to Gallen's side. "I'm with you, Gallen!" the bear called in his deep voice, and a young female bear padded along beside him. Gallen was glad to finally meet Grits.

Maggie Flynn was calling, "Out of my way! Get out of my way!" and Gallen could see her trying to break through the crowd over by the inn. Within moments she came huffing through the crowd with nothing but a small valise in her hand.

Her uncle Thomas nearly skipped at her side, and he came bustling up with his own bag in one hand, his lute over his shoulder, smiling. "'Tis good that I didn't even have time to unpack!" he told Gallen.

Then he bowed to Gallen's mother and handed her his purse. "Everything that I own is now yours, good woman. Spend the money in good health."

Some wights had moved in behind the crowd. They'd gotten into the stables across the street from the inn, and they pulled out the bodies of the dead Vanquisher and Everynne's defender, then carried them toward the sea.

Father Brian pushed his way through the crowd, a look of profound fear on his face as he studied the wights who'd gathered behind Gallen. He looked as if he would speak, but he managed to say only, "God be with you, Gallen. I don't know what's happening here."

"Perhaps it's best if you never know. Look in on my mother from time to time, will you?"

Together, the little band began moving through town, and the townspeople parted to let them pass. Some of them shouted out, "God be with you, Gallen, Maggie," and "Go with God!" Their voices were high and troubled, like the voices of small birds that call querulously in the night.

It was obvious that the townspeople did not understand what was happening, but they were afraid. Only witches and sorcerors and those who knew too much were ever taken by wights, and they never returned.

Gallen looked about the town with a profound sense of loss, feeling as if someone had died. He wondered at his own numbness, at his sense of mourning, and knew that it was because everyone he had ever known, everyone he had loved and trusted and played with and hated, all of these people with their odd quirks and petty vices would be dead to him now.

And thus it was that he walked stiffly out of town, an army of wights dogging his step, a few loyal friends beside him. None of the townsfolk followed, for most of them feared that Gallen and his friends were going to their deaths, and none wished to share their fate. Gallen took out his glow globe and squeezed it, let it light his footsteps as they made their way into the forest.

Thomas stopped at the edge of the wood and whispered, "I want to give them one last song, Gallen."

He sang thunderously, yet sweetly,

"Many roads I've traveled down,
And many more I'll follow,
Past lonely woods, and shadowed fens,
And fields too long a-fallow.

But when night breathes on the land,
When fear makes my walk unstately,
I'll remember you, my friends,
And good times we've shared lately."

When he finished, Thomas waved goodbye, and the whole town shouted farewell.

"That was kind of you, Thomas," Maggie said as they walked, "to send them away with a song. It eased their hearts."

"Ah, well," Thomas said, "being as it costs me nothing, a song always makes a fine parting gift."

After an hour they reached a secluded glen at the foot of a mountain. Lichens hung thick on the trees, and the leaf mold was heavy.

There, sheltered under the dark pines, lay Geata na Chruinne, an ancient arch of dark stone with dancing animals and glyphs carved into its side. The forest was alive with the blue and green lights of wights, circling the small group.

The air around the arch was cold, and Gallen fumbled through his pack until he found the gate key. He picked it up, realized that he didn't even know how to use it. He handed it to Maggie, asking, "Show me how to work this thing."

She thought a minute, punched in a sequence of numbers on the key, and suddenly the arch shimmered. A pale lavender light shone beneath it. Maggie handed the key back to Gallen and took her uncle Thomas's hand. "Come on. This way," she said.

They walked through together first, followed by Orick.

The small female bear stood and watched Orick go, apparently too afraid to follow. She had not voiced a word since they'd left town. Gallen bent and whispered into her ear. "There are marvelous worlds beyond the gate, but if you come, it is doubtful that you will ever return to this place." He could see the confusion in her eyes.

"Tell Orick goodbye for me," she said, then she licked Gallen's face.

He sighed deeply, patted her head, then walked to the gate. She gave a short growl, lunged toward him just as he stepped into the cold light, and he realized that she had come too late, for she couldn't enter behind the key-bearer. Then he felt the familiar sensation of winds blowing, as if he were a leaf borne by turbulent storms between worlds.

Nine

Orick stepped through the opal wind between the worlds and found himself in a clearing surrounded by a lush forest, thick with undergrowth. A cool dawn breeze whispered through the trees. Overhead in a sky full of lavender, twin suns rose above the forest, weaving shadows in the woods, while white birds swirled among the trees calling out in creaking voices.

Thomas was staring up with mouth open, and Orick remembered his own sense of awe upon first visiting Fale. "'Tis a sight to behold," Maggie whispered. And Thomas nodded, too dumbfounded to speak.

Orick looked behind him and suddenly a glowing white form appeared, like a mist streaming through the jungle, then Gallen strode into view, his face rigid and worn. The gate could not be seen from this side.

Orick waited, hoping that his bear friend Grits would come through, but the female had stayed behind. Orick gave a little bawl, and weaved his head back and forth as he tried to catch a scent of her.

"I'm sorry, Orick," Maggie said softly, coming to his side. She knelt by him, touched his brow. "She seemed so nice. And you've been looking for love so long. I had hoped she would come."

"That's all right," Orick grumbled. Maggie seemed so distraught that he wanted to calm her. "I couldn't hope for any better from a she-bear. I left her alone with those sheriffs. How could I have hoped she would be more true to me?"

"She wanted to come, Orick," Gallen said. "But she was afraid. Don't blame yourself."

Maggie scratched behind his ears, and Orick licked her hand in gratitude.

Thomas stared about at the skyline. His lute case was strung over his shoulders, and he held to the strap with both hands, a gesture that showed his insecurity. Tall creepers climbed some of the trees, and a few orange birds began chattering loudly as they fed on berries.

Gallen knelt on a clump of grass, pulled out his map of worlds—a thin piece of film that showed a three-dimensional representation of Fale with tiny red gates displayed at various points. "We're not far from a gate to Tremonthin," he said, a tone of relief in his voice. "It's about two thousand kilometers. We'll need to go into town, hire a vehicle."

"What is a kilometer?" Thomas asked.

"Just a stupid way to measure things," Orick grumbled.

"It's a little less than half a mile," Gallen said.

"Do you think it's safe to go into town?" Maggie asked. She had put down her pack—for they'd just walked with them for an hour—and she was looking to Gallen.

Gallen shrugged. "I'll not lie. It has been only a week in this time-line since you and I defeated the Lords of the Swarm. The Dronon should have abandoned their military installations here on Fale, but that doesn't mean that we're safe."

"Well, now, you're the optimist today," Orick said.

Gallen hung his head, downcast. Maggie knelt next to him, touched his knee. Orick looked into Gallen's pale blue eyes, and for a moment he felt as if he were looking into the eyes of a stranger, there was so much pain behind them.

"See here, lad—" Orick told Gallen, "just because you've

got kicked off your own home world, you don't have to wilt. Things can't be worse than last time we were here."

Gallen smiled up at him. "Aye, you're right, Orick. But we must take care. We have enemies here—men who were evil before the Dronon ever set hand to corrupt them. Lord Karthenor and men of his ilk may hold power, for all we know."

"Och, well, if he does," Orick said, "I'll bite his butt so hard he'll never want to sit on a toilet again!"

Yet Orick's playful threats could not brighten the mood. Karthenor had been a powerful servant to the Dronon rulers, perhaps powerful enough to wrest control even after the Dronon retreated.

"So, Gallen, you've taken my money and led me astray, have you?" Thomas said. "I thought you said this was a decent sort of place, where folks live forever?"

"I also said there were great dangers here," Gallen reminded him. "Some folks here do live a mighty long time, but you still have to take care. . . ."

"Ah, don't listen to him," Orick said. "It's good enough for the likes of us. You'll never taste better food, and they pass it out free to strangers as a courtesy. Why, it's so easy to grow here, that they esteem food as nothing. That's why they give it away."

"Really?" Thomas asked, his face showing that he doubted Orick's every word. Now, some bears have a reputation for stretching the truth, but Orick had never been that kind of bear, so Thomas's raised brows got Orick riled.

"It is indeed the truth!" Orick said. "And I'll tell you something else: there's wonders here that a pudding-head like you couldn't imagine—"

"Tell me about them as we walk, then." Thomas laughed, and with that laugh, Orick looked up. It seemed to him that Thomas was somehow a younger man, less weathered and worn than he had been just hours before, and Orick began to tell Thomas of the things he'd seen on his last trip here.

Maggie donned her own mantle and the cinnamon-colored robes of a technician. In moments they were off, striding through the forest. Gray lizards skittered from their feet, and as they marched, Orick used his keen nose to follow the trail they'd blazed on their journey here two weeks earlier.

Orick told Thomas of the wonders he would behold here on Fale—of starships and men who wore wings, of teaching machines and ancient merchants who lived for ten thousand years, of machines that let one speak with the dead or breathe underwater, and of horrifying weapons that could burn worlds to ashes. He described the armies of insectlike Dronon that had infested the place and boasted of the heroic efforts of common people who sought to end their tyranny. He told how Gallen had defeated the Dronon Lords of the Swarm in single combat, when even the brilliant Lord Protector Veriasse had failed the challenge, and Orick minimized his own part in all these affairs. For a long while he described the Tharrin woman Everynne, who now reigned as Maggie's regent, as far as the Dronon were concerned, over the ten thousand worlds.

From time to time, Orick would pause along the path to eat a slug or a large wood snail. In two hours he had just begun to fill in the details of what Thomas should know when the group reached a small cliff that looked out over Toohkansay, a sprawling purplish-green city grown from a corallike plant. It stretched like beach foam across the hills, spanning a wide river.

They climbed down the cliff and walked to the city along a ruby road, past rich farms. Hovercars and magcars sped past them, much to the wonder and dismay of Thomas.

And when they reached the outskirts of the city, little had changed. They could still smell the sweet fragrance of foods from a roadside cantina, music swelled from the city walls, and within the shadows under the city gates they could discern human-looking inhabitants from various stock (the impish Wodari with their large eyes, tall bald men out of Bonab who wore nothing but tattoos), along with gold serving droids that still reminded Orick of men in armor.

Several Lords of Fale sat together at one table in the shade of the cupola outside the inn. They wore the multicolored robes of merchants, with masks of palest lavender.

Thomas stopped and surveyed the scene, his mouth gaping

in wonder, as if he'd just reached the gates of heaven and feared that Saint Peter would come out and wrestle him for the right to enter.

And as the group approached the archway that led into the cantina, one woman looked up from her table and gasped, "Gallen? Maggie? Orick?"

Orick had never seen the woman before, of that he was certain, but immediately the diners at all the tables turned to stare. Here and there among the crowd, people shouted, "It's them!" "They've returned!" "Welcome!"

And suddenly a human tide surged from the inn, people shouting, hugging them, giving thanks. A Lord of Ethics, wearing her purple robes of office, rushed to Maggie and fell at her knees, kissing them and then kissing Orick's paw, thanking them all for their part in ending the long siege by the Dronon.

As the cry went up, a clamor issued from the city, and soon there were hundreds upon hundreds of people shouting the good news, their voices swelling and blending together in a roar.

When Gallen had first defeated the Dronon's Golden Queen and her escort, he'd received accolades from the ambassadors of ten dozen worlds, but Orick had never witnessed anything like this, not this overwhelming, spontaneous outpouring of gratitude.

Someone picked Gallen up on his shoulders, and for one moment Orick saw his golden hair limned in the morning light. Orick suddenly envied the man—a hero on ten thousand worlds—while Orick didn't even know if he'd won the title of Primal Bear of Obhiann and Morgan counties. Only two days before, Orick had been reading the parable of the talents in the Bible, and he wondered if he himself was progressing as God would have him. So often, Orick was content to be—well, just Orick. And somehow that didn't seem enough. He silently vowed to do better.

But just as suddenly, Orick too was lifted by strong hands, and he and Gallen and Maggie and Thomas were carried upon human shoulders into the city.

Orick bawled out for the people to let him go, for it was

rather precarious for a fat bear to be carried by humans, but to his delight, they ignored his pleas.

Orick looked forward, and Gallen smiled, pleased but embarrassed by this show of affection, and Orick felt glad for him. Gallen had been cast off from his own world, but it appeared now that he'd won back more than he'd lost.

Maggie, for her part, looked resplendent, a huge grin on her face that you couldn't clean off with lye soap. And Thomas shouted to Orick in glee, "Some welcome, eh, Orick?"

They entered the city of Toohkansay with great fanfare and were treated to feasts. And that night, painters decorated the sky with incandescent clouds of plasma in Gallen's and Maggie's honor. A band of twelve people from various worlds played beautiful instruments that could sing as sweetly as birds or cut a man to the heart, and Thomas took up his lute and played and sang with them, astonishing the people of Toohkansay with his prowess. Upon hearing a ballad that Thomas had composed, a Master Musician honored Thomas by giving him his own mantle, as "just recompense" for the performance. As soon as Thomas had placed the silver mantle upon his head, his eyes began to water as he learned the music of the universe.

Shortly afterward, Thomas was forced to ask Gallen to take him to his rooms for the night, for he needed seclusion.

"I think it's time for all of us to make a night of it," Gallen said.

The mayor of Toohkansay himself offered to escort them to an inn that had the finest rooms in the city, and when they reached the door, he asked Gallen if there was anything he needed for the night.

Gallen said, "I need access to an ansible. I must talk with Lady Everynne."

"Even with an ansible, it takes several hours to send messages so far," the mayor said. He was a tall, bald man whose skin shone as if it were oiled. "Is there a question you have, so that we can ask a response?"

"She set me a task. Tell her that I would like more direction. I'll want to review her response in private."

"As you wish," the mayor said, then he departed.

Gallen and Maggie took one room as man and wife, and they went in.

Orick and Thomas were each given separate rooms across a wide hallway, and they stood for a moment. Thomas closed his eyes and whispered, "Ah, Orick, have you heard the fine music here?" And Orick knew that Thomas was listening through his mantle.

"I've heard some," Orick said.

Thomas shook his head, as if words could not convey what he wanted to say. "I can hear the music of ten thousand worlds, composed over the past thirty-eight thousand years. . . . All of my life has been so . . . cramped, so stilted." Hot tears were flowing from his eyes, and Thomas was weeping bitterly. "How could I have been so blind? There is so much to explore!"

"How do you mean?"

"We're babes, Orick! On Tihrglas, I thought I was at the end of my life. But I'll need an eternity to perfect my skills as a musician, and another to compose my songs!"

Orick looked up at Thomas, at the gray streaks in his hair, and he could see that the aging man was at the beginning of his own incredible adventure. At this very moment, Thomas had his foot stuck in the door of heaven, and he was set to put his shoulder to that door and force it open.

"Well, then," Orick said, for lack of anything better to say, "it's good night to you."

Orick went into his own room, and he sat and thought. Thomas, right now, Orick was sure, was in his room getting his head crammed full of knowledge, probably weeping his eyes out for joy. Gallen was hailed as the hero of ten thousand worlds and was most likely frolicking with the woman he loved most in life.

And Orick, well, Orick tried to sleep on a soft bed, but found it to be too odd. It was large enough, but it hadn't been made to hold a bear, and he sank so low into it that he kept having a spooky feeling that he might drown. So instead he lay on the floor beneath an open window, watching the galaxies pinwheeling overhead, and skyships streaking through the night like meteors. He wondered if he would ever find happiness.

When Orick had been a cub, his mother once told him a tale. She'd said that the hummingbird was the sweetest-tasting of all fowl, for it alone of all birds fed upon the nectar of flowers. She'd said that the sweetest honey tasted bland in comparison.

And so Orick had taken to hiding in a thicket of summer lilies, leaping up after hummingbirds whenever he heard the trill of their wings. But no matter how well he hid, or how quickly he leapt, the hummingbirds would always lift themselves just out of his reach.

Orick drifted asleep, dreaming of jumping, jumping, leaping impossibly high to catch honey-scented hummingbirds, which he held gingerly in his teeth, savoring them.

He heard a chiming noise as Gallen's door opened across the hall, and Orick got up groggily, stepped out into the dark arching corridors of the inn, where gems in the ceiling lit the dim way.

Gallen was standing in the corridor, fully dressed in the black of a Lord Protector.

"What are you about?" Orick asked.

"Shhh . . ." Gallen signaled for Orick to follow him, and they crept down the familiar streets. It was soon obvious to Orick where Gallen was heading: to the quarters where Lord Karthenor dwelt with his aberlains.

But when they reached those offices where Lord Karthenor had enslaved Maggie and dozens of other workers, the buildings were stripped bare. The Dronon guards were gone, the machinery removed.

Gallen walked through a dozen dark rooms, until he reached the last, then stood, staring into nothingness.

"Couldn't sleep, thinking about him?" Orick asked.

"I wondered if he was still here. He would have heard that Maggie and I were back."

"From the scent, I'd say he's been gone a while," Orick said. "The aberlains probably left the day the Dronon pulled out."

"Maggie says that the women on this world will conceive children built in the image of the Dronon hive," Gallen said distantly. "Some women will have swollen bellies, and they will be breeders, giving birth to six or eight children at a time, as if they were hound bitches.

"Other women will be born to labor, never able to give themselves to a man in love, barren except for an irresistible craving to work from dawn to dusk.

"Some men will be thinkers and planners.

"And some men will be born to war, bred to fight and hate and bully others into worshiping the Dronon Golden Queen. And all of this happened because people like Lord Karthenor were willing to sell mankind's secrets to the Dronon.

"In all probability, we will suffer for a thousand generations for what Karthenor and his aberlains have done."

Orick didn't understand much about how Karthenor and his aberlains manipulated unborn children into becoming something so strange, but he knew that Karthenor had done unmentionable evil. He'd known it from the moment when Karthenor had placed his Guide upon Maggie's head, enslaving her so that she could be his worker. "Aye, no beating would be great enough to suffice for that man," Orick grumbled.

Behind them, someone cleared his throat, and Orick turned. A man stood in the shadows in a corner, a man wearing the robes and mantle of a Lord Protector. His robes had so blended into the night, that Orick had not seen him. And Orick could still not smell his scent. "Perhaps he is already paying a penalty," he said.

Gallen turned and studied the stranger.

"I'm Laranac," the man said, "a Lord Protector for this world."

"Do you know where Karthenor is?" Gallen asked.

"He left in great haste, I believe, when the Dronon evacuated, taking many of his creations—and his slaves—with him."

Gallen frowned. "How can that be? I've been in a Dronon hive city; the stench of their stomach acids fills the air. And the acids dry into a fine powder that blankets everything. A closed ship would be—impossible to bear."

Laranac nodded. "Their kind and ours were not meant to live together. Karthenor knew that. Yet he will suffer for his choice, constantly burning from the acids on the Dronon hive ships. The nanodocs in his blood will keep him alive, but at what price? I suspect his exile is a great torment to him."

"A fit ending for the man, as far as I'm concerned," Orick said. "Death would have been too nice."

"No, this is not his end," Gallen whispered, "only a reprieve in torment. Such a painful exile will only madden him, make him want to return that much more quickly."

"And so I keep watch on this place," Laranac said, "hoping for his return. I found a cache of weapons and credit chips hidden in a secret room behind that wall. If Karthenor returns, he will come searching for it, but all he will find is me. I will give him death, when next I see him."

"What of the law?" Gallen asked. "Will you give the man no trial?"

"His memories were on file, along with his gene samples, so that the Dronon could rebuild him if he died. Those memories were all the evidence we needed. Karthenor has already been convicted and sentenced to death. I wait now only to mete out his punishment."

Orick considered this bit of news on how evil men were tried here on Tremonthin, and he thought it much better than what had happened with Gallen, back home.

Gallen smiled up at Laranac. "You'll not mete out his punishment, if I get to him first."

"That is unlikely," Laranac said.

Gallen mused, "I am Lord of the Swarm. If I asked the Dronon to turn him over, they would do it on a moment's notice."

Orick did not like the idea of having to deal with the Dronon. He never wanted to see one of their black carapaces again.

Laranac smiled back at Gallen. "Then do it. Karthenor is a dangerous man, and the fact that he is on a Dronon starship hardly hinders his work. He must be stopped."

"Soon," Gallen said. "I'll make arrangements. But I've urgent business elsewhere for the moment. If it takes a week for him to be delivered, I'm afraid I can't be here to meet Karthenor at the spaceport."

"I can," Laranac said. "Send for him."

"I will, first thing tomorrow. Until then, keep watching this place," Gallen said. "And I shall sleep better tonight."

Gallen turned to leave, but Laranac caught his arm. "Be careful," Laranac whispered fervently. "A new government is forming on this world, one that recognizes the Lady Everynne as Semmaritte's heir and as a rightful judge. They are eager to join once again in the Consortium of Worlds. But there are other voices crying to be heard on the councils. There are other Karthenors on the loose—brutal people who lost profit and prestige when the Dronon evacuated. Such people would not bear you into the city upon their shoulders. They would rather trample you under their feet."

"You think I am in danger?" Gallen asked.

"The mayor of Toohkansay is protecting you now, the best he knows how. But if you left soon, you would be doing him a favor—and perhaps you would save your own lives."

Gallen nodded almost imperceptibly. Gallen and Orick returned to their chambers, and when Orick was alone, he offered up more than his usual nightly prayers.

The next day dawned bright and clear. Gallen sent a message to Everynne to be relayed to the Dronon Vanquishers, asking that Karthenor and any other such humans carried away in Dronon ships be returned to their home worlds for judging and sentencing.

For a bit in the morning, Orick was edgy, watchful, but the mood soon vanished like the morning mists burning off the wide river. The celebrations continued all throughout the day, and Orick found it difficult under such circumstances to believe that anyone would wish Maggie and Gallen harm.

On the contrary, at every turn people sought Maggie and Gallen out to offer favors. The finest clothiers arrayed Gallen, Maggie, and Maggie's honored uncle Thomas in their best wares, and perfumers brought their most exotic scents. Musicians and actors played before them, while chefs plied them with fine food and technologists brought tokens of knowledge for Gallen and Maggie to place in their mantles.

Those who were poor came and told tales of woe, describing the horrible tyranny they had suffered under the Dronon. Those who were weak, or deformed, or belligerent, or brave had been annihilated under Dronon rule. Their bodies were processed for fertilizer by unfeeling Dronon overlords.

And so the poor people of Fale told unending tales of woe, then thanked Gallen and Maggie. From all across the planet, the grateful people of Fale came to give honor.

The whole affair was dizzying and extravagant beyond anything that Orick had ever dreamed, and all through the day he watched Gallen, gauging the look upon his face. He seemed worn, worried, and not until that evening when the brewers of Fale convinced him to try their dearest vintages of wine did those lines of worry begin to ease.

That night, as they returned to their rooms, the mayor of Toohkansay walked with them once again, and he was laughing, smiling. Thomas had his lute out, and he sang softly as he walked.

Outside the door to Maggie's apartment was a large, intricately carved crystal vase, holding one perfect white rose with petals so lustrous they looked like pearl. A note beneath the flower said, "A Token of Our Esteem."

"Ah," the mayor said, "it looks as if the hotel has left you a special gift."

Thomas cooed in appreciation, and reached down for the vase, but the mayor said, "Let me get that for you!"

As he touched the vase, the petals on the rose somehow changed. They whirred and spun like a pinwheel, and blurred into the air, striking him in the face. Blood and flesh spattered across the hallway, and there was cracking as the rose cut through his skull, then rose petals exploded outward.

The mayor's head seemed to implode, the broken skull sagging in on itself, and he fell face first to the floor.

Maggie screamed and backed away, and Orick looked up. Thomas stood in shock, holding his wrist. A delicate-looking petal of rose had lodged in his wrist, like a knife blade.

Gallen spun, looking down the hallway, as if expecting attackers to come, and in seconds, four men rushed down from both ends of the corridor, all of them with weapons drawn. They looked at the mayor, watched down both sides of the corridor.

One of them was shouting into a tiny microphone at his lapel, "Security breach, code one! Man down!"

The men took defensive postures on either side of the corridor, placing themselves between Maggie and any would-be attackers.

In another minute, a dozen more soldiers arrived, including several of the green giants like the "demon" that Thomas had displayed at the inn. The sight of those creatures dismayed Thomas more than anything, so the soldiers were forced to rush Thomas and the others into their own room, where they waited for a medic, who used clamps and nanoware to begin healing the cut ligaments in Thomas's wrist.

Thomas just sat on his bed during the whole procedure, cursing the folks who had done this.

"It was nanoware," Maggie said to herself once in the room. "They were after me and Gallen."

"Aye," Thomas said, "it looks as if you've made some enemies here, while collecting worshipers."

"But I don't understand," Maggie whispered. "They could have found so many easier ways to kill me—a bomb, a poisoned scent in the flower. Even if they'd wanted to use nanoware, there were so many things they could have done. They could have stripped every atom of copper from my body . . . torn away my ability to remember—any one of a thousand things. So why the rose?"

"They weren't just trying to kill you," Thomas suggested. "Perhaps the saboteur wanted to do more than kill you. He wanted to send a message."

"Of course," Gallen said. "Whoever put the flower there believed that killing Maggie would be pointless. Her memories could just be downloaded into a clone. So the flower was a message from her enemies."

"But what does it mean?" Orick asked.

The medic who was attending Thomas's wound looked up.

"Beware of beautiful appearances," he said, with almost too much certainty. "Things are not as they seem."

"Are they warning us away from the Tharrin?" Gallen asked. "Lady Everynne?"

"That may be. Not all people trust the Tharrin. Though they are beautiful, they are not truly human. On the other hand, perhaps the rose was not meant as a message to you," the medic said. "Perhaps it was a message to the rest of the world. This weapon was intended to kill Maggie, and she too is beautiful. Perhaps the killers were trying to warn the people of Fale away from her."

"You're talking gibberish, man," Orick said, certain the medic was on the wrong track. Maggie was not a leader on Fale. No, the rose had to signify the Tharrin, but Orick knew the Lady Everynne well. The Tharrin were good folks, and only a person with a warped mind would fear otherwise.

The medic shrugged. "I'm only making wild guesses. The only person who really knows what the message meant is out there somewhere." He waved toward the city.

He applied some nanodocs to the wound, then bandaged it, and left.

When they were alone, Gallen took an object from his robe—a white metal triangle with a lens set at each corner.

"You've a message?" Maggie said, taking the contraption from his hand.

"The mayor gave it to me earlier. It's from Everynne." Maggie set the thing on the floor, and asked the room to lower the lights.

"Everynne," she called softly, and suddenly the image of Everynne was standing in the room, her dark hair gleaming, resplendent in a pale blue gown. Thomas gasped at her beauty, and Orick studied the fine bones of her jaw, the keen intellect behind her eyes. In the brief weeks since Orick had last seen her, he found that time had blurred her image, so he tried to burn the Tharrin woman's image into his memory.

"I had suspected that you would call me, Gallen," the holoimage said, "and I will give you what little help I can. I need you to go to Tremonthin, a world like yours where mankind has rejected most technologies, with one exception: in the City of Life the Lords of Tremonthin have dedicated themselves to developing life-extending technologies. There they download memories into clones of those worthy for immortality. There, they fight disease and suffering. And for twenty millennia the world has had but one export—children who are engineered to live on worlds that other humans cannot inhabit, or who are engineered to fulfill roles that other humans cannot. Many of these altered people live on Tremonthin still, for the Lords of that world do not force their creations into exile but give them their choice of staying or leaving.

"My ancestors, the Tharrin, were created on Tremonthin eighteen thousand years ago to be judges and rulers of mankind, and for this reason Tremonthin was one of the first worlds that the Dronon sought to conquer. It appears that they murdered all of the Tharrin there, but one survived with the help of technicians from the City of Life. And she has been hunted by a thing called the Inhuman.

"I have no information on the Inhuman. It seems to be a secret society, formed by the descendants of genetically up-graded people. We lost ansible contact with Tremonthin years ago, but rebels working on a ship that visited the City of Life in the past three months were able to smuggle out the small recording that I sent you, along with a request that the rebellion send a Lord Protector. They must have known that Veriasse and I were traveling between the world gates, for the message says that someone will meet you at the gate.

"Gallen, this will be no easy task. Those who are genetically upgraded and who choose to remain on Tremonthin are often banished from human lands, and in those lands the fiercest variations of mankind thrive.

"I would come with you if I could, Gallen," Everynne said, and her voice caught a little as she said it. "Since I don't know the dimensions of this problem, I fear the worst. Certainly, the rebels on Tremonthin were desperate, for they sent their plea knowing that the Dronon would almost certainly discover the recording. Still, they hoped that one Lord Protector, alone, could handle their problems—as I also hope.

"Be strong, but be wise," Everynne said. "Come back to us alive."

The message ended, and Gallen stood looking at the holograph thoughtfully.

"Well, we'd better get going," Orick offered after a moment of silence, hoping to prod the others into immediate action. It would feel good to be back in Everynne's service, to be doing something important.

"The mayor spoke with me earlier," Gallen said. "He'd readied a flier. We can leave in the morning."

"But folks are waiting for us!" Orick said.

"They've been waiting for months," Gallen countered. "We'll need our rest. They can wait one night longer."

Thomas had been sitting quietly, watching the holograph, and he cleared his throat. He was waxing the tips of his moustache, twirling them thoughtfully. "Gallen, Orick, Maggie—you may do as you please. But I'll be staying."

"No you won't," Gallen said. "There are only four people on this planet who know where Maggie and I are going—and all of them are in this room. And sometime in the next few weeks, at least one Dronon hive queen will come hunting for Maggie, and I'll have to be at her side to protect her. I'd rather they didn't find us, so I can't leave any witnesses behind. So, you see, sir, that I can't let you stay!"

Gallen's jaw was set, his eyes stony. Orick knew that look. It was the same look that hill robbers always saw just before Gallen pulled his knives and gutted them.

"I'll not have you talking down to me in that tone," Thomas said. "I've got my own dreams in life, my own path to take, and I don't fancy that running off with you will get me where I want to go. It appears to me that you three are just targets for trouble: you bring it down on yourselves wherever you go, and I'm not a fighting man. If I stay long in your presence, I'm sure to get killed."

Thomas quit twirling his moustache and tentatively held his

bandaged wrist, clenching and unclenching his fingers experimentally.

"You'll be under my protection," Gallen said forcefully. "I've
never lost someone who was under my protection."

"Well, it's mighty convenient that you weren't hired by that
fellow who is lying dead out in the hall, isn't it?" Thomas
grumbled. "We wouldn't want to ruin your reputation."

Gallen frowned at the haughty tone in Thomas's voice.

Orick realized that this argument was beginning to escalate.
As a bear studying for the priesthood, he felt it his duty to calm
these folks.

He rose up on his hind feet, catching their attention. "I'm
sure that Thomas is no coward, Gallen. After all, he's smarted
off to every mayor and usurer in Tihrglas for forty years. So, if
he doesn't want to come, he must have his reasons."

"I know what he's after—" Gallen said, "he's after a
comfortable retirement!"

"I'm sure you misjudge the man. . . ." Orick soothed, but
Thomas began laughing, deep and hearty.

"Oh, Orick, Gallen has judged the man right! I've *earned* my
rest. The food here is good, the people gracious . . ."—he
flexed his fingers experimentally—"for the most part. And,
frankly, I'm a paying customer. I paid to come here—not to go
to someplace worse off than Tihrglas!"

"Nevertheless, that's where we're going," Gallen said, as if
the discussion were final.

"Look," Thomas said. "I'm an old man. You can't be
ordering me about!"

"You were quick to order *me* about when it suited your
fancy!" Maggie countered.

Gallen was staring icily at Thomas, and he took the older
man by the collar. "You're coming with us," Gallen said. "I'll
leave no witnesses behind—at least not live ones. This isn't a
game I'm playing, Thomas. If you stay here, you put us at risk,
and I'll not be looking over my shoulder because of you! Once
this is all over, I'll bring you back here, if you want, or send you
to any other planet!"

Thomas fixed him with a gaze, and Thomas's own face took

on a closed look. Orick suddenly found that he didn't trust the man. "So, the ferryman has taken my money, and now he plans to row the boat where he will! Well, it sounds to me as if you're cheating me out of my life savings, Gallen. I commend you for that. I admire a man who is willing to take what he wants." He sighed, and his gaze turned inward. "All right then, Gallen, I'll come with you to your damned world—but it *is* a comfortable retirement I'm after. I'll find me a nice inn and settle down for a bit, work on my music. When you're done with your task, you can come back and bring me here, if I so desire. Agreed?"

Gallen nodded, and the two men shook hands.

Thomas stood taller, stretched and yawned. "Very well, then. I suspect that tomorrow will be a long day. Wake me in the morning."

Orick sighed in relief, now that the matter was settled. Gallen, Maggie, and Thomas went to their rooms.

Sometime well before dawn, Maggie rushed back into Orick's quarters, waking him. Orick had never seen her so mad; she had tears in her eyes.

"Orick, get up! We've got problems. We just got another message from Everynne. We've got to leave for Tremonthin now! The Dronon are here, and I just went to that lousy Thomas's room. He left us a goodbye note, and ran sneaking off sometime in the night!"

"Oh, damn him!" Orick grumbled, realizing that Thomas had only made a pretense of being reasonable. She held a note in her hand, and Orick read it quickly.

Dear Maggie:

Now, don't be cross at me, darling, but by the time you read this, I'll be off on my own adventures. I'm afraid I'm getting old and plump, and if you don't mind, I'd rather spend some time on a nice, safe world like this. You go ahead and tramp down the dark roads, if that's what your heart is after, but for me, I want nothing more than a warm mug of whiskey by the fire, some soft music, and a woman who loves me just for warming her bed.

I know that Gallen is worrying that I'll tell someone about you folks going you-know-where, but I promise not to whisper a peep about it, even in my dreams. So don't you fret. And don't waste your time trying to hunt me down. I've eluded my share of assassins in my time, and I know how to disappear when I want to.

Now, I must say that I've been pleased to be making your acquaintance, Maggie. You're a fine-looking woman, and I'm glad you're a Flynn. But you do have your mother's way about you. I sometimes think my brother drowned himself just to escape your mother's vile temper. And if I know you, you're probably so mad right now, I could fry an egg on your forehead. But someday, maybe you'll thank me for leaving.

With no apologies,
Thomas

Maggie placed a holoprojector cube on the floor, then went to Orick's pack, began throwing it together.

The holoprojector flared to life, and an image appeared—a Dronon Vanquisher with a dusty black carapace and glistening amber wings. The insectlike creature squatted on four hind legs, and its forward battle arms were crossed on the ground. The Dronon's head was to the ground, so that his forward eyes looked at the dust while his backward eye cluster pointed upward. It was the Dronon stance of obeisance.

"Oh, great Golden, admired by all," a translator said in English while the Dronon's mouthfingers clicked over the voice drums beneath its jaws. "I bear messages of congratulations from the Tincin and Tlinini, Lords of the Fourth Swarm; and from Kininic and Nickit, Lords of the Fifth Swarm; and from In and Tlik, Lords of the Third Swarm; and from Cintkin and Kintiniklintit, Lords of the Seventh Swarm. All of these speak their adoration, and announce their intent to challenge you and the great Gallen O'Day to combat for the right to rule the Sixth Swarm of Dronon."

The image faded, and Everynne stood in the creature's

place. "Maggie, I wanted to give you and Gallen time to prepare, to rest. But that time has been cut short. I received this message, and immediately afterward registered a power fluctuation to the Gate of the World. The Lords of the Seventh Swarm are coming, and they know you are on Fale. They may be there already. Flee."

Orick's heart began beating hard. He had imagined that in time, Golden Queens from within the swarm that Gallen and Maggie nominally controlled would grow and demand to battle for the right to govern, but he had not considered that lords from the other swarms of Dronon would seek them out.

"They're all coming for you," Orick muttered, in shock. "The Dronon attack only those that they believe are weak. They must think that you and Gallen are the weakest lords of all."

"We are," Maggie said. And she handed him his pack.

Ten

After notifying Orick of the danger, Maggie rushed to her room, then took off her nightgown and dressed in the burnt-orange–colored robes of a Lord of Technicians and donned a pale green mask to hide her face. Gallen threw her nightgown in her bags.

After she dressed, Maggie stood for a moment, trying to wake, thinking furiously. She wondered where Thomas might have gone. Her uncle seemed willing to cause her any amount of trouble. She doubted that he would willingly betray her—his notions of the duties to kin would extend too far for that—but Maggie knew too well that what he was willing to tell and what he would be forced to tell were two different things.

"Quickly," Gallen said as he took Maggie's hand and they rushed out the door. "My mantle is picking up Dronon radio signals. The Lords of the Swarm are heading for the city."

Orick was in the hall. Gallen did not slow for him, but as they hurried down the corridors, Gallen kept watching down side passages, as if hoping to find Thomas wandering the halls. "That old fool will cost us dear," Gallen murmured. "The Dronon will have the city in an hour."

In two minutes they were on the roof of the city, where half a dozen fliers were parked. Gallen rushed to them, spoke his name and commanded the fliers to open.

Only one of the fliers obeyed his command—a four-man flier. Maggie jumped in the pilot's seat, while Orick scrambled to fit into a space entirely too small for a bear of his bulk.

"Hurry! They've reached the city," Gallen shouted. As if to emphasize his point, emergency sirens began whining all across the city. Orick squeezed in, filling two seats.

"Head north at normal air speed. We don't want to attract attention," Maggie commanded the flier's on-board intelligence while Gallen took out his map and looked for the coordinates to the gate to Tremonthin. The flier lurched into the air, and Maggie looked down.

An army of Dronon Vanquishers was marching in the night, carrying lights before them. They churned and seethed, like ants seen from a distance. They had nearly reached the city. Fortunately, the entrance to the Gate of the World was too small to allow them to bring in their own heavy fliers, and Maggie sighed in relief.

They surged upward for ten minutes, then slowed. In that brief time, the flier had traveled a thousand miles, and in moments they were on the ground beside an ancient metal arch in a northern desert. The rocks stood out in sharp relief all around them, and in the distance, Maggie could hear wild dogs barking. The night was warm, yet she shivered.

Maggie commanded the on-board intelligence of the flier to erase its memories of this trip, then sent it back to the city, arching up toward a high cloud whose edges were silvered in the moonlight.

Maggie stood breathing the air of Fale for a moment as if she were readying to plunge into cold water, then pulled out the key to the Gate of the World and began entering codes. The air under the gate shivered a brilliant magenta.

"Remember," Gallen said. "We are traveling in disguise. Do not mention our names."

Maggie took her bags, handed Gallen the key, then walked into the magenta light. She felt the familiar sense of being lifted impossibly high into the air, and in a moment she was standing in a field yellow with ripe wheat, white with the bitter-smelling flowers of wild carrots. Tall daisies with beer-colored hearts swayed in the wind. They were in the folds of a valley, and on the hill behind her, golden oaks swayed.

Maggie could hear the distant sound of a marketplace, the cries of street vendors, the bawling of goats. She glanced over her shoulder. A light building rose above the oaks not two hundred yards away—a curious temple the color of the wheat, with five spires rising high above the hill. Banners flew from each spire, red with images of twin orange suns. Along the parapets of the temple walked a man, a broad-shouldered man in a red tunic, with thick braids of golden hair. Maggie studied him a moment, vaguely distressed by his appearance, until she realized that the man could be no less than nine feet tall.

White ghosts blurred into existence at Maggie's side, as if emerging up from the grass, and suddenly Orick and Gallen stood beside her.

They stood for a moment, looking about, and Orick growled, pointed to Maggie's left. On the next hill, a Dronon's walking hive city squatted on six giant legs, like some great black tick. The incendiary gun turrets that bristled on its back were unmanned, and had in fact been stripped off, but the red lights at the hatches glowed like squinting eyes.

Maggie found herself suddenly wary. The hive city was uninhabited as far as she could see. Yet it served as an unsavory reminder that this world had been under Dronon control only days before.

"Where do we go now?" Orick asked, looking about.

"To find the Lady Ceravanne," Gallen said uncertainly. There was a depression in the hill, a hollow where someone had perhaps mined rocks. Gallen went to it, hunching down beneath the shelter of an odd, twisted green stump to get out of sight of the temple walls. The others followed. Gallen reached into his bags and brought out his map of Tremonthin. It showed two large continents near each other, and from the map Maggie could see that they were on the eastern coast of the northern continent, but the map did not show cities, for it was far older than cities, so it showed only images of the approximate terrain and the nearest gates.

Maggie studied the map. "Ceravanne could be anywhere, thousands of miles from here."

"The Dronon can't have left more than a week ago," Gallen pointed out. "A Tharrin will be precious rare on this world. If Ceravanne is near, perhaps others will know of her."

But Maggie was not so certain. This world was nearly as backward as her home on Tihrglas. She looked up the hill and noticed that the stump above them had a faded rope tied to it, with a small leather purse attached. She wondered if it had been left there on purpose. Perhaps there was a letter inside, bearing instructions. She began climbing toward it.

Gallen sighed heavily. "I want to travel secretly," he said, hunching lower into the grass, "stay on back roads and sleep in the woods."

"And if I had your face, I'd keep it hidden, too," Orick jested, trying to lighten Gallen's mood. "Any sack would do fine."

"The young man has a fine face," a strange whispering voice said. The voice was almost a groan, or the yawn of a waking man. And most startling of all was that it came from the stump!

Maggie looked higher, and saw that the tree stump was staring down at her. The creature that watched them was the most amazing thing she had ever seen: it had deep brown eyes set high up on the uppermost ridge of its long, narrow head, and leaves crowned its top. Its long arms and legs each had many knobby growths, so that no two joints were at the same height. And it had been holding its hands up toward the sun as if it were praying, or warming itself. Each long hand had many fingers. Its mouth was a leathery crack at the bottom of its head, and two holes in its face might have been a nose. But Maggie could see no ears on the creature, and it wore no clothes. She could see no sign of sex organs or an anus.

"Soooh, you have come at last," the creature said slowly. "But I am patient, as *she* is patient."

"She?" Gallen said. "You mean Ceravanne?"

The green man did not answer, but instead looked down in concentration. It twisted its right leg, pulling many toes from deep in the rocky yellow soil. Then, with equally great effort, it pulled its left leg free from the earth.

Its skin looked like forest-green leather, and the three-pronged leaves on its head rustled as if blown in the wind.

"What are you doing?" Orick demanded, as if he were questioning a young rascal.

"Drinking rainwater, tasting sun," the green man answered.

"And who are you?" Orick asked.

"I have no name, but you may call me Bock, for I am of the race of Bock, and we are all one."

The green man swiveled, and began walking slowly down the gully on long legs that covered a great distance. In two steps it was staring at them in the hollow.

"So, you have taken shelter?" the Bock addressed them. "Sitting with backs to the wall, facing out." It seemed to consider this for a moment. "That is a human trait." Maggie had never noticed it before, but it was indeed a human trait to take such a stance, one that humans shared with bears.

"Aye," Gallen said, climbing out of the hollow, eyeing the Bock.

"You speak strangely," the Bock said. "Were you born speaking this way, or did you learn to speak by listening to your parents?"

Maggie had never heard of anyone who had not been born knowing how to talk. "I was born speaking thus," Gallen muttered. He rested his free hand on his dagger.

"Good," the Bock said, his strange eyes widening at Gallen's threatening action. "Then you are not from feral human stock, but have had some genetic upgrading. I see that you also wear heavy clothes, which speaks of a strong *enclosure* quotient."

"A what?" Gallen asked.

"Humans of most subspecies seek enclosure," the Bock said in slow, even words. "They house themselves in cavelike enclosures at all opportunities, and drape their bodies in bits of hide or vegetation. The amount of covering they desire is a guide to their enclosure quotient, and this can help me make a judgment as to how *human* the specimen is."

"You mean that different people want to wear different amounts of clothes?" Gallen asked.

"It varies by subspecies of human," the Bock said.

"That's mad," Gallen said. "We wear clothes to protect ourselves from the weather."

"You are a Lord Protector," the Bock said, half a question. "The weather is warm. Why don't you take off your clothes? You don't need them here."

"I would rather keep them on," Gallen said. "I need the hood, to hide my identity."

"No one will recognize you," the Bock assured Gallen, putting his long green hand on Gallen's shoulder, pulling back his robe to expose flesh, and Maggie counted nine fingers on that hand. "Here on Tremonthin, you are unknown. You may show your face freely. You may show your whole body freely."

The Bock's actions were strange and frightening, but Maggie could also sense that it meant no harm. Its touch was not rough or lecherous. It seemed instead to be—*perplexed* by Gallen. Curious about him, and totally alien.

Gallen stared up at the creature, shrugged his shoulder away from it. "Why are you so intent on taking off my clothes?"

"Why are you so intent to keep them on? Does the thought of your nakedness frighten you?" Gallen didn't answer, and the Bock whispered, "What kind of fear must you possess to be a Lord Protector, to feel so threatened that you must kill all the time?"

"Gallen's not afraid of anyone, you green galoot," Orick said.

"It's all right," Gallen said, studying the Bock.

"Soooh, if you are unafraid," the Bock said slowly, "take off some of your clothes. You wear your weapons as casually as another man wears his belt. Take them off, and your robes also."

Gallen smiled up at the creature's challenging tone. He unbuckled his knife belt and dropped his weapons, watching the Bock carefully. He then pulled off his robe and mantle, stripped off his tunic so that he wore only his hose and tight black boots. The Bock made a gasping noise as if in approval. "Some subspecies on this planet could not divest themselves of clothes or weapons so easily," he said. "Their enclosure quotient is too high. But if you are truly courageous, you will come with me now into the marketplace, unarmed."

He turned and began walking uphill. Gallen didn't move, and the Bock reached back and took his hand, leading Gallen. "No one will harm you. You will be in the company of a Bock."

He led Gallen forward, and Orick growled. "What about us?"

"Stay here," the Bock said. "We will return shortly. Gallen should come naked into this world."

"Wait one minute!" Maggie said. "I don't know if I like the idea of you taking off with that—thing! Leaving us alone!"

Gallen looked up at the Bock quizzically, then glanced back at Maggie. "I . . . don't think he means us any harm," Gallen said.

"No," the Bock said. "We wish no harm, to you or anyone else."

"But is it safe for us to be alone here?" Maggie asked.

"No one disturbs the temple grounds by daylight," the Bock said. "I have been here for weeks, and only the priests come into this field. But people like you would best seek shelter at night." The Bock took Gallen's hand and led him off up the hill and into the trees.

Maggie and Orick waited in the little hollow until one hour passed, then two. Heavy clouds rolled in. Still, Gallen did not return with the Bock.

Near sunset it began to rain, a light warm drizzle. Minute by minute, Maggie began to worry that perhaps the Bock was not as harmless as he seemed, that perhaps he had set some kind of a trap. He'd said he would be back before dark.

As darkness drew on, a huge gonging rang out, and the cries of street vendors in the village over the hill went silent just as the rain stopped. The thick gray clouds created a false darkness. It seemed somehow spooky the way the vendors all stopped crying out so suddenly.

Whenever Maggie mentioned the time, Orick had encouraging words to say. "Gallen will be back shortly. He won't get lost. Nothing bad has happened." But at last, Orick admitted, "I don't know what Gallen's thinking, but he should be back by now!"

"Shall we search the city?" Maggie asked. "You can probably track Gallen by scent."

Orick nodded uncertainly, began sniffing. Maggie bundled up Gallen's packs, wrapping them all in his robe. They climbed over the hill, to the back of the temple, walked around it, and looked out over a large bay filled with sailing ships. Tall, elegant stone buildings surrounded the bay, and the nearer hills were filled with homes made of fine wood. Twin suns had just set golden in the distance. The air carried the smoke of evening fires and the tempting odor of food cooking, heavy with the scent of ginger and curry. Night was coming quickly.

Overhead, the clouds were whipping away, and ragged patches of evening sky came into view, showing a small scattering of stars.

"Don't worry," Orick said softly. "I'm sure I'll find Gallen soon."

Maggie shook her head violently. "Don't give me that. Something's wrong. Gallen wouldn't just leave."

"Perhaps that Bock creature has him jumping through hoops somewhere," Orick said.

"I don't understand Gallen sometimes," Maggie said as if to herself, "running off unarmed with some strange . . . *thing*, on a world he's never set foot on."

"Och, he's a young man," Orick said. "You have to let them act the part of fools—you couldn't stop them anyway."

A wind was blowing in off the sea, carrying an evening chill. Orick stood just beside Maggie, close enough so that she could feel his body heat. She trembled slightly, stroked his back.

Down the street several blocks, a man turned a corner, walking toward them, but when he noticed them, he immediately turned back, ducking behind a house.

Orick licked his lips, raised his nose in the air to taste the scent. Maggie started forward, but Orick stopped her. "Wait a minute, darling," he whispered. "You had better strap on one of Gallen's swords and a dagger. I've got a cold feeling that an unarmed person wouldn't last long on these streets at night."

Maggie reached into the bag, pulled out Gallen's vibro-blade, felt it begin to activate as it registered her body heat on the handle. She strapped on a knife belt for good measure.

"What should we do?" Maggie asked.

"I'd feel more comfortable in a nice crowded building," Orick said. "This is a port. Surely there's a hostel down at seaside."

"I've decided to stay out of off-world inns," Maggie whispered. "Every time I go in one, I get into a hell of a lot of trouble."

"Well, a young girl traveling with a vicious bear to protect her, what kind of trouble could she get into?" Orick reasoned, and he led the way, heading through the broad streets toward the sea.

After a half mile, they entered the business district, where four-story buildings lined the street, each with its own elaborate columned portico. The doors were all locked. By the docks they found an inn where they could see inside broad windows. A cheery fire was set in a large hearth, and the inn was so crowded that many of the patrons stood around drinking and laughing, unable to sit down at a table to eat. Maggie took the door handle and began shaking it, trying to get in, but the door was locked. She rapped it with the butt of her dagger, and a man with a thin face came to the window beside the door, shaking his head, shouting, "Too dark! Go away!"

"Let us in!" Orick called, but the innkeep turned away. Maggie could tell when a man acted out of fear and when he could not be pushed. She didn't bother rapping at the door again.

Maggie wandered out into the middle of the street, looking both ways. It seemed safer out there, where no one could creep up on them unawares. It was getting quite dark now, and moths banged softly against some of the more well-lighted windows. A mosquito buzzed at Maggie's neck, and she slapped it.

"Which way do we go?" Maggie asked. "North or south?"

Orick stood sniffing. "Back over the hill," Orick said. "I can't taste Gallen's scent at all. Maybe they'll come back for us."

But if Gallen were here on the streets, Maggie figured that she'd spot him half a mile away, and it seemed likely that he'd be coming down the street to find her. Maggie turned up the north road, and Orick followed. A bat swooped in front of them, dipping twice for mosquitoes. Maggie welcomed its presence, figuring that for every mosquito it ate, there was one less mosquito to dine upon her.

Just as the bat swooped in front of them a third time, something enormous fluttered over Maggie's head—something large enough so that its wingspan could have been no less than fifteen feet. Orick bowled Maggie forward, and as she fell she saw the creature grab the little bat out of the sky with a quick snatching motion of one wing.

Then the dark creature flapped up the road where Maggie and Orick had been heading and landed atop the portico of a building.

Maggie blinked. The creature had the wings of a bat, and a bat's catlike ears. It looked for all the world like a bat itself, except for its milky golden eyes. It sat on the portico, staring at Maggie and Orick, and gingerly began feeding on the bat it had caught.

Maggie got up off the muddy road, dusted off her hands, then slowly advanced. The creature sniffed the air as she approached. "Niccce night," it whispered as they neared. "The sstarsss glimmer like firesss in the bowl of heaven." It glanced up. "And the moonsss cassst their golden light on the earth."

Something about the way the creature spoke bothered Maggie. There was a threat behind its words, and she felt as if she should answer. The creature tore a wing from the bat, stuffed it in its mouth and began crunching the tiny bones.

Maggie looked up at the sky. There were no moons shining,

and she guessed at the coded message the bat-thing had given her. It had said the word "golden," and immediately it brought to mind the golden color of the Dronon's hive queen that Gallen had killed a couple of weeks before. She stammered, "Yet their light is not so great as that cast by our Golden Queen."

The creature on the portico looked at her long, stopped tearing apart its prey. Instead, it took the remainder of the body, stuffed it in its mouth, and swallowed the bat in one gulp.

"My brother and sissster, how goesss your hunt tonight?" the creature asked.

"The streets are empty, as you see. We've found no one," Maggie said, praying that she answered correctly. Maggie felt tense to the breaking point. If this creature chose to attack them, there would be no way to escape it. Not with all the doors in town locked against them. She'd have to fight, and she was no great hand with a sword.

"In the harbor liesss a ssship, the third to the north. I sssaw a hatch open, and men insssside were making merry. They think themsselvesss ssecure."

Maggie forced a smile. The creature's intentions were clear. It expected Orick and Maggie to prey upon those men, in the same way that it preyed upon the bat.

"Thank you," Orick said, touching Maggie's hip with his snout, turning toward the harbor. She could hear the tautness in his voice. "Come," he whispered to Maggie. She could tell that he was frightened, that like her, Orick only wanted to get out of there.

We're in this deeper than I'd imagined, Maggie realized. They'd come to this world seeking the Inhuman, and if she guessed right, the Inhuman had found *them*—in a matter of hours.

Maggie forced herself to turn, follow Orick on legs that felt as unresponsive as wood.

The bat began whistling, an odd, meandering tune that sounded more like some code than music. Maggie silently prayed that no one was listening, for she felt sure that if other creatures like this one were near, they would attack. She slipped Gallen's dagger from its sheath. Sometimes, when things had been slow in the inn back home, she had sat in the kitchen with John Mahoney, throwing knives into a target on the wall, above the bread table. John had always insisted that it was a skill that could come in handy someday. Maggie was fairly accurate at a distance of thirty or forty feet, but this creature was more like sixty feet away. Still, it was her only chance.

She hefted the knife half a moment, testing its balance, then whirled and threw high, fearing that the knife was heavier than she was used to.

The knife sailed through the air, and the batlike creature jumped. The heavy knife glanced off the creature's face, and it squealed and fell from the portico, flapping its wings as it tried to fly.

In half a moment Orick was there, leaping atop the creature with all of his weight. She heard the sickening snick of bones cracking when Orick landed, and Orick took the creature's head in his jaws before it could cry out. Orick swung his mighty head back and forth, decapitating the creature, then he slapped the dead body and lunged away in disgust. Then changed his mind and pounced on it again.

"Enough, enough! It's dead!" Maggie cried.

Orick looked at her and roared, choking out strangled sounds, shivering violently.

"Come—come away from here," Maggie said, and she turned.

They hurried north, up the broad avenue, away from the bloody mess behind them, running from the horror of it rather than searching for Gallen.

Somewhere in the air high above and behind them, Maggie heard a shrill whistle, as if from a seaman's pipe—but the sound moved toward them. She glanced back, and in the light of three small, swiftly rising moons saw a huge bat-shape flapping toward them.

In a moment it was overhead, and it landed on a tall building before them, out of throwing distance. It held something shiny in its mouth, and the shrill whistle came again.

Maggie froze, turned to head back down the street, but three men were rushing up the street behind them—if men you could call them. Two were large men in dark robes—too large to be human, but a third hairy man with a misshapen head was hunched low on the ground, running on its knuckles.

Maggie glanced forward, saw another huge brute rush into the street ahead of her.

"This way!" Orick growled, gingerly nipping Maggie's arm in his teeth to guide her. They ran to the nearest shop, and Orick charged the door full force. The door splintered and broke into pieces, but Orick had hit his head against a metal crossbeam that held. The poor bear was knocked unconscious, and he lay there like a sack of flour.

Maggie glanced both ways up the street, saw the four men closing the distance rapidly. She climbed past Orick. Orick lay on the ground in a tumble of splintered wood. He was groaning, and looked up at her weakly, squinting, then his head sagged to the ground.

Maggie turned and brandished her sword, weaving the weapon forward. She'd seen how much damage it could do. It could rip through a human body as easily as slicing melons. From inside the shop, the streets seemed washed in moonlight.

The great hulk reached the building first, stood gazing in the doorway, looking down at Orick, who was still unconscious.

In seconds, the others stood outside the building, panting. One of the men smiled, said easily, "What do you think you're doing? Running? What do you fear?"

"Not you," Maggie said, brandishing the sword.

One hulk held a club. He went to a huge window of the shop where bowls and urns were displayed, and began shattering the glass, widening his access to Maggie.

"Was that your handiwork down the street?" the first man said, a worried expression on his brow. "That poor scout. Not much left of him now."

Maggie glanced at the broken panes in the window. One piece thrust upward like a tooth. Absently, the hulk outside kicked it, breaking it off.

"Stay back!" Maggie warned. "Move along." Her hands were sweaty, and she gripped the hilt of the sword more tightly. The sword seemed to hum, reacting to her fear.

The man in the doorway laughed uneasily. "Come with us. A pretty young thing like you, you belong with us."

"Ah, I'll bet she's human," the hulk said. "She wants nothing to do with us."

"Is that it?" the smiling man asked. "Are you too good for us? Are you sure? I can show you something beautiful. I have a Word for you. You might like it." He reached into the pocket of his tunic, and she knew she did not want to see what he brought out.

Orick moaned at her feet, shifting the shattered door as he tried to get up, then he fell down, and Maggie realized that he would not get up, would not be able to come to her aid. And Maggie recalled something Gallen had once told her: when opponents know that the odds are vastly in their favor, they never expect you to leap into battle.

With a shout, Maggie bounded over the windowsill, swinging the sword with all her fury. The blade caught the hulk at the midriff, slicing through his belly. She whirled and let the blade arc into the smiler, slicing him in two before he could get his hand out of his pocket. Suddenly, Maggie was on the sidewalk, dancing past two dead men.

The hairy man on his knuckles shrieked and tried to leap backward, throwing his hands up to protect his face, and Maggie whacked off his hands while slicing open his face, turned to her last foe who shouted, "Ah, damn you!" and leapt backward.

He drew his own sword ringing from its sheath, and from the cornice of the building above them, the batlike creature blasted its shrill whistle three times.

The swordsman didn't give her a second to think, merely advanced on her, his sword blurring in the moonlight. Maggie was far outmatched in swordsmanship. She stepped back, and in her haste stumbled over the corpse of one of her victims.

The swordsman pressed the attack, swiping maliciously. She managed to parry with her own blade. His sword snapped under the impact, and hers flew from her hand, landed three yards away.

Her attacker jumped at her, landing a foot on her chest,

knocking the air from her. For a moment, Maggie's vision went black from the pain, and she raised her head feebly. Her attacker held his broken sword, its jagged edge lodged in her Adam's apple.

"Here now, sweet lady," he panted. "You see, all of your resistance has come to naught. I never wanted to hurt you." Maggie looked up into his face, and a shock went through her. Though the man was tall, his narrow face was a pale yellow, and he was unnaturally handsome, lustrous, almost as if his face were cast in ceramics. And there was a kindness to his voice. He believed what he said. He didn't want to hurt her.

He struggled with his free hand to untie a pouch wrapped to his belt, opened the pouch and pulled out something small and silver that glittered in the moonlight. It moved like an insect, a large praying mantis perhaps, but its body was sleeker, longer, and more angular.

"Here is the Word. Let it set you free!"

He put it on her chest, and the creature poised for a moment with one huge claw ready to stab into her chest. Then, carefully checking each direction, it began stalking toward her face.

Eleven

The Bock led Gallen over the hill and into a city market, on a wide street where canvas tarpaulins fixed to poles provided some shelter. Under the tarps, small, tan-colored men and women haggled with customers over the prices of exotic fruits and trays of fishes. The locals wore short colorful tunics that left their legs exposed. On their shoulders they wore hooded half-capes made of soft, oiled leather.

The vendors' stalls smelled strongly of curry, anise, saffron, vanilla, and pepper—salt and spices beyond number. The pair moved past brass potmakers, past coils of hemp, bags of wheat, down toward some docks where they had to pass human guards.

Forty ships had put into port, and the docks were awash with all types of cargo—bales of wool and cotton, silks and hemp. Crates filled with beans and furniture, ingots of brass and steel. The Bock explained that most of the people in the crowd were nonhumans, come to trade from far-off lands.

A batch of red-furred sailors in heavy leather armor were unloading a scow, singing a high nasal song. Gallen looked at them in wonder, feeling that something more was wrong with them than their fur, when he realized that they had no ears.

Among bales of cotton, a dark woman dressed in yellow silks sat upon a palanquin that was at the moment unattended. On a long metal chain she held a pitiable creature, an emaciated girl with greenish skin and sad eyes who squatted naked atop a coil of hemp. There were no other men about to bear the palanquin, and as Gallen looked at the woman, she squatted on her hands, and smiled at him. She moved in an odd manner, scratching her arm with her teeth in a way that was distinctly unlike anything he had seen before, and as she stared at him with glimmering eyes, the look of undisguised lust in her eyes frightened him, for Gallen understood immediately that she did not lust for his flesh, except to eat it.

"What is that?" Gallen asked in disgust, leaping back from the woman.

"That is a Herap," the Bock answered. "Among her people, ten men are born for every female. Once she mates with a man, she dines on him, if she can."

Gallen was truly dismayed by all of this, and soon the oddities he noticed among the locals—grotesquely enlarged chests, huge grasping toes, violet skin—all began to meld together in his mind, a seething collage of monstrosities.

A warm shower started, but despite the downpour, the people milled about freely, oblivious to such weather. If it had truly been the Bock's determination to simply parade Gallen through the streets, it could have taken Gallen back to Maggie then. But instead the Bock led him resolutely past the marketplace, down toward a district where the buildings began to close in, stone houses flanking the narrow streets, each house with its pillars and portico protruding out so far that they had to walk around them.

"Where are we going?" Gallen asked at last, wiping the rain from his face.

"Consider for a moment," the Bock answered, "but do not speak your guess." And Gallen knew that they were going to see Ceravanne.

The Bock led Gallen down around the bay, and over a hill, farther up the coast. The city extended on for miles, stretching among the hills, and Gallen realized that they had been only at the very southern tip of it. The sky began to darken, and the streets emptied far too quickly, until few people walked the streets, and those who did glanced about furtively and would duck into alleyways when they saw Gallen and the Bock approaching.

"This part of the city isn't safe," Gallen said.

"If you wore weapons or more clothing, this would be a dangerous neighborhood," the Bock answered. "But obviously you are carrying no money. A half-naked man and a Bock—no one would bother with us. Besides, are you not a killer?"

"A Lord Protector," Gallen answered uncomfortably.

"A killer," the Bock argued, a hint of distaste in his voice.

"And you disapprove?" Gallen asked.

"I am a Bock. We respect all life."

"You must eat."

"I have a mouth so that I may speak," the Bock answered. "Beyond that, I take nourishment from the rain and the soil. I cannot comprehend killing. Life is precious—in all its forms. Unfortunately, not everyone agrees with me. Some peoples are esteemed as less than others. For example, in the wilderness of Babel, there are creatures called the Roamers. Their ancestors were humans, but the desire for enclosure was bred out of them, and they were given hair and great strength and stamina, so that they might thrive in the wilds without shelter. They wear no clothes, and many in Babel think of them as somehow less than human, animals. The Roamers do not have human rights—access to human technology and the human system of justice."

"That doesn't seem fair to me," Gallen said. "Why, back home, every man can have his day in court."

"But for many subspecies of human," the Bock countered, "the human system of justice itself is unfair. It requires them to think and act like humans—something they cannot do. And so we cannot hold them to human laws."

"But what if a nonhuman kills someone else?" Gallen said. "Certainly you can't just allow that."

"All beings are held accountable equally," the Bock answered. "In such cases, our courts hire a champion to hunt down the offender, and slay it."

And suddenly Gallen knew why he was here. "The Inhuman . . ."

The Bock glanced at him sideways, the wide portion of his head swiveling. "Yes. Champions have been sent to Babel to hunt the Inhuman, but they never returned, and still its power spreads. That is why our leaders requested a Lord Protector from off-world, someone licensed to use weapons that we keep restricted here."

"So you want me to hunt down and slay this Inhuman?" Gallen asked.

"*I* want nothing of the sort. Whether the lion or the jackal wins this conflict does not matter to me. It does not matter to the rocks and sky and water. I see little difference between the goals of the Inhuman and your goals, nor do I see any difference in your methods for gaining control. Ceravanne says that your people fight for freedom, but freedom is an illusion, so long as the light within you is encased in a body made of dust. You are all slaves to your animal desires—"

"And you're not?" Gallen asked.

"I am not an animal," the Bock said. "That is why the Tharrin . . . worship me." Gallen caught his breath at this last bit of news, for he imagined the Tharrin to be the highest life-forms in the galaxy. It had never occurred to him that the Tharrin would look up to other beings, much less that they would so admire another species that they would worship it. For the past hour, Gallen had felt that the Bock had been trying to show him something, had been trying to get across a message that somehow wasn't connecting. Now Gallen focused more attentively.

"Gallen, I desire that both sides find a path to peace, nothing more." The Bock stopped in a narrow alley. A chill wind swept through the alley, and overhead several pigeons flapped about, trying to find the best roosting spot on the crumbling stone lip of a roof. Gallen could see over the edge of town, and the suns setting out over the ocean were shining on some near hills. He could see the front of the temple near where the Gate of the World opened, and near the temple's huge doors, a huge brass disk reflected the dying suns. Two giants in yellow robes began to beat the disk with great clubs, so that the gong flashed golden like the wings of a fiery bird, and the sound of its gonging echoed over the town. There was silence for the moment. "Those giants are called Acradas. In many ways they are wise, but each night they try to call the suns back, fearing that unless their sun disk tolls, the suns will never return." The Bock hesitated, and Gallen pitied such ignorant creatures. "You and I look at the Acradas, and we think them strange. As you are to Acradas, I am to you. My thoughts are incomprehensible to you, and you and the In-human are equally alien to me. But we—each of us—are held prisoner by our own bodies. We sense the world in our own way, and we act toward it in ways that our mind allows. No man can truly be comprehended by another. Here on our world, in the City of Life, our people design new forms of humanity to inhabit other worlds. They have created over five thousand subspecies of human. Many of them have far-reaching enhancements that cannot be detected by eye alone, and with others, apparently major enhancements are merely cosmetic. For some subspe-cies, their paths of thought so differ from those of mankind that they cannot be held accountable to the laws that govern life here in the human lands. Still, their lives are precious to them. They cannot help what they are, and they cannot change it. They are not capable of being human, but you, Gallen O'Day, I hope will look upon them with empathy and understanding."

"You want me to *judge* the Inhuman?" Gallen asked.

The Bock whispered, "Many people have been absorbed by the mind of the Inhuman. Few of the people who have become Inhuman did so of their own free will. For each Inhuman that you meet, you will have to decide whether to slay it or let it live." The Bock sighed, and its mouth opened and its eyes half closed.

For a moment, it gave an expression of such profound sadness that Gallen feared it would break into tears. "And yet,

Gallen, I suspect that you will have no chance to reason with or prevail against this . . . thing. The Inhuman is powerful, and if the rumors we hear are true, it controls hundreds of thousands of beings. . . ." The Bock glanced up, then whispered, "See, there is one of its scouts now! They come to the city every night!"

Gallen looked skyward, and from the clouds above a dark form swooped, a wriggling tatter of night that suddenly resolved into a creature flapping on batlike wings. As Gallen watched, he almost imagined it to be an enormous bat. And suddenly he knew why the streets here cleared at dusk. The servants of the Inhuman owned the night.

"Quickly now," the Bock said. "We must get indoors."

Gallen had a sudden cold fear, and he wondered if Maggie and Orick were all right. He would need to get back to them soon.

Gallen stopped, unwilling to go any farther with this strange creature. The Bock turned and looked at him expectantly, waiting for Gallen to follow.

"Wait a minute," Gallen said. "What of Maggie and Orick? Shouldn't we go back for them?"

"Soon, soon," the Bock promised. "All in time."

And Gallen wondered. He was a stranger to this world, still unsure of its dangers. The Bock knew more than he did. Perhaps the fact that the Inhuman was sending scouts to the city at night did not mean that Maggie was in danger—but Gallen had seen the fear in the eyes of the locals as they hurried off the streets.

"I'll go no farther with you," Gallen said.

"Please, hurry," the Bock said. "It is not much farther—a moment more."

Gallen hesitated, greatly torn. But Maggie had Orick to guard her, and Gallen suspected that another moment would make little difference. Reluctantly, he followed the Bock.

The Bock led Gallen to the side entrance of a building, and they stepped under the portico and hurried down a maze of dark hallways until Gallen was completely turned around. Then the Bock stopped and whispered a name at a door that looked like all the others. "Ceravanne."

Gallen heard a bolt sliding, then the door opened, and behind it stood a young woman wrapped in a dark cloak that hid most of her face. Yet Gallen could see the precisely sculpted cheekbones and brow that marked her kind. He found himself wishing that she would speak, so that he might hear her voice. Her dark eyes were haunted, and she looked at Gallen hopefully for a second, then turned and led the way into a dusty store room filled with barrels and crates, moving with a delicate grace that could only belong to a Tharrin.

Gallen entered the room behind the Bock, feeling extremely ill at ease. As he stepped through the doorway, the door closed a little and a large man moved in behind Gallen, placing a sword at the side of his neck. "Far enough," the man said, putting just enough weight on the blade to force Gallen to step sideways and back. "Face the wall."

Gallen stood against the wall, bridling at the thought. He'd come here unarmed, without so much as a knife or his mantle. His legs were shaking, and Gallen forced himself to breathe deeply, hold down his anger. The guard kept the sword to the back of his neck, then ran one hand through Gallen's long hair, checking carefully around the base of his neck. "He's clean, milady," the guard said. "No weapons, and no scars near the neck."

"The Lord Protector, Gallen O'Day, did not come alone," the Bock told Ceravanne. "He brought a woman and a bear. I left them behind with the weapons, as ordered."

The guard stepped back, and Gallen glanced at the Bock, realizing that this seemingly innocuous creature had a duplicitous streak to it. "You tricked me," Gallen said.

"Ceravanne asked me to bring you to her alone, stripped of weapons," the Bock answered. "But I asked you to come so for my own reasons."

So the Bock and Lady Ceravanne worked at cross-purposes, and Gallen realized that he might be working at cross-purposes to them both. The Bock wanted the Inhuman left alone.

Ceravanne perhaps sought only to stop its encroachments. And without knowing anything about the Inhuman, Gallen had halfway decided to kill it.

Ceravanne was about to speak, but she stopped, as if a sudden thought had occurred to her. "Bock, isn't it getting dark out?"

"It is late," the Bock agreed.

"But—Gallen's friends, where did you leave them?"

"In the field, at the opening to the gate."

Ceravanne frowned, plainly worried. "Bock, we can't leave them for the night—the Inhumans . . . !"

"I will go get them," the Bock said.

Ceravanne said, "Can you retrieve them before full nightfall?"

"If I hurry across the fields, over the hill!"

"Rougaire, you go with him," Ceravanne said.

The guard, a giant with a bulbous red nose and weathered features, put one hand on his sword and said, "Yes, milady."

"Should I go, too?" Gallen asked.

Ceravanne frowned. "No," she said after a moment. "I think not. I still need a guard. And if your friends stayed put, the Bock and Rougaire should reach them soon enough. Four people traveling together in the early evening are not in great danger—especially not when Rougaire is among them."

The giant Rougaire took a heavy robe from atop a nearby crate and put it on, then strapped his swords to his back. Gallen studied the man's movements. He was all strength and no grace. When he was ready, the giant handed Gallen one of his swords, a weapon that seemed just a bit too long and heavy for convenient use.

"For you, sir," Rougaire said, bowing deeply.

"I'd rather have one of your daggers," Gallen said. The giant frowned a bit at Gallen's choice, then took one of his daggers from its sheath at his knee and handed it to Gallen. It was large enough for Gallen to use as a short sword. Gallen just held it, for he'd left his belt with Maggie and had nowhere to put the weapon.

"Thank you, Rougaire," the Lady Ceravanne said to the guard. "Go quickly!"

The guard bowed to her, then hurried out in company with the Bock. Gallen bolted the door behind them.

Ceravanne studied Gallen, and the haunted look did not leave her eyes. She appeared to be a child of thirteen or fourteen, but she held herself with a dignity, a wisdom, far beyond her years. Her platinum hair cascaded in waves down over her shoulders, and she watched him from green eyes, paler than any eyes he'd ever seen or imagined. She wore a delicate white dress with white birds embroidered upon it, and she looked like something not quite human, like a fragile fairy bride in a dark glen. But there was the pain in her eyes, and Gallen wondered idly how many cloned bodies she had worn out.

"I'm sorry for asking the Bock to bring you stripped *and alone*," she said. "I asked him to bring you alone because curious children sometimes follow the Bock, and I didn't want them tagging along. The Bock . . . is very wise in his way, but he does not think on our level. He often takes the things we say too literally, and he does not comprehend the import of our struggle. He meant no harm, and I hope that no harm will come of it."

"My friend Orick is handy in a fight," Gallen said, trying to put her at ease, still uneasy himself. "I suspect they'll be all right."

"I am not worried that they will be injured or killed," Ceravanne said. "I'm worried that they will be infected by the Inhuman."

"Infected?"

"The Inhuman sends agents—small creatures—to burrow into their victims from the back of the neck, and then the creature infects its host with the Inhuman's propaganda, downloading information into the victim's brain. Those who have recently been infected will bear a scar at the base of the neck."

Ceravanne went to a large barrel, used a match to light a

single candle, then set it on the barrel. She sat down cross-legged at the base of it, and motes of dust rose up, floated in the light.

"I asked the rebellion to send someone I could trust. Can I trust you?" she asked.

Gallen stared into the child's eyes, and his heart felt as if it would melt. He had forgotten how powerful the scent of a Tharrin woman could be, had forgotten how the pheromones she exuded could tug at his sanity. One look at her frail, perfect figure, and he wanted only to fall to his knees, pledge his fealty. And because she was Tharrin, because she was bred to rule in kindness, he could see no reason not to do so. Yet Gallen remembered the deadly rose in its glass last night, someone warning him against trusting the beautiful Tharrin? He stood aloof from her. "Of course you can trust me."

"You are new to our world," Ceravanne said. "I forget my manners. Is there anything you need? Food, drink?"

"No," Gallen said.

"I suppose you have questions?"

"Your friend, the Bock—he said that you Tharrin worship him. Is this true?"

"Worship?" Ceravanne answered, and the question seemed to make her nervous. She shook her head and looked away a bit guiltily. "I'm afraid he does not understand all of the nuances of our language. I revere him, certainly. I respect him, seek to emulate him. He is my teacher, and I love him as a friend. . . . Perhaps 'worship' is close to the right word." She looked at him squarely. "I do not worship him any more than you worship the Tharrin, I suspect. Do you worship the Tharrin?"

Gallen puzzled at the question. In many ways, he almost did. He found that when he was in their presence, he could not help but serve them faithfully. He admired them. He had loved the Lady Everynne. Still . . . "No," Gallen said. "I do not trust them completely. I have learned that despite all appearances, we are not the same species."

Ceravanne smiled wryly at that. "In some ways, I trust the Bock completely. He is a man of peace, who can do no harm.

But it seems that I cannot trust him to fetch a Lord Protector to me, without botching the job."

Gallen changed the subject. "Why does the Inhuman want you?"

"I'm Tharrin," Ceravanne answered. "And therefore am born to lead. The Inhuman may want me as a leader."

"I am surprised," Gallen admitted. "With the Dronon gone from this world, I would have thought you would be a Lord Judge, wearing a mantle."

"No," Ceravanne said. "The human lords in the City of Life act as judges on this world, not me. I act as a counselor to them only—should they seek my counsel. I have not held much power for the past several centuries. Still, I am the last of the Tharrin here, and so the Inhuman seeks to control me.

"Beyond that, what I can tell you about the Inhuman is mostly guesses. We began to hear rumors of it three years ago. At first it was only one or two odd reports, borne from the interior of Babel by nonhumans who came with wild tales. The lands there are very rugged and backward, and we imagined that it was only some new religion. But when our leaders sought to send scouts to the area, the Dronon opposed us. Among the Rebellion, there was some talk of sending our own scouts in secret, but we erred—we ignored the rumors for the moment, and concentrated instead on fighting the Dronon.

"So the Inhuman seemed to grow slowly, until last year. Among the peoples of Babel, there is a race called the Tekkar, a brilliant people, engineered to live on a brutal world so hot that men can only safely move about at night. They have purple eyes that see in the dark, and they are themselves stealthy and dark. Within weeks, all the tribes of Tekkar were converted, and then they began to attack their neighbors by night, converting those they could, slaying those who opposed them."

Gallen said lowly, "The Bock showed me some of the peoples who live here, and he warned that some were more powerful, more vicious than humans. Yet I wonder: the Tharrin are peaceful people—why would you create such beings?"

"Once again, you overestimate my influence," Ceravanne

said. "The human lords in the City of Life choose which races to create, which attributes are needed for those who will inhabit other worlds. Some of the beings they've created were designed before the Tharrin were born. Others I see as abominations that should never have been formed. Still, I have long sought to maintain peace between our various races."

"You were telling me about the Inhuman?" Gallen said.

"Yes. It was about a year ago that the Inhuman sent its first scouts to the City of Life, where I had been in hiding from the Dronon for many years. The agents of the Inhuman tried to abduct me, but I resisted to the death, and my faithful followers downloaded my memories into a new clone.

"Then sailing ships began arriving from Babel, ships filled with refugees, and they warned us of the darkness growing in the land of Moree. Only then did we begin to recognize the true size of the danger, but we could not mount an attack against the Inhuman. The Dronon still ruled here, and they refused our pleas. At first, we thought they were only refusing to take sides in a local squabble, so we sent out scouts then, in secret. Even I went with that first scouting party, but most of our people were killed, and those who survived returned as Inhuman converts who betrayed the Rebellion by pointing out our operatives. Some small bands of our people went to war secretly then, but they were no match for the Inhuman.

"Then three months ago it became apparent that the Dronon were openly siding with the Inhuman. They put a marching hive city in each of our ports so that we could not mount an offensive. We could not defeat the Dronon's aircraft and walking fortresses with spears and swords.

"And so we began to lose hope. We thought we would all be consumed—until a few days ago, when the Dronon left our worlds. And suddenly our hope is reborn!"

"And what is the Inhuman's cause?" Gallen asked.

"It was created for the purpose of convincing mankind that our species can coexist peacefully—as subjects within the Dronon Empire."

"So the Dronon created the Inhuman?"

Ceravanne frowned. "Not exactly. It is beyond their technology—in some ways, it is beyond ours. Here on Tremonthin, we have adopted a simple way of life. Nearly all technology is proscribed, except that which is used in the service of extending life. In the City of Life we download memories into clones, perform our great work of adapting mankind to fit within alien ecosystems. Because it is our sole technological export, our life-enhancing technologies are among the best in the galaxy. The Dronon incorporated our technologies into the Inhuman. Some of our scientists aided them. We found the perpetrators, and those who aided them willingly have already been dealt with. The rest are working to undo the damage."

"You say that the Dronon helped create the Inhuman," Gallen said. "What is the Inhuman?"

"The Dronon saw that with the thousands of subspecies of mankind living on this world, it was the perfect place to experiment, learn which breeds might most easily integrate into their society.

"So they made an artificial intelligence that stores the memories of Dronon technicians, along with those of non-humans from our southern continent.

"And this artificial intelligence is struggling to infect our people with a new world view—a complex web of memories and beliefs and lies that lead those infected to convert to the doctrines of the Inhuman," Ceravanne sighed. "We couldn't fight such sophisticated weaponry."

"Then why don't you get better weapons?" Gallen blurted out. "Bring in forces from off-world."

Ceravanne looked pointedly at Gallen. "Our world is distant from others. Even with the fastest ships—and such ships are on their way—it will take months for help to arrive. Even then, it will be hard to mount an attack on Babel. It was created as a refuge for nonhumans, and many of the species there fear us. If we attacked in force, they would see it as an invasion and would seek to turn us away. So even those we count as allies could turn against us. But more importantly, many of the nonhumans in Babel are genetically upgraded. They are stronger and faster than us, tougher, and often more cunning. We could not defeat them on their own ground. We can hardly hope to repel an invasion."

"So you want me to sneak into the southlands and destroy this Inhuman, this machine?" Gallen asked.

Ceravanne studied him a moment, then looked down at her feet. Her jaw trembled, and an expression of utter hopelessness crossed her face. "Oh, Gallen, I wish that were all I was asking of you. . . ."

Gallen went to her, knelt and put his hand on her shoulder, trying to comfort her. She looked up, reached up with one hand and stroked his cheek, then kissed him softly.

For one long moment, he allowed it—reveling in the sweet, intense taste of her lips—then pulled back sharply, as if he'd been struck. He wiped her kiss from his mouth with the back of his arm, yet the scent of her pheromones lingered, and he had to remind himself that as a Tharrin she was made so that he would love her. "I, I—" He fumbled for an explanation. "I'm married."

"I need you!" Ceravanne said fiercely. "I need you to give yourself to me completely. Gallen—I don't know everything about the Inhuman, but I believe that it is more dangerous than you or I can imagine. It isn't just a machine, it is a technology that has fused the minds of millions of beings—and they will oppose you. It is not just the machine, it is the talents and wisdom and hopes of all those people. I can't tell you what I think I must ask you to do for me! But I need you to trust me. If my guess is correct, it will be harder than anything you can imagine. I need you!"

Gallen studied her face. It was obvious that she planned to face this challenge with him, that she did not want to reveal her part in this fight. It annoyed him that she would hold her plans so secret, but looking into her eyes, he suddenly realized that he trusted her. "It seems that I do trust the Tharrin completely," Gallen said. "Or at least I trust you. I'll do whatever you ask—but don't ask me to give you my heart."

"I need *that* most of all!" Ceravanne whispered fiercely. "I need a Lord Protector to serve me wholly. Listen: in Moree there is a leader, a very powerful person that the servants of the Inhuman call 'the Harvester.'"

That name struck a chord in Gallen, and he found his heart pounding. He was sure he'd never heard of this Harvester—yet he suddenly remembered something, a bit of information that only his mantle could have planted in his memory.

"Are you sure it's human?" Gallen asked. "A thousand years ago, on a planet from the Chenowi system, a few hundred machines were built, machines called the Harvesters. They are nanotech devices which carry downloaded human memories. They can assume dozens of forms, change colors. They were designed to be the ultimate assassins. Over the centuries, most of them have been destroyed. But on a low-tech world like this, a Harvester would be almost invulnerable. It's possible that one survives here."

This bit of news seemed to disconcert Ceravanne. "I—never considered such a possibility," she said.

"I'll have to kill it," Gallen said, almost certain that this Harvester was more than a mere person.

Ceravanne looked up at him, startled, and there was resignation in her eyes. Though she was a Tharrin, and could never bring herself to harm another, she understood the need for killing at times. Still, she seemed tormented. "I hope it does not come to that," Ceravanne whispered, and Gallen wondered at her naïveté. "But if it does, it won't be easy. At the very least, I suspect that you will bear scars from this—scars on your soul, scars that you will abhor. I . . . am loath to ask this of you."

"I've killed before," Gallen said calmly, wondering what Ceravanne knew of this Harvester, and even as he said it, he remembered the three men back home, the empty-headed oafs who had forced his hand by testifying against him. He still felt marred by those killings, stained.

Twelve

When Orick woke at the doorway to the store, his vision was blurred. He could smell the cobbled roads thick with dust and tiny flakes of dried manure from sheep and some other animal, and Orick wished that he could stand up and walk on his hind feet, put a little distance between himself and that unclean scent.

A whistle blew, and its sound was a cold wind that froze Orick to the heart.

The Inhuman, Orick remembered. The hair on the back of his neck bristled, and Orick opened his eyes, spotted Maggie in a patch of moonlight, lying on her back in the street, corpses stacked around her. A tall fellow hunched over her, holding what looked to be a broad dagger at her throat.

Orick lay for just a moment, and suddenly there was a shout from down the street, the way they had come. Two forms moved in the shadows—one was the familiar shape of the Bock, the other was a giant, and they were running, but they were too far away to help Maggie before the villain could cut her throat.

Orick jumped up and charged, digging his claws into the

floor planks for all the purchase he could get, bounding forward so that parts of a broad wooden door were flung away from him.

Orick roared, and the fellow glanced up from Maggie, then fled down the road, between two buildings. Orick lunged after him, and the fellow grunted and zigzagged into the shadows.

A giant bat swooped in front of Orick, trying to distract him, and Orick stood up, swatted at the creature, catching a corner of its wing. The bat veered away clumsily.

Orick was so angry he felt as if he were invulnerable, as if he could run forever, and he continued to chase Maggie's attacker, rushing till he could nearly take the man's neck in his teeth.

The fellow glanced over his back, shouted "No!" and, in a burst of redoubled speed, made it around a corner and jumped over a high wall.

Orick came up short against the wall, knowing he couldn't make it, and decided that it was best to go care for Maggie.

He rushed through the streets to Maggie, found her on her back, holding some strange insect in her hand, keeping it at a distance. Her face was pale, frightened. The giant and the Bock stood over her, gasping for breath.

"What is that thing?" Orick asked. The insect was mantis-like in appearance, but its front legs were oversized. Maggie had them pinched firmly.

"I'm not sure," Maggie said. "It looks like a machine, but I'm not sure what it does."

"That is an Inhuman's Word," the giant said in a deep voice, taking the thing from Maggie's fingers and smashing it. "It turns a man into an Inhuman. You had better watch out. There might be more."

The giant immediately began dusting off Maggie's back while watching for the bugs on the street.

When he was sure she was clean, Maggie retrieved Gallen's sword. One of the insects was there beneath it. It began to scurry over the cobblestones, so she swatted it with the flat of the sword. After more searching, she decided there had only been two Words. Up the street from them, that damned batlike creature had made it to the top of a building, and it blew its whistle in three sharp bursts.

Maggie looked up at the giant bat. "Shut off the whistling already, damn you!" she shouted. "If any more of your black-hearted friends come around, we'll give them just what we gave the others!"

The scout looked down at them in the moonlight, his eyes glowing golden. He growled, "You'll pay for dessstroying the Wordsss." He let his whistle dangle from a chain about his neck, glared at Maggie for a moment, rubbed his face with the little black hands at the joint of his wings, then hurled himself from the building, swooping just over their heads.

Orick wished that Maggie had been carrying a stick or something. One good knock on the head would have busted the creature's skull open like an acorn.

"I am sorry that I got back so late," the Bock told them, waving its arms emphatically. "When we reached the meadow, you had already left. We've been looking everywhere for you!"

Maggie shook her head. "No harm done," she said, hefting her packs. "Let's go." They began hurrying north, but the Bock was striding along slowly. The giant walked ahead, leading the way, his huge sword in hand. He stopped at each side street, checking both ways.

"Can you hurry?" Maggie said, trying to help the Bock along by pulling at its arm.

"I'm sorry," the Bock said. "I have no energy after dark. There were huge clouds at sunset, and it slowed us. I should have found you long ago!"

Orick looked at the creature—half man, half plant. They could not leave it behind, and they could hardly wait for the thing to move at its own pace.

Maggie was sweating heartily from her fight, from her fear. She looked at Orick a moment. "Orick, could you have a go at giving him a ride?"

Orick considered. His ears were ringing, and he felt woozy from the bump on his head, but he could probably carry the man. Still, just because he had four legs, it didn't mean he'd let people treat him like a pack mule. "All right," he grumbled, "but it's undignified."

Maggie helped the creature on. Orick ran with Maggie at his

tail, and they managed to make good time with the giant leading the way.

They were running into the wind, and once Orick smelled the fresh scent of strangers ahead. Orick called to the giant, then turned aside, lurching off around several blocks, certain that he'd avoided an ambush. As if to prove his point, moments later he heard excited whistling behind him as the batlike scout realized what had happened. Just then, the giant had Orick duck into a little side alley that led to a warehouse, and within moments they were inside.

Maggie closed the door tight behind her, threw the bolt home, and sagged against it in the dark. There were no lanterns, no lights in the building at all, and the dark was utterly impenetrable. Orick half turned. He could smell her warm sweat, and she was breathing hard, as much from fright as from the exertion. He couldn't smell any other people in the hall, though Gallen had passed here shortly. There would be no ambush waiting ahead of them.

"Orick?" Maggie said. "Where are you?"

"Here," he grumbled.

"Come here, where I can touch you."

Orick ambled to her, and Maggie petted his snout affectionately. It was one of the most intimate pettings she had ever given him, and he closed his eyes, relishing the way she scratched him. He groaned with pleasure, and Maggie bent down and kissed him full on the snout. "Thank you," she said. "You're welcome at my table anytime. You really saved me."

And at those kind words, Orick's heart warmed. He led Maggie, the giant, and the Bock down the maze of twisted halls in something of a blur, until he got to a door. He could see candlelight winking through the cracks, and the Bock called out softly for Gallen.

Gallen slid the bolt, pulled the door open, and at sight of the blood on Orick's face he cried, "What happened to you?"

Maggie told them then of their skirmish with the servants of the Inhuman, and Ceravanne frowned and paced the room, then had Gallen and Rougaire check Orick and Maggie for neck wounds.

When she was satisfied, Ceravanne shook her head, plainly worried. "I had hoped to wait here for a few days so that we could provision our trip at our ease, receive counsel from the Lords in the City of Life. But we will have to leave first thing in the morning."

"Why?" Orick asked.

"Their scout has your scent," Ceravanne said. "It will call its fellows, and by dawn there may be a dozen or more of them hunting for you and Maggie. The Inhuman will not hold harmless those who have slain its members. We must flee at dawn."

Thirteen

———

Zell'a Cree heard the shrill warning of the scout's whistle from over a mile away, and rushed through the darkened streets until his infrared vision could make out the fiery forms of his men. He came upon the corpses of his men, his pack brothers, lying in pools of their own blood. Their bodies glowed like faint embers, and the blood still hot in their veins was like twisted rivers of light under their skin.

Besides the scout Ssaz, who sat nursing an injured wing from the stone gutters of a building, three other hunters from Zell'a Cree's pack had gathered—two were unnamed Tekkars, swathed in black robes cut at the thighs, wearing tall leather boots tied above the knees. The Tekkars' purple eyes gleamed darkly from their shadowed hoods. The third was a small man named Ewod who might have been human, except that he wore fur-lined winter robes on a balmy evening and his skin was pale yellow. He stared at the ruined corpses and shook, and Zell'a Cree watched him closely. He had seldom seen so much fear upon the face of a man.

Zell'a Cree felt calm himself. Fear had been bred out of his people thousands of years ago. He had never wakened with his heart thumping from a bad dream, had never felt an uneasy tingling at the sound of running feet in a dark alley. And now, looking at his brothers, he felt only sadness, a profound loss at such a waste.

He went to the corpses, closed the staring eyes. "The wheel turns, and we must now travel the road without you. Come to us when you can," he whispered to the dead, bidding them to seek rebirth soon, then reached into his travel pouch and brought out wafers of bread and placed one in the mouth of each of his dead comrades to feed them on their spirit journeys.

Zell'a Cree was disturbed by the sounds of the little man, Ewod, crying, and Zell'a Cree also wanted to weep at the waste of life. But as leader of this hunting pack, he could not afford the luxury.

"Don't dawdle," the scout Ssaz hissed at them from its perch, its canines gleaming as gold as its eyes in the moonlight. Zell'a Cree could smell the sweet copper scent of its blood, but couldn't immediately see the wound. "The humansss may return, hunting usss thisss time!"

"What happened?" Zell'a Cree spoke only in a hushed whisper. All of the men here had hearing far keener than any human.

Ewod said, "Me and my brothers chanced upon a bear and a young woman, and we thought they would make easy converts. The bear wounded himself trying to escape, but the girl came at us with a sword and slew my brothers before they could react."

"Fools!" one of the Tekkar spat, his voice the sound of loose gravel shifting under one's feet. Because the Tekkar did not name themselves, Zell'a Cree was forced to bestow names upon them in order to keep them straight. He called this one Red Hand, for the man had his right hand dyed red. "They should have taken more care. They deserved to die!"

"No one deserves death," Zell'a Cree said.

"The humans who did this deserve to die!" Red Hand countered. "We must make an example of them, teach the humans to fear us."

Zell'a Cree knew that the humans no longer walked abroad at

night because they were afraid of his hunting pack, and it was only that fear that made it possible for his people to penetrate so deeply into the human lands. If the humans banded together and went abroad in the dark, his hunters would be no match for them. But the humans did not know this, and so fear protected Zell'a Cree's men. He could not gainsay Red Hand's argument, no matter how repulsive he might find it.

"What do the rest of you think?" Zell'a Cree asked, hoping that the imaginative Ewod might be able to find a reason to extend mercy.

The second Tekkar, whom Zell'a Cree called Garrote because the man always kept a garrote wrapped at his waist to use as a belt, said, "If an Inhuman kills a human, the humans send their assassins to take vengeance. We should do no less."

"And if we kill these humans, will we not be lowering ourselves to their standards?" Zell'a Cree said. "The way of the Inhuman is a way to peace."

"Yes," Ewod said nervously. "I tried to tell the humans that. But they feared the Word."

Zell'a Cree glanced at his men. "The Inhuman does not seek vengeance, it seeks converts above all. Yet justice must also be done. We shall hunt this woman and offer her a choice: she may accept the Word, or lose her life."

Zell'a Cree held his breath a moment, and his men grunted their assent. The Tekkar immediately raised their heads, trying to catch the woman's scent, but whereas their night vision was stronger than Zell'a Cree's, his sense of smell far outmatched theirs. He could smell the woman now, the subtle aroma of strange perfumes about her, like nothing he'd ever come across before. And he could smell the bear, its heavy fur.

He rushed down the street, under the cover of darkness, his men flitting behind him like shadows. For nearly an hour he tracked them through the streets. It was a difficult task, even for Zell'a Cree, for it was not long past dusk, and the odors of thousands of travelers were still fresh on the night air.

Their scout flew ahead, and once he spotted the humans and they tried to set a hasty ambush, but the humans turned aside from their course.

Still, it was not hard to pick up their trail again. Zell'a Cree held to the exotic scent of the woman, a scent utterly alien, until at last he came to a warehouse that covered most of a block. It was an old stone building that had once been a great covered market, but now the huge arched doorways had been filled with new brick, leaving but one small opening under a portico.

Bending near the door, Zell'a Cree tasted the scent—and discovered the earthy vegetable odor of Bock. He inhaled deeply, closing his eyes, so that he would remember those smells, recognize their owners as if they were old friends.

Zell'a Cree pulled on the door, but it was barred inside, as he'd expected. He backed up, looked at the building from outside. The old warehouse had two high windows that were barred. Ssaz was already at the bars, tugging on them. But the batlike creature didn't have the strength in his hands to pull the bars loose.

"We could pry open the door," one of the Tekkar suggested, breathing down Zell'a Cree's neck. The Tekkar's voice was annoyingly loud to Zell'a Cree's sensitive ears.

"We don't know if they're in there," Zell'a Cree said. "They may have left another way. Besides, if they remained within, they may have accomplices. I can smell several people who have entered here recently."

He nodded toward the Tekkar. "Each of you circle the building, checking for other doors. If you catch the woman's scent there, call us. Do not try to fight this woman alone. I will go up on the roof and listen for them, see if I can hear them inside."

He only hoped that the Tekkar would follow his orders. The Tekkar had been bred for life on a violent world, and were prone to viciousness. Both of the men were likely to kill their prey without notice. And given their skill in battle, their blinding speed, the woman would not stand a chance against them.

Zell'a Cree's ancestors were designed for life on a world where the air hung so heavy it would choke humans, and the gravity would make the blood pool in a human's legs till the vessels burst. It was a dark world, swathed in eternal mists, and so Zell'a Cree's ancestors had been gifted by the Immortals with compensations—eyes that could see in the dark, a sense of smell as keen as a wolf's, hearing as sharp as an owl's.

Zell'a Cree looked more human than any of his companions, but even now, the sensitive hairs in his ears twitched, and he listened for the sounds of voices.

"Ssaz, fly up and make certain that our prey does not leave the building," Zell'a Cree whispered. "Ewod, you hide in the shadows and watch this door. I'll try to find them inside."

The scout unfurled his wings and leapt into the air, swooping down and then flapping madly. Zell'a Cree grasped the rough stone walls of the building with his fingertips, finding chinks in the stone with his fingers and toes, then climbed up quickly two stories to the roof, crawling over the moss-covered slate tiles, listening, trying to catch a scent.

In moments his knees were wet and bore cuts from the slate roof, but he hardly noticed, he was so intent. Several times he heard the sounds of rats in the rooms below him, their shrieking voices and feet padding over the wooden floors, but Zell'a Cree passed them by, straining to hear above the softly gusting wind, until at last he heard voices echoing in a room beneath him, and he stopped.

The night was nearly silent, and the humans below him, with their dull senses, were utterly unaware. ". . . The Inhuman will not hold harmless those who have slain its members." A girl was speaking, or a young woman, more likely. He imagined that it was the swordswoman speaking. She had a commanding voice, which was at the same time soft and mellifluous. "We must flee at dawn."

"Are you sure you want to come with us?" a young man asked. "It will be a long trip, and if I'm to protect you, it seems to me that the best way to do that is to leave you here."

"I need to come," the young woman replied. "Many servants of the Inhuman respect the Tharrin. You will need their help in finding the Harvester. You'll get that easier with me around. Besides, we requested a Lord Protector simply because I can no longer trust anyone here. The number of those who have been converted by the Inhuman are growing. I would not count myself safer here than in your presence."

"What of the giant, Rougaire? He seems trustworthy."

The woman lowered her voice, and by this Zell'a Cree guessed that the giant must still be in the building, and the woman did not want him to hear her words. "Trustworthy, yes, but he is not your match as a warrior. In battle he is both as graceful and as dangerous as a dancing elephant. Still, he has a great heart. But if we are to win through to Moree, we will require stealth, and Rougaire lacks that capacity."

"And will the Bock be coming?"

"No," the Tharrin said. "He's ill-suited to travel and is incapable of defending himself in an attack." She hesitated. "And what of you? You say the High Judge sent you here. How did you earn her trust?"

"Maggie and I killed the Lords of the Swarm, and Maggie banished the Dronon from the human worlds."

There was a pause, and Zell'a Cree sat openmouthed at his good fortune. To find a Tharrin and the new human Lords of the Swarm both at once——it was incredible. "You did that?" the Tharrin asked.

"Aye," the young man said, and his voice was weary. As if to change the subject, he said, "You said the servants of the Inhuman will be hunting us. Will they attack tonight?"

"That is doubtful," the Tharrin said. "Maggie killed several of them, so they will respect her for that. And now she has reinforcements, while the hosts of the Inhuman are scattered in their hunting packs. No, I think it more likely that they will band in larger numbers——then try to hunt her down. That should give us time to escape."

"How can we manage to escape them undetected?"

"Our best hope is to travel quickly, over water," the Tharrin said. "The scouts have keen noses, but they are blind in the daytime. We can flee at dawn, but we cannot leave our scent on any road leaving town. With luck, they will search the buildings here in town for a couple of days before they realize that we are gone. I think we should set sail in the morning, on the first ship that sails with the tide."

Another feminine voice broke in, a young woman, "Gallen, the beds are made up. . . ."

Zell'a Cree inched away from the room, taking immeasurable care not to make a sound. The rainwater trapped in the moss had wet his tunic so that he shivered with the cold, but when he was well away from his prey, he merely turned on his back and looked up at the stars and three small golden moons that whirled dreamily through the sky like juggler's balls. He breathed the sharp air, and considered. A Tharrin, a Lord Protector with his woman—the newly proclaimed Lords of the Swarm—all heading toward Moree to do battle with the Inhuman.

What better converts could he desire?

Zell'a Cree thought furiously, considering his resources. Here on the frontier he had nearly run out of his copies of the Word. And Zell'a Cree wondered if even the vicious Tekkar would be a match for a Lord Protector. Here, Zell'a Cree lacked the necessary resources for a confrontation, both in technology and in manpower. But if the humans were heading toward Moree . . .

"When you reach the Harvester's throne," Zell'a Cree whispered, "you will bow before it."

Fourteen

Once they reached the shadowed recesses of the warehouse, the Bock was dismayed at the sight of blood on Orick's brow, so while Ceravanne and Gallen talked in the other room and Maggie and the giant made up beds nearby, the Bock lit an oil lamp and set it on some crates. Then it brought forth a pouch of blue dust from its belt, and began slowly rubbing it into Orick's wounds, his sticklike finger probing tenderly.

"I see blood," the Bock exclaimed, "but your hair is so dense, I cannot find a wound."

Orick wasn't sure if he should tell the creature that he healed quickly—ever since Maggie had fed him some capsules of nanodocs that would extend his life for a millennium or more.

"What is that?" Maggie asked of the powder, looking up from one of the bedrolls.

"Healing Earth," the Bock said. "It will ease the swelling, mend the cuts. It is a small wound. He should be well in a few hours."

Maggie came and pinched some of the dirt in her fingers. "Where does it come from?"

"Legend says that ages ago, the Immortal Lords brought it

from the City of Life and put it in the land. Now it is there for the benefit of all people, to be used in curing all wounds."

"Nanodocs," Maggie whispered, looking at the powder. "Does it extend one's life? Regenerate nerve tissue?"

"No," the Bock said, leaning away from Orick. "Only the Immortals in the City of Life have that power. But it cures wounds, mends bones. If you travel, you will find the Healing Earth in many places, beside the springs where the ground is wet."

Maggie nodded thoughtfully, then said, "I'm going to let Gallen know that the beds are ready." She went back behind the crates, into the main room.

The Bock stood perfectly motionless, slightly hunched, and there was a vacant look in its eyes.

"Are you all right?" Orick asked.

"Pardon me," the Bock said. "I fell asleep. I'm exhausted. I must rest soon." The Bock stepped back into a corner, raised his arms up toward a dim window, and stood with eyes squinted, unfocused.

The Bock began asking questions, in his slow way, about Orick's habits, his interests in theology and the possibility of becoming a priest. And with each question, the Bock grew steadily more incredulous, more awake and more interested.

The Bock asked, "So you have been working with Gallen for three years, yet never has he paid you? If you receive no compensation, why do you stay with him?"

"Oh, Gallen does buy me an odd meal now and then, but there's more in this world than money," Orick said. "After all, the Bible says that it's easier for a camel to get through the eye of a needle than for a rich man to enter the Kingdom of Heaven. I'd have to be a wretched creature, indeed, to base my relationship with someone on money."

"So why do you work with him?" the Bock said, his brown eyes gazing steadily at Orick.

"He's my friend."

"So you remain with him for companionship?" the Bock said, as if it were an alien concept, vaguely understood.

"Of course."

"But what of your own kind? Why do you not seek out other bears for companionship?"

"Oh, I don't know," Orick grumbled, not wanting to admit the painful truth. But he was an honest bear, so he continued, "On my world, bears don't run together. Mostly the males eat too much, and they wouldn't want to share food with me. The females love to have us during mating season, but they commence snarling soon afterward, and then, well, they just won't have you around, and they let you know it."

"Have you sought company with many females?" the Bock asked.

"Some," Orick admitted. "There was one I met just before I came here. I had hopes for her."

"You wanted to bond with her?"

Orick hesitated to admit to such a crazy notion. "Marriage is an honorable and holy state . . . or at least that's what the Bible says."

The Bock stopped, and in the dim lamplight he opened his mouth wide in surprise, as if he had just had a fantastic idea. "You are human, Orick!" the Bock said excitedly.

"I'm a bear!" Orick argued.

"Few of us are what we seem," the Bock said. "Our flesh is our disguise, hiding our desires and notions. Many who seem human are mere shells, so why should it be improbable that a creature such as yourself, who inhabits the form of a bear, would be a human at heart? Your thoughts, your beliefs and needs, are all those that a human would understand and agree with. And if you are human at heart, then by our law I have the right to extend the invitation: you may live within our society and enjoy the blessings of human company."

"Great," Orick murmured. He'd had human companionship for his whole life. It didn't seem a great privilege. "So what does that get me?"

"A great deal," the Bock answered. "Few nonhumans may ever enter the City of Life and obtain the blessings granted there. You will find many nonhumans here in the port, but they cannot travel the roads beyond. Instead, they must leave with their ships, returning to exile in Babel."

The Bock seemed so distressed by the plight of the non-humans that Orick found himself sympathizing with them. He imagined how things must be in Babel, a seething madhouse of incompatible species, preying upon the weak and upon one another, a vast continent laid waste by perpetual warfare. Orick's heart went out to such creatures, for he understood what it was to be outcast, to never belong.

"So," Orick grumbled. "Gallen will be surprised when I tell him that I'm as human as he is."

"Are you sure that he *is* human?" the Bock said.

"Why, what else would he be?" Orick asked.

"He could be many things," the Bock said. "I have not yet determined whether he is human, and so I cannot grant him the privileges that come with humanity."

"Why, that's the most absurd thing I've ever heard!" Orick said.

"One's flesh is often a disguise," the Bock countered. "On your home world, did you not often meet others whose thoughts and actions seemed strange to you—so strange as to be incomprehensible?"

Orick considered the blackguards who had tried to frame Gallen. Orick couldn't quite understand how someone would go to so much work to destroy another. It just wasn't in his nature, and on that count, Orick had to agree. Outwardly, men looked the same, but on the insides they could be strangers.

Maggie, Gallen, Ceravanne, and the giant Rougaire came back at that moment, and Orick said in glee, "Did you hear that, Gallen? The Bock says I'm human!"

"Well"—Gallen shrugged—"I've always known you were a better man than me, Orick, but I wish you would do something about that excess body hair."

Orick chuckled, but Ceravanne said quite seriously, as if she were offended, "Do not take the Bock's word lightly, Orick. For five hundred years, this one has been a Lord Judge in the City of Life. A million times he has judged the subspecies of peoples who came before him. In many ways, this Bock knows you better than you know yourselves. If he has proclaimed you human, then he is granting you legal rights and protections. This is a great boon, though you may not know it."

"Well, thank you, then," Orick said to the Bock.

Ceravanne turned to the Bock and said softly, "You know a human when you meet it. So, what do you think of Gallen O'Day?"

The Bock blinked and looked at her from the corners of his eyes.

"I approved the bear, Orick, as human. Not Gallen. As for Maggie, I cannot make a determination, since I have spoken with her so little," the Bock admitted.

"And why do you not think that Gallen is human?" Ceravanne pushed him.

"I sense within him . . . a struggle. He desires to become more than what he is."

"So perhaps he is only a human with high aspirations?" Ceravanne countered.

"Perhaps," the Bock agreed. "I suspect that his are a strong-willed people, with only minor genetic upgrades, very close to feral humans in temperament. I could name him human," the Bock said, "but I am loath to place him so low on the scale of sentient life."

Ceravanne laughed daintily and half lowered her eyes, as if at a private joke. "I suspect you are right," she said to the Bock. "To be a Lord Protector, one would have to be more than human." She lowered the flame on the lamp, then with the giant in tow made her way to the other room.

Orick lay tasting the scent of cobwebs and thinking of the spiders spinning their webs above his head. He was unable to sleep for a long time.

The next morning, Orick woke to the cries of gulls and the smell of sea fog, a salty tang that seeped through every crack in the floor boards and clung to every fold of the blankets. Rougaire the giant had roused the others, and they grabbed their belongings then made a quick breakfast of bread and cheese from Ceravanne's pack.

Gallen and Maggie sat alone and talked for a moment by the

door with the giant, while Ceravanne had gone to the back room with the Bock.

Orick went to tell them that breakfast was ready, and what he saw surprised him: Ceravanne and the Bock stood in the dim light shining through a small window, and Ceravanne was holding the Bock's long fingers, looking down at them, like a shy lover.

Orick stopped in the shadows of a crate, and the Bock said, "Are you sure you want to go with them? They killed so easily last night."

"I too am horrified by their violence, but what can I do?" Ceravanne asked.

The Bock thought a moment. "For three hundred years you have studied with the Bock, learning the ways of peace. You are more one of us than you are of them."

"Three hundred years . . ." Ceravanne echoed. "It is time I return to my people, and teach them the ways of peace. If I can." Orick wondered at the words "my people." Was she saying that the nonhumans of Babel were her people?

"We are our bodies," the Bock said. "I fear that you cannot teach peace to these creatures. And I fear that the violence you must endure in their presence will maim you. Should that happen, do not hesitate to seek us out. In the woods, in the high mountain glens, you can find peace with the Bock."

Ceravanne had been holding the Bock's hand, and suddenly she bent forward and kissed it. "Three hundred years among the Bock—passed all too quickly. . . . I often wish to see the world as you do. I often wish that I could be you."

Suddenly the Bock's face twisted into a mask of profound regret, and he reached out his long fingers to stroke her hair, cradle her head in his hand. "We are our bodies, with all their hopes and dreams, all their limitations. But you, Ceravanne, even among the Tharrin—you are special. . . ." The Bock wailed in its own tongue, "Assuah n sentavah, avhala mehall—" and Ceravanne stepped back as if astonished at this.

"I love you, too," Ceravanne said. "As much as I have ever loved."

The Bock reached up to its head and fumbled among the

green leaves at its crown, then plucked something loose and held it out for Ceravanne. It looked like a small greenish-tan nut, something that Orick hadn't noticed before among its foliage.

"You are going away, and I may never see you again. Should you need a Bock, plant this seed, and in time I will be with you once again."

Ceravanne took the seed gratefully, held it close to her chest as if it were precious. The Bock reached out his long fingers, cradled them around her hair so that she looked as if she were caught in the bushes, and then the Bock leaned forward. His face overshadowed hers, and he kissed her softly on the lips.

Ceravanne wept.

Orick sneaked back to Gallen and Maggie, unwilling to tear the Bock and the Tharrin away from each other. In moments, Ceravanne came out of the back room and placed the seed in her pack, then ate a brief breakfast.

When she finished, she hugged the giant Rougaire and said, "You can see us off at the dock, but afterward I need you to go to the City of Life. Tell the Immortals there that the Lord Protector has come, and that we have gone to confront the Inhuman. If our task is not accomplished by mid-winter, they will have to prepare for war in the spring."

The giant nodded, and they made one last quick search of the room.

Ceravanne wrapped her hair back with a red rag, then pulled her hood forward low over her eyes. She got some soot from a corner, dusted it on her cheeks and under her eyes, making her look worn and wasted. Obviously, she was assuming a disguise.

"Won't people recognize you as a Tharrin?" Gallen said.

"Most people alive today on this world have never seen a Tharrin," Ceravanne said. "And so I tell them that I am a Domorian dancing girl. They look much like the Tharrin. But few people ever even question me about my race. I wear a young body, and children are often ignored, invisible."

She pulled her hood up, affected a slumped posture, a slightly altered body language that somehow completed her disguise. Orick was amazed at the transformation.

Then they hurried out of the warehouse into the streets, and crept to the docks in a dawn fog so thick that they could not see a dozen paces ahead.

It felt good to be on the road again with Gallen and Maggie and a Tharrin, and Orick was somehow eager for action, so he was disappointed when they reached the docks without incident and were able to quickly purchase berths on the second ship they found heading toward Babel.

Because of the thick fog, they had to take the purser's word as to the seaworthiness of the ship; he described it as a lofty five-masted clipper—a worthy ship whose wood held no worm, a ship that could outrun pirates.

So with trepidation they left the docks as several crewmen rowed them to the ship in the fog. The Bock and Rougaire stood on the docks and waved goodbye, seeming to recede into the mist.

Once aboard the ship, the purser escorted them to their berths in three of the six small cabins near the captain's quarters, then excused himself to handle other business.

A brief inspection showed that the ship was all they had been promised—comfortable, immaculate. The ship was already heavily laden with goods, so Orick and Maggie went up to the weather deck in the fog and watched one last time for sign of the Inhuman. Dozens of sailors came aboard in small boats, many of them obviously drunk.

"Watch for a man with bright yellow skin," Maggie breathed into Orick's ear, and Orick sat, listening to the creaking timbers of the ship, the water slapping against the hull. Certainly, most of the crew was made up of an eccentric lot. Dozens of small, bald men with red skin came aboard wearing little more than breechcloths and knife belts. They were filled with nervous energy and were soon everywhere, manning the lines, checking the ties. A dozen grim-faced giants in leather tunics, all armed with oversized bastard swords, seemed relegated to the more strenuous tasks of hoisting sails.

Other crewmen were more eccentric—tall men with tremendously large pale yellow eyes. Black men with horny growths sticking up under their long white hair. Two men with black hooded cloaks came in the last boat, so tightly bundled that they looked as if they wanted their faces hidden, and Orick strained to see the color of their skin. When they climbed up the ladder to the main deck, they moved with incredible swiftness. He glimpsed bare arms the color of slate. One had tattooed his right hand red.

The men passed Orick and Maggie on their way below deck, and Orick caught a glint of their eyes—a deep purple. The second of the pair bore a tattoo of a white spider between his eyes.

And though neither man had the markings that Orick sought, he found that the hair on his neck raised just a bit, and he fought the urge to turn and see if the men were staring at him. When at last he did turn, they had gone off into the fog, yet he wondered what those men might be able to see with such eyes.

When the last sailors boarded the ship, Maggie breathed a sigh of relief. "Thank heaven," she whispered. "Not a yellow man nor one of those bat people among the lot."

The crew weighed anchors and hoisted a single sail, and the ship slid out of port slowly, still under cover of the thick fog.

And Orick soon forgot the chill he'd felt at the sight of the dark-cloaked men. Now that they were away, he found that his heart was light. He heard children laughing out over the water, and spotted some tots—little girls and boys swimming among the many jellyfish alongside the ship. He was amazed at the children's speed, till he noticed that they wore no clothes, and they had tails like fishes.

"Hello!" Orick called to them, and the children laughed and waved at him and Maggie, shouting, "Hello, funny man! Hello, funny lady!" Then one of them threw a jellyfish and they all dove deep, as if they were afraid that he and Maggie would hurl rocks at them.

"Oh, do you think they'll come back?" Maggie cried in delight, and they watched the white-tipped waves for a time, but saw no more of the water children.

Maggie and Orick ambled over the decks for the next half hour till they reached the open sea, where the air swirled and the oppressive fog was left behind.

Orick's spirits soared as they came out under blue skies. The giants began hoisting all sails, and when they filled with air, the ship suddenly surged over the water.

Orick glanced up to the white sails, full of wind, his heart thrilling, just as three giant bat shapes swooped out of the fog to land in the rigging.

He cringed and Maggie cried out, and they moved a bit to see where the creatures went. All three of them scurried to a roofed crow's nest, where they began to cover their eyes with their wings, hiding from the sun.

One of them shouted, "All clear! Night watch out!" then blew a seaman's whistle.

Orick had heard that voice dozens of times in the fog, but never realized that it came from one of the loathsome batlike scouts.

"Hah, they're just part of the crew," Maggie laughed in mock relief. "Who better to sit watch in the crow's nest?"

"A crow would be better," Orick growled, recalling how the scouts had blown their little seaman's whistles in town. "I don't like the looks of them!"

"You can't damn them for their looks," Maggie said, studying the creatures as they huddled in their dark nest.

Her red hair was flying in the wind, and she brushed it out of her face. "Just because they're scouts, it doesn't mean they're Inhuman."

"But it does mean that they're ugly, and I'd just as soon not have their kind near me!" Orick grumbled. "I've seen no good from them."

Maggie whispered, "Speak softer. There's no telling how well they hear." She bent closer, and Orick listened tight. "Orick, those things may not be Inhuman, but it's just as possible that they are. We're on a ship full of people from Babel, and it's likely that at least one of them, and probably more, are Inhuman."

Orick grumbled, turned away, and padded over the deck, his claws scratching the well-scrubbed planks. Maggie's voice had sounded calm enough when she talked of the creatures, but Orick noticed how quick Maggie was to follow at his heels.

That evening, Orick and the others dined at the captain's table. The dinner was a fine feast, with a unique wine that both stimulated the mind and elevated the mood, and along with it they had plates of candied meats, five types of melon, sweet rolls, and breads with cheese baked in them. Orick was delighted, for he seldom found a table larger than his appetite.

In the captain's cabin, the brass lamps kept the room well lit, and the captain had only two other guests at the table—a fat merchant and a shy albino girl.

Captain Aherly sat at the far end of the table from Orick, with a steward boy in a gray smock at one shoulder and his nervous bodyguard at the other.

They made polite conversation for a while at dinner, and Orick was plainly curious about the other guests at the table, so he was almost relieved when the captain said to Gallen, "I've never heard someone who spoke quite the way you and your friends do."

"They're from the village of Soorary, in the north," Ceravanne put in, covering for them.

"Ah, a far country," the captain said, plainly trying to disguise the fact that he wasn't satisfied. "So, do you travel to Babel on business, or pleasure?"

"Adventure," Gallen said. "My friends and I are out to see the world, and I understand that a lot of it is south of here."

"Hah." The captain laughed. "Well, if you're going south, there are some sights that will have your eyes popping out."

"What of our other guests?" Gallen asked. "Why are you aboard?"

The albino girl, a shy girl who had not spoken all evening, looked to the merchant as if asking him to speak, but when he remained silent for too long, she leaned forward and said softly, "I went to the City of Life, for Downing."

Ceravanne supplied the proper response. "You seek resurrection? I hope you were judged worthy!"

The girl looked away demurely. "I was not. They read my

memories, but felt that my contribution to society does not merit—" She choked off the words.

Orick felt a small shock go around the table, and wondered what it would be like to be judged unworthy of future life. It would be as bad as getting a death sentence, he decided.

"You are young yet," Ceravanne said. "Redouble your efforts. All is not lost. I am but a lowly Domorian dancer, yet I got the Rebirth."

The young woman looked at Ceravanne, gratitude in her pink eyes. "As one whose skin is young, but whose eyes are old, I appreciate your reassurance. But—I am considered to be a great teacher among my people. I have worked so hard. I don't know what more I can do. . . ."

She abruptly drew her head back, a graceful gesture, like the movement of a deer in a forest, and Orick realized that she was not shy or reticent as a personality quirk, but that her timidness went much deeper. Her life might well be defined by it.

"Be kind and generous, as is your nature," Ceravanne offered. "It is said that the Immortals value such more than other accomplishments."

The albino woman lowered her eyes, blinking them as a sign of acceptance.

"Perhaps, instead more life, seek meaningful death," the captain's bodyguard said, pacing across the room. The guard, a woman named Tallea, was like a panther, stalking to and fro, and she spoke in quick, sharp tones, as if unable to slow her speech down. She was well muscled and wore a short sword on her right hip and a dueling trident on her left. Her decorative tunic of gray with blue animal figures was covered by a thin leather vest. All in all, her clothes seemed to be merely functional rather than protective. Despite her pacing and her bunched muscles, she seemed serene.

"A meaningful death?" Gallen asked.

Tallea paced across the room, flexing her hands. She wore many rings of topaz and emerald. "Among Roamers, death is accepted. It comes to all, even those who run long, as Immortals do. They say, is duty of young to live, to care for herd. But when you old, is duty to die, to free others from caring for you. Death, like life, should have purpose. So, seek meaningful death."

"And how would you do that?" Gallen asked.

"Life has meaning only if serve something greater than selves. Give life in service."

"You mean, in battle?" Gallen asked.

The woman half nodded, half shook her head. "Maybe. Or in work."

Captain Aherly laughed. "You must forgive Tallea. She is a pure-bred Caldurian, but she is also a devotee of the Roamers, with their odd ways."

"Why do you want to be reborn as a Roamer?" Ceravanne asked.

The woman turned, her dark hair flying. "Peace. Caldurians never at peace." She turned away, began pacing.

"And what great thing do you serve?" Ceravanne asked.

The Caldurian woman shot a glance over her shoulder, a bright-eyed, mocking look. "I raised in wilderness of Moree, but I left. I serve truth."

There was an uncomfortable silence at the mention of Moree. By saying she'd left to serve truth, the woman seemed to be openly siding against the Inhuman, and none of the others at the table would dare be so bold. The burly merchant who was sitting beside Orick spoke evenly. "My name is Zell'a Cree. I'm a trader myself. For fifteen years now, I've been traveling."

"And what do you sell?" Gallen asked.

"Oh, this and that," Zell'a Cree said. "It used to be that trade was good between continents, but now, most folks don't want to go to Babel. I keep thinking it's time to get out of there, come home and settle down."

"So you are human?" Orick asked, somehow unnerved by the man. All evening, Orick had found that Zell'a Cree sat a bit too close. And now, his tone of voice was off—too mellifluous. The women had just been talking about death and hope, their deepest fears. Yet this man's tone hinted that such things did not bother him. It struck Orick that the man lacked social graces, or some quality that Orick couldn't quite name. At the very least, he didn't know when to keep his mouth shut.

"Yes," Zell'a Cree said, affirming his humanity.

"Liar," Gallen countered, unaccountably furious at the man.

The fellow raised an eyebrow, but did not recoil at the accusation. Gallen raised a hand, as if to strike him.

Zell'a Cree just looked at him calmly. His pupils did not constrict. He did not tremble or sweat.

"You're not human," Gallen said. "You don't even know how to fake it. You have no fear at all, do you?"

"Here, now," the captain said. "We all have our secrets. I make it a policy never to dig too deeply into the private lives of my passengers. A man's subspecies is his own business. Why, I even have a pair of Tekkar aboard—the black-hearted devils."

Gallen put his fist down, but carefully watched the burly Zell'a Cree.

"Tekkar?" Ceravanne asked, and Orick could tell by the tone of her voice that these Tekkar had a nasty reputation.

The captain's face took on a closed look. "Aye, two of them. I invited them to dinner, but they declined, so they're holed up in their cabin. They said that they too went to the City of Life, seeking the Downing."

"But you think they have other schemes in mind?" Gallen asked.

"A Tekkar?" Captain Aherly laughed. "You think they would get the rebirth? Weasels will sooner get reborn as doves."

"Is this what things have come to?" Ceravanne asked. "You knowingly transport agents of the Inhuman?"

"It's not something I can prove or disprove," Captain Aherly said. "I may suspect that a man is a scoundrel, but even the guards at the City of Life will turn no man back who desires the Downing. As long as we keep the gates of the city open to all, I can't prove that the Tekkar have no business in Northland."

"I suspect," Ceravanne said, "that the Immortals would have closed those gates to the Tekkar—if not for the presence of the Dronon. Now that the Dronon have fled, the Tekkar will not be allowed into the northlands."

"A shame, a shame," Captain Aherly said, "that things had

to come to this. Ah, it's not like the old days, when the Tharrin judged men honestly, and there was goodwill among peoples."

"You believe there ever was such a time?" Zell'a Cree said. "Some say that it is a myth."

"The harbor at Tylee has old dry-docking facilities for a hundred vessels," Aherly said. "But I've never seen more than ten ships put up at any one time. There must have been more people coming and going, not too long ago."

"It's true. There was never such fear or animosity between peoples when I was young," Ceravanne said. "The gates to the City of Life were unguarded, as were the ports. People traded freely, and it seemed we were rich."

"If ever there was such a time, it is long past," Zell'a Cree said.

"You were born after the Dronon came," Ceravanne said. "Ask the old ones you meet, they will tell you. Our world was at peace."

"Yes," Captain Aherly said. "It's true that we had some peace, an unequal peace. There was always peace in Northland. But even without the Dronon, it was harder to come by in the south. You can't let people like the Tekkar mix with folks like . . . the Champlianne here"—he waved to the albino woman—"and hope to have any peace. You might as well raise wolves in the rabbit pen."

"Yet even the Champlianne had the faithful Caldurians to protect them," Ceravanne said, looking up to the warrior woman who paced the floor. "And as long as the Caldurians are strong, there can be peace again. Especially now that the Dronon have fled."

"Ah, the Dronon have fled but the Inhuman remains," Aherly said. "And I fear that those who desire peace will be swept away before it. Those who have just come from the City of Life say they have seen preparations for war. Armies gathering in Northland."

Maggie gasped, unable to hide her astonishment.

"It makes sense," Zell'a Cree said. "With the Dronon gone, someone will have to take charge."

"I have heard this rumor, too," Ceravanne admitted reluctantly, eyeing Gallen for his reaction. "But mark my words, the Immortals will not let their human soldiers cross the oceans. They will not carry their war to the Inhuman, whatever the provocation."

"Pity, Inhuman does not feel same," the Caldurian guard said. "No one has counted people of Babel, but they outnumber humans. They will strike first, and they will strike hard. Humans can't stand against them."

"You seem certain," Ceravanne said, setting down her fork, watching the Caldurian for a confirmation.

The Caldurian shrugged. "I hear things."

"What kinds of things?" Ceravanne asked.

"Rumors." Aherly laughed, too nervously. "Rumors are all you've heard."

The Caldurian studied his face, and seemed to take a warning from it, as if perhaps it was unsafe to speak further. "Rumors," she agreed.

That night in Gallen and Maggie's room, when the waves rode high and the boat tossed on the sea, Orick lay sprawled on the floor while Ceravanne reclined on his stomach, as if it were a pillow. Gallen and Maggie gathered round and held a council, speaking softly.

"What is this about a war?" Gallen demanded from Ceravanne, his voice almost a hiss. "You said nothing about it last night!"

"It's a rumor started by the Immortals," Ceravanne said. "So long as the hosts of the Inhuman believe that we have troops massed and prepared, we hope that they will not march against us. Meanwhile, we are trying to gather armies. A muster has gone out. Our lords fear that now that the Dronon have left, the Inhuman will try to seize power. As to whether the Inhuman has gathered armies, we do not know. So far, we have heard only rumors, no more substantial than those we have spread ourselves."

"What if those rumors are true?" Gallen asked, incredulous. "You want us to march into an armed country?"

"We have no choice," Ceravanne said. "But think of this: if

armies are now gathering, a muster could work to our advantage by drawing soldiers away from Moree. It could aid our quest.

"Gallen, you must understand something," Ceravanne said. "We don't know how many foes we are up against. As the Caldurian told you, the people of Babel have never been numbered, and we can't even guess how many have joined the Inhuman. But there is one thing we do know: we know the quality of their troops. The Tekkar are swift and brutal in ways you cannot comprehend. They live in dark warrens carved into the stones, and no one can guess their numbers. They alone would sorely test our defenses. Their swift-winged scouts can fly long and far, coordinating armies in ways that we cannot match. And there are thousands of lesser races in Babel, each with its own unique strengths.

"Gallen, the message we sent to the rebels was recorded six months ago. It took a long time to contact you. I've been waiting for you now for months, and you may have come too late to do much good. It may be that we cannot avert a war.

"I fear that the hosts of the Inhuman will sweep across Northland, and the human hosts of Tremonthin may be decimated.

"But no matter what our quest may accomplish, we must at least try."

"If I'd known this last night," Gallen said, "we could have hurried!"

"Hurried where?" Ceravanne said. "It would have been foolish to try to leave port in the dark, even if we'd had a trustworthy captain handy who was willing. We left as soon as we could, and we cannot make the wind blow us any faster. We've hired a lofty ship—but until we reach port in Babel, you and I have no power to even begin the race to Moree.

"Gallen, there may be more dangers ahead than I have told you, depending on our route. There are peoples in Babel who do not think as we do, and we may be unsafe among them. Some, like the Derrits, are uncivilized and eat other peoples for food. Some, like the Tekkar, are civilized and more brutal. And we are just as likely to find unexpected friends. It has been five hundred years since I left Babel, and I do not know what people occupy the lands now. Mostly, I fear the Inhuman and its Tekkar. But I do not want to burden you with possible dangers."

"Tell me this, then, at least," Gallen said. "Why are you here? Why did you insist on coming? Why do you insist on facing the Inhuman yourself?"

"I came for many reasons," Ceravanne said. "I came because you need a guide, and few in the human lands could do this. I came because I fear that you may not have the heart to do what is required, and I hoped to give you strength, and to help rally the people of Babel to our need, if possible." She leaned closer and said softly, "Gallen, it is not enough to destroy the Inhuman—I have come to undo the damage it has wrought."

"Ooh! How can you do that?" Gallen asked.

"I'm not sure," Ceravanne said. "I can only try." She plainly did not want to say any more.

"Right, then," Gallen mumbled. He turned away from her in frustration, bit his upper lip. There were volumes that needed to be spoken between them, but they would not be spoken now. "We must take stock of our situation.

"What did you think of our dinner guests tonight?" Gallen asked, looking between Ceravanne, Orick, and Maggie. "It seems to me that other folks had secrets to keep. Not just us. I don't trust Zell'a Cree."

"Why not?" Ceravanne asked.

"He claimed to be a merchant, but when I asked what he sold, he didn't tell. Every merchant I've ever met is quick to grab your collar, and if he's any good, he'll try to unload half his wares before you get away. That man is no merchant, and he's no human."

"He is a Tosken," Ceravanne said. "Outwardly, he can pass as human. Inwardly, he is something else entirely. Still, they are a peaceful people."

"You don't think he is dangerous?" Gallen asked.

"He has no fear—of death, of pain, of strangers. And because he has no fear, he is not likely to harm us."

"And what of the captain?" Maggie said, bending down close to Gallen, taking his hand in hers. "He practically admits that he transports those who are in league with the Inhuman."

"If he were secretly in league with the Inhuman, would he admit to transporting them?" Ceravanne asked. "No, I think he is like any merchant. He would rather make money than ask dangerous questions."

"And if he is loyal only to money," Orick said, "then he's loyal only to those who pay the most—or last. As long as our purse has a bottom, I won't trust him."

"Tallea said she was loyal to the truth," Maggie whispered.

"Yes," Orick said, excited. "A curious sentiment. Which truth, do you think? And why did she leave Moree? To escape the Inhuman?"

"She's not loyal to the Inhuman," Ceravanne said.

"How can you know?" Maggie asked.

"She wore no belt."

"What do you mean?" Gallen asked.

"Tallea is a Caldurian," Ceravanne said. "Her people are often called 'the Allies.' They were created long ago—long before the Tharrin were formed—by corporate warlords who sought total devotion from their workers. When they are young, Caldurians may bond to a certain patron, and they remain faithful throughout life. And when they bond, they wear a belt as a sign of their bondage. She is not bonded to Captain Aherly, or to anyone else."

Orick looked at Ceravanne appreciatively. She seemed to have a keen eye, and he saw now that her presence on this journey would be invaluable.

"Which means that she might hire her services out to us," Ceravanne considered. "She would make an excellent escort."

"Wouldn't you rather have a man?" Maggie asked. "Someone who is stronger?"

"A Caldurian woman is stronger than a man of most other races," Ceravanne said. "You saw the rings on her fingers? Six master rings of emerald for her swordsmanship. Four rings of topaz for staff. When a Caldurian proves equal in training to a master, he or she gets a ring. To win more rings, they must cut them from the fingers of their dead foes.

"She is an accomplished warrior, and it is rumored that the Caldurians cannot be turned by the Inhuman."

"Why not?" Gallen asked.

"Some think that it is because they are so highly disciplined," Ceravanne said. "Others think that their minds are just too different from ours, so the Word cannot function properly with them. It is whispered that the Inhuman does not even bother to try to convert them now. Instead, they are killed outright."

"I don't know about the rest of you," Orick said, "but I'm getting nervous with all of this talk. I think there's trouble on this ship. I saw those Tekkar. Even without your warnings, I knew they were dangerous."

"Yes," Ceravanne agreed. "The Inhuman is with us, but does it know of our plans? Will it seek to thwart us?"

"I don't think any of them followed us from the city," Maggie said. "Orick and I watched the boats, and we saw no familiar faces."

"That's a good sign," Gallen agreed.

"But the Inhuman is often subtle," Ceravanne warned. "Just because you do not see it, that does not mean it isn't here. We should take care. We should stay to our cabins as much as possible for the duration of the trip, and never speak openly about our quest again. I know that it is much to ask for you to agree to such seclusion, but it should only be six or seven days till we reach Babel."

"Well?" Captain Aherly asked.

Zell'a Cree pulled his head away from the cabin wall where he'd been listening. "They don't suspect either of us strongly," he whispered. "But they are wary of the Tekkar."

"You should have left the Tekkar in Northland," Aherly said. "They'll be nothing but trouble. They've already asked my permission to kill some of our guests. I denied them, but they're thirsty for blood."

"Yet we may need their services before this is over," Zell'a Cree whispered. He considered. He had only three copies of the Word left in his pouch. He couldn't harvest all of the souls in the neighboring cabin. But perhaps he didn't need to. The bear was expendable. Still, most unwilling converts would fight the Word, and there was no way to be certain that three copies would be enough.

"The Tharrin woman, Ceravanne, is beautiful," Aherly said. "I have often longed to see a Tharrin. And yet I find that if I had seen this one on the street, disguised as she was, I would have passed her, never knowing what she was, knowing only that she was lovely." His tone became hard, commanding. "Whatever happens, I don't want you or your men to kill her."

"She's more than just beautiful, she's useful. I'll order the Tekkar to stay in their room," Zell'a Cree agreed.

Aherly shook his head in bewilderment. "Are you sure these people are what you say they are? Gallen and Maggie look like . . . well, just nice kids. Not Lords of the Swarm. And Ceravanne looks like their younger sister. They're practically children!"

"Were we not children before the Inhuman claimed us?" Zell'a Cree said.

"Well, yeah," Aherly fumbled.

Zell'a Cree sighed, obviously fatigued. "We'll find more copies of the Word when we reach port. It seems that time is against our friends. From now on, at night we will put the sails at quarter mast."

"You bastard!" Captain Aherly said. "I've got cargo to carry. You'll cost me days!"

Zell'a Cree scowled at the man. Aherly might be Inhuman, but he was still greedy, a vice that Zell'a Cree could not claim for himself.

"If you have complaints about how I treat you," Zell'a Cree whispered dangerously, "perhaps you should take them to the Tekkar." Zell'a Cree was a broad man, incredibly stocky, so that even in spite of the fact that he was not much taller than Aherly, Zell'a Cree seemed to dwarf the captain.

Aherly's jaw quivered, and Zell'a Cree studied the movement . . . wondering if he could learn to simulate fear.

Fifteen

That night, Gallen wore his mantle to bed. The heavy metal ringlets were uncomfortable, and the many tiny knowledge crystals dangling from it tinkled when he moved his head. But he cared little for sleep this night. He needed knowledge, and so he lay thinking for a long time, wondering how best to speed their trip to Moree.

With his mantle's many sensors, he could see around the room clearly, and he let the mantle heighten his hearing, until the creaking of timbers and water lapping the hull were well amplified. Maggie slept beside him in the narrow bunk, facing the wall, and Gallen enjoyed the sweet scent of her off-world perfumes.

He lay curled against her, smelling her hair, just holding her.

Outside, there was the occasional sound of a scout calling his reports, and the scurry of feet over the weather deck.

Gallen tried to call up files about the Tekkar, but he was using Veriasse's old mantle, and Veriasse had never battled that race. His mantle carried information about the planet Tekkar—a fiendishly hot world where near-sentient dragons hunted by night. Gallen could guess at the specifications one might set in creating a subspecies to dwell on that world, but the reasons for colonizing the place at all were baffling.

And so after a bit of study, Gallen let his mantle seek files on other subspecies he would find on Tremonthin—size, coloration, distinctive features; visual, auditory, and olfactory sensitivity; speeds and strengths; various traits. The information he received was very discomfiting. He found that many races had been boosted for sensitivity, for dexterity, for intelligence, for fierceness.

The Lords of Tremonthin were designing subspecies to colonize thousands of worlds in this galaxy and beyond, yet Gallen saw that the attributes given to some made for incredibly dangerous combinations. He shook his head in wonder, wishing vainly that Ceravanne and the other Tharrin would have had more control over such decisions.

Late in the night, Gallen suddenly became aware of soft footsteps outside his door, and he realized that for several minutes he had heard stealthy sounds—the creaking of timbers at long, infrequent intervals.

For a moment, he watched his door. He'd thrown the bolt home before retiring, but he watched the door handle. His mantle let him see it clearly in the dark, and Gallen silently willed the mantle to let him view the scene in infrared.

He spotted two people standing on the other side of the door—their form revealed by the warmth of their body heat striking the planks.

For a long time they stood, then one of them gently pulled the wooden door handle, testing to see if the door was locked.

Gallen silently sat up, pulled his knife from his sheath, and began stalking toward the door, thinking to pull it open, surprise the men.

He slid his feet across the floor, careful to make no sound, and his mantle detected none.

But suddenly the man at the door froze and distinctly hissed to his companion, "The Lord Protector!" They turned and fled above deck.

Gallen rushed to his door, threw it open, and raced above deck. The deck was cluttered with the lines and mast, dozens of nooks where someone might hide. There was a swift, cold breeze outside, and a dozen sailors were on deck, but Gallen couldn't be certain which of them had been at his door. He looked at them in infrared, and their bodies seemed to shine while flames flickered across their skins as if they were demons from hell.

He addressed one giant who stood at the wheel above him, back turned. "Did you see anyone come up here just now?"

The giant looked over his shoulder. "No. But I heard a noise. Could have been someone."

Gallen nodded. There was no one else close enough to have been keeping watch. He looked up, noticed that the sails were at quarter mast.

"Why are the sails lowered?"

The giant shrugged. "Cold wind from up north, I guess. Might bring a squall. Captain said to lower them. It's his ship."

Gallen pulled his tunic up tight around his throat. It was a cold wind. Very cold.

He looked to the deck to see if there were any prints. The blackguards' body heat should have left its mark. But the men had run too quickly, and he could see no trail. At least the sensors in his mantle weren't strong enough to pick it up.

He asked the mantle to give him an olfactory boost, but this was a feature of his mantle that Gallen had not used before, and the heavy odors that came to him meant nothing.

He grunted, went below deck, and bolted his door. Maggie had slept through the whole thing.

Gallen lay back rehearsing what had just happened, and he could not recall making a sound that would have alerted the intruders. He had his mantle play back the recorded sounds of the incident, and there was nothing that could have alerted the intruders.

Which meant there was but one alternative: they had to have seen him. His foes could see infrared.

But far worse, Gallen realized, was that even though he had

kept his mantle and weapons concealed, his foes knew that he was a Lord Protector.

The next morning, Gallen asked Orick to check the corridor, see if he could track the intruders by scent. But the cabin boy had already come through the hall that morning, swabbing the decks with lye.

So Gallen went to the captain's quarters to speak with Aherly, and Orick followed. Gallen had hoped to meet the captain in private, but his bodyguard, Tallea, was there. The captain sat in a stuffed chair at his desk, writing in his log, and Tallea stood at his shoulder, her eyes alert, muscles bunched.

Still, Gallen felt he needed to speak now. "Two men tested the doors to my room last night, trying to break in," he informed the captain.

Aherly looked at him askance, his balding head gleaming in the light from the portal. "That's a substantial accusation. Was anything taken, anyone harmed?"

"No," Gallen said. "But they did try my door."

"Did you see them? Could you point them out to me again?"

"I didn't see their faces, but they were of normal height."

"Of normal height?" Aherly pursed his lips. "That's not much of a description."

"And I know that they can see in infrared," Gallen added, hoping to narrow the field.

"It's a common trait in Babel—or even in Northland, for that matter." Aherly shrugged. "Half of my crew has it—all of the night watch. I insist on it, for safety's sake. I would love to resolve this situation, but—is there anything more I could go on?"

"Nothing," Gallen said. "Except—could it have been the Tekkar? Were they out last night?"

"I'm sure they were, but it would prove nothing. The Tekkar prefer darkness, and they sleep during the day."

Gallen stood thinking, and Captain Aherly said, "Look, sir, I don't know what I can do about this matter. But it does concern me. So, I have but one question for you: do you feel unsafe on my ship? Do you feel threatened in any way?"

Whoever had tried his door last night knew Gallen was a Lord Protector. And if he knew that, he would almost certainly know Ceravanne's identity, and Maggie's. Gallen could not ignore that threat, and it was so horrific that he wished he could hide it from his companions. At this moment, he wanted nothing more than to get off this ship. "I do," Gallen admitted. "I feel threatened clear down to my boots."

The captain frowned. "Then there is only one thing to do. I deal with many kinds of people, some who feel threatened by things that are real, others who feel threatened by things that are imaginary. . . ."

"Och, here now," Orick grumbled, "Gallen's not one to go about imagining devils and banshees—"

"Oh, I didn't mean to imply . . ." the captain said, studying Gallen's eyes, "I just mean that—it is . . . it is my policy to make all of my customers feel safe aboard my ship. Welcome and secure. Which is why I hire the Caldurian.

"Would you feel safer if I assigned Tallea to watch your rooms at night?"

Gallen studied the warrior. She had short dark hair with streaks of gray, and deep brown eyes that were very intense. She moved with a grace and power that he only someday hoped to match, and Ceravanne had said that the woman could not be Inhuman.

"Yes," Gallen said. "I would feel safer."

"Good," Aherly smiled. "She will be outside your doors from dusk to dawn." He began to fumble with a drawer of his desk, as if he would open it. "Uh, look," he grumbled. "I assure you that I want to catch these intruders as much as you do. I try to run a clean ship. I pay my crew well, but it may be that one or two of my men—or even some of the other passengers—were intent on pilfering. If that's the case, it's bad for my reputation, you see?"

Gallen nodded, for he could ask no more of the man, but as he turned away, he muttered under his breath, "That's not the case."

He went back to his cabin, and called a meeting. When Ceravanne heard his tale, she was terrified.

"Are you sure that the intruder called you 'Lord Protector'?" Maggie asked Gallen.

"Certain," Gallen answered. "I was wearing my mantle. I've played back the recording a dozen times."

"Then the Inhuman's agents are on the ship, and they know who we are," she said.

Orick looked at the porthole, then at the door, as if the Inhumans would come piling in at any moment. "What can we do?"

Gallen had been sitting cross-legged, but he pulled his legs up, wrapped his arms around his knees. "I see only one thing that we can do. I have to find the servants of the Inhuman, and eliminate the threat."

Ceravanne said, "Perhaps you're wrong in imagining that it is the Inhuman. Perhaps these intruders know only that you are a Lord Protector. We were gone from our room for a time last night. Perhaps someone entered the room and went through your pack, found your mantle and incendiary rifle."

"Perhaps," Gallen admitted. "But I think you are only hoping for the best. If they were thieves, why didn't they just take my things, then?"

Ceravanne could come up with no answer.

"There are lifeboats aboard," Maggie said. "We could sneak off the ship some night, try to make it to shore."

"The night crew can all see in the dark," Gallen countered. "To them, you glow like a firefly. You'll not get off this ship unnoticed."

"Then we'll have to be patient, and courageous, and wait," Ceravanne said.

"For what?" Orick demanded.

"For them to come to us," Gallen said.

Sixteen

They sailed that week without further incident, and after a couple of days, the group began to rest easier. During the days they walked the decks of the ship, but in the evenings none of them journeyed abroad.

Orick in particular soon began to wonder. After five more days without a sign of trouble, he began to wonder if Gallen had not dreamed of the danger.

So Orick took to scrambling across the decks longer and longer during the days, watching over the railing as porpoises leapt in the waves and salmon swam in lazy circles, tantalizingly close to the surface of the water.

Each day, the sun came up clear and bright, and the wind filled the sails. Orick spoke to some of the sailors—the red-skinned men of Penasurra were boisterous and always had a joke handy, while the strong Annatkim giants seemed more wistful, always dreaming and talking of their homes in the White Isles far to the south and east.

But it was the warrior Tallea who sat night after night guarding their rooms who most captured Orick's interest, and so one night, he went to speak to her.

He opened the door to his room, found her in her accustomed position outside, standing in the light of a small oil lamp. Orick just stood for a moment, looking at the woman, embarrassed.

She watched Orick's face. "You want from me?" Tallea said.

"I'm curious," Orick said freely. "You're a Caldurian, but you devote your life to following the teachings of Roamers—so that means that when you die, you hope to be born again in a Roamer's body?"

"If I worthy of honor, yes, my memories put into body of Roamer."

"I knew that some folks could be reborn into young bodies made from the old," Orick said, licking his lips, "but I never imagined that they could give you a *different* body. Could I be reborn—as a human?"

"Perhaps . . ." Tallea said doubtfully. "Body is shell. What lives inside, is important, judges say. But rebirth not granted to many. Immortals in City of Life, they judge. Sometimes strangely."

"What do you mean? How do they judge strangely?"

"They read memories, thoughts. Sometimes, person not given rebirth, even when all other peoples think person should be. Judges make hard for person who is not human to get rebirth."

"Maybe it's not just the actions they base their judgment on—but also thoughts and desires," Orick said, "so that everyone who knows the person thinks well of him, but the judges at the city don't. That's how I'd handle it, at least." And that's how God does it, Orick thought.

"Sometimes," Tallea admitted, shaking her head as if to say he was wrong, "I think humans judge human ways, not peoples' ways."

"What do you mean?" Orick asked, licking his nose. He could smell something annoying in the air—lye soap.

"I abhor violence, but excel at it," Tallea said. "Among Caldurians, those who fight best are honored. They would be reborn. But among humans, those who *serve* best reborn. We do not value same."

"Then you feel cheated by the humans?"

"They gave life," Tallea said. "How I feel cheated?"

"Because your people die young?"

"You forget, I am devotee of Roamers. They own nothing. No land, no clothing, no honor. Not even lives. This is wise, to know you cannot own life. It passes."

He left then, but Orick could not help but wonder at the Caldurian.

After a week, Ceravanne began to worry. "We've been at sea too long, with such strong winds," she said. "It's but a five-day journey to Babel under such winds. We must be off course."

Yet when she spoke her fears to the captain in his office, he only scratched his bald head and muttered, "Aye, we're not making good time. We're heavily laden, and that slows us. And we've faced some strong head winds two nights in a row. Give it a day. We'll find land tomorrow."

But it was two days before they sighted land, just after dawn, a line of blue hills barely discernible where the water met the sky. But the scouts knew those hills. The ship was still two days from port.

It rained that afternoon, and everyone was forced to remain inside for most of the day, so it wasn't until evening that the weather cleared. Gallen seemed tense, his muscles tight, and he stared into the darkness.

Maggie knew he was thinking about Moree, wishing that the ship was already there. To ease his tension Maggie convinced Gallen to walk with her under the moonlight.

So it was that they left their room in the evening, well after dinner. The Caldurian, Tallea, stood outside their door, a solid presence.

And as they went topside, Tallea touched Maggie's hand and whispered, "Take care. Tekkar are out."

Gallen was wearing his black-hooded robe, with his mantle concealed beneath. He had his knives and his fighting boots, though he wore no gloves. Maggie felt safe in his presence, so she merely nodded at the Caldurian.

They walked under the moonlight, talking softly, and Maggie

held Gallen's hand. As always, his touch was electric. They hadn't made love yet that day, and under the cold stars, she welcomed his touch. They went to the bow of the ship, and stood looking off to sea. To the south she could see the lights of a city sprinkled over a distant hill.

The boat rocked gently, and for a while they stood and kissed, long and passionately. So many times during the day, while Gallen worked out with his swords in their room until the air was filled with the humid scent of him, Maggie found that her lips hungered for his. But now she hesitated to give herself to him too completely, to satisfy her cravings, for she felt the weight of other eyes upon her. Yet she trembled under his touch, and for a while, it was good.

She leaned into him, and her breasts crushed against the strong muscles of his chest. She drew back his hood so that the links of his mantle gleamed in the moonlight, and the memory crystals in it shone with the reflected light of stars. He wore the metal netting over his blond hair, and she considered taking it off so that she could run her fingers through his hair, but decided against it and only bit his ear. "I'd give you more of a honeymoon tonight," she whispered, "right here, if no one were watching." She whispered the words only to tease him, for she knew Gallen to be a gentleman with more self-control than she sometimes wanted him to have.

But she felt him tense, look around, as if to find some handy corner where they could be alone. Suddenly he drew back from her and asked, "Why are the sails at quarter mast?"

Maggie looked up. The evening breeze was cool and steady, without a sign of clouds in the sky. There was no threat of storm, no reason for the sails to be lowered.

"Look at this," Gallen said, gazing over the bow. "We're nearly dead in the water!"

Suddenly a feeling of dread came over Maggie. They'd been aching to reach port for days, and the trip had taken them at least three days longer than expected, though the winds had seemed good the whole time. And even though the captain had complained of head winds at night, she'd never been aware of them.

Gallen looked up over the deck to the helmsman and asked, "Why aren't we at full sail?"

"The captain orders them lowered after dark," the fellow answered, a giant of a man.

"And why would that be?" Gallen asked.

The giant shrugged.

"Has he always lowered his sails at night?"

"Just this trip," the giant answered.

"Gallen," Maggie whispered. "Something smells. Do you think the captain has cost us time on purpose?" But she couldn't imagine how that could be. They'd never spoken of their need to make haste in public. Could the man read minds?

"Aye, the captain," Gallen whispered. "I think I'll have a talk with him."

He took Maggie's hand and began leading her along the weather deck. Aft of the forecastle were two stairs on each side of the ship, leading down to the main deck. The moons were low on the horizon, and shadows from the sails kept the main deck as black as it could get. On a ship back home, the sailors would have rigged a lantern for light, but there was none here. Maggie dreaded having to feel her way down the steps in the darkness, but Gallen stopped, squeezed her hand.

Barely, she saw something black moving in the shadows—a cloaked form.

"Get out of our way," Gallen said evenly.

The shadowed figure barely moved, and Maggie saw light glint from a steel blade. "Get out of *our* way, Lord Protector," a mocking voice replied. It had a hissing grate to it, and Maggie was sure that nothing human spoke with a voice like that. The ship listed as it wallowed in a trough, so that for a brief moment she saw figures in the moonlight—two black-robed Tekkar, sitting on the opposite stairs.

Gallen pushed Maggie back with one hand, drew his sword and a dagger.

"Oh, a wicked man, a wicked *human*," one of the Tekkar laughed.

"With a *big* sword!" the other mocked.

Maggie glanced behind her. There were four crewmen

walking along the weather deck toward them, clubs in hand. She stiffened.

"I know—they're coming," Gallen whispered.

"Let, let us through!" Maggie cried.

"We're not stopping you," one of the Tekkar said. "We have no business with you—for now. Go and talk with the captain, if you wish. . . ."

Gallen crept forward cautiously, and Maggie followed so close behind she could feel the warmth of his body.

Just as they reached the doorway to the cabins, Zell'a Cree opened the doors, stood for a moment backlit from a lamp in the hallway. He yawned, then seemed to realize that something was amiss.

"What's going on?" Zell'a Cree asked, looking to the Tekkar. "I thought you two were confined to quarters?"

Maggie realized that Zell'a Cree had known something she did not. She hadn't known that the Tekkar were confined to quarters. Maggie thought it odd that the captain hadn't told the others this comforting bit of information.

One of the Tekkar leaned a bit closer so that light from the hallway fell upon him—a menacing figure all draped in black. Maggie could see just a bit of the man's face, eyes gleaming like wet stones, a white spider tattooed into his forehead. "Even weasels must come out to hunt," the Tekkar said. And then Maggie knew that these men had heard them talking through the walls. The Tekkar pointed. "This *human*—thinks we are a problem, so he wants the captain to tell us to go away. But we know the captain does not like to be disturbed after dark. We thought we'd stop him from squawking."

"You like the hunt, don't you?" Gallen said to the Tekkar. "It's not enough to just kill. You like to bully your prey first. Like cats, batting around dazed mice. Och," Gallen laughed low and dangerous, "I've known plenty like you. Well, come and get me." Gallen thrust his sword forward, letting the tip move in slow circles. The Tekkar was ten feet away.

"Meow." The Tekkar smiled. Then he lurched forward and spun back so fast it baffled the eyes. One second he seemed to be attacking, the next he was over behind the rigging.

"Watch out," Gallen breathed to Zell'a Cree. "We're coming past."

Gallen began to inch past the heavy man, and Zell'a Cree turned his back to the Tekkar and reached up and put his hands on Gallen's and Maggie's shoulders. "Here, here," he said, "let's all be reasonable. Surely there's no cause to draw weapons!"

Gallen slipped past him, drew Maggie into the corridor. Zell'a Cree seemed taken aback by his quick retreat, and he leapt into the hallway with them as if afraid to be on the main deck in company with the Tekkar.

Gallen slammed the outer door, throwing home the bolt. Zell'a Cree stood beside the door dumbly, as if pondering what to do next. The guard Tallea stood at the far end of the hall, a small oil lamp at her feet casting a comforting glow.

Gallen went to the captain's cabin and knocked at the door until it opened.

"What's the matter?" the captain asked groggily through a cracked door.

"Have your lads hoist sails," Gallen said. "I want no more delays from you."

"What do you mean?" Aherly cried.

"I mean, you've ordered the ship to sail at quarter mast every night. I want the sails hoisted."

"What?" Aherly cried, indignant. "I gave no such orders! Wait a moment. Let me get my clothes."

Maggie wondered if this were all a mistake, if some crewman had sabotaged the journey by giving false orders in Aherly's name. He closed his door and bolted it tight. For two minutes Gallen and Maggie waited, until Gallen rapped on the door again with his knife handle. There was no answer from the captain. And Maggie was left to wonder if he was merely frightened of Gallen, or if he was indeed in league with the Inhuman.

The door was made with thick planks, and it hinged on the inside. Maggie doubted that they could break it easily.

"Go," Gallen growled to Maggie. "Warn the others. We're getting off this ship now!"

"Careful," Tallea said at Gallen's back, and she drew her own sword, stepped between Maggie and Zell'a Cree. "He's of them! I in captain's office when he came aboard. He said you would seek passage on ship."

"How did he know we'd choose this ship?" Gallen asked, eyeing the heavy man.

"He knew you traveling, so he bought every berth on every ship. He set trap for you!"

Zell'a Cree stood down the hall, his hands behind his back. Before Maggie knew what was happening, he opened the door to his own room and leapt inside, slammed his door shut, and held it tight as Gallen threw himself against it, trying to knock it open before Zell'a Cree could lock it.

Zell'a Cree threw the bolt home, and Gallen cursed and kicked the door.

Tallea stepped forward and watched the doors, said to Gallen, "Go to cabin and pack. I guard."

Gallen pulled up his hood, glared at the door that Zell'a Cree had fled behind. He stood for just a moment, frustrated, then cried out as if in pain. He threw back his hood, rubbed the back of his neck.

His hand came away bloody, and he looked at Maggie, stricken. For one moment he wobbled, and cried "What's happening?" then Gallen crumpled to his knees.

Maggie rushed to his side. He was looking around, dazed, and Maggie pulled his long hair away, studied the back of his neck. There was a sickly purplish welt under his skin, with blood dribbling from it, as if some pus-filled boil had popped. She couldn't imagine that thing having been on his neck without him noticing it, and then suddenly the whole welt heaved, as something moved under his flesh.

Maggie's stomach turned at the sight, and she gasped.

"Maggie?" Gallen asked. "What is it? I can feel something moving! Something's burrowing into my head!"

There was a crackling noise of bones chipping away from his skull, just beneath the flesh.

"Ah, Christ," Maggie muttered, and her first impulse was to

take a knife and cut into his flesh, pull out whatever was burrowing into him.

Tallea rushed over to Gallen, looked at him, aghast. Then she reached into the hood at the back of Maggie's cloak. "Careful," she said.

She brought out a creature that could have been a mantis, with a wide body and a single spade-shaped arm. She held the back of its body gingerly between two fingers.

"The Word is inside him," Tallea said. "The Inhuman is inside him."

"Ah, God," Gallen gasped, and he dropped to the floor, reached behind his neck, tried to pull the thing away.

Tallea dropped to her knees in front of him, peered into his face, curious. "You fight it!" she whispered fiercely. "You must fight!"

"Help me! Help me!" Gallen cried, and his plea terrified Maggie. "I feel it moving in my head." She had never seen him plea for help, had never seen him despair. His eyes grew large, and beads of sweat dotted his forehead.

Maggie fell to her knees, held him close, so that he rocked back and forth, his face buried against her breasts. "It's all right. You're all right," she whispered, yet she could not keep the tone of panic, the pure desperation, from her voice.

"How do you know?" Gallen cried.

"Some resist Inhuman's Word," Tallea insisted. "They not die. They not injured. You must say no to Word!" She took the insectlike machine in her hand and crushed it with emphasis.

Gallen looked up at the Word crushed between her fingers, and his eyes became vacant, as if his mind were far, far away.

Then his attention snapped back, and he looked up at the women, as if embarrassed. "My mantle? The Inhuman is trying to communicate to me through its Word, but my mantle has blocked the transmissions."

There was infinite relief in his voice, yet the precariousness of his situation was not lost on him. Maggie could see by the manic gleam in his eye that he was horrified. Maggie had never seen Gallen like this—so terrified, so utterly alone, and she clung to him as he climbed to his feet.

"It was Zell'a Cree," he whispered fiercely. "The bastard slipped those things into our hoods when we were outside!"

Maggie knew that it must be true, but there was little they could do about it. Gallen ran and leapt, kicking Zell'a Cree's door, but the door held. He kicked at it again and again, then looked over his back at Maggie. "Damn, they build solid doors here!

"Get packed, and get the others," he said, and there was a fury in his voice. She dared not argue.

Maggie ran into her room, threw her things together, and helped Ceravanne pack.

By then Orick was in the hallway, drawn by the noise, and Maggie came and stood at the back of Tallea, vibro-sword in hand.

"Do you think we can make it out?" Gallen asked Tallea.

"Inhuman seeks converts, not corpses," Tallea said. "They might let us go. But if choose to kill—" She shrugged, as if to say that neither Gallen nor anyone else could stop them.

Maggie pounded on the door of one last passenger—the albino girl who was too frightened to leave her room during most of the trip, but the girl would not open her door now.

Gallen rushed up to the end of the hall, peeked through the door's small window out over the deck, then backed up slowly. "They've got half the crew out there."

Tallea nodded. "We should wait. I can't see well in dark."

"I can lighten things up for you," Gallen said. He grabbed his pack from Maggie, pulled out his incendiary rifle, and connected the barrel to the stock.

He opened the door and fired once. Burning white plasma streamed out, bright as the sun, and sprayed over the crowd, dousing the mainmast. Gallen shouted for the others to follow, and he leapt out onto the main deck.

Silently, Tallea raced out after him, followed by Orick and Maggie. On the quarterdeck, one Tekkar was a seething inferno. For a moment his skeleton remained standing, blazing like a torch, the bones fusing together, and then the skeleton crumbled. Several of the small red-skinned sailors had taken minor hits as plasma splattered from the rifle, and they screamed and spun about, madly dancing as they tried to escape. But with plasma heating to ten thousand degrees on their arms or torsos, even a minor wound was cooking them alive.

The bottom of the mainmast incinerated in a moment, and the sail began to topple forward, held only by the rigging. Maggie shouted for Ceravanne to follow her.

Ahead of her, Gallen and Tallea were in a deadly duel, pitted against a dozen hosts of the Inhuman. Maggie saw Tallea lop the hand off one red-skinned foe, stab a giant in the eyes with her dueling fork. Gallen cut a giant down at the knees, and engaged two black sailors with bony ridges on their foreheads and long white hair.

The remaining Tekkar, a man with his hand tattooed red, rushed forward, his body a blur, and stabbed one of his own men in the back to move him out of his way as he sought to engage Gallen.

In seconds, the two were spinning madly, exchanging parries and thrusts. Maggie had imagined that with his mantle—which helped speed Gallen tenfold and which had the fighting experience of six thousand years stored in its memory crystals—no one should have been able to challenge him in single combat. But for fifty seconds the two traded punches and kicks, slashing and blocking with their swords, and it soon appeared that the match was even.

Each blow was jarring, so that when Gallen parried the deck rang with the sound, and Maggie was surprised that the swords didn't splinter under the impact. And Maggie knew that Gallen was strong. He'd been training as a guard from his childhood, and his wrists and arms were far thicker than a normal man's. Yet each blow by the Tekkar would knock Gallen back.

One sailor swung a pole at Gallen's feet, trying to divert his attention, and the Tekkar dove in low, throwing his whole body forward in a deadly lunge, sword thrust outward. Gallen parried the sword away with his knife, and blood went splashing over the deck—though Maggie could not see whose—then the Tekkar's body slammed into Gallen, knocking him back onto the deck.

For a moment they struggled together, the Tekkar on top trying to wrestle Gallen's knife away, and it was growling.

Orick rushed to Gallen's aid, but a sailor moved in to intercept him.

Maggie tossed the vibro-sword at the sailor, so that it flew end over end. It caught the man in the neck, slicing him open, and Orick barreled past, jumped on the Tekkar and bit his shoulder.

In that second, Gallen wrested the knife away and brought it up into the Tekkar's kidney with a violent jerk, so that the blade shot upward, spraying blood.

Then Gallen shoved so hard that the Tekkar flew back three yards and lay clawing the deck. Gallen surged up into the fray. He gutted the sailor who'd swung at his feet, leapt and kicked another in the head so hard that his neck snapped. Four sailors rushed away from him, and Maggie turned to see how Tallea was doing.

The woman knelt on the deck, holding her guts in with one hand, astonishment on her face. Three bloody-handed sailors advanced on her, aiming for a killing blow.

Maggie had no weapons, but without thought she shrieked and leapt forward, tossing her pack. It hit one man, driving his own sword back so that it split his nose.

Then Maggie was in front of them, shouting furiously, "Get out of my way, or I'll cut your nuts off and send them home to your wives!"

All three sailors stared at her, seeing that her hands were empty, yet somehow not trusting their own eyes.

And Maggie had a sudden thought. There were thousands of subspecies in the southlands, more than any one person could know, and you couldn't always tell the dangerous ones by looking at them.

"Believe me, friends," she threatened. "You don't wrestle a woman of the Coola, and walk away alive."

The three servants of the Inhuman stood watching her, uncertain. Maggie raised her hands and bared her fingers threateningly, as if she had talons on them, and two of the men actually backed away.

One of them leapt forward with a roar, jabbing his sword swiftly for a killing blow. Maggie heard a gasp behind her, and suddenly the Caldurian's own sword darted out, caught the tip of their foe's sword and knocked it away with a flourish. With a deadly lunge Tallea let her own sword slide up the attacker's arm, till it bit deep into the sailor's ribs. The last two foes turned and fled, knowing themselves to be no match for Maggie and the wounded Caldurian.

The sails had become sheets of flame, and suddenly the mainmast fell forward, crushing the forecastle, sending up a shower of sparks.

And then Maggie was running, pulling on Tallea's arm. The warrior woman slumped to the deck, crying weakly, "Leave me!"

And Maggie pulled her up, shouting to be heard above the flames. "Not for a fortune. I want to hire your services, if you live through this!"

"Agreed," the Caldurian said.

Someone pushed Maggie from behind, and she looked back. Orick had her pack in his teeth, and Ceravanne was stooping to grab Gallen's incendiary rifle. Gallen was leaping toward them all through the flames.

Maggie saw with relief that the timid albino girl had come out, that she was running to the far side of the ship.

In a moment, Gallen was beside Maggie, half carrying Tallea. They rushed to the aft of the ship, found sailors lowering a lifeboat. It had just hit water, and already some of them were scurrying down the rope ladders to get in.

Gallen aimed his incendiary rifle, shouted to them, "Go on, all of you. Get away from the boat!" And the sailors stopped. One man leapt off the ladder, began swimming for shore, while another raced back up to the deck. The sailors at the ropes all rushed to the far side of the ship, hoping to get to the other lifeboat before the ship burned.

Gallen stood on the weather deck, keeping the sailors at bay, while Maggie and the others climbed the rope ladders down to the boat. Maggie held the Caldurian in her lap, for the woman had saved her life, and with her own hands she pushed the woman's intestines back in place. The Caldurian's brown face was a mask of pain, and she looked up toward the stars, her dark eyes fixed, unfocused.

Then everyone was in the boat, and Ceravanne was pulling at the oars, splashing them all with water in her hurry to leave. Gallen stood in the prow, balancing on a seat, incendiary rifle in hand.

Fire-lit smoke streamed across the water, and the ship was a roaring inferno. Maggie looked up. The batlike scouts were circling the burning ship, and Orick said to Gallen sadly, "You can't let them get away, lad. It's a man's work you have to do."

Gallen nodded, took his incendiary rifle, sighted for a second, and fired into the sky. Plasma streamed high, lighting the darkness, and hit one of the scouts, splashing enough so that a second also fell.

A third wheeled out over the water, and Gallen fired. But the scout was far away by then, and it dodged the incoming plasma.

Gallen fired twice into the ship for good measure, and Maggie watched several men throw themselves overboard. A dozen men rowed into view from the far side of the ship, and Gallen fired into their boat at a hundred yards. The plasma rushed toward them, a bolt of lightning, and for ten seconds after the hit, the sailors sat burning in the inferno, flesh melting from bones, so that they were skeletons that crumbled in the furnace.

And then the horror of what had just happened—of the murders Gallen had just been forced to commit—fell upon Maggie like a solid weight, like an invisible stone falling from heaven. She saw him standing with head downcast, shoulders limp, limned in the light of the fires.

"Oh, god forgive us," Ceravanne whispered, and then it was over.

They were rocking in the lifeboat, and the sea was fairly calm. Gallen made a little whining noise, a cry of shock and disgust and fear, and he let his rifle clatter to the hull of the boat.

Men were out in the water, swimming for their lives, and the flaming ship was sailing to oblivion, making a sound like the rushing of wind, while spars and timbers cracked. And Maggie knew that some of those men were her enemies, servants of the Inhuman, and it was dangerous to show them any mercy. She knew that they should row out there and cut the men down.

But none of them had the heart for it. Gallen shook his head, muttering, "I know what I'm fighting for, but what in the hell am I fighting against?"

No one answered. Instead, Ceravanne brought out her bag of Healing Earth and began to administer to Tallea. Maggie watched out the back of the boat, to a cloud on the horizon, and at that moment, she saw that the Inhuman was but a shadow, a vapor. Every time they tried to strike against the Inhuman's agents, they faded back and disappeared. She wondered how they would be able to strike against enemies who would not face her.

As Gallen took the oars and rowed toward the distant shore, where the city lights dusted the hillside like flour, Orick began reciting the last rites for those who had died.

Zell'a Cree dove deep beneath the burning ship, and looked up. It seemed for a second that the sky was aflame—or as if the water had turned to amber that scattered the sunlight. Then he climbed for the surface, broke through.

The burning ship roared like a waterfall, and Zell'a Cree floated a moment, floundering, then a wave lifted him and he saw a dark ball floating in the water. He swam to it. It was Captain Aherly, his bald head lolling as if it had been crushed.

Zell'a Cree clung to the floating corpse, and gritted his teeth, looked up at the scouts who were wildly flapping about the ship. All of its masts were aflame, and there was nowhere for them to land, yet the scouts seemed to be circling in the hope of helping survivors.

One of them spotted Zell'a Cree and dove toward him, just as a finger of light arced up from the sea. The scout turned into a flaming skeleton that dropped like a meteor, splashing not far away.

Poor Ssaz, Zell'a Cree thought. Some of the sailors were getting away in a boat, and another finger of light touched them, sent them screaming into torment.

And then Zell'a Cree was nearly alone in the water. Dead, nearly all his men were dead, and of those in the water, he couldn't guess how many might make it to shore. One lone scout had escaped.

Zell'a Cree fumbled for the bag tied to his belt, feeling the contents. His last Word was there, whole and safe, more precious to him than diamonds. Zell'a Cree let his eyes adjust, until he could see Gallen's little lifeboat tossing in the waves, and beyond it the lights along the distant shore, and then he struck out.

It would be a far swim, but Zell'a Cree was Tosken. He ripped the bag from his belt, put it between his teeth, and his mood grew foul as he followed the boat.

Seventeen

The wind and current carried the lifeboat east for many miles, so that as Gallen began rowing, they drew farther and farther from the city.

Ceravanne lay in the boat, stunned by what had happened. She carried the memories of her own suicides, suicides that she had been forced to endure in order to evade the Inhuman, but she had seldom seen such butchery. She'd seldom actually seen men seek to annihilate one another, and she was shocked to the core of her soul.

There was nothing to do but tend to the wounded. She administered the last of her Healing Earth to the Caldurian. The woman had a slash across her belly. It was long, but ran little deeper than the flesh at its deepest point. No vital organs seemed to be hit. Still, Ceravanne did not know if the woman could heal.

Maggie was talking to Tallea, trying to keep the Caldurian calm, her mind occupied. "Are you well? Are you comfortable?" Maggie asked. "Here, let me move, so you can lean your head back."

Tallea leaned her head back at an odd angle, and after a

minute seemed to register the question. "Comfortable. I'm comfortable."

Maggie held her hand over Tallea's wound, and blood seeped through it. It was a large wound, too big for the Healing Earth to help much.

"Is there anything more that you can do?" Maggie asked Ceravanne.

"No," Tallea answered, apparently believing that Maggie had asked a question of her.

Ceravanne considered. The nanodocs in her own blood were far more potent than the Healing Earth, but she was proscribed by law from giving her blood to a nonhuman. The nanodocs could establish a colony in her, which would extend her life by decades. Ceravanne pulled a knife from Tallea's sheath and cut her own wrist in violation of the law. Then she let the blood flow into Tallea's wound. In a moment, Ceravanne's own bleeding stopped as the nanodocs closed her cut.

"That is all I can do for her," Ceravanne said. "It may be enough, if no vital organs have been punctured."

So Maggie held the woman as Gallen rowed the boat, long into the night. Soon, Tallea faded to sleep.

In two hours, while the moons were riding high, they landed upon a rocky beach where a large creek spilled into the ocean.

Gallen, Ceravanne, and Maggie carried Tallea from the boat, then dragged the boat ashore into deep brush, and set it down.

Ceravanne helped Maggie form a bed of leaves under the shelter of a large tree, and they placed Tallea in it. Orick was gathering wood, while Gallen made a small fire with matches from his pack.

When he got it going, everyone sat beside it for a while, and Ceravanne looked over to Tallea. She was surprised to see the woman conscious again, watching her from the corner of her eyes.

Ceravanne went to her side, to see if the Caldurian needed anything.

Tallea clutched at Ceravanne's robe and whispered, "Life brings joy, only if serve something greater than selves." Her voice was weak.

"Yes, you said that to us several nights ago," Ceravanne said. Ceravanne looked at the woman helplessly. "Is there anything you need? Water, food?"

Tallea shook her head fiercely and whispered, "A year ago, you came to Babel. I served you then. Not well."

Ceravanne caught her breath, studied the woman's face. "Yes, one of my clones came here, before I was renewed," Ceravanne whispered low enough so that the others would not hear. "It was lost, and never returned. What happened to it?"

Tallea wet her lips, looked away, and closed her eyes. "Dead, I think. That one dead. I wanted to tell when I saw you, but I not want Inhuman to hear." She coughed, then winced at the pain in her side.

Ceravanne bent low, brushed her lips over the woman's forehead, and held her for a long time.

"I need rope, to use as belt," Tallea whispered.

"You don't have to bind yourself to me," Ceravanne whispered. "I don't want slaves."

"I not slave," Tallea wheezed. "I ally. I serve freely."

"But the clone you served is dead. I am not that woman."

"No, I not be bound to you—to Maggie."

Ceravanne looked at Tallea, taken aback.

"She saved me," Tallea said. "I promise live for her."

"You promised wisely," Ceravanne said. "Sleep now, and keep your promise. When you wake, I will have the belt for you."

Ceravanne gently laid Tallea's head back down, then went back to the fire. The others were still all wide awake. "I wish we had more blankets for her," she said, nodding toward Tallea. Maggie had put a thick robe on the woman, but it was hardly enough, and the blankets had gotten wet in the bottom of the boat. They'd have to sleep without for the night.

"When my fur is dry, I'll lie next to her," Orick offered.

Ceravanne laughed. "And may I sleep on the other side of you?"

"If you do, you'll do so at your own risk," Orick said. "I tend to toss and turn in my sleep. I'd hate to squash you."

"I'll take the risk," Ceravanne said.

No one spoke for a minute, and they all sat gazing into the fire. At last, Gallen said, "I'll hike into town in the morning and buy a wagon, if we've got any money. We'll need it to carry supplies—and to get *her* to a doctor."

Ceravanne said, "Her fever is low. If she makes it through the night, she should do well. There's nothing more that a doctor could do. Still, she will need a wagon. She won't be walking much for a few days."

The others spoke on for a while, but Ceravanne began to tire. She went and lay beside Tallea, and sometime later she woke. Orick was beside her, his fur all warm from the fire. The bear put one big paw over Tallea's chest, and Ceravanne hugged him from the other side, lay for a moment, watching his chest rise and fall. He began to sing in his deep voice, a song she guessed that bear mothers would sing to their cubs on his home world:

"Little bear running,
little bear running,
with burrs in your hair,
and dirt on your paws.

May your spirit linger,
long may you wander
in woodlands hallow
with dirt on your paws."

When he finished, Ceravanne realized that it was a song to comfort dying cubs, and her heart ached to think that anyone should have to compose such a verse. Yet she was glad to have Orick here, comforting the woman in his own way.

When Orick and Ceravanne went off to sleep, Gallen and Maggie rested together beside a small fire that flickered and twisted among a few sticks.

Gallen sat in the darkness far under the tree, and Maggie lay in the crook of his arm, holding the crushed Word, its white metal body limp in her fingers as she scrutinized it. Aside from

Tallea, only Maggie knew that Gallen had been infected by the Inhuman, and she seemed greatly distressed, unable to sleep.

Gallen tuned his mantle, listening as far as its range would extend, calling upon its sensors to amplify the light until it seemed that he sat in daylight, beneath cloudy skies. Yet there was a surreal quality to his sight. He could see mice hunting for food among the leaves in the distance too clearly, their body heat glowing like soft flames. And small deer in the near hills shone brightly. The songs of ten thousand crickets and katydids filled the woods, and he could hear the rustling of mice under dead leaves. No people lurked nearby.

Yet despite his sensors, Gallen was worried. Even with ample warning, Gallen feared the servants of the Inhuman. The fear gnawed at him, kept him awake.

When battling on ship, he'd found the giants and the red-skinned sailors to be no great challenge, but he had come close to dying in the grasp of the Tekkar. The little man had been incredibly fast, incredibly strong, and he had the focus of one who does not fear death but only wishes to kill. While struggling with the creature on the deck of the ship, Gallen had watched the white spider tattooed on the Tekkar's forehead. As the man grimaced and struggled, the legs of the spider had seemed to move as his skin stretched and tightened. And Gallen realized that the man had done it purposely, seeking to frighten him. The Tekkar had worked its hand slowly, inexorably toward Gallen's esophagus, despite Gallen's best efforts to fight the creature off. It had been playing with him, Gallen was sure, lengthening the seconds until it took Gallen's esophagus in hand and crushed it.

Gallen did not want to frighten the others, but he worried, for it had only been their combined strength that let them defeat one Tekkar.

"How are you feeling?" Maggie said, still looking at the machine in her hand. She wore her own mantle. "Your head—is it all right?"

"I can't feel anything moving in it anymore," Gallen said, and even to himself his voice sounded stretched, hollow.

"What are you going to do?" Maggie whispered. "You can't just ignore it. The Word isn't going to go away."

"What are our options?" Gallen asked. "What have you learned from the Word that Tallea found?"

"It's a fairly simple device," Maggie said. Maggie had on her own mantle, and she was studying the creature as a technologist would. "Its body has a few sensors—smell and sight only, as far as I can tell, and the main shell is built with invasion in mind. Its streamlined build helps it get under the flesh quickly. Beyond that . . ." She pried off its largest arm, with its spade-shaped blade, then pulled off the head. Something like a green-blue gel oozed out. "On the inside, it's all nanoware interface. The Word is designed to burrow into your skull and create an electronic sensory interface."

"So the Inhuman can send its messages?"

"Yes," Maggie said.

"Can it control me?"

"It's more primitive than a Guide," Maggie said, referring to personal intelligences that were designed to enslave their wearers. "It's not large enough to carry the machinery needed to take total control of your central nervous system. I believe it simply carries a message to you. The Word."

"What if I resist it?"

Maggie considered. "It may punish you. The nanoware sends circuitry, strings of neural web, into your brain. It might activate pain and pleasure centers—cause fear, send hallucinations. But if Tallea is right, people *can* resist it. If you resist it enough, I suspect that the circuitry may just fry certain nerve sites, activating them over and over until they burn out. Once that happens—there's probably nothing more that it can do."

She tried to make it sound easy, as if freedom were only a thought away, but Gallen knew that it would be much tougher than that. He could resist it, but if neurons were getting fried, then he'd have some brain damage as an aftereffect. But it was better to die for his friends than to live for the Inhuman.

"I have to see if I can fight it," Gallen said. "I have to test it. I've had my mantle knocked off in battle before. I can't let myself get in a position where I'm fighting on two fronts at once."

"I know," Maggie said, and she threw the dead Word into the brush, turned to look up in his face. She kissed him slowly, and the reflected firelight flickered on her face. He breathed deeply, relishing the clean scent of her hair, the faintest hint of perfume.

"I'll ask my mantle to shut down its signal block for two minutes," Gallen said, silently willing the mantle to stop. His ears went numb, as if all the sound in the world—the song of the katydids, the rush of the wind, the bark of a distant fox in the darkness—all disappeared. Then his legs buckled from under him, and Gallen tumbled to the ground, looking out, struggling to hear the sound of his own heartbeat, and he could not move, could not speak. He was vaguely aware of Maggie grabbing him, trying to lift him up, hold him in her arms.

And then the visions started, and Gallen remembered. . . .

He was in a beautiful village in Babel growing up in a home that was a work of art, a mansion formed of stone and wood. As a child he would watch the cornices of his bedroom, which were sculpted by hand, and he would imagine that the animals and people carved there would speak to him of their lives in wood. And he remembered his ancient grandmother, draped in robes of purple silk with black lace, the black feathers woven into the white mass of her hair. She was greatly venerated for the cloth she wove and dyed, but he loved her for her sweet voice as she sang him to sleep, and he loved her even more for the attentiveness with which she listened to the tales he would tell from the lives of the wooden creatures carved on the cornices of his room. Once, his grandmother had told his father, "He will be great among the Makers, for with him, the art is not something that he sees, it is something that he lives."

He remembered the green fields of his childhood, where the yellow cows on his father's farm drank from elaborately decorated brass containers shaped like moons and suns and stars and boats all set out on the green pastures.

He learned in time that his people were called "the Makers," and in his village, creating things of beauty was the goal of every person. They did not seek to own beauty or horde it—only to create it. And not only were the things of their hands beautiful, but the thoughts of their hearts, the lives that they lived, also were shaped and molded into beautiful forms.

And so Gallen remembered that from the youngest age he desired to do nothing but shape stone, to release the people and animals and gods hidden under stone—whether he was carving walnut-shaped tubs from marble or forming statues of giant whales that seemed to be leaping out of lawns. As a child, he would seek the hills where cliff faces were exposed, and there he would chisel and smooth the granite, creating wondrous scenes of gods from his private pantheon, battling their demons.

By the age of twelve, he was given his name and his rank—Koti, a master craftsman. He was one of the youngest ever to become a master, and small, brown-skinned Makers from all across Babel came to study at his feet, learn his techniques.

By the time he was forty, sixteen thousand students he had, and great was their work—greater than that of any Makers who had ever lived.

At the Tower of Serat his pupils worked for seventeen years to carve scenes from the tales of the life of the hairy prophet Janek, and tell of his ascent into heaven on the back of a flaming swan from that very pinnacle. Though the tower was six hundred feet tall, the Makers worked every inch of the stone, until it became one of the great wonders of Babel, so that millions of people undertook pilgrimages to gaze upon Janek at the top of the tower, his long beard whipping in the tempest as he straddled the back of the giant flaming swan.

When he finished, Koti took his pupils to the edge of Andou, where the river Marn flowed in from the Whitefish Mountains. There a great sea of rounded boulders had lain for millions of years, deposited by glaciers.

Koti's students worked diligently among the boulders for twenty years, carving each of them into great images from their tradition, showing the War of the Gods that would someday come, when Goddess Peace would finally put down the Dark Spirit of Strife, when Fertility with her many orifices overcame the sexless Barrenness, when all the ten thousand gods of virtue ascended to their rightful domain.

The place was renamed Valley of the Gods, and one could walk through it for weeks staring at marvel after marvel.

And Koti did not only create great works in stone, he married a wise woman who had a talent for shaping lives. They loved one another passionately, and well Gallen remembered the countless times they wrestled as one while making love in their garden bed, under the evening stars at their summer home. His sweet wife Aya gave birth to eleven talented children, so that together Koti and Aya became a great patriarch and matriarch, admired by all.

After sixty-two years, Koti's body grew frail even though he was still young, for he had worn it out in the service of his art and of his family and of his people.

By then, Koti's fame had grown so great that his own people built him a throne and begged him to slough off his mortal body so that he could reveal himself as a god, for the works that he had designed for his apprentices were not only apparently without number, they were also without equal.

But Koti convinced the crowds to stifle their acclaim, and he prepared for death.

And so it was that the Makers gathered fifty thousand men and women, and they bore Koti's ravaged body upon a pallet carved of sandalwood, and they sailed with a thousand ships across the sea, as he lay dying.

Together they marched to the City of Life, where the great columns of crystal memory rose high and haughty and gray against the white mountains on the skyline.

His people came arrayed in their finest garments of scarlet, and they swung golden censers of incense before his pallet, filling the sky with sweet-smelling smoke of green. The drummers and flutists played before him, and women danced with bells on their feet and tambourines in their hands, their voices rising in haunting music.

At the City of Life, he had his memories recorded and gave the humans samples of his skin, and fifty thousand people wept upon the stairways to the Hall of Life and petitioned the human lords to prepare a new body for the greatest of Makers.

And there the memories of Koti ended, but the memories of his disciples were recorded thus:

And so the humans studied Koti's works, studied his memories, and they judged him: "We know that Koti's work is magnificent in form, but it is flawed in content. His work is filled with boundless passion, but we fear the images of the gods he has formed. We fear that his work will fuel a dangerous resurgence of idolatry. He has impeded the cause of mankind, and therefore will not be reborn."

And so his disciples took Koti home and tried to nurse him back to health, but on the cruise home, Koti was so humiliated by his treatment at the hands of the humans that he swore to eat no more. Because of his poor health, he died within the week.

So all Makers swore a vow that none of them would ever go back to the human lands seeking rebirth, and none would sell their wares to humans. Since the greatest of them had been judged unworthy, the Makers knew that mankind esteemed them as dust.

Gallen felt the weight of Koti's life in a great surge. He lived through the passion, the genius, the years of toil, the intense love he'd felt for his family, all in moments, gained the insights that Koti had had, then witnessed the final humiliation and death.

And Gallen knew, he knew surely, that mankind had judged Koti wrongly, that they had been blind to his greatness.

And suddenly, the colors swirled in his head, and Gallen began to recall the life of Doovenach, a humble woman of the Roamers, the hairy people of the plains.

She had been born under a weathered oak tree in a warm rain, and had lived her life on the open plains beneath the sky. As a child, she had learned the call of the thrush, the scent of the rabbit. And during the summer storms, when forks of lightning beat the earth, the tribe would huddle under wide trees, and Doovenach would huddle under her mother's sagging breasts and watch the dark clouds, listen to them growling.

For countless days she had wandered the golden plains, under Tremonthin's suns, harvesting handfuls of wild oats, rose apples, and black peas. She grew to hate the biting black flies that followed her herd, never realizing that they were so tormented only because her people had a law against bathing— for when one bathed in the infrequent pools of the grasslands, he dirtied water that others might drink.

But mostly, Doovenach remembered a sense of peace that flowed as wide as the prairie, and she remembered the good times hunting for mice to eat with her sisters, or the time that the tribe wandered east all summer until they reached the end of the world, where it dropped over cliffs to salty water, and together the whole tribe jumped off into the ocean and swam about every day until the weather turned cold, then they climbed out and headed west for another three years until they bumped into the mountains.

At times it would rain or snow, and Doovenach would huddle beneath a tree, her furry hide wet and cold, and she would curse her life on such miserable days.

Like others of her tribe, she had been born into a society that knew no possessions. Her people ate the wild grasses from the plain, hunted with sticks and rocks. When they brought down a deer or an antelope, they squatted and cut the fresh meat with knives, divided it equally among all.

Other races sometimes hated them, for the Roamers could not understand the concept of ownership. If they found a cow in the wild, they would eat it. If trees were filled with fruit, they fed. And afterward some person of another tribe would come and claim that they owned this cow or this tree.

And so Doovenach remembered times when other peoples would chase the Roamers and beat them. They once found a field of peas, and men with clubs came to chase them away, and when one of the men hit Doovenach's mother, his long club also struck Doovenach's baby brother, crushing his skull.

And she remembered a time when her people wandered into

a town, hoping to drink from the troughs where horses drank, and people in hats and tunics and dresses laughed at her nakedness, and their children threw rocks at her. Doovenach found a beautiful dress as blue as her eyes drying on a bush, and she tried to put it on, but some people came out of a house, shouting, and their dogs bit her legs and drove her away.

And when she was eighteen and beautiful so that the males of other clans wanted to mate with her too much, Doovenach ran away and crossed through a great town, and while she was hungry, she went into an inn and began to feed from a table.

The people of that town gathered around and laughed at her nakedness, and a man claimed that she was eating his food. She tried to run then, for she feared he would beat her, but he only laughed and said that he would trade her for the food, give her something good, then he took her into an alley and beat her and savagely mated with her.

When he finished, he threw coins on her, and other men from the inn also came and mated with her, too, ignoring her cries but leaving more coins, until at last when the men had all finished, a wench from the inn came and explained to Doovenach how to use the coins.

Doovenach had never owned anything. It seemed to her that her very bones whispered that the root of all evil came from lusting after the possessions of another. And her very bones told her that the earth and all of its riches belonged to all. And because Doovenach had never possessed something to call her own, she had never learned the great secrets of exchange.

But once she learned this great secret, Doovenach returned to her people with money and sought to teach them. She told them that their lives would not be so harsh in the winter if they took money into town and bought food, and she explained that they could mate for money, but her people could never seem to comprehend her words. Or perhaps they never believed them.

So Doovenach returned to the city and rented a corner in a stable where she could sleep in warm straw, close to the sweet smell of horses. She made money by breeding with any man who would have her, and she learned to both take and give great joy in the act. Many were the men who would suck at her hairy breasts and cry out in ecstacy as they made love. And though she never bore children, she helped care for children of the streets who had no homes. For many years she studied other races and learned their ways.

Often in the winter, younger Roamers would come in off the plains and Doovenach would share her food with them, let them sit under her shelter, but the others never learned her ways. They respected her and knew she was wise, but she was wise in ways that they could not comprehend.

And so, when Doovenach began to grow old and ugly and could no longer earn much money, she journeyed to Northland with a friend and sought rebirth, hoping to be young again, hoping to become a teacher for her people.

The human judges in the City of Life recorded her memories and took her skin sample, and Doovenach's memories ended there. But she gave money to her friend, and her friend's memories were also recorded. After many days the humans passed judgment on Doovenach, saying, "Although you claim to be a devotee of human ways, you have never understood anything but the most surface concepts of capitalism. You have rented the barest shelter in a stable, and sometimes bought food, but beyond that, you have never gained any possessions, never sought to obtain the virtues that would assure rebirth."

"But I have advanced the cause of mankind," Doovenach protested. "I gave joy to many men."

The human judges said: "You sold them pleasure. You were only a whore, catering to their most basic instincts." And they sent her away.

Doovenach shrugged, and she was not angry. She had lived her life, and she reasoned that if the humans had given her another, then perhaps on some cosmic scales the universe would have been thrown out of balance, and someone else would have had to go without being born.

But after that, the Roamers did not go to the human lands seeking rebirth, for even the wisest and most human among them had been found unworthy.

And the colors swirled, and Gallen began to recall the life of Entreak d'Suluuth of the bird tribe. And just as suddenly, he was in the night again.

There was a searing moment of pain, and Gallen found himself lying on the ground. He could smell grass and mud. There was a familiar weight of his mantle on his head and shoulders.

The night felt so strange, so cold. Gallen struggled up, until he could see Maggie squatting over him, her dark red hair limned by moonlight. She was holding his hands.

"Oh, Gallen, are you all right?" she asked. Gallen's mantle heightened his vision, and he could easily see the lines of worry in her face. In the darkness the pupils of her eyes dilated to a seemingly unnatural width.

Gallen struggled to his feet. It was well past midnight, and silver-lined clouds rolled across the night sky. Two minutes. He had been under for two minutes, and in those moments, he somehow felt the weight and pain of two lifetimes. He'd tasted the flavor of those lives, of people's feelings, in a way that he'd never imagined. "We are our bodies," the Bock had said. And Gallen wondered if that creature really understood the depth of those words—understood the sense of peace the Roamers felt in traveling the wide earth, or the passion the Makers felt while kneading mud for the potter's wheel.

Gallen recalled dozens of experiences, all whirling like butterflies in his head—Doovenach tasting wild anise for the first time; an old man of her tribe dying of hunger. Koti as a young man, painting a tin glaze over a pot before it went into a kiln.

Gallen felt as if he were tumbling, tumbling; his emotions were still jangled. He felt exultation that was somehow displaced, without a reference to any experience he could imagine. Right now, he thought he should be feeling relief at getting free of the Inhuman, or disgust at his own humanity . . . or something. But the Inhuman's probe seemed to be stimulating his emotions directly.

"I . . . can't think. I can't think!" Gallen said.

"Why not? What are they doing to you?"

"Memories—" Gallen said. "I'm remembering lives."

"The Dronon made the Inhuman, and they don't want you to think!" Maggie said, squeezing his hands. "Whatever the Dronon show you, they don't want you to think. Gallen, I know how memories are recorded. They can be edited. They can be misremembered. It's easy to fake them. But even if these are genuine, the Dronon don't want you to think: you might disagree with them, and the Dronon don't tolerate that."

Gallen looked up at her, knew that she was speaking what she believed was the truth, yet dangerous thoughts kept flooding through his mind, welcome snatches of memory. He felt far more experienced in life, far wiser than ever before. He reveled in his new memories, as if they were a new great cloak that weighed heavily on his shoulders, but was yet new and comforting. The memories that the Inhuman offered were sweet and exotic and tinged with pain, and he hungered for more.

Maggie was human, and she accepted the human agenda without question. But neither she nor Gallen had ever looked beyond the human agenda. Neither of them had really considered whether the benevolent Tharrin were running the universe in the best possible way. Gallen remembered the deadly rose, left as a warning on Fale. And now, Gallen recalled the lives of the people of Babel, saw how their lives were thrown away, how their needs were ignored. They suffered. They suffered. Ignorance, poverty, lawlessness, death. The humans of Tremonthin could protect the people of Babel, sweep all of these ills away, but they did not.

"Maggie," he whispered. "I need to go under again. I need to know more!"

"Not right now," Maggie said, squeezing his hand. Her eyes were frightened, and he knew that she didn't want him to ever go under again. "Give your head some time to clear. Rest."

"Soon, then," Gallen said. "I want to go under soon."

Maggie's eyes were large and frightened, but Gallen suddenly knew that there was nothing to fear. The Inhuman had never sought to kill them, had never sought to harm them. Gallen felt dazed, as if he were whirling, and he knew he was too tired to stay awake much longer.

"Promise me," Maggie said, her voice tight, "that you won't go under again without telling me. Promise me that!" She took him by the collar, held him, her lips just inches away from his.

Gallen gazed into Maggie's wide eyes, and wondered how he would tell her of the things he'd seen, the things he was beginning to guess—about the Inhuman's beautiful plans. . . .

Eighteen

When Maggie woke at dawn, Gallen was gone. She hoped that he had not tried to wrestle with the Inhuman once again. Whatever he'd felt the night before, she had seen in his face that the Inhuman was more dangerous than she'd imagined. It had seduced him in only a moment, and she feared that he had wakened hungering for its touch.

She stalked around the camp all morning, wondering if she should tell the others, wondering if Gallen would come back at all. She retrieved the broken Word from the bushes where she'd thrown it the night before, then went outside of camp, put her mantle on, and Maggie silently asked her mantle to feed her information on the creature—its probable functionality.

Immediately, the mantle showed her a schematic for the creature, detailing the known hinges in its joints, its sensory apparatus, its own brain and system of energy storage. The body of the Word was just a simple machine designed for invasion. It was too small to be self-aware, and therefore would try to complete its only task rather doggedly, and stupidly, at times.

But the information she needed most was not available. Once

the creature invaded its host, the nanoware inside was extruded into the host's brain, and that nanoware could not be studied without microscopic sensors that Maggie's mantle did not have.

So Maggie asked it to make a guess about the most logical functionality of the thing based on current technology. The mantle suggested that the system required several components: an antenna system to receive signals; an amplifier to boost the signal; a power system to power the amplifier; and a neural interface that would let the Inhuman's message be sent directly to the brain.

Beyond those four systems, Maggie didn't know what else the Word might have incorporated into it. But Maggie considered each of these systems, wondering how to sabotage them.

The antenna was first on her list. Her mantle said that since the human body already worked as an antenna, receiving radio signals due to the electromagnetic field created by ionized salts within the body, the Word would need to do very little to actually receive the signals. The body already could receive signals, it just wouldn't recognize them. But solar interference during the day might distort signals, weakening them to the point that they would be worthless. And beings living underground might not receive the signals at all. And the Dronon may have taken these factors into account.

Her mantle whispered that the human body could be greatly enhanced as an antenna by temporarily introducing small amounts of metallic salts, and Maggie suspected that such metallic salts would disperse evenly throughout the body.

But the main thing that the Word needed was not a better antenna, but a good amplifier, and that amplifier would be powered by converting body heat into electrical energy.

Maggie noted that the servants of the Inhuman had kept the Word close to their bodies, kept them warm, and she suspected that the biogenerator was concealed in the body of the creature, probably with the amplifier. If she could get that biogenerator to cool, the Word would die.

But the Word had burrowed to the base of Gallen's skull and had actually inserted itself inside the skull, making it almost impossible to remove.

Gallen had said that he felt it "moving in his skull," and Maggie had the very disturbing notion that he might have been right. Once the creature made its entrance at the base of the skull, it might well have moved higher into the brain to protect itself.

Once there, it had little difficulty sending a chain of nanoware devices into the brain and spinal column, forming new neural pathways so that it could send its message to its host.

Once there, the Word had only to receive its signals from the Inhuman, then convey the information to Gallen. He recalled two lifetimes in only two minutes, which suggested to Maggie that an incredible amount of information was being downloaded rapidly.

But those possessed by the Inhuman were not being controlled individually, of that she was sure. If they were all connected through a transmission network, they would have been able to send and receive information instantly, coordinating their attacks without even voicing commands.

But back in town, the hunting packs of the Inhuman had relied upon their scouts to convey verbal communications.

Which meant that the Inhuman, once it fed its propaganda to a host, released the host, expecting it to act at its own discretion.

The Word. . . . Maggie recalled how her attacker in Northland had talked about it almost reverently, as something to enjoy. And Gallen had been seduced by its touch, and now craved to hear more. When she'd first looked at his face, he had been filled with joy and peace and loss. His eyes had been shining with an emotion she hesitated to name—ecstacy.

And Maggie realized that the entire process, rather than being dark and frightening, had been designed to be something far more palatable for its victim—perhaps even something desirable. Perhaps that was why the Tekkar were converted so quickly; instead of running from the Inhuman, they embraced it joyously.

Maggie considered the Word, as she walked up a steep incline, wondered how to combat it.

If she were a surgeon and had the proper equipment, perhaps she could have destroyed the neural network. But she wasn't prepared to perform brain surgery out here in the woods. Likewise, she couldn't risk trying to open Gallen's brain to get to the Word's amplifier or biogenerators.

She wondered if it might be possible to damage the Word, corrode the nanoware with chemicals—but her mantle whispered that such an attempt would be dangerous. The nanoware would be more resistant to most chemical attacks than Gallen's own body would. Doubtlessly, with the many human subspecies on Tremonthin, the Dronon would have created the Word to be suitable to a broad spectrum of creatures.

"The nanodocs in Ceravanne's body form an artificial immune system, designed in part to rid the body of excess metals," her mantle whispered, and Maggie considered. It was possible that the nanodocs could—over several days—corrode the Word, but her mantle also whispered that it would take the nanodocs from a liter of Ceravanne's blood three days to have much effect. It was hardly a workable solution.

Which meant that Maggie had to figure out how to disable the antenna. Her mantle had suggested that metallic salts would stay in the body for only a few days. And she realized with a start that this was all the Inhuman would need: it was probably designed to download its information in a matter of hours, then never be used again. In fact, Maggie realized that it probably *couldn't* be used at long distances after a few days, not if the antenna system were only temporary.

Her mouth became dry, and she grew more excited.

Is there a way to get rid of these metallic salts? she wondered.

"You cannot attempt to deprive him of them," the mantle whispered, "for he needs some to live. But if you feed him small amounts of potassium chloride and large amounts of water, his body should flush out any of these metallic salts quickly, within a few days."

Beyond that, Maggie could guess what to do. In the daytime, the natural solar activity would help Gallen's mantle block the radio waves. In fact, Maggie suddenly realized why the Inhuman attacked after dark—so that their victims would be converted immediately, instead of having to wait for the night.

And after dark, it would help if Gallen could get underground, where the Inhuman could not communicate.

So Maggie realized that she would have to begin flushing the excess salts from Gallen's system. Until that was completed—a task that her mantle suggested would take a week—Maggie would have to do what she could to lower Gallen's susceptibility. They could probably travel during the day, but at night they would have to seek shelter underground.

And still, given all of that, the Inhuman's Word would still be lying dormant within him. Once Gallen got close to the Inhuman, or close to one of its transmitters, the Word would no longer require a strong signal, and it would be able to overwhelm him.

"One battle at a time," Maggie told herself. "I must fight one battle at a time."

At noon, Gallen returned to camp with food—a plump goose, a burlap bag filled with apples, plums, pears, squash, new potatoes, and a pouch of cherry wine.

Gallen passed the food out, then told the others, "There is a road just south of here, with a farmhouse. The master of the house was good enough to sell us some stores, but no wagon. We're twenty kilometers east of a fair-sized town. I'll buy a wagon there, and drive home tonight. Keep your heads low. We've no way of knowing these folks around here, whether their intentions toward us would be foul or fair."

Maggie watched his eyes as he spoke, and she could detect no change in his features, no change in how he acted toward them. If he'd been seduced by the Inhuman's Word, she could not tell. She could sense no struggle.

Maggie told Gallen that she would come with him to town. Orick said he also wished he could be off with them, but he looked around camp and decided that his greater duty lay here, to guard Ceravanne and Tallea in case an armed mob came searching for them.

Maggie was getting ready to leave, eating a brief lunch of plums and raw corn, and Ceravanne was caring for Tallea.

Orick began plucking the goose with his teeth—a thankless job that he complained would leave down stuck between his teeth for days.

When Maggie finished eating, she and Gallen climbed the hillsides through the thick woods until they reached a dirt road wending through forests at the foot of the mountains.

Gallen seemed somber, distracted.

"Tell me more about what happened last night?" Maggie asked, hoping that he would at least acknowledge that something had changed.

He said, "It doesn't matter. They were just someone else's memories, someone else's thoughts. I'm over it now."

He hurried his pace, as if he were angry, and looked about. She could tell that he was still deep in thought, deeply troubled, trying to work things out.

She told him then of her own studies, and the things that the mantle had revealed, how they would need to travel during the day and go underground at night, how he could reduce his own reception of the Inhuman's signal by drinking heavily to rid his body of any metallic salts that the Word introduced.

Gallen's eyes began to tear at that news, and when they passed a small stream, he knelt on all fours and drank to his fill. Afterward, Maggie took his hand as she walked with him, and the sun was shining, and the road was clear, and she felt somehow relieved, hopeful that all would be well.

Maggie had not known what to expect in Babel. She'd imagined armed encampments, each city a fortress. But as they walked along the dirt road, past stands of alder, maple, and oak, the hills seemed little different from her home in Tihrglas. The autumn colors were on the trees, and the soil smelled rich.

And in each little valley that they came to, a few quaint cottages huddled. Most of them were of gray stone with round clay shingles. The hay houses and sheepfolds and dovecotes were made of mud and wattle, with thatched roofs made of reeds.

Instead of armies, Maggie saw children working beside their parents at cutting wood for the winter or bringing in the corn.

In the afternoon they came to one green valley, where the emerald grass had been cropped short by the sheep, and Maggie stopped and looked out. The maples and alders lit the hillsides with flame. Three houses clustered together on the side of a hill at the foot of the valley, and a small smokehouse was letting its blue smoke rise lazily up. The scent of cooking sausages was strong. And beside the road, where a bridge spanned a clear river, a dozen naked children were swinging from a rope into a wide pool. Some of the little boys had thick red hair, almost fur, that covered most of their bodies, and one little girl had a face that was strangely deformed—with eyes that were unnaturally large, and a heavy brow that jutted over them. The children were screaming and laughing, splashing water at each other, and for a moment, Maggie grasped Gallen's hand, forcing him to stop.

"Look," she said. And Gallen suddenly became wary, scanning the hillside.

"No, you muffin, look at those children—this place!"

"Aye, it's a pretty valley," Gallen admitted.

"I . . . I think I could be happy here," Maggie whispered.

Gallen looked at her askance. "Here? But I thought you loved fiddling with gadgets—technology. There's nothing here for you, nothing like that. You'd be splitting logs and butchering pigs just like back home. You—your neighbors wouldn't even be human, damn it, Maggie!"

"I know," Maggie said quietly. Her sudden change of heart surprised even her, and she remembered the mischievous grin she'd seen upon the Lady Semarritte's face when she'd told Maggie of Tremonthin. Somehow, Semarritte had known that Maggie would like this place.

"I don't understand," Gallen said. "If you want to live on a backward planet, there are valleys just as pretty as this back home. I know a place near An Cochan. And if it's a stone house you want to live in rather than a house-tree, well, one could be built."

"No," Maggie said. "It wouldn't be the same. On Tihrglas, you can't go to the City of Life to be reborn. On Tihrglas, you're told what you must be. But here——" She suddenly got a glimmer of what it was she really was after, and she waved toward the motley assortment of children. "Here you'd never want for interesting neighbors. They'd be nothing like you, and they'd never try to tell you how you must act or what to wear."

"You're not making sense, Maggie," Gallen said, shaking his head. But he stared out across the valley, thinking, considering what it would be like, and his voice had held no conviction. "What about the Tekkar, and the other warrior races? You would be scared to step out of your door at night."

"Och, and who would be so bold as to come threatening the household of Gallen O'Day?" Maggie asked. "I know you, Gallen. You wouldn't mind it a bit, finding some village in the wilds and becoming a sheriff, keeping the peace for those who want it. . . ."

Gallen said no more. But as they walked on, he eyed the homesteads and hamlets and the fertile valleys keenly, looking beyond the exterior, as if considering the possibilities.

In the late afternoon, the road became cobblestone and wound down out of the hills to the sea, leading to an oddly shaped granite bluff, where the road led into a vast cave.

There were a few buildings perched next to the bluff—a sizable stable, some shops, but no houses—and people were going into the cave with wagons filled with wood and produce. Maggie realized with a start that the inhabitants of this city all lived within that monolithic rock.

She studied the place a bit—some rounded pillars had been carved into the rock, and they thrust up high, carrying a bit of smoke. In other places, holes had been gouged into the roof, giving light and air. In some holes, she could see through to whitened walls.

As with the temple she'd first noticed back in Northland, this place was built by someone who had no concept of symmetry. Each of the chimneys was a different height, and the windows were each shaped in their own ways. And yet there was a gracefulness, a peaceful organic feel to the structure, that was both comforting and inviting.

Cormorants and gulls wheeled out over the gray ocean, and

the skies were getting dark, promising rain. Maggie and Gallen went down to the city.

Under the arching entrance, they could see the city before them—a vast cavern filled with people and noise and the smells of smoke and sweat and fish. The rock had been carved away so that long stone staircases led away under great arches. The walls were not only painted white, but crystals had been set in them, casting light back like stars.

Between the skylights and the guttering lamps on wrought-iron posts placed strategically beside the roads, the caverns sparkled with light.

Maggie looked up, and along the roads going up the hill were side corridors, where people of a dozen races lived. Children screamed and played in the corridors, and clothing was left along stone walls to dry.

There was the smell of seawater in the air, and off to the right, a path led to the ocean. There, on broad stones at the sea's edge, sea people swam through an underwater channel, bringing up fresh fish and crabs. Maggie saw a gaggle of hooded merchants who were bartering loudly for the fish, offering brass bracelets and sacks made of fine cloth.

Directly ahead, just above sea level, a central pillar, like an enormous stalagmite, filled the middle of the complex, and carved at the column's center were several shops and a large pub where a dozen burly giants guzzled mugs of beer at wooden tables. The delicious scent of fish and sausages filled the air.

As Maggie and Gallen headed toward the pub, a grizzled giant approached. He wore a green tunic over black leather pants, and had a rope tied around his waist. His dark brown hair was tied back, and he wore beads of aqua and cardinal woven into it. His enormous beard spilled down his chest, thinning into a ragged wisp at his belly. It wasn't until he was nearly on them that Maggie realized how truly large he was— eight feet tall, with broad shoulders. He wore a short sword on his hip, but he handled himself like a man who wouldn't need weapons.

"My name's Fenorah," he grumbled, studying Gallen's sword. "Welcome to Battic, where land kisses the sea."

"Thank you," Gallen said, lifting his chin high to stare the man in the eye.

"We're a peaceful town," Fenorah said, scratching his nose. "I'll be straight with you. You carry a sword, and from the way you wear it, I'd say you know how to do more than split kindling with it. And there's blood on your boots—and I'd rather not know how it got there. But these are my folks, my town. There's peace here."

He looked deep into Gallen's eyes, as if trying to gauge what lay beneath their cool blue surface.

"I appreciate an honest man," Gallen said. "And I admire one who seeks peace. As long as I'm given it, I shall give it in return."

The giant laughed, slapped him on the back. "You look hungry from the road. I saw how you eyed the pub. May I buy you dinner? We've the finest flounder you'll taste on the coast." Gallen hesitated, but Maggie could sense something in this giant, a lack of guile, that she found refreshing.

"We would be honored," Maggie said, and the giant took her arm, led them into the pub, where they dined on sea bass roasted in rosemary and a fruity wine. Other giants like Fenorah lumbered around.

Fenorah talked long and boisterously, asking Gallen's business. When Gallen said that he wanted to purchase a wagon and draft animals, Fenorah called a serving boy and ordered them, as if he'd been ordering dinner, and the boy rushed to fetch them.

Then, Fenorah took them down to the "docks," the stones where the sea people rose from the dark waters, their tails flashing silver, and there Fenorah talked to Gallen of the city's trade agreements.

He showed Maggie and Gallen a great cavern where the annual fairs were held, where images of the city's founders were carved in three giant stalactites, so that their beards were hanging shards of stone. Fenorah then took them to the upper chambers above the city, where small swarthy men and women of the Ntak race still carved, singing in high voices as their picks and hammers rang, with each blow extending the city back deeper and deeper into the bones of the earth. The giant seemed to Maggie to be enormously proud of his city. He was obviously a man of wealth, a man of worries. And at last when they were in the far upper recesses of a cave, looking back down over a vast stairway of a thousand feet, and the ringing of hammers and picks below them rose like some strange music, Fenorah motioned for Gallen and Maggie to sit on a rock. Then, with a grunt, he knelt down beside them, and stared down into the distance.

"Gallen, my friend," the giant whispered, his voice a mere grumble, hard to be heard over the ringing hammers, the piping music. "There was a ship that burned last night, a ship not far off the beach. Its sails lit up like a bonfire, and we could see it sailing as if it would fall off the edge of the world."

"Aye?" Gallen asked, curiously.

"Aye," the giant grunted. "The sea folk went to investigate, and they brought back some survivors." The giant sighed, measured his words. "They told . . . stories, about a swordsman with two beautiful women. They hinted that he was a great warrior, and that they would pay well for his capture. Too well."

"And what did you tell them?" Gallen said.

"I sent them away, though I've thought better of it since. They had broken none of our laws, and yet . . ."

"And yet what?"

"And yet I found it hard to spare them their lives." Fenorah dug his hand into the stone at his feet, broke off a small boulder. Maggie had not seen any sign of a chink in the stone, and even Gallen caught his breath at witnessing the giant's tremendous strength. "The thing is, Battic is small for a sea town, and distant from other cities. We don't even have a port. And we've been careful to watch one another, protect each other. Perhaps for this reason, we have escaped the Inhuman's scrutiny. We have been . . . beneath notice. But I fear that now the Inhuman will turn its face our way, if it is searching for you. It's a small fear, perhaps unfounded."

Maggie took all of this in. If the agents of Inhuman had been turned loose from town, then perhaps they would be out in the countryside, hunting even now. She suddenly feared for Ceravanne, who had only Orick to protect her. More importantly, she understood that Fenorah, despite his great strength, was asking them to make a hasty retreat.

"I suspect," Gallen said, "that such fears *are* unfounded. Did you see which way they went?"

"Four of the Inhuman's servants went to the south, toward the wilderness of Moree," the giant whispered. "Five to the woods to the east."

Maggie caught her breath. Despite their best efforts, the Inhuman's agents were still searching for them in greater force than she'd imagined. It would be easy for a few servants of the Inhuman to find others like themselves, raise the countryside against them.

Fenorah studied them from the corner of his eyes. "I . . . have to admit that I am not above spying on a stranger. When the nine were alone in the medic's chamber, I listened to them from the hole above. They spoke of a Lord Protector who should not be allowed to reach Moree."

Gallen did not answer for a moment. "Even if it is true that you have escaped the Inhuman's scrutiny so far," he said, "it will not remain so forever. Unless the Inhuman is destroyed, you and your people will be found."

"And what can one man do against it?" Fenorah grumbled. "I fear that the Inhuman is more powerful than you know."

Gallen said, "There is more than one warrior here, unless I miss my guess. Perhaps you and some of your kind would join me."

Maggie held her breath, for she wished that this strong man would come with them. An army of them would be formidable.

"I am of the Im people," Fenorah said. "I could not travel inland with you, away from the sea. Me and my brothers cannot drink your fresh water. We would die after a few days' march."

Maggie's heart fell, and she wondered what Gallen would do without the giants' help. Somehow, though she had not admitted it to herself, to go into that wilderness alone seemed . . . unthinkable.

"Then let me have a wagon," Gallen asked, "and tell no one that I came this way."

"Done." The giant nodded. He looked at Gallen from the corner of his eye once again. "And more. I'll come with you, and bring my brothers, so long as your road leads by the sea. The Inhuman will have to show some restraint, with us at hand."

"I accept your offer, gratefully," Gallen said.

"Good." The giant slapped his knee and he got up, took Maggie's hand and helped her to her feet.

"One thing more," Maggie said. "Among the survivors, did you find a pale woman?"

"The Champlianne?" the giant said. "Aye, she's safe."

"She's not Inhuman, I don't think," Maggie said.

"Neither do I. She's well, resting in my own house," Fenorah assured her. "My wife is caring for her."

Maggie found herself suddenly weeping in relief. As far as the others on the ship went, she had trusted none of them, but she hated the thought that this innocent woman might have died in the skirmish. Gallen put his arm over Maggie's shoulders, hugged her for a moment.

Then Fenorah led them back down the long stairs, to the mouth of the city, where the serving boy had readied a fine wagon carved of cherrywood, with ornate scrollwork and bas-reliefs of trees and dancing rabbits on every panel. Gallen slapped the wagon, commenting on its fine Maker build, and Maggie wondered at his knowledge of it.

To pull the wagon, Fenorah had provided a beast that Maggie had never seen before, nor ever imagined. It stood tall as a horse, but was built more like a cow. It had a great hump at its shoulders, and while most of it was a creamy golden brown in color, shaggy black hair covered its head. Its small horns curved like those of a ram, and it glared about with small red eyes. It was both a fearsome creature, and powerfully built.

"What is this thing called?" Maggie asked.

"A travelbeast," Fenorah answered, obviously surprised that she did not know. "His kind are greatly prized. He has greater endurance than a bull, and greater speed than a horse. He sees in the dark, and is smart enough to understand a few small words." He hissed a little lower. "And he will trample anyone who gets in his way."

Maggie climbed up into the seat of the wagon, saw that it was lightly loaded with baskets of fruit, a barrel of salted fish, and plenty of blankets.

On impulse she grabbed the giant, hugged him tight. "Thank you," she whispered fiercely, and found herself fighting back tears once again.

"It is my pleasure," Fenorah said, and he went to find some men. In half an hour, six of the giants had gathered. Three ran out ahead of the wagon, while three others followed close behind.

Then Gallen nodded and slapped the travelbeast with the reins, and they lurched off, out the door of the tunnel. The twin suns were already down outside, and the moons had not yet risen. Clouds scudded across the sky, obscuring the stars. In the darkness, she could barely see the broad backs of the giants, rushing ahead into the shadows.

Gallen hunched at the reins, his face an unreadable mask in the darkness, and she felt distant from him. She could sense a change in him, a new uncertainty that he dared not voice.

As the wagon rattled over the cobblestones up toward the woods, Maggie had a sense of foreboding. It was dark under the trees, so dark that she could hardly see her hand in front of her face, and somehow she sensed that she was crossing into a darker realm than she could have ever imagined.

Nineteen

As night fell, Zell'a Cree ambled along the rutted roads east of Battic. His men had been following the road since just after dawn, sniffing for the scent of Gallen O'Day and his party. They'd crossed forty kilometers of mountain, hugging the coast, and never caught a whiff of him.

Forty kilometers seemed too far. Zell'a Cree knew that the currents and the wind had carried the little lifeboat east along the coast, and for a good time, he'd kept them in sight as he swam.

Still, they should have landed somewhere closer to Battic. But Zell'a Cree's nose didn't lie: they hadn't set foot on the road.

They're learning, Zell'a Cree realized. They must have known that if they walked on the road, I would catch their scent. And the coastline here was so rocky in places, that Zell'a Cree could not easily hunt them by following the beach.

He wondered idly how it would be to be a human—living in a world where the senses were so limited, where sight and smell and hearing were so dull. Humans must feel terribly vulnerable, terribly open to attack, and they would have to be wary at all times. No wonder they had developed fear as a basic component of their emotional makeup.

Yet Zell'a Cree could hear a twig snap a mile away, and at night, even in a deep fog, the heat of living things blazed like torches. Zell'a Cree did not need to suffer from mankind's irrational fears. He was better than that.

At dusk, he stopped, weary to the bone, and said to the three other men, "It may be that we have passed the Tharrin's trail. I for one believe that we should go back."

"Bransoon told us to head east. He's first mate," a sailor grumbled, a small red-skinned man with yellow eyes.

"But we've been walking all day, and still have no sign of them," Zell'a Cree said. "Don't you think it likely that we passed them already?"

"Maybe," the sailor said, scratching his ear with a long knife. "But what if you're wrong? What if they're a kilometer down the road, or five kilometers? The wind and current are strong. Maybe they decided to follow the coast by boat. If they're ahead of us, and we turn back now, we could lose them. But if they're behind us, most likely they'll just come down the road right into our arms."

Zell'a Cree studied the men. It seemed just as likely to him that Gallen and the others would run off into the woods and never be found again. There were hundreds of small hamlets scattered throughout these mountains, with roads going everywhere. It would be easy to lose them on back roads.

The three sailors seemed nervous, and they kept looking east, as if in a hurry to be off. "I'm not sure that you men want to find Gallen," Zell'a Cree said. "I think you're afraid of him."

One sailor licked his lips. "It's not healthy to tangle with him, that's for sure. What can four of us do against him?"

And Zell'a Cree had to admit that tangling with the Lord Protector had proven to be an unhealthy pastime.

"Aye," the others agreed. "We're heading east, and when we find the next town, we'll notify someone in authority that Gallen may be coming. Then I for one will sit and have a long beer, and thank my ancestors to be quit of this mess."

Zell'a Cree saw his mistake. He couldn't trust these men to

hunt Gallen properly. In all likelihood, the first mate and his men would just as soon never meet Gallen again, either. But there was a reason why Zell'a Cree had been given his own hunting pack to lead. He had to trust his own wits, his own instinct. "I'm going back," Zell'a Cree said, "to check the road again."

And he turned back, heading west. It was cool under the trees at night. Even for a Tosken it had been a long day. He felt worn through, but he picked up his pace and began jogging along the road.

At a farmhouse, he suddenly caught the scent. Gallen, Maggie, Orick, and some others had come out of the road here, just minutes ago. And the smell of Im giants was heavy all around. In the dark, he could see warm glowing footprints where someone had stood by the road for a bit—a giant— waiting for the others to come.

But at the roadside, the scent suddenly became very weak. Gallen and the others were not walking, they were riding.

And Zell'a Cree detected the heavy, malodorous fur of a travelbeast. Since the creature had not passed him, it must have gone west toward Battic.

Zell'a Cree redoubled his efforts, running over the hills, pumping his legs with a fury. If Gallen had fallen in with Im giants, and if he had a travelbeast, then any creature afoot would be hard-pressed to catch them.

So he ran as if to outrace the wind; Zell'a Cree stretched his legs, letting them pump in steady rhythm, the sweat pouring down his face. "I am Tosken, I am Tosken," he repeated over and over as he pounded the dirt roads, racing under trees past farmhouses where dogs rushed out barking and snapping and then finally fell back in defeat when they tired. Zell'a Cree's mind retreated from thought until there was only the race.

He heaved great, gasping breaths. He'd been made for great strength and great endurance, but he had not been formed to breathe such thin air as this planet offered. Most times, it did not bother him, but running, the constant pumping of legs, wore him down.

In an hour, he reached Battic, and dared not take the tunnel into the city—not if Gallen was with the Im giants. At Battic one road branched south, and the first mate and his men were to have followed that road. A second road went west.

Zell'a Cree scrambled over the hills, until he found the exit heading south, and there he did not find Gallen's scent. Which meant that Gallen had anticipated an ambush, and he was circling around it.

Zell'a Cree raced through the woods till he reached a hillside above the west road. There the woods had burned away in ages past, and only low brush survived on the stark, windswept hillsides. He could see parts of the road for six kilometers, and there, at the edge of his vision, burned the forms of the racing giants as they sprinted down the road, protecting their wagon.

Suddenly, the wagon stopped. The giants waited for a moment, glancing about anxiously.

A man climbed up in the back of the wagon and stood looking toward Zell'a Cree. He wore a dark robe, and wore a sword at his back. Gallen O'Day.

To most peoples, even the Im giants, Zell'a Cree would be invisible at this time of night, at such a distance. But Zell'a Cree had been running, and he imagined that the heat of his own body must be radiating like a torch. Yet of all those below him, only Gallen O'Day could see him.

The tricky little man could see in infrared. Zell'a Cree had had no idea that the Lord Protector possessed such talents.

They stood for a moment, gazing at one another across the distance, and Gallen raised an arm, as if to wave, then suddenly clenched his fist, drawing it downward—one of the secret hand gestures of the Inhuman—a beckoning call. Then the wagon lurched forward, the travelbeast rushing over a hill, and was gone.

For one moment, hope flickered in Zell'a Cree. If Gallen knew the hand signal, then he had been infected by the Inhuman. The Word had indeed entered him.

Yet something was wrong. If Gallen was Inhuman now, then why did he run? Why did he not bring the others so that they too could be converted? The only answer seemed to be that

Gallen had been strong enough to resist the Word. Had Gallen beckoned him in mockery?

Zell'a Cree licked his lips, angry. Sweat poured down his face, and he gulped for air. He'd been two days without sleep, and he'd just run twenty kilometers. He could go no farther tonight. He let himself collapse into a sitting position.

So Gallen O'Day was not as blind and helpless as other men. He had more resources to draw upon . . . and he had resisted the Word.

Zell'a Cree considered his own resources. He imagined the roads south, drew a map in his mind. The Inhuman had given him a great gift—the memories of a hundred lives lived and wasted. Over six thousand years of memories. Twelve of those lives had been spent in cities and villages between Battic and Moree. He recalled childhoods spent playing on obscure tracks, the life of a tinker working between towns, the days of a Thoranian guard who traveled with a tax collector. Zell'a Cree concentrated, recalling each road, each main track.

Gallen might go far west to avoid detection, but he was in a hurry. If he went too far, he'd have to cross the Telgood Mountains, and that would cost him many days. At the most, Gallen could go four hundred kilometers out of his way, but then he'd have to go south, closer to the hosts of the Inhuman.

Sooner or later he'd turn up on the road to Moree. Zell'a Cree had no choice but to race south now, checking for Gallen's trail, hoping to enlist other servants of the Inhuman in his quest.

Perhaps I've been too naïve, Zell'a Cree considered. I'd hoped to take Gallen alive, but he really isn't as essential as Maggie and the Tharrin. The practical thing would be to kill him.

Once the decision was made, Zell'a Cree felt an enormous calm.

Twenty

As the wagon stopped, Orick looked up at Gallen, saw him study the distance behind them, then make the strange pulling gesture at the sky as if trying to wrap clouds in his hand and draw them to earth. Gallen's expression was distant, and Orick could see that some heavy burden was upon him.

"Gallen, what's wrong?" Orick asked.

"Nothing . . ." Gallen said, obviously disturbed himself. "It's just—I saw Zell'a Cree behind us."

"How far?" one of the giants asked, drawing his sword as if to do battle.

"He's back several kilometers—at Battic."

The giant grumbled, sheathed his sword, and took a moment to swab the wagon's axles with grease from a bucket.

Gallen turned and sat back down in the driver's seat, urged the travelbeast forward, and the giants began running. The travelbeast was terribly strong, much faster than a horse. Although the huge wagon carried four people, a bear, and supplies, it fairly sang over the roads. The craftsmen who had built it had invested a great deal of time in carving every panel, and they'd spent equal care in designing the suspension. Orick had never ridden in a wagon that was its equal, and he was grateful for the smooth ride, not for his own sake, but for Tallea's. The warrior's wounds had healed at the surface, but the giants had carried her from the camp to the road, and every jarring step was a pain for her.

So as they raced through the night, Orick lay beside her, keeping her warm, singing to her.

Everyone was silent. Since Maggie and Gallen had been hiking all across the countryside, when they tired the giant Fenorah took the reins and Ceravanne sat hunched beside him with her cloak draped tightly about, to keep out the cold. Gallen and Maggie lay in the back of the wagon.

Gallen stretched out beside Orick under a blanket, with Maggie beside him, and Orick could feel a certain tenseness in Gallen's muscles.

Orick took a moment to consider, trying to remember how far a kilometer was. He was still not accustomed to measuring things as the starfarers did. When he was satisfied that Zell'a Cree was far away, he breathed deeply, quietly, trying to get back to sleep, but it wasn't much use. They traveled under the clouds for a while, and then the stars came out—a vast panoply far brighter than the dim stars back on Tihrglas.

Maggie was looking up at the sky, too, and she whispered, "Ah, Gallen, look at all of the stars."

"We must be close to the galactic center here, closer than we are back on Tihrglas—"

"Not much closer," Maggie said. "We're on the far side from Tihrglas, closer to the Dronon worlds. They're out on the rim, but we're halfway to the galactic center here, a little above the spiral. See that bright band—how wide it is?"

And Orick saw. Indeed the Milky Way was but a dim river of stars back on Tihrglas, but here it took up the whole night sky. The starlight alone was enough to see by, fairly well.

"Gallen," Maggie whispered, changing the subject, worry in her voice, "what was that hand signal you gave Zell'a Cree?" Orick could barely hear the question over the sounds of running feet, the creak of wagon wheels, the jostling of springs.

"I don't know," Gallen whispered.

"What do you mean, you don't know? Is it something you learned from the Inhuman?"

"I really don't know," Gallen said. "I was just standing there, and it came to me. It seemed the right thing to do."

Maggie seemed to take this in, and Orick realized that they were discussing something private, something dangerous. What would Gallen have learned from the Inhuman? Orick wondered. They were whispering, and with the way the backboard for the driver's seat leaned, it would baffle the sound for Ceravanne and Fenorah.

Maggie sat up and readjusted her pack, using it for a pillow. "I wish we were underground this night, Gallen," she said. She looked at Orick.

"Orick, are you still awake?" Maggie asked.

"Huh, ah, yes." Orick yawned.

"Oh, good night, then," she said; she rolled over.

Orick saw his mistake. If he'd feigned sleep, then Maggie and Gallen would have kept talking. Instead, Maggie drifted into a light sleep. But Gallen lay for a long time, his muscles rigid, until the rumble of the wagon lulled even him to sleep. Orick roused enough to look over the backboard, and a hundred yards back, the giants were running three abreast behind the wagon, a strong, comforting presence.

Orick lay watching the sky, and the marvelous wagon moved so gently over the road, he felt that he was floating under the stars. They passed through several small towns, and each time, dogs would bark and geese would honk, and then they'd be left behind. But then the trees closed over them, and for a long time there were no houses to pass. They were moving deeper and deeper into the wilderness.

A few hours before dawn, they came to the sea and clattered over a long bridge, then at some woods along an empty beach the giants stopped for the night. Two of them stayed up as sentries, watching the road, and the others built a small fire and napped. Ceravanne and Fenorah camped under a tree, while Orick slept in the wagon with the others. At dawn Orick got up, while the giants fixed breakfast—salty corn cakes covered with peaches, dried apricots, and cream.

Orick walked along the road, and quickly realized that they were on a small island between two branches of a river. And on the island two enormous cliff faces, each over two hundred feet tall, were carved with the images of eagles. One eagle, with its wings raised, faced the north sea. The other, with its wings folded, looked upriver, its beak wide as if it were screeching.

And the bridge they had crossed was a marvel—nearly a mile of vast granite pylons held stonework that was intricately carved along the side with a massive frieze that displayed images of grotesque gargoyles, squatting and grunting as they shoved handcarts over the bridge. The images were somehow both comic and beautiful. And the bridge was enormously wide, enough so that four or five carts could have gone abreast.

On the far side of the island was a shorter bridge, just as intricately decorated, and Orick suddenly saw why the giants chose to camp here: the island could be easily defended.

Orick climbed a steep, pine-covered ridge until he reached the top of the eagle that gazed out to sea. There, on the head between the eagle's wings, he found Gallen sitting, dangling his feet as if unaware that he was perched above a deadly drop. Gallen wore the black gloves and boots of a Lord Protector, along with his robe that would stay black unless he willed it to change some other color or let it blend into whatever background he happened to be standing in.

Orick climbed beside him, sat gazing out to sea, resting his muzzle on his paws. The double suns had just risen, and the sea was flat, smooth, a deep, pristine blue. Orick could see salmon finning in lazy circles out in the water, and cormorants were flying out to sea, shooting just above the waves.

Orick said, "Did you see the bridges?"

"Indeed." Gallen sighed. "This place is called Profundis, and those unbreakable bridges were carved long ago by a race called the Thworn. If you look west, on that bluff over there, you will see the walls to an ancient city, Tywee." Orick looked over to a dome-shaped bluff beside the sea and noticed for the first time some crumbling walls among the trees. "Eight hundred years ago, a young man named Omad fell in love with a beautiful princess, and she agreed to marry him if he took her armies and unified this region. He did so—by making pacts and trade agreements, so that never a drop of blood was spilled. And after their wedding he wisely built the bridges—not only to facilitate travel in his own lands, but to keep enemy ships from sailing upriver into the heart of his realm.

"You see, this river accepts drainage from all the land within a thousand kilometers in any direction, and so it is the major artery leading south into the heartland."

"Did the king build these statues, too?" Orick asked.

"Yes. A bloody, barbaric race called the Dwinideen were great seamen, and they had often raided deep into the fertile inland. As the bridge was being built, the Dwinideen harried the craftsmen, slaughtering many people, much to the dismay of Omad. But the Dwinideen were superstitious, and they feared Capúl, the sky god who appears in the shape of a fish eagle. They believed that if one dies, and the fish eagle gets at the body, the eagle will carry off the dead person's spirit to be eaten so that the dead can never be reborn. So the King of Tywee carved this statue, and when next the Dwinideen attacked, Omad took thirty of the Dwinideen captive. With his own hand he hurled them from the eagle's head to the rocks below, crying, 'Thus shall my enemies die!' There were many fish eagles living here then, as there are now, and they fed on the carcasses. Afterward, the Dwinideen feared this place and never returned. For the rest of his days, Omad regretted that he was forced to shed blood to protect his kingdom."

Gallen fell silent. His voice seemed grim. Almost, Orick thought, as if he were grieving for the long-dead king, and there was pain in his eyes, a quiet wisdom that seemed out of place on Gallen's features.

"Hmmm . . ." Orick said, wondering how Gallen had learned so much. Gallen must have spoken of this place with the giants.

In the distance, toward the ancient city of Tywee, Orick saw the white flashing of wings as a fish eagle swooped to grab a fish from the water.

"If this bridge is so important, why isn't there a city here now?" Orick asked.

"The kingdom fell into ruin. It was attacked from the south, by men who came out of the desert. The villagers who live here now are weaker men, too divided to stand against their overlords. They pay a small tribute and live in relative peace."

"And who might these southern warriors be?" Orick asked, knowing that they would have to go south soon, and might have to pass through their lands.

"Can you not guess?" Gallen said. "They're the Tekkar."

Orick licked his lips. "I don't like the Tekkar." He'd known that they served the Inhuman, but somehow he imagined that they would be far away—not a present danger. "Will we meet more of them soon?"

Gallen said, "We made good time last night. A hundred kilometers since sunset. And it's a beautiful, clear day. We'll go a hundred more kilometers before the day is done. But we are almost a thousand kilometers from the desert, and the Tekkar do not like climates as cool and wet as this. It will be a few days before we find them."

Orick grunted in relief, and Gallen sat brooding, looking out to sea. Orick headed down between the dark pines to see if breakfast was ready. Squirrels were out in the morning sun, searching for nuts, chattering. At the foot of the trail, Orick found Maggie.

"Have you seen Gallen?" she asked.

"He's up top."

"Is he all right?"

"Quiet," Orick said. "He just seemed to want some time alone, to think."

Maggie bit her lower lip and frowned. She glanced up the trail, then headed up in a hurry.

Orick watched her leave, and something in her face bothered him. She'd been panicked, as if she didn't trust Gallen to sit and think for five minutes.

Orick almost headed to camp, but curiosity got the better of him. Maggie was nearly running up the steep trail, darting between trees.

Orick turned and rushed after her, but halfway up the trail, Gallen met Maggie coming down, and Gallen had obviously seen Orick. The two of them walked down together, arm in arm, and Orick tagged along, certain that once again he had missed out on a chance to hear their secret conversations.

When they got back to camp, the Im giants all sat around a small cooking fire, circled by dark trees. Their tunics were stained by sweat, and they smelled none too sweet to Orick, but the humans next to them didn't mind. Breakfast was ready, and they passed out the corn cakes, tasty enough fare for the road. Even Tallea was up to sitting a bit while she ate. It felt good to Orick to be in the daylight, with the sun shining on his fur.

Ceravanne addressed them all as they ate. "Today we must make some decisions. The roads to Moree are many, and each is fraught with its own dangers. We've come west out of expediency, but how far west shall we go? And when do we head south? I walked abroad in this land many years ago. The hills and mountains look little changed, but rivers have turned, old roads are forgotten and new ones are unknown to me. So I think it best to ask our friends, the Im giants, for their advice, and to ask Tallea the Caldurian for her help."

"I not been to this land," Tallea said.

"I know the roads along the sea," Fenorah said, "and I know the roads inland by reputation. You could head south this morning at Marbee Road. It's a wide road built upon a bed of stone, and it follows the river where it passes through many small hamlets, and borders many a field. The folk along the way are friendly enough, and accustomed to strangers. But I fear it is a dangerous road for you: the hosts of the Inhuman have already gone south on Battic Road, and Marbee Road will meet it in one hundred and twenty kilometers. They may be waiting for you there or beyond. Still, if you hurry, the chances are good that you could keep ahead of them."

"What other choices do we have?" Ceravanne asked.

"Beyond Marbee, fifty kilometers, lies the Old King's Road," Fenorah said. "It is a winding road among the hills, built to connect old fortresses, many of which no longer exist. But there is many a farmstead along it, and a few villages."

"And some places along the road often flood," Ceravanne said.

"In the spring, this is true, but the roads should be clear this time of year," one of Fenorah's men protested. "But once again, it meets Marbee Road in two hundred and forty kilometers, at High Home. Beyond that, the next best trail would be the ancient highway at the foot of the Telgood Mountains. Only a few wild people live in those mountains—Derrits and the like. The road is mostly unused and has gone to grass. Some would claim that it is no longer safe, but I have hunted along its trails, and a sturdy wagon should make it through."

"I know that way well," Ceravanne said. "In younger days it was called the Emerald Way. The caravanserais would come out of Indallian, and at night when you camped in the valleys you would see the lights of their fires burning like winding rivers of stars along the hills."

"That could not have happened within the past three hundred years," Fenorah mused, a faraway look in his eyes, "though my grandfather recalled those days—the glory and the wars."

"Indeed, it was the richness of this land that destroyed it," Ceravanne said.

"If Derrits along road, road not good," Tallea said. "Troublesome people."

"What are Derrits?" Orick asked.

"They . . . are solitary giants," Ceravanne said, "built for life on a sterile world. They are very strong, and very cunning."

"They're cowards and killers," Fenorah said, glaring, grasping the hilt of his sword as if he wanted to cut one down.

"Eat other people," Tallea said. "Build traps."

"They can eat just about anything—from carrion to raw soil," Ceravanne said, "and they will eat you, if you're alone and fall into one of their pits."

"We can't use that road," Maggie said, "not with a quick-running animal."

"I agree that it is a dangerous choice," Ceravanne said thoughtfully. "But beyond that old highway, there are no roads south until you cross the Telgoods. They're a high mountain range, and we couldn't cross easily."

"Six hundred kilometers," Fenorah said, "just to cross the

mountains, and that land is so distant, I do not know the roads there."

"I have been there," one of Fenorah's men said. "The roads south are good, better than any we have here, for the Lords of Telgood keep them. But the mountains also veer west, and if you go to Moree, then you will be spending much time in the high passes. The wingmen live there, and it is not safe to travel in parties as small as yours—especially without bows."

"More importantly," Ceravanne said, "we would be traveling hundreds of kilometers out of our way. And we need to hurry."

"So," Gallen said, "it sounds to me that perhaps our best choice is the Old King's Road. It gives us a chance to race against the Inhuman, and it sounds safer than the far roads, more civilized."

"But therein lies another danger," Ceravanne said. "If we pass through hamlets and villages, undoubtedly we will meet more servants of the Inhuman. Do you suppose that they pose no threat?"

"All roads may lead astray," Orick said, "and the longer we sit here, the more dangerous they become. I think Gallen is right in his choice."

Ceravanne looked to Fenorah, as if the giant held the final word. "The choice is yours, dear lady," he said. "No one should make it for you."

"Then I will follow Gallen," Ceravanne whispered. "Still," she said more loudly, "there is another matter we must consider. And that is the question, Who of us shall go? We know that the servants of the Inhuman are rushing ahead of us, we know that they will be prepared. If any choose to come, they will be risking great danger. So, I have spoken with Fenorah, and he has agreed to let any who desire return to Battic." Her eyes rested on Maggie.

"None of us will return to Battic, I wager," Maggie said. "None of us are cowards."

"Yet there is good reason to consider the offer," Gallen said loudly, and he stood, resting his hand on the hilt of his sword. "For one among us has already been infected by the Inhuman's Word, and all who travel are imperiled by it!"

Orick looked around the camp. One of the Im giants leapt to his feet as if ready to attack the traitor, and Ceravanne looked from Gallen to Maggie, her face a mask of fear.

"Who?" Orick cried.

"*I* am infected, my friend," Gallen said, and there was a sadness in his eyes. "Forgive me. The Word burrowed into my skull while we were aboard ship, and the Inhuman has been sending messages to me for the past two nights."

"And what kind of messages does it send?" Fenorah asked, scratching his thick beard.

"It sends memories of lives spent and wasted. It tells me that the world is unfair, and that the peoples of Babel have been treated shabbily. The Inhuman cries out for justice, and reparation, and equality. But the humans of Northland will hear none of it." Gallen paused and closed his eyes, looking inward. "The Inhuman teaches me to be ashamed of my own species, and to mistrust them and the Tharrin who lead them." There was a long moment of silence.

Tallea, who had been leaning weakly against a tree, pulled herself forward, fixed her eyes on Gallen with desperation. Until now, she had always spoken crisply, breaking off her words and her sentences. But now, as if to emphasize their import, she spoke as others on Tremonthin did, in her harsh voice. "You can fight those voices, Gallen," she said. "I know those who fought and won. At first, when you hear those voices, see their memories, it is like falling into a great darkness, and your own small voice is a tiny light—"

"No," Gallen growled. "It is like falling into a vast and yawning light, and *my* voice is the small darkness!"

"Why did you keep this infection hidden from me?" Ceravanne demanded.

"Because I hoped that my mantle could defeat it. Because I believed that it could jam the frequencies that the Inhuman sent its signal on."

"And your mantle fails you?" Ceravanne asked.

Gallen looked away to the north. "The Inhuman is switching frequencies, sending messages in short bursts. I have . . .

memories flowing into me, like water gushing through a swollen dike. In the past few hours, I have recalled five lifetimes."

"No, Gallen!" Maggie cried. "It can't have!"

"But it has," Gallen said.

"I don't understand," Maggie said. "The Word shouldn't be sophisticated enough to do what you're saying."

Gallen shook his head, and there were tears glistening in his eyes. "Apparently we have underestimated the Inhuman once again. The Word *is* sending signals in coded bursts. My mantle tries to block them, but when it does, the Inhuman then begins sending on a different frequency. My mantle doesn't have enough power to block both signals."

Maggie frowned in concentration. "This is worse than anything I feared." She took his hand and looked up into his face steadily, searching his features. "We can stop this! We can stop it! We could—take you underground."

"Aw, and what use would it be, my love?" Gallen shook his head. "You can't just hide me away from it. I'm fighting. My mantle is fighting, but it cannot stave off the attack. I must warn you: you go to battle the Inhuman, but by the time we get to Moree I may be Inhuman."

"The Inhuman's Word can be defeated, as Tallea said—" Ceravanne intoned hopefully, "by those who are strong of purpose, by those who are wise. I can help you defeat it."

Gallen glanced at her, and there was a gleam of anger in his eye, and Orick's heart froze at the sight—anger at the peaceful Tharrin, a folk who'd never done Gallen any harm.

"Thank you," Gallen said coldly. "But I do not want your help."

"Why?" Ceravanne asked, unable to hide how his tone had hurt her.

Gallen's face took on a closed look. "I'm not sure I trust you—or any Tharrin."

Two of the Im giants got up, throwing the remains of their corn cake to the ground, confused and hurt by Gallen's words. They brought their hands to their short swords, as if ready to do battle over such talk. And Gallen half pulled his own sword.

"Wait!" Orick said. "Gallen here has always been a trusty

lad. I've never seen him back away from any bandit or outlaw! So if you're going to draw swords on him, you'd best be sure of your cause. And you'd better be ready to die."

"Orick is right," Ceravanne said. "Put your weapons away. We are all friends here. I'll not force Gallen or anyone else to serve me."

Ceravanne stared deep into Gallen's face, and the giants rested, seeing no immediate danger. But Gallen held his own sword halfway drawn, as if ready to sweep the blade free. The sunlight shone on Ceravanne's platinum hair, and her pale green eyes reflected the light like cut gems. The sunlight caught her blue-white dress, and it gleamed like a bolt of lightning here under the dark pines. In spite of her strength and wisdom, she looked like little more than a frail child who could be easily swept away, and Gallen's sword was nearly out. If Gallen had wanted to cut her down, he could have put a swift end to her.

"If you are willing to go to Moree to risk your life, then I will walk beside you," Ceravanne said. "I know that the Inhuman teaches that I am its enemy, that the people of this world are but pawns in our hand. But you can trust me, Gallen. I desire harm for no one. I've come to bring peace to this land, not war. I have long been a friend to the people of Babel."

The Im giants stirred restlessly at these words, studying her, and Fenorah said hopefully, "Unless I miss my guess, you are an Immortal? But I am not sure that I have heard of a Tharrin who was a friend to Babel."

"For three hundred years I have been studying with the Bock," Ceravanne whispered. "And for over two hundred years before that, I exiled myself. But I lived here before your grandfather was young—for two thousand years. In Chingat they called me the White Lady. On the island of Bin I was Frost Before the Sun, and in Indallian they called me the Swallow— she who returns. If you have memories from the Inhuman, Gallen, then you have heard these names, and you know why I have come here!"

"By the gods!" Fenorah swore. "The Swallow has returned from the dead! The Immortal is with us!" And the giants of Im all fell to their knees. Some lowered their eyes in respect, while others stared at her in amazement. One man drew his sword, as if pledging it to her service, while the others set their weapons on the ground before them, as if swearing to put them away forever. It was obvious that all of them knew her name and her reputation, but none of the giants was certain how to react.

For one moment, as the giants sat with their heads lowered, it looked as if Ceravanne stood among a field of huge boulders.

And to Orick's utter amazement, Gallen himself, who seemed but a moment before ready to draw his sword on her, suddenly opened his mouth in surprise and fell to one knee at Ceravanne's feet, as if she had slapped him for some insult and he were begging her forgiveness. He watched her steadily. "I know of the Swallow, and how her gentle people fell in ancient days at the hands of the Rodim," he said, "but I have not heard that she was a Tharrin. Truly, you are a friend of the people." Gallen's voice became husky. "I would be more than honored, if you would accompany me to Moree."

"My Lady," Fenorah said, "will you again build the Accord?"

"For long I've tried to bring peace between all peoples," Ceravanne said. "And the Accord was my best effort. When the Rodim slew whole villages, I could hardly bear it. In anger I turned my back on them, and let my disciples ruin them. The slaughter was horrible, and I could not live with what I'd done. I had sought peace by giving in to war. For centuries I have been in the North, studying the ways of peace at the hands of the Bock, purifying myself. But now I must return to my people. The Tekkar and the Inhuman are forming a deadly alliance, one that could shake the stars."

"I would fight them with you," Fenorah said, and all of his men shouted, "Aye."

"Then draw your weapons upon no man, except in self-defense," Ceravanne said.

"But—how can we fight the servants of the Inhuman without drawing upon them?" one giant asked.

"Your people are tied to the sea, and I forbid you to shed blood. But that does not mean that you cannot fight. There are ships in the harbors of Babel preparing for war," Ceravanne said. "Set them afire. See that the Inhuman does not cross the ocean. And in every ear, with everyone you meet, tell them that the Swallow has returned to build the Accord, and that she begs human and Inhuman alike to lay aside their weapons."

"But the Tekkar will not listen to you," Fenorah said. "They are as deadly and vile a race as ever the Rodim were. We cannot let them live."

"How do we know that we cannot reason with them, if we have not tried?" Ceravanne said. "They are violent and cunning and bloodthirsty. But their men love their women as passionately as you love your own wives. And their mothers love their children."

The Im giants shook their huge heads in disbelief, doubting that the horrid Tekkar could share any brotherhood with them.

But Fenorah looked to his men. "Anabim, Dodeo, the Swallow has spoken her wishes. I charge you to return to Battic and raise some men. Go east along the coast, and set fire to any ships that are preparing for war. And tell people what you have learned here today—that the Swallow has returned to rebuild the Accord. It will set fire to their hearts."

The two giants turned and ran from the grove, heading toward the bridge east.

"You know, Great Lady," Fenorah said, "that news of your presence will put you in greater peril. It now becomes imperative for the Inhuman's agents to kill you, lest some among their numbers give you aid. Legends of the golden days of the Accord abound, and long have we hoped for your return. Still, some people may be slow to believe that you have returned. In past years, there have been rumors. . . ."

"What kinds of rumors?" Ceravanne asked.

"It was said that you had died and that the Lords of the City of Life would not let you be reborn. It was said that they feared a new Accord. It has even been said that the Inhuman has sought to rebuild you, so that you will come and lead it to victory."

"Those were lies spread by the Dronon and their Inhuman," Ceravanne said. "The Dronon tried to kill me when they learned that they could not turn me to their violent ways, when

I would not champion the cause of the Inhuman. Four times the Rebellion brought me the rebirth, and each time I tried to return south to my people, but the Inhuman stopped me."

"Of course," Fenorah said. "Some had guessed as much, and all will be glad of your return." He lowered his head in thought. "Look, when I heard the Servants of the Inhuman talking yesterday, making plans in their cave, I knew only that they sought to turn you because you are a Tharrin, and because you brought a Lord Protector to fight them. I am sure that they did not know your real name, or the full scale of your mission."

"I have been careful not to reveal that until now," Ceravanne said.

"Well," Fenorah said, "what I mean to say is—we had planned to take you inland for a hundred kilometers. But maybe we could go farther."

"Yes," one of the giants echoed.

"And what will you drink?" Gallen said. "Without seawater, you will die of thirst in a matter of days."

"We could buy sea salt in the villages along the way, and add it to fresh water," Fenorah said. "I have gone far inland in such a manner. Indeed, I brought a small pouch of salt just for such an emergency."

"Bless you," Ceravanne said, and tears suddenly shone in her eyes. "But I fear that it would put you in danger. Four giants, all searching for sea salt in those small villages? No, I would be asking too much."

"One giant, then," Fenorah said. "I am Lord Sheriff for this region, and I will accept the risk. I will run two thousand kilometers at your side, all the way to Moree."

"There are vast deserts between here and Moree." Ceravanne shook her head. "You will not find the salt you need to purchase, and even water may be scarce. No, my faithful friend, I cannot accept your life as a sacrifice."

"It is mine to give," Fenorah said.

"Then give it in service. Two hundred and eighty kilometers you may come, to High Home, where the Old King's Road meets the Marbee Road. If we are in peril from the Inhuman's servants, that is where we will most likely find them, and I would welcome your protection."

"Agreed," Fenorah said. "And now, we must be on our journey, for every second matters."

With that, the giants leapt to their feet, and in a moment the travelbeast was harnessed. They did not clean their cooking pans, only pushed them under a bush for later retrieval, then Orick and the others climbed into the wagon.

The giants were no longer content merely to run loosely behind the wagon. Instead, two of them got behind and pushed, and in moments they were off, the wheels singing down the road, the travelbeast lowering its head and huffing as its hooves thundered over the bridge.

Orick looked out over the broad river, saw the folding wings of a fish eagle as it dove, and he gazed along the cliffs at the gray statues of the birds that rose above the trees, gazing out to sea, in to land, their wings and heads splotched green and white and yellow with lichens. Gallen sat beside Orick, an old friend and confidant, yet now Orick knew that Gallen was a stranger. Indeed, the man he'd befriended and trusted most was gone, if Orick understood correctly, becoming submerged under layer after layer of other beings.

Orick recalled how Jesus once met a man near the region of the Gadarenes who was afflicted with demons, and he spoke to the man, asking his name, and the man said, "Legion, for we are many."

And Jesus commanded the demons to depart, and they begged to enter a herd of swine. So Jesus allowed it, and two thousand pigs immediately ran downhill into the raging sea and were drowned.

Ah, Gallen, Orick wondered. Will you let your demons pull you into the sea? And Orick wished that he were a priest, with the authority to cast out demons. Indeed, Gallen needed an exorcist now, as deeply as any man ever did.

But I've always been too weak to accept the priesthood, Orick realized. Too much tempted by the things of the world.

Orick looked at Gallen, all draped in black. And he

wondered if he might yet have to fight Gallen at some lonely spot down this road.

Orick could not examine such possibilities for long, and somehow he found himself mourning for lost Profundis and the people who had lived in hard-won peace under these sun-drenched skies. For he knew that, like them, he would never see this place again.

Twenty-one

For two hours that morning the giants ran west along the coast as Gallen drove the wagon. When the road abruptly turned south, heading between two low hills, the giants stopped to rest. All four of them went down to a calm sea, as blue and sparkling as sapphires, and waded into waves up to their chests. For ten minutes they stooped and slowly drank their fill. Afterward, each of them bathed, then clambered back up the long sandy beach, looking refreshed, but as bedraggled as if they'd washed up in a flood.

Then the group headed south through the wooded hills. Tallea was healing nicely, and she and Orick took advantage of the opportunity to rest, while Ceravanne only sat gazing out the back of the wagon.

Maggie had time to wonder. According to Gallen, during the previous night his mantle had begun picking up memories in short bursts, so she put on her own mantle of technology and questioned Gallen about the problem.

"Gallen," she whispered as the travelbeast charged down the dirt road, rounding a corner, "you said that the Inhuman is switching frequencies, trying to communicate with you. Did it do that only last night, or has it continued today?"

"It kept up until just past dawn," Gallen said, "then it stopped."

That was good news, at least. As she'd imagined earlier, the Inhuman's ability to transmit seemed hampered in daylight, so it would be safer to travel by day. But she didn't like the fact that the frequencies were changing at all. "Dammit, Gallen, the Word is more complex than I thought: at the very least, it is equipped with a transmitter so that it can communicate with the Inhuman."

"But how much can it communicate?" Gallen said. "Is it just telling the Inhuman 'I'm here,' or does it send more information?"

Maggie considered. She'd thrown away the broken Word she'd had in camp yesterday. If she had it in hand, she might have been able to find its memory. Most likely, it would have been a small crystal, and by knowing its size, she would have been able to calculate exactly how much information was stored in the Word. But she knew that it couldn't have stored much. *If* the Word's memory was large at all, she'd have noticed its crystal earlier. Which meant that it wasn't equipped with much memory—probably just enough to walk and move and recognize potential targets. It was probably not much smarter than an insect, and it might have had a transmitter in it just so that it could let the Inhuman know when to begin sending messages and whether they had been properly received.

But what bothered Maggie was that the Word didn't *need* much memory to do some rather devastating things. With its transmitter, it *might* be able to download Gallen's memories, his thoughts and ideas, and inform the Inhuman. It *might* be able to send direct transmissions to let the Inhuman know what he saw, what he smelled, what he heard.

In other words, without his knowledge or approbation, Gallen could very well lead them all into a trap, all the while believing himself to be fighting the Inhuman's sway.

"Gallen, I don't know how much the Word in your skull might be able to communicate with the Inhuman," Maggie said hopefully. "But from what I've seen, the agents of the Inhuman don't work in concert. Information doesn't seem to be transferred directly between people. So that transmitter can't be sending much."

"But . . ." Gallen said, "I can tell that something worries you."

Maggie leaned close to Gallen and a wave of dizziness passed over her. What she was about to say was so horrific, so undesirable, that she could hardly express her fears. "If the Word has a transmitter built into it, I've got to believe that it was put there for a good reason. I don't know how much memory the Inhuman has. It couldn't possibly hope to control a million or fifty million people all at once, so it downloads thoughts to you and lets you all act as if you were autonomous. But what if you're not? What if the Inhuman *could* read your mind? What if it could take control of your body the way that Karthenor's Guide took control of me? It wouldn't take a lot of memory for the Inhuman to control a couple dozen people."

"That can't happen to me," Gallen said. "My mantle is blocking its transmissions—at least during the daytime."

Maggie looked meaningfully at Gallen and considered the problem. She didn't want to speak so openly of such possibilities in front of Gallen and the others. She wanted to believe—she needed to believe—that the Inhuman had weaknesses, controllable limitations.

She whispered to her mantle, You have transmission capabilities. Can you help Gallen block the Inhuman's signals?

Done, her mantle whispered. Static will be transmitted in a steady burst. Maggie understood that as long as she stayed within three meters of Gallen, the mantle would add an extra layer of protection.

Maggie silently asked her mantle to provide a schematic for the Word's transmitter, and the mantle provided her with an image. The transmitter, it indicated, would most likely still be inside the metal body of the Word that had burrowed into Gallen's skull. Because it was powered by a biogenic cell, the transmitter would have to be very weak, and would best communicate at ultralow frequencies, lower than those normally used by mantles. Maggie's mantle was unable to read any such frequencies emanating from Gallen's Word. And Maggie wondered if the Word was conserving energy. Perhaps it recognized the futility of trying to communicate during the day.

So Maggie sat next to Gallen, her mantle leaning up against his shoulder, and she rested as he drove.

During the late morning they began to pass others on the road—farmers with handcarts traveling to markets, old men with barrows carrying bundles of firewood, children herding pigs along the road.

Each time they passed such folk, the travelbeast was obliged to slow for safety's sake. And on the occasions when they passed some small hamlet in which buildings made of stone seemed almost to stoop out into the streets, the beast was brought to a walk.

But once they passed such villages, the race would begin anew, and the giants ran. They startled herds of wild pigs sleeping under the oaks by the roadside, and often deer would bound away at their approach, crashing through the brush.

Thus in the early afternoon they topped a long grassy hill, and rested under the shade of an oak. The wooded valleys spread out wide below, thick with oak and alder. As far as they could see, the land looked barren of habitation.

With heavy hearts, three of the giants stopped, begging Ceravanne's pardon for leaving. "You will have to go in the care of Fenorah from now on," one young giant apologized, "though he's not much good for anything but eating your stores."

The giants were covered with sweat, but Ceravanne stood in the back of the wagon and leaned out, kissing each on the forehead. "Go with my blessing," she said, "and know that I am grateful for your service."

The travelbeast was winded, and it lowered its shaggy head and began tearing great clumps of grass from the ground. One of the giants took a bag of rotting pears from the back of the wagon and fed them to the beast, explaining that if it was to run all day, it would need something better than grass to eat.

Then the giants turned as if to walk back toward the sea, but they were slow to leave. And for her part, Maggie was sad to see them go. With them at her side, she'd felt safe, like a child in its father's arms. One of them told a joke that Maggie could not hear, and the three laughed.

Gallen stood in the wagon and shouted in a strange tongue, "Doordra hinim s Duur!"

The three giants turned as one, raising their fists to the sky, and cried, "Doordra hinim!" Then they smiled, as if with renewed energy, and raced away.

Fenorah chuckled. "Stand tall in Duur! Indeed. Where did you learn that old battle cry? The Im giants abandoned the ancient tongue centuries ago."

Gallen took a seat, but his eyes flashed, and he looked up into Fenorah's face. "I learned it a few hours ago," he said softly. "From a man who has been dead for five hundred years. He served beside the Im giants, and with them he hunted Derrits in the mountains of Duur until he swore fealty to the Swallow, and for her slew the Rodim."

Gallen fell silent and his eyes lost their focus as he gazed inward. It was a magical thing for Maggie to see him as a boy one day, then suddenly turning into an old man the next, with too much pain and too much wisdom in his eyes.

Gallen began to sing, and though Maggie had heard him sing a few tavern songs, in the past she'd never thought him to have a fair voice. But now he sang in a voice that was both beautiful and startling, like the scent of a fresh rose filling a room in late autumn, and Maggie realized that it was a talent he'd learned from the Inhuman.

> *"In Indallian, the peaceful land,*
> *among dark pines glowering,*
> *the hills were hollowed by Inhuman hands*
> *in the days of the Swallow's flowering."*

"Hold," said Ceravanne from the back of the wagon, and she reached out and touched Gallen's hand, silencing him. "Please, Gallen, do not sing that song. It is long forgotten by those who dwell here, and . . . it hurts too much. Perhaps if it came from the voice of another bard—but not you. You remind me too much of Belorian."

"He has been dead for many centuries," Gallen said. "I would have thought that time had brought you peace."

"Not today," Ceravanne whispered. "The memories of him seem fresh today, and the pain still hot. If you must tell your friends of Indallian in its days of glory, I beg that you do not sing of it around me."

"What's Indallian?" Orick asked.

Gallen waved toward the wild hills before them, golden with fields of grass, green with forests. "All of this is the land of Indallian—from the rough coast to the ruined halls of Ophat beside the city of Nigangi, and beyond, even to the deserts south of Moree where the Tekkar dwell. Long ago Ceravanne ruled the empire from the great city of Indallian with her consort the good King Belorian, until the Accord fell. Even today if I judge right by Fenorah's account, their love is remembered as the stuff of legend."

"It is spoken of," Fenorah said beside the wagon, "though I must confess that I have not heard that song. And the Land of Indallian is no more, while its capital is spoken of with dread."

"Belorian was more than a consort," Ceravanne said as if to correct Gallen. "He was my lover, my husband in all but name—for by the laws of his people, we could not marry. Yet our love was fierce, before he died."

"I do not understand," Orick said to Ceravanne. "Your people can bring the dead back to life. Why is he not beside you now?"

"Because," Ceravanne said, "a man is more than his flesh. He is also his memories, his experiences, his dreams and ambitions. And shortly after Belorian died in battle, the crystals that stored his memories were destroyed, and that is a far truer and more permanent death than the sloughing off of the flesh. We could rebuild his body, but we cannot remake the man." She looked sharply at Gallen, as if to censure him for bringing up such a painful subject, then turned away.

In the uncomfortable silence that followed, Gallen urged the travelbeast forward with some strange words foreign to the human tongue. The beast responded as if Gallen had spoken in its own language, and it rushed through the hills.

And as Maggie rode that day, she watched the land roll by. Often she would see ancient lichen-crusted stones tumbled in the grass as they passed some ruin, and twice they passed ancient fortresses that sprawled upon the hills, covered with moss, with oaks growing in the courtyard, their branches reaching over the stone walls like great hands.

As the day drew to its close, a brief squall blew over, and Fenorah, unwilling to risk that his travelbeast should injure itself by slipping in the mud, decided to set camp in an old fortress, in a great hall without doors or windows. So they brought the travelbeast inside.

The walls were made of huge stones, a meter thick, carved so that various grooves fit together. Maggie suspected that the stone might not deter the Inhuman's signal as well as a dozen feet of solid dirt, but she hoped it would serve nearly as well. She found the most secluded corner and directed Gallen to sit there and rest.

Dried horse dung left by the mounts of previous travelers served as ample fuel to set a small fire, and Fenorah brought out stores for dinner. They had not had a formal meal since early morning, and everyone was tired, and the poor giant was most weary of all. He curled into a corner while Maggie cooked dinner, and he fell asleep before it was done.

After a brief dinner Ceravanne withdrew from the group, going out a back hall that led to a tower. Outside, the rain was falling steadily, hissing as it struck the leaves of trees, and the heavy scent of moisture pervaded the room. It was chill and dreary.

"That song you began to sing today," Orick said. "Will you sing it to us now?" And Maggie hoped that he would, for the sound of music would do her heart good.

Gallen sang in a low voice the same tune he had begun earlier in the day, and Maggie was amazed at his voice, at the easy grace and power in it, as if he'd been born to sing.

He sang of Indallian, the riches and glory that made it the

envy of all the world. He sang of the peaceful peoples drawn by the Swallow to form the great Accord, where each species had equal voices in the open counsels.

But then the Rodim came, a greedy race lured by tales of the rich deposits of emeralds and gold found in Indallian, and they ravaged whole villages, looted and burned the caravanserais.

The Swallow's love, Belorian, was a strong man, and he sought to protect his people by arming them. But the Swallow urged him to counsel with the Rodim peacefully, to reconcile with them, bring them into the Accord.

Yet when Belorian met with the savage chieftains of the Rodim in their mountain camps, they slew him and put his body upon a pole, then danced through the night, proclaiming victory over the land of Indallian, and they sent their armies to Belorian's throne at the city of Indallian, where they heaped contempt upon the dead by destroying the crystal that held Belorian's memories.

Ceravanne was there, in her tower, and she witnessed the abuses committed upon her people, and upon her lord. Then the Rodim's head chieftain ravished Ceravanne in Belorian's bedchamber.

Because of the atrocities, the peaceful peoples of Indallian gathered together and slaughtered the armies of the Rodim without mercy, then fell upon the villages of their women without restraint and murdered their children, removing the Rodim from the face of the land.

Many went to the Swallow, asking her to have mercy before the final slaughter of the Rodim, hoping to spare some remnant of the race.

But Ceravanne turned away so that not one child remained.

And when the Rodim were all dead, the Swallow put a single red rose upon the grave of Belorian, and another upon the grave of the chieftain of the Rodim, to signify that she forgave him and his people, though she had not spared them. Then she proclaimed a year of mourning for the Rodim who lay dead, and for those who were forced to kill them.

None who beheld her could miss the horror on her face, nor deny her torment. And hours later the Swallow disappeared, and her crystal scepter was found in the mud of her courtyard. Many thought she had chosen to die rather than live without Belorian; while others imagined that she was so horrified by the genocide that was done in her behalf that she turned her back on mankind forever; but her friends swore that she would return when her grief had run its course, and so the legends said that someday she would come back to lead the Accord.

"Four hundred and eighty years ago the Swallow left rich Indallian," Gallen intoned. "And still her heart knows no peace. Yet in songs and legends, people here remember the days of the Accord."

Maggie looked toward the door that led to the tower, understanding why Ceravanne sought refuge in silence. Ceravanne had said earlier that her love, Belorian, was fresh on her mind, and Maggie felt the pain of knowing that she was surely losing Gallen to the Inhuman, just as Ceravanne had lost Belorian to the Rodim.

Gallen lay beside Maggie and stared into the fire, unable to sleep for a long time. Sometimes, he thought he could hear snatches of whispers, and he saw brief visions, tatters of memories that belonged to other people. But the song of the Inhuman was weak tonight, possibly because of the storm. Even as this thought struck Gallen, he heard the distant rumble of thunder, confirming his suppositions.

He got up quietly so as not to rouse Maggie, and he put some twigs on the fire.

"How many lives you recall?" Tallea whispered, letting the sound of her voice fill the night.

"Just the seven," Gallen answered. Then to fill up the silence that followed, he said, "I wonder how many more the Inhuman has in store for me."

"A hundred lives to be remembered," Tallea said. "You fortunate, remember them slowly, over days. Should be easy."

"Yes." Gallen smiled wanly. "I'm fortunate." A cold shiver of fright wriggled down his backbone. He went to his pack, dug around for a moment, then pulled out a thin film of translucent material and applied it to his face.

His face suddenly shone like blue starlight as he put on the mask of Fale, and he stood for a moment, his black robes draped over him, weapons bristling on his back and thighs. He recalled how the witnesses at his trial back home had imagined he was a sidhe when thus garbed, a magical being with malevolent intent, and now Gallen could indeed feel it. With his face gleaming in the dark like a ghost, there was little human left in him. He looked like a thing.

Gallen stood at the door, as if he would walk out into the night rain, and for a moment he wanted to do that, just walk away into the dark and the cleansing rain that was sweeping down in misty sheets.

Instead he went to a back corridor of the great hall. The floors were thick with dust and moss, old leaves, and the husks of pine nuts carried in by squirrels.

He stood for a moment, testing the air to see whether the Inhuman would try to send him more memories. But there was nothing. It seemed that for the time being, he was free.

Using his mantle's night vision, Gallen negotiated the passageways until he found some stairs curving up the wall of a tower. Muddy footprints showed that Ceravanne had been here recently, and though Gallen mistrusted her, he felt drawn to her.

He climbed the winding stairs for twenty meters, till he found a room that opened at the top. There, several arching windows were still intact; weathered stones surrounded casements that had long ago rotted into dust. Ceravanne stood beside one such window. Ivy grew in dust on the floor, so that she stood as if in a meadow, surrounded by foliage, staring out into the rain. Her back was to him, and she shivered.

Gallen went to her, stood for a moment. He could feel the heat of her body near his, and he inhaled her clean scent. He knew that it was only pheromones that drew him so vigorously, yet he found himself wishing to hold her, to comfort her.

"I hoped you would come," she said, and she turned. With the light amplification provided by his mantle, he could see that she'd been crying, and she stared into his face, at the mask, and he wondered what she saw. A blue glowing phantom, with dark holes for eyes.

She took his hands, held them lightly, and studied his face. She was breathing heavily, and she said, "That song—I have to ask—from whom did you learn it?"

"From a minstrel named Tam, who lived here ages ago," Gallen answered.

"But this man, did he remember me? He didn't know the Swallow in person?"

"You were but newly gone when he composed the song," Gallen said.

"And Belorian? Did he know Belorian?" Her voice was nearly hysterical, as if she hoped for some word of her long-dead lover.

"No," Gallen whispered. "He never knew Belorian."

Ceravanne gasped and began weeping, fell against Gallen's chest. "Ah, I thought he had. I thought you remembered his face." Then she sobbed from the core of her soul, and Gallen clumsily put his arms around her, tried to ease her pain.

"So many tears, for one long dead," Gallen whispered.

Ceravanne looked up, stroked his chin. "You look much like him," she said. "When we first met, I kissed you inappropriately. I guess I wanted you to love me. Being near you has been hard. Forgive me if I've offended you with my affection."

Gallen licked his lips, stepped back. He'd been aware of Ceravanne, of her graceful movements, of the longing glances she sometimes gave him. He'd imagined that it was all a ploy, a sly attempt to manipulate him. And the Inhuman, with its clever tongue, whispered that this was true—another cruel attempt by the Tharrin to ensnare him. Gallen had never dreamed that Ceravanne could really have felt anything for him, and now he saw that he was but a shadow to her.

"I'm sorry." He found himself unaccountably apologizing. "I didn't know."

She looked at him oddly, as if wondering if he told the truth. "Of course you couldn't have known." She turned away. "What of Maggie? Have your feelings for her changed?"

"Today, I learned of the most marvelous people, far to the south. The Yakrists, they are called, and they care for others more than they care for themselves. They love one another perfectly, and as I lived the life of a Yakrist, I came to understand how weak and imperfect my love for Maggie has been."

"So your feelings for her *are* changed?"

"I will try to be more . . . understanding of her needs," Gallen said. "Perhaps if I were Inhuman, I would love her more perfectly."

Ceravanne nodded, obviously distraught, and Gallen realized that she had hoped he would answer differently, that he would say he was abandoning Maggie.

"And you believe that by enslaving others, the Inhuman is showing that kind of great love?"

"Ceravanne," Gallen whispered. "I think there is something you should know. The Inhuman is not completely wrong, here. It only wants us to understand one another, to help one another."

There was a cruel laughing, something that Gallen could almost not imagine hearing from Ceravanne's throat. "Don't tell me that," she whispered fiercely. "I've seen what the Dronon are up to. They care nothing for us, nothing for each other. They love only their Golden Queen, and they serve her ruthlessly."

"And yet they want peace," Gallen said. "They want us to unite with them, and they're offering . . . so much in return."

"What are they offering?"

"Life. Rebirth," Gallen said. "They're going to open restrictions on giving rebirth to nonhumans. And anyone can be reborn into the body of their choice, experience life as they desire.

"And peace!" Gallen continued. "In the past, the people of Babel have been slaughtered in ruthless wars, with everyone trying to conquer their neighbors. But among the hosts of the Inhuman, everyone will live fuller lives. I know what it is to be a Yakrist, and now that I know them, I could never harm one of them. That is what the Inhuman offers, a knowledge of our own brotherhood. And the Dronon will take care of the people of Babel."

"Gallen," Ceravanne said, looking at him as if he were mad, and a knife of fear stabbed him, for Gallen wondered if he was mad. "The Dronon don't care for us," she said reasonably. "You can't imagine that they do. When their own infants are sick or crippled, they grind them up to fertilize their fields. You're trying to make sense, but the Dronon are using your own compassion against you. And it's damned unfair of them to ask you to be compassionate, when they lack that capacity themselves. They don't want to free us from our wars and infighting, they want to create nations of slaves with them as our masters. All of the technologies they offer to benefit mankind are technologies we've already developed. If they succeed in taking over, just watch them. They'll give rebirth only to those who serve them best. And they want you to feel good about it."

Gallen listened to her words carefully, tried to hold on to them, but somehow their meaning evaded him. I used to think like she does, Gallen realized. But when? It seemed to him that his fears of the Dronon had stemmed from a dream—a long time ago. Something about Maggie, wearing a Guide, while trapped in a Dronon fortress. But just at the moment, he couldn't recall. Instead, a more pressing argument came to mind. "You are no more human than a Dronon is," Gallen said, brightening. "Why should you rule us?"

"Because humans created me for that purpose," Ceravanne countered. "And I crave to serve them. But unlike the Dronon, I never force my rule on anyone. If humans desire to elect a human leader, that is their option. But the Dronon will not let you serve as equals. They will never accept human leaders."

There was a long pause, and Gallen listened to her words but could not understand how any sane person could arrive at her conclusion. He finally managed, "The Dronon will accept *us*. Maggie and I, we are the leaders of the Sixth Swarm. We could take our rightful place, show them how to live together with us in harmony!"

"But humans don't want to live with *them!*" Ceravanne said.

"Agreed, most of them don't," Gallen whispered, and there

was an unusual intensity in his voice. He felt almost as if his mouth moved of its own accord, and he merely listened to the words it said. "But what of the people of Babel? They are not humans. Can't you see how your policies afflict them? They have no sense of purpose, so few social bonds across tribes. They have no law, no access to technology. You created them, then abandoned them. They need what humans and the Dronon have!"

"Gallen, I was not formed to be a judge of the peoples of Babel. I *can't* take care of them, any more than the Dronon could. I don't understand all of their needs, all of their hopes. I don't even force my judgments on humans.

"But let me ask you this, Gallen. Is it our obligation to govern other peoples, or to find a purpose in life for them, or to be their friends?" Ceravanne asked, and her voice was desperate. "You are human, from a world not unlike Tremonthin: who ever tried to give you a purpose in life? Who ever protected you? Can't you see—all of these things that you say the humans owe the people of Babel, in your own country, you don't even force them on your own children. It would be wicked to do so. If these people in Babel want law, then they have to figure out how to create and enforce their own laws. They weren't designed to live by human standards, and I can't take the right to govern themselves away from them."

"But you deny them life. . . ." Gallen objected, angry that she would not or could not see his point.

"And we deny most of our own people more than one life," Ceravanne said. "Even the best of us often only get our lives extended by a few decades."

"But the humans of Tremonthin created these people," Gallen objected. "You owe them!"

"Since we created them, doesn't it stand to reason that they owe us for the blessing of life?" Ceravanne countered. "Think of it. Do we owe them more than we owe our own children? Even for our own children, we make no guarantees. We make no promises of love or acceptance or wealth. No society can promise all of these things to its individuals. Happiness comes as a reward for a life well lived. It cannot be an entitlement."

."But . . ."

"There are no buts," Ceravanne said. "Gallen, all of your thoughts, all of those confused feelings, those are just the Inhuman talking. Those notions don't make any sense when you look at them closely. But the Dronon want you to believe them. The Dronon want you to believe that their Golden Queen will take care of us. But you've seen what the Dronon offer on other worlds. They want to feed off us, as parasites. Gallen, the Dronon showed you the lives of a few folks. They told you a story, providing the sights, the smells, the emotions. They told you a lie.

"But more importantly, I want you to realize that you are spouting dangerous dogma that doesn't necessarily follow from the information you've been given. Think about it, and you'll know I'm right. The Dronon are teaching you on a subconscious level, altering your thought patterns. The memories they feed you only serve to cover the deeper alterations, and to make you think that you changed your mind on your own."

Gallen was stunned. She had all the answers, all waiting in her hand like needles to prod him with. It seemed obvious that she had argued against the Inhuman before. He felt confused, and a buzzing sounded in his ears, sounded so loudly that he had a hard time thinking. He wanted to speak against her, but he could not think what to say next. The room seemed to be spinning, and Gallen found himself wanting to take Ceravanne by the throat, shake some sense into her. For the moment he seemed certain of only one thing: she was his enemy.

He grabbed her neck and pushed her against the wall. "Liar! Deceitful little vixen!" he said, and the room spun mightily so that he wondered if he could even stand. In his mind, her presence registered only as some hateful creature, a woman with long skeletal hands, groping for him.

Ceravanne hit the stone wall and slid down, her mouth open as if she would cry out, her eyes wide with fear, and Gallen knew that if she spoke again, he would have to silence her. Lightning struck outside—once, twice, a third time.

But the Tharrin only sat heavily in the ivy leaves. For a long moment, she only breathed, and Gallen's anger began to pass.

The room quit spinning, and Gallen's mantle whispered, Seek shelter below, next to Maggie, quickly! And suddenly Gallen knew that the Inhuman had been communicating with him, trying to download its arguments directly into his mind.

Gallen stood gazing down at Ceravanne. "Don't hurt me," she pleaded, and she folded her arms, sat gazing up at him, a helpless child.

Gallen found that his sword had unaccountably appeared in his hand. Some time in the past minute, he had drawn it. And he'd been prepared to kill her, without thinking.

He shoved it back into his scabbard, and he wanted to run then, wanted to rush down the stairs and hide in the woods for what he'd almost done. He felt terribly embarrassed.

"Forgive me," he whispered, white shock registering in his brain only as numbness. "The Inhuman can be . . . subtle."

"You're forgiven," Ceravanne said with a tiny nod. She reached up her thin hand, so that he could help her up.

He took it, pulled her to a standing position. His heart was hammering with fear, and something else. . . . The air in the room was moist and closed, and Ceravanne's scent was thick. She was trembling, frightened, and he wanted to ease her mind. So he kissed her hand, looking into her eyes. She was small and pale, like a porcelain figure. Her hand, when he kissed it, tasted sweet. He'd almost forgotten how sweet the taste of a Tharrin could be.

Ceravanne reached up, and she was shaking, leaning against him. Her whole body trembled. She gazed deeply into his eyes. "You see," she whispered desperately, "that I was right when I told you that I needed your heart. If you do not give it to me, the Inhuman will take it. Gallen, give me your heart!"

She kissed his chin experimentally, then brushed her lips against his. A burning passion rose in him, and Gallen kissed her full on the lips, pulling her close. She drew tight against him, her flesh folding into his like a lover's, her arms embracing him. All thought retreated, and for one moment, there was only that passionate kiss blossoming like a field of wild poppies in his mind. Every nerve in his body tingled, her touch was lightning, and she groaned, tried to pull him to the floor there among the ivy.

Desperately, he pushed her away. "No!" Gallen cried. "I am married to Maggie!"

And he fled across the room from her, stood by the doorway. Ceravanne was on her knees now, breathing heavily, gazing at him, stunned. "No man has ever rejected me," she said, hurt in her voice.

He turned for the door, and she said, "If it is Maggie you want, then be faithful to her, Gallen—remain as faithful to her in Moree as you have been tonight."

Gallen hurried down the stairway, almost running. When he reached the bottom he found the fire still going. Tallea was hunched over it, putting in some more dry dung. Everyone else had gone to sleep, but Gallen stayed awake for the rest of the night while the others rested. He stared off into the rain, letting the full powers of his mantle keep watch while he remained on guard duty.

And through the night, ghosts came, the memories of people long dead, and they took him on journeys he could not sleep through and could not hope to escape. He felt like a child on a sandy beach, with water rushing in upon him with tremendous force, and with each crashing wave, the sand beneath him would shift, so that he felt as if something essential were being dragged away.

It did not matter where he stood in that little room. It did not matter that his mantle tried to block the signals. The Inhuman was overpowering him moment by moment, so that sometimes while the others slept, Gallen sobbed or cried out softly.

Long before morning, Gallen woke the others, and they headed south.

Twenty-two

By dawn the companions were on the road again, and Tallea felt . . . decent for the first time in three days. She was able to sit with little pain, and in fact could feel herself mending, and to her it seemed miraculous. As a Caldurian, she tended to heal fast anyway, but the Immortal's blood had worked wonders on her wounds.

More importantly, the support that these people had given her was working wonders on her spirit. A year earlier, when Ceravanne's other self had come to Babel, Tallea had hired on with her band, had led them into the wilderness of Moree, and there she lost them to the Tekkar. At the time Ceravanne had not announced herself as the Swallow. Indeed, Tallea had only thought her to be a beautiful woman, traveling as a companion to the valiant swordsmen who sought to destroy the Inhuman.

But one night, when they had neared Moree, the Tekkar ambushed their small band. Many good men died before their swords cleared their scabbards. Tallea herself had been sorely wounded and left among the dead. And Ceravanne, beautiful Ceravanne had been carried away into Moree where the Tekkar would do unspeakable things to her.

For a year Tallea had been serving on ships, waiting for a new band to make its way into Moree. And this time, she vowed, they would slay the Inhuman. For a year she had suffered alone on the ships, refusing to bind herself to anyone. It was an untenable situation for a Caldurian, and only her training, her devotion to the ways of the Roamers, had helped her survive.

Yet now, as they rode in the oversized wagon through a gray dawn, she could not help but feel concerned. It seemed that some cosmic balance was being maintained. Minute by minute, her pains decreased, and she blossomed to greater health.

Minute by minute, Gallen was crumbling, falling in on himself like an old house toppling under its own weight.

He hadn't slept all night, and during the morning he just sat, huddled in the driver's seat of the wagon, his mouth slack as he stared into nothingness. The travelbeast was guiding the wagon more than Gallen was.

Orick whispered to Maggie about it. "There is a horror on Gallen's face that I've never seen before. Gallen has always been a feisty lad—nothing like this."

And so the travelbeast ran on, its head rising and falling as it drew the wagon along the bank of a winding muddy river. Ceravanne took control of the wagon for a while, and Maggie took Gallen and cradled his head against her breast tenderly, and he stared out the back of the wagon, at the trees falling behind.

Gallen muttered, "Eighteen . . . eighteen. My defenses are crumbling."

Maggie said that her own mantle whispered insistently that it was doing all it could to block the Inhuman's transmissions. And when Maggie asked Gallen to tell her about this latest life he had lived, he said nothing for many minutes.

"God, I wish I were home," Maggie whispered in his ear. "I wish we both were home, that we'd never come. This trip is changing us, destroying you."

"So the journey changes us," Gallen said wearily, surprising Tallea by responding at all. "You can't walk from your house without your hairs growing whiter. You can't walk down to the gate without taking a risk. And from the death of the old, the new is born."

"This isn't a walk to the gate," Maggie said. "Ever since you went to the teaching machines on Fale, you've lost some of yourself, some of your accent. Now, you hardly sound as if you're from Tihrglas at all."

Gallen said no more for a long time, and Ceravanne, who was sitting up front, exchanged worried glances with Maggie.

One of the rear wheels began squeaking a bit, and Tallea climbed up, ignoring the stabbing pains in her side, got the swabbing rod out of the grease, and daubed each wheel.

No one spoke for a long time. They passed through several small villages in the space of a few hours, and Fenorah stopped at the largest to grain the travelbeast and to purchase salt, food, leather for shoes, and a number of small items that they had not had a chance to carry.

All during that stop, Gallen went and stood leaning against a hitching post, and the townsfolk took great pains to avoid him. Even a pair of yellow dogs that were running together crossed to the far side of the street.

As Fenorah began loading the wagon in preparation to leave, he glanced at Gallen and mumbled, "Only twenty demons in him, and he's ready to crumble. If an apple spoiled in our food barrel, would we not throw it out?"

"What you saying?" Tallea asked.

Fenorah nodded toward Gallen. "I'm worried. He's a danger to us now—perhaps more dangerous than he knows. If we left him, I do not think he'd notice."

And Tallea realized that Fenorah truly was entertaining thoughts of leaving Gallen behind. Sometimes, it seemed that people who were not of the Caldur were so unaware of how the tenuous threads of friendship could bind people together, lend them support. To her, those feelings were almost a visible thing, they were so strongly felt.

"Now he needs us most," she said, struggling into a more comfortable position. "Servants of Inhuman want you reject him, so he turn to them for companionship."

Orick pricked his ears forward and stood still for a moment.

"You're right!" Orick shouted in a voice that echoed from the buildings, and he got up from the bed of the wagon and stood clumsily with his two front feet on the backboard. "This is no time to turn our backs on him."

He jumped from the wagon, ran to Gallen's side, and stood, wrapping his paws around Gallen's shoulders. By applying his weight, he pushed Gallen to the ground. "I've had enough from you!" Orick said, putting one great paw on Gallen's chest. "You spirits, I adjure you to come out of this man, in the name of the Father, the Son, and the Holy Ghost. Amen!"

Gallen grunted, gave half a laugh, and his eyes suddenly cleared, as if he'd wakened. "Orick, I wish it were that simple!"

"Och, well, it was worth a try," Orick growled, looking from side to side as if for another answer. "Look, Gallen, my friend, you remember your Bible: and if Satan can appear as an angel, then it's no great feat for the Dronon to disguise themselves as our friends. But I tell you, Gallen, even if you had a head made of straw and a belly full of whiskey, I'd expect you to know better! When the Dronon came to Clere, they didn't pass out bags of gold and welcome us to paradise. They chewed off John Mahoney's head, and shot Father Heany, turning our priest into a puddle. And on Fale, they didn't come ask Maggie if she'd like to be their slave. They put a Guide on her and dragged her off—me fighting them tooth and claw. You know better than to trust a word they say!"

"Get off me," Gallen choked, "I can't breathe!"

"I'll not get off you until you start making sense!" Orick growled, and he put both front paws on Gallen and bounced his weight on him experimentally, as if to prove the point. "I don't care whose memories are rolling around in your head, Gallen. Your own memories are in there, too. You've got to take control of yourself!"

Gallen stared up at Orick, and there was a bleakness to his countenance, a look of utter desolation, and then a smile crossed his face, and he began laughing. It was not a happy laugh, though it held a tone of relief. "Well said, my dearest friend. I hereby take control of myself."

"Good," Orick grumbled, "'cause I'd hate to have to crush

you." He backed off Gallen's chest, sniffed the air. Then reached down and nipped at Gallen's mask, pulling it halfway off. "And take off that ugly mask."

Gallen crumpled the blue mask, put it in a pocket of his robes. Then he rolled over, began climbing to his knees. Orick bit the collar of his robe and began dragging him forward playfully, growling, "Come on, into the wagon with you." By now, a dozen locals began gathering to watch the spectacle, creeping out of shops, openly asking one another what was going on, and for their benefit Orick said loudly, "We'll have no more public displays of drunkenness, young man!"

Orick climbed up to the wagon, and in moments they were off.

Gallen looked to be himself, smiling around at his friends, and he put his arms around Orick gratefully, and for the moment, Tallea knew that they had him back.

When they passed out of town, beneath the shade of chestnut trees that lined the road, Gallen looked up at Ceravanne. "You told me once that you could help me fight this. I need your help."

Ceravanne, who had been sitting up front to drive, turned back around, pulled the reins and brought the travelbeast to a halt, then set the brake. "Lean your head into Maggie's lap, and stare into her face."

Gallen lay back, so that his long golden hair spread about Maggie's lap, and he gazed up into Maggie's face. Ceravanne climbed down beside them, and the back of the wagon bed was suddenly crowded, but Tallea herself did not mind the close bodies. It reminded her of her childhood in the crèche at Wind Mountain, sleeping with her sisters among the pile of blankets in their dormitory.

"Maggie is the woman you love," Ceravanne said softly, and only the gentle hiss of the wind through the trees competed with her voice. "You have loved her since you were children, and you gave your heart to her long ago. Look into her eyes and concentrate, try to recall every detail of her face, and remember that she is the one you have chosen to give yourself to. . . ." She hesitated, and Gallen stared into Maggie's face, his mouth working as he silently spoke to himself. Cool clouds were scudding overhead, and the wind played delicately in Maggie's hair. Ceravanne's voice was fragile, dreamy. "Maggie is the one you've loved forever. Tell this to yourself, over and over. A hundred times is not enough. A thousand times is just the beginning. A hundred thousand times, you must repeat this, though it take the next year of your life."

Gallen stared up at Maggie for a long time, and she held his face. The sun shone through the clouds on him, and Tallea could see on his nose the pale remnants of freckles that might have been more pronounced in childhood. He had a strong jaw, and clear blue eyes, and for a few moments, all the pain and worry seemed to leach away. Maggie was holding Gallen's chin, stroking it, and he was gazing up into Maggie's eyes. So Gallen did not notice when Ceravanne reached down and brushed his lips with the back of her forefinger.

Tallea had heard much about how the touch of a Tharrin could calm a person. Indeed, Gallen licked the back of Ceravanne's finger, sensually, kissed it, thinking it was Maggie's caress.

Then Ceravanne pulled her finger away gently, took Maggie's hand and moved her forefinger into the same position, and he kissed it. Suddenly his eyes became clear, focused, and he stared at Maggie, unblinking, for several moments, then fell asleep.

He rested for a long time in Maggie's lap, and Maggie said, "What did you do to him? Put him to sleep?"

Ceravanne shook her head. "No. He has hardly slept in three days. I think that we just eased his mind enough so that fatigue finally took him."

"But what did you do?"

Ceravanne said softly to Maggie, "Every woman's touch can have a power over man, but a Tharrin's touch is very strong. There are . . . agents, pheromones in my skin that he craves, that can cause him to bond to me. I exude them at all times, but I do so more when I am afraid. It's a defense mechanism that your ancestors gave me. He tasted those pheromones, but it was your face he was watching. He will be more strongly bonded to you now."

"I envy you that power," Maggie whispered.

Ceravanne shrugged. "Don't envy me. I think that it is a power that causes as much harm as good. It has saved me at times, but it ill serves the men who throw their lives away in my defense. I envy you his love, for it *is* you that he loves above all others." She watched Gallen sleep for a bit, and whispered, "He will hunger for your presence as never before, and you must stay close to him. Still, the draw of the Inhuman is strong. He may need more treatments before this is over."

She climbed out of the wagon bed, got back up front into the driver's seat again, and eased the wagon out slowly.

"I'm glad he's resting," Orick said, watching Gallen. "I know that if Gallen were thinking straight, he'd never doubt us." Orick was lying on his stomach, resting his nose under his paws, watching Gallen thoughtfully with his sad brown eyes, like some great dog studying its injured master. The sight of it warmed Tallea's heart, for she valued faithfulness above all traits, and instinctively she knew that Orick would never betray Gallen or be unsteady. Orick looked right at Tallea and said softly, "Thank you for reminding me how to be his friend."

The way that they were sitting, his rump was near her hand, and she patted his rear paw. In response, he began licking her ankle with his broad tongue, and she found this show of affection . . . curiously sensual.

For a moment she looked around at these strange companions—to strong Fenorah up ahead of the wagon, running in his rolling, lumbering gait; Ceravanne at the wagon's reins; Maggie and Gallen, resting together with eyes closed; while faithful Orick lay at Tallea's feet.

It seemed remarkable to her how these people had a way of weaving themselves into her heart, with a song, a sigh, a touch.

Tallea's Caldurian instincts were having their way with her. Perhaps it was only because she had denied bonding with someone for so long. Perhaps she would have chosen to serve these people anyway. But she felt a sharp need to protect them.

The wagon left the wide valley and began heading up a long road again, into some lonely hills where the trees grew thick and wild. It was a likely place to find Derrits or Sprees, or some other wild animal.

Tallea pulled her sword from its scabbard, a blade heavy near the guard for parrying, and deceptively long and thin, for thrusting. The sunlight gleamed on its edges, and the blade was in fair condition, but over the past few days Tallea hadn't felt well enough to take proper care of it. It had been nicked and blunted in the battle at sea, and she'd managed only a cursory cleaning the day before.

So as the wagon rolled ever closer to Moree, she took her stone from its pouch tied at her back, and began grinding out the nicks, honing the blade to razor sharpness, buffing off the rust, and she considered. If they were going to Moree, she'd need a bow and some arrows.

The travelbeast was running steadily through the brisk air, over the rolling hills. At the rate they were moving, they'd reach High Home by nightfall. She hoped to buy some weapons there.

Twenty-three

In the early afternoon Zell'a Cree had reached the mountains a few kilometers north of High Home when he limped to the junction to the Old King's Road.

He'd killed two stolen horses to get here, and he'd run without much sleep for most of the past two nights. His right boot was held together with a strip of cloth torn from his tunic.

But his work was paying off. South of Battic he had met up with five servants of the Inhuman who had given him a Word. And more importantly, last night he'd spotted a scout, flying high beneath the clouds. With a gesture he had pulled it to earth and asked it to carry a message south, warning the Inhuman that a Lord Protector was coming.

With that done, Zell'a Cree had felt a great sense of relief. The scout flew south, and it would deliver its warning long before Gallen's wagon got to Moree. Still Zell'a Cree could not rest. He wanted to capture this band himself.

Marbee Road met the Old King's Road at the mouth of a small valley where an old wooden bridge crossed the river, its boards whitened by the summer sun. Zell'a Cree stood for some time, tasting the scent of the air. There was no stench of travelbeast, no perfume of the Tharrin or taste of the others, but it was hard to tell for certain. An orchard had been planted here many years ago—Zell'a Cree recalled it from the memories of Anote Brell, a soldier who'd died six decades past—and still there were many apple trees growing on both sides of the road. The smell of the pungent, fallen apples filled the air, so much so that Zell'a Cree could smell little else.

Still, after a bit, he felt sure that the wagon had not passed. More good news. If the Tharrin's company had not passed, he had managed to stay ahead of them.

He hurried along the road south to High Home, and soon began climbing the long hills. He was well up into the mountains by now, and the air was growing thinner, too thin for a Tosken to breathe comfortably.

Yet Zell'a Cree managed the climb until he reached the crown of the mountain and stood in the small hamlet. Iron ore was mined from ridges above town, so that on the upper slopes there were red holes gouged in the earth, and the miners had tunneled deep into the hills. Down below town, sheep farmers grazed their herds on the green slopes.

The homes here in town were not your standard northern fare. They were built of heavy stone, mudded over on the outside with a white plaster the color of bones, topped with tile roofs that were an ash-gray. The houses kept cool in the hot summers when the wind blew out of the desert, but in the winters when the snow flew, the folks hereabout would have to fasten tapestries to their walls and stuff straw behind them to provide insulation against the cold.

In the summer, frequent cool winds blew down from the mountain slopes so that High Home had a reputation among desert folk as something of a mountain resort with "healthy air," a place where the rich could escape the blistering summer months.

But now it was fall, cool but not unpleasantly so, though the three fine inns in town were fairly deserted, as were the streets. In the summer, the streets would have been filled with merchants out to sell their wares, but now there were only a few shops open, their doors thrown wide in invitation to potential customers.

Zell'a Cree asked around until he found a bootmaker who was willing to throw together something cheap and durable.

In the bootmaker's shop, Zell'a Cree put his foot on the thick leather for the soles and let the old man scratch his cutting marks, then they chose something more supple for the uppers. In moments the old man had cut the leather and begun sewing, when Zell'a Cree heard the rumble of hooves and the clattering of wheels.

He glanced out the window of the shop toward the wide avenue, and his heart skipped a beat.

Sure enough, Gallen's wagon rolled into town, the huge travelbeast frothing at the mouth from its exertions, one lone giant in the lead, the chest and armpits of his tunic stained with sweat.

The suns were setting, and the Tharrin's company cast long shadows over the cobblestone streets. The white stone buildings gleamed intensely in the sunlight, and Zell'a Cree ducked behind his doorpost and listened.

"The travelbeast needs grain and rest," the giant told the others, walking up to set the wagon's brakes. "He's nearly done in for the night, and won't be able to carry you much farther along these mountain roads. We might as well eat here—the inns are highly renowned."

"Thank you," the Tharrin said, as the giant took her gently by the waist and set her down from the wagon. "I don't know how we can repay your generosity."

"Your safety is repayment enough," the giant said, and Zell'a Cree nearly laughed. The others were climbing down from the wagon now, and Gallen O'Day stretched sinuously, reaching for the sky.

Zell'a Cree put his back to the doorpost, so that none in the company would have even the slimmest chance of spotting his silhouette in the doorway.

Darkness, a lonely town, and Gallen unaware. And in my pouch, two copies of the Word. Zell'a Cree could not quite believe his good fortune.

And yet, and yet he was worried. He felt alone with his troubles. New converts often rejoiced at the sense of fullness that communion with the Inhuman gave them, the sense of boundless knowledge, the feeling of buoyancy, as if they were children who had been lifted up and were looking at the world from the height of tall shoulders. But in time, that sensation wore thin. After years of not hearing from the Inhuman, one sometimes felt lost, cast adrift. It was said that some great leaders were in constant communion—the Harvester, certainly, and the commanders of the armies and navies to a lesser extent. But not Zell'a Cree. Not once over the long years since his conversion had he heard the sweet voice of the Inhuman. And at this moment, he wished that he could be certain of the correct course—to let these people proceed to Moree, where the Inhuman could arrange a more appropriate reception, or to kill Gallen now and seek to convert the others.

He stood for several long minutes, pondering his choices, then peeked out again. The company had gone inside, with the exception of the giant, who was busy unharnessing the travel-beast.

Zell'a Cree crept back to the bootmaker's bench. "Just sew up the right boot for now," he said softly. "I'm in a hurry."

The bootmaker glanced up at him in surprise and grunted, "Don't think I can have it done by dark, and I close soon."

"In the morning, then," Zell'a Cree said. He checked out the door. The giant was leading the travelbeast away to the stables down behind the inn. The suns were falling rapidly, and in the cool evening air, some crickets had begun chirping. A few people scurried along the streets, heading home. Even here, the Inhuman's agents were known to hunt at night.

Zell'a Cree pulled up the hood of his cloak, covering his face, and hurried across the shadowed avenue to the wall of the inn. From its shade, he could see the wooden stables in back, down a small hill. The giant had reached the stables, and he opened the broad doors, took the beast inside.

Zell'a Cree knew that he had to get Gallen alone, had to strip Ceravanne of her protectors. The giant himself was a formidable adversary. The Toskens were smaller in stature than the Im giants, and were not so strong, though they could endure greater hardships. And as a Tosken, Zell'a Cree knew no fear.

He ran down to the stable, slipped into the door. His eyes did not need to adjust to the dark. He saw the giant plainly enough, stooping over a feed bin, dumping in a bag of grain. The travelbeast was already stabled, nuzzling the feed.

The Im heard Zell'a Cree's approach, turned his head partway. "May I help you with your beast, sir?" Zell'a Cree asked, taking the role of stablehand, hoping that the giant would not recognize him. "Does it need water, or a comb?"

"Aye, it will take a couple of water buckets," the giant said, not bothering to look back, dumping the whole sack of grain into the bin.

"Good enough, sir," Zell'a Cree said, only a step behind.

Zell'a Cree grasped the haft of his sword, pulled it free, and plunged the blade deep into the giant's back, just beneath his rib cage. He'd hoped to hit a kidney, send the giant into deadly shock, but the Im shouted and spun, hitting Zell'a Cree in the head with the bucket.

There was a moment of pain, and horses began neighing in fright, kicking at the doors to their stalls, and Zell'a Cree found himself struggling up from the stable floor to his knees. The giant had taken a step to the middle of the room, and he pulled the sword from his back, stood gazing stupidly at the blade.

Zell'a Cree jumped up, rushed at him, but the giant bellowed loudly and took a step back. Zell'a Cree tried to pull the sword from the giant's hand, and for one brief moment they struggled together, both of them fighting for the blade.

The short sword twisted from Zell'a Cree's grip, and the giant made a weak stab. Zell'a Cree leapt backward as the sword slashed at his midriff.

The giant stood, panting as if from long exertion, holding the sword. He sagged to his knees after a minute, dropped the blade, then fell facedown into the straw.

The horses were all neighing frantically now at the smell of blood, and Zell'a Cree knew that the noise would draw attention. He had hoped to commit a nice quiet murder.

Instead, he grabbed the short sword, stabbed the giant in the back of the neck to sever his spinal cord, then rushed to the rear door of the stables and stood panting, trying to get some air.

He wondered whether anyone had heard the giant's bellowing. He did not know if he should run now or set a trap for Gallen and the others.

Gallen had settled into his seat at the inn and ordered dinner. The place had few patrons, and they were all sitting up in front of a little puppeteer's theater, where marvelously decorated puppets used to play a tale about a greedy king who was being robbed by some highwaymen. Gallen could not hear all of the dialogue, but two of the highwaymen were speaking aside to one another, and it sounded as if they were the king's own wife and daughter, robbing the man in the hopes of curing him of his greed.

Gallen had just asked his mantle to amplify the sounds of the room, hoping to hear the puppeteers, when he heard Fenorah cry out.

He jumped from his seat, seeing the surprised faces of Maggie and the others. He had been trying so hard for the past few days to seem normal that he did not want to cause them alarm. "Trouble!" Gallen said, then he went tearing out a back door, where two cooks stood looking toward the stable.

"I'm sure I heard yelling, back here!" one said, though neither seemed inclined to go see who had screamed.

Drawing his sword free from its scabbard, Gallen raced down to the stable, pulled the door open, and let his mantle magnify the light, show him the scene.

Fenorah lay in the straw, facedown. Gallen rushed to him, found blood flowing all down the back of his neck, soaking into his tunic. Gallen could see no sign that he was breathing, and for a brief moment, stinging tears came to Gallen's eyes. The giant had never harmed anyone, had sought to do only good. He'd shared his food, given of his time and wealth.

"Goodbye, my friend. The wheel turns without you for a

while," Gallen whispered into his ears, and realized that he had subconsciously chosen to voice a death farewell common to the people of Babel.

He bit his lip, tried to calm himself. He was afraid, for he could feel the weight of years on him. He felt that he was struggling to control the voices inside him—strong Amvik of the Immatar, a scholar and physician, wanted Gallen to check Fenorah more thoroughly for signs of life. "Turn him over. Try to revive him," the doctor warned, but Gallen knew it was no use. Even if he managed to revive the giant for a few moments, he had lost far too much blood.

Gallen noticed that someone had stepped over the body, making bloody footprints in the straw, and had rushed out a back door, leaving it open.

The horses and the travelbeast were standing quietly in their stalls, looking out. Gallen glanced upward to the haylofts and empty stalls where tack and fodder were stored. He listened closely for any sound of the murderer, then took one last look at Fenorah.

The Inhuman has done this, a voice whispered at the back of Gallen's mind.

Gallen went to look out the rear door with a heavy heart. Suddenly he heard movement to his side, and his mantle warned him to duck. Gallen spun in time to see Zell'a Cree exploding out of a stall where hay had been piled high. The stocky man had been hiding under the hay, and he threw some at Gallen's face.

Gallen almost did not see the blade of Zell'a Cree's sword, arcing through the flying straw, but fortunately he had his own blade up high enough to parry the blow.

Zell'a Cree's sword hit Gallen's with such force that Gallen barely held on. The blow knocked Gallen back a pace, and Gallen spun away from Zell'a Cree's charge, feigning a loss of balance as if he'd fallen, then he whirled as he fell and thrust his own blade up into Zell'a Cree's chest, a brief, biting kiss that left the tip of Gallen's sword bloodied.

Gallen rolled to his feet and sat, hunched low, his sword weaving slowly before Zell'a Cree's eyes.

Zell'a Cree spotted the well-bloodied sword, and seemed to react more to it than he had to the touch of the steel. His free hand rose up to his chest, and his eyes grew wide in surprise at the severity of the wound.

"Damn your hide for that! I'll split your belly and strangle you with your own guts!" he cried, and he kicked a bucket at Gallen.

Gallen dodged it easily, and waited en garde. "Come, then," Gallen hissed, "and find out why I'm a Lord Protector!"

Zell'a Cree almost rushed him, but instead halted, watched him warily. And in half a second he turned and fled out the back door, slamming it behind.

Gallen ran to give chase, but when he threw himself against the door, it wouldn't budge. Zell'a Cree had bolted it from outside.

Gallen rushed back to the front, then circled the stable and stood gazing over the valley. Along a trail downhill were dozens of stone houses and buildings with white stucco exteriors, many with low courtyards where someone could easily leap a wall to hide. Bright stars pierced the indigo sky, and Tremonthin's three small moons were rising all in a close knot, shining like molten brass over the countryside. Gallen could see far to the south, across a great valley where dark hills rose as forested islands from a moonlit sea of fog.

There was no one on or near the road, no sign of Zell'a Cree. But in infrared Gallen's mantle detected hot points of light on the ground, splashes of blood.

He stooped low and ran, following the trail. A dog began barking far ahead, perhaps a kilometer off, and Gallen wondered if his quarry were getting away.

He raced low a couple hundred meters, responding to the voice of Fermoth, a great hunter who whispered that he should be quiet, refrain from alerting his quarry, and Gallen found a bright pool of blood on the ground on the far side of a stone well. Zell'a Cree had rested here momentarily, dripping blood over everything.

More bright flecks beckoned farther on, and Gallen began stalking through dark alleys, over a wall. His prey moved like a fox—backtracking and zigzagging, and Fermoth whispered to Gallen, yes, yes, this is how I would do it. This is the direction I would go, till Gallen wondered if the shared experiences of the Inhuman might not be a disadvantage to his quarry.

Gallen reached the far end of town and began circling back along a hill, at which point even Fermoth wondered what the quarry was up to, and Gallen began to wonder if Zell'a Cree was Inhuman after all.

Yet it was obvious that Gallen's quarry was failing. Perhaps he was no longer thinking clearly. The droplets of blood were getting brighter, warmer. The man was slowing, weakening, until Gallen felt sure he was near, and that he would be weak, and dying, when Gallen found him.

Gallen felt confused. He was beginning to understand the servants of the Inhuman. Indeed, he thought that they might be friends, or that at least they thought themselves good. None of the voices inside Gallen were evil. They had just been people who were concerned with living their own lives, people who wanted to continue living. And though Zell'a Cree had killed Fenorah and was an Inhuman, he was also someone like Gallen who had become infected against his will. Gallen recalled the Bock's warning, in which he told Gallen that at times he would have to choose whether to kill an Inhuman or spare it. And as he hunted, Gallen's resolve to kill Zell'a Cree weakened.

Yet Fenorah had also been innocent, had not deserved to die, Gallen reminded himself. And Gallen could not understand how it was that basically good people could do this to each other.

After nearly twenty minutes, he reached an alley behind a store.

Blood was smeared on a white stucco wall in the moonlight, and Gallen could see droplets on the dusty road. He heard the sound of coughing ahead.

He rounded a corner, and a beefy man was there in the moonlight, lying on his side in the alley, his pale eyes looking almost white. Zell'a Cree. He held his wound and lay gasping, bubbles of blood dribbling down his chin.

Gallen held his sword point forward, carefully stalked up to the man, to the *Inhuman*, he reminded himself, and he stared into the man's face. We share so many memories, Gallen thought, looking into Zell'a Cree's eyes. The Inhuman struggled to run, moved his legs about feebly, and stared forward into the dust, his eyes blind. He breathed furiously, and small puffs of dust rose up near his chin. His face contorted in a grimace, and beads of sweat stood out on his forehead.

"Boots. Boots are inside building," Zell'a Cree whispered to Gallen, as if it were terribly urgent, and Gallen could smell the tanned leather scraps outside the back door of the bootmaker's shop. Indeed, Zell'a Cree's right boot was tied together with a scrap of cloth. And Gallen suddenly realized that this man had circled back to town to get some new boots.

Now that Gallen had caught him, he considered stabbing him again, but didn't have the heart. Gallen shared the memories of twenty lives with this man, and all of those people had lived extraordinary lives. They were not small-minded killers.

"Damn you," Gallen said. "Why did you have to stab Fenorah?"

Zell'a Cree didn't answer. Gallen suspected that Zell'a Cree had taken a mortal wound. Yet Gallen could not afford mercy. His friends' lives might still be at stake. Gallen stuck his sword at Zell'a Cree's throat, demanded, "How many of you are stalking us? Where are your men camped?"

Zell'a Cree did not answer, merely turned his head up at the sound of Gallen's voice.

Gallen put the sword to his chin, and asked again, "How many more are you?" Zell'a Cree said nothing, and Gallen wondered if he were past talking.

"Join us," Zell'a Cree breathed, "and we will stalk you no more."

So Zell'a Cree still felt himself at war and would give up no information. Gallen respected that. He studied the creature. Zell'a Cree looked human, simply a beefy man with pale eyes that were much like Ceravanne's. He could have been a baker or an innkeeper in any town that Gallen had ever visited, and Gallen felt ashamed at wanting him dead.

"What did you do, before the Inhuman converted you?" Gallen asked.

"I . . . farmed," the big man panted. "Apples. I make, uh, cider."

"I think you're going to die," Gallen admitted softly. "There's little that you or I or anyone else can do to stop it now. I can let you die slowly, in your own time, or I can take you quickly." He let the tone of his voice ask the question.

"Slowly," Zell'a Cree asked. "Life is sweet. Savor it."

Gallen was dismayed by the answer. How could life be so sweet that you looked forward to coughing up your own blood for five minutes? But the voices of the dead within him bubbled up, all of them clamoring, "Yes, yes, life is sweet." They craved it, even a miserable few moments of pain.

Gallen looked back toward where he imagined the inn might be. He was tempted to leave Zell'a Cree on the road, head back to check on the others, but he was acutely aware that Zell'a Cree had lost his life at least twice: once when the Inhuman had converted him against his will, and once when Gallen had plunged a sword into his lung.

So Gallen sat down in the dust, prepared to wait with Zell'a Cree, stay with him to the end.

"Forgive me," Zell'a Cree asked, grunting, his words raising small puffs of dust. "I never wanted to hurt you . . . anyone."

Gallen wasn't sure what to answer, but settled for "I know."

The voices of the Inhuman rose within Gallen, crying out across the centuries, "Join with us."

Gallen felt torn. For several minutes Zell'a Cree only lay breathing, gasping at an ever more frenzied pace, droplets of sweat rolling down his face into the dust. At first, Gallen feared the man, but Zell'a Cree made no move against him, seemed less and less capable of moving at all. He wheezed for a bit, and coughed until fresh blood began foaming from his mouth.

Zell'a Cree closed his eyes and began weeping, concentrated on breathing.

"Let me take you now, friend," Gallen said. "There's nothing left to savor."

"Please . . ." Zell'a Cree mumbled after a long moment, "water. A drink first. Then kill me."

Gallen looked about. His own water skin was back in the wagon, but there was a rain barrel under the eaves of the shoemaker's roof. Gallen went to the barrel, found that it was nearly full. He sheathed his sword, cupped some water in his hands, and went back to the dying Zell'a Cree, put his hands down under Zell'a Cree's lips.

The dying man didn't take the water. Just lay there breathing heavily, lapsing into sleep.

"Wake up," Gallen said. "I brought your water."

"Unh," Zell'a Cree grunted, twisted his head to try to get his lips to the water. Gallen held his hands down lower, and to his surprise, Zell'a Cree tried to sit up to drink, put a hand on Gallen's shoulder as he steadied himself.

Gallen held his hands to the man's mouth, let him drink it for a moment, and Zell'a Cree leaned back against the wall, his eyes focusing on Gallen. He seemed only a bluish shadow in the moonlight, all colors washed from his face, as if he were already fading into dust.

The cicadas and crickets began singing in the still night, and a little breeze whipped through the streets, raising the hair on Gallen's back.

Zell'a Cree smiled weakly, stared up at the sky, and Gallen thought he would die now. "Thank you," Zell'a Cree whispered as if addressing the universe, and then he looked into Gallen's eyes. "It has been so long . . . so long since I have heard the voice of the Inhuman . . . but now, I know what it wants me to do."

Gallen leaned closer, curious, and looked into Zell'a Cree's eyes. "What does it want from you?"

Zell'a Cree reached up quickly, and there was the jingle of metal rings as he pulled at Gallen's mantle. Gallen grabbed at the Tosken's wrist, but like the Tekkar he was immensely strong—so their struggle lasted only a brief second, then the knowledge tokens flashed in the moonlight as Zell'a Cree ripped Gallen's mantle free.

It went sailing through the air and clanked against the wall of the bootmaker's shop, and Gallen gasped and drove his sword into Zell'a Cree's neck.

For one moment, Gallen still could not feel the Inhuman's presence. He was not lost in strangers' memories, and for a brief few seconds he dared hope that the Inhuman would spare him, and he lurched toward his mantle in the moonlight.

And then there was a surging in Gallen's ears, dozens of voices clamoring, as if a tide were swelling from a distant shore. His arms and legs fell out beneath him, and Gallen could almost imagine that someone had reached into his body and pulled his spirit free. He felt disconnected—the sounds of crickets and cicadas suddenly ceased. Gallen crumpled to the ground, barely conscious of the fact that his head bounced off the dirt street.

And he felt them come leaping and tumbling after him, the hosts of the Inhuman, the ghosts with their iron will. Until now, they had taken him gently, slowly, but now he could feel something akin to desperation emanating from the machine, the desire to crush him before he could resist.

Far away he heard a desperate shriek, a harrowing wail that shook him and demanded aid, but Gallen hardly recognized that it was his own voice.

It had been thirty minutes since Gallen jumped up and rushed from the inn. Maggie and the others had gone down to the stables where they found poor Fenorah lying in a pool of blood.

Ceravanne was still beside his body, weeping, while Maggie tried to comfort her. Orick had headed south along the outskirts of town with Tallea, sniffing Gallen's trail.

At last Maggie went and stood outside the barn, hoping to see Gallen's shadow against the white stucco walls in the moonlight.

A maid from the kitchens was up at the inn, beckoning to her, urging Maggie to "Come back indoors, where it's safe!"

Then Maggie heard Gallen's bloodcurdling scream.

Gallen's voice rang out over the small town, echoing from the hilltops and from the buildings so that she couldn't be sure where it came from. Almost, it seemed to rise from the earth itself, but she thought it might have come from a ridge to the west.

Maggie's heart began pounding, and she looked about frantically. She wondered if it really had been Gallen's voice—it had been blurred and distant, after all—but she knew that it was. It sounded like a death cry, as if he'd taken a mortal wound in the back, as Fenorah had done. She raced toward the sound for a moment, looked about hysterically, realized that anyone who could have killed Gallen could also kill her.

And yet it didn't matter. If Gallen was dead, she didn't really care to live anymore.

So she ran uphill, west toward the ridge, and began searching. For an hour she wandered through town, investigating every street, until she met Orick and Tallea coming up from the south of town.

"Maggie, girl, what are you doing out here?" Orick demanded.

"I heard Gallen scream," she said.

Orick and Tallea looked at each other. "We heard a shout some time back," Orick said, "but I couldn't say it was Gallen's. It sounded to us as if it came from the north."

"No sign of Gallen?" Maggie asked.

"Whoever he was chasing," Orick said, "knew how to cover his scent. He ran me in circles, and his scent didn't stick to the dust. And Gallen's wearing that damned cloak of his, which hides all smell. So we've lost their trail."

Maggie filed that information away. She hadn't known that a Lord Protector's cloak masked his scent.

"Maybe Gallen went back to inn," Tallea said, and Maggie realized that she *had* been gone for over an hour. If Gallen were hurt, he'd have gone back to the inn, if he could.

And it seemed her last hope. So they went back to the inn, down to the stables. A maid from the inn had brought a lantern down, and Fenorah had been washed and turned on his back. A clean quilt was stretched out over him, but it was too short for the giant, so that it covered his feet, but not his face.

Shivering from a chill wind that was beginning to blow down

the high mountain passes, the companions sat in the stable, waiting for Gallen's return for several more minutes, until at last Ceravanne said in her clear voice, "All things pass away. It is time, my friends, to consider the possibility that Gallen is gone, and what that means to the quest." She stood above Fenorah, and the lantern's sharp light reflected from her angular face. She seemed somehow washed out, unreal under such light.

"Are you saying we should leave without him?" Orick grumbled, rising to his hind feet. He sniffed the air once again, as was his habit when he felt nervous.

"I hesitate to say it," the Tharrin answered. "Gallen has not returned, and almost two hours have passed. I doubt he would stay away so long, if he were able to return to us."

"And if he's dead, killer waiting for us," Tallea muttered, resting her unsheathed sword by letting its tip settle into the floorboards under the straw.

"And that means we have little choice but to press on as quickly as possible," Ceravanne whispered. "But there is something else we must consider. If Gallen is dead, then his killer may have taken Gallen's mantle. We will have someone with the powers of a Lord Protector hunting us, and he will have access to all of Gallen's memories. He will know where we plan to go, what we plan to do."

"So you want us to stay and see if we can find Gallen's body," Maggie asked, "just to make sure we get his mantle?" And she knew Ceravanne was right. Knowledge is power, and the Lord Protector's mantle would be a powerful weapon if it fell into the hands of the Inhuman.

"I think," Orick said, "you're all worried for nothing. If Gallen is dead and his enemies took his weapons, why haven't they come after us? He had his mantle, that fancy sword, and his incendiary rifle."

Maggie clung to his words, knowing they made some sense, hoping he was right. "Gallen may still be hunting," she said at last. "He's thorough when it comes to blackguards. He wouldn't let one give him the slip."

"Aye, that's possible," Orick grumbled. "Down in County

Toorary, Gallen tracked a cutthroat for three weeks, chased him two hundred miles."

Ceravanne licked her lips, looked out the open door southward. "Perhaps we should wait," she said. "But there is something just as portentous that could have happened. Gallen has been very . . . deep in thought these past two days. We all know that his loyalties are wavering, hanging in the balance. He may have joined the Inhuman, or he may have gone in search of solitude while he considers his future course."

Maggie wanted to deny this, wanted to slap Ceravanne for even bringing up the possibility, but this too seemed very likely.

"I don't think he'd leave me," Maggie said, her voice small in the close darkness of the stable.

"I would hope not," Ceravanne offered, and she took Maggie's hand in hers to offer comfort. "But he is under great pressure. You must remember that he is living with many other voices inside him, rich recollections of other loves. Those who become infected by the Word, they sometimes become lost in the . . . history that the Inhuman offers. Their small voices are drowned out by the bitterness and despair of the Inhuman. And I fear that Gallen may be susceptible to this. Those who are most susceptible are those who are weak of purpose, or weak of mind, and those who are simply inexperienced—the young. Gallen is neither weak of purpose nor stupid, but he is young."

"You forget," Gallen said loudly from the far end of the room, "the others who are equally susceptible to the Inhuman's domination."

Maggie turned, and Gallen stood in the front doorway to the stable, all draped in the black robes of a Lord Protector. Yet there was something terribly wrong. The way he stood—with a certain swaggering confidence as he leaned casually against the doorpost—was nothing like Gallen. Indeed, a terrible light seemed to blaze from his pale blue eyes, and he wore the mask of Fale. Yet strangest of all was his voice. It sounded deeper, and it resonated more, and all of his accent was gone. Where a few weeks ago he'd been a charming boy from County Morgan, now an older and wearier man stood. It seemed to Maggie suddenly that a stranger was wearing Gallen's body, and that Gallen stood smiling, mocking their fears for him.

"What others are susceptible to the Inhuman?" Ceravanne asked.

Gallen waved his hand at her. "The trusting," he spat, then waved to Orick. "The naïve. And those who are actively evil."

Gallen reached into the pocket of his robe, pulled out his mantle, and its black rings and silver stones glimmered in the moonlight. He draped it over his head.

"So, you are Inhuman now," Ceravanne whispered, and Maggie found her heart pounding within her. "But you have never been any of those—naïve, trusting, or evil."

Gallen straightened, and he seemed taller and more menacing to Maggie as he crossed the stable, gazed out to the south, over the wide valley below with its shroud of fog that glowed like gauze in the moonlight.

"Yes," Gallen said, staring to the south. "The Inhuman has tried to claim me as its own." For a brief moment it looked as if he would collapse, and he held to the door frame as he struggled for control. Maggie could see the old Gallen. "And, my friends, it is good for us all that the Inhuman has finished its task—else I would not have suspected its plans, and we would have walked into a trap.

"Maggie, come here."

Maggie went to his side and followed his eye. He took off his mantle, placed it on her head. "Listen to the radio frequencies on the higher end of the spectrum," he said, "and look south to Bern's Pass, beneath that far mountain, four hundred kilometers from here."

Four hundred kilometers? she wondered. She couldn't imagine seeing that far. But Maggie concentrated, and the mantle brought a faint sound to her ears, bursts of radio signals squealing undiscernible messages. It was a code.

She looked to their source, beneath the far mountains that suddenly appeared in her mind as she gazed, and Gallen's mantle magnified the distant image. Something vast and black was crawling down a mountainside.

"Dronon hive cities," Maggie realized, "crawling toward us."

"Yes," Gallen said. "They are far away, but they're coming. Part of the memories the Inhuman gave me came from a Dronon technician. All those who join the Inhuman know how to use Dronon technologies, and now that the Dronon have been forced to abandon this world, leaving the hive cities behind, the Inhuman hosts have taken them up. With these they will march against Northland, for the hive cities can also swim across the oceans, and here in Babel their guns are not dismantled."

"So the Dronon who abandoned this world betrayed it, leaving behind weapons for the Inhuman to use." Gallen breathed deeply. "Ceravanne, your people are in far graver danger from the invaders than even you had imagined!"

Maggie was watching the distant image of the Dronon hive city, crawling down the mountainside like a huge spider, when a second crested the ridge. And then she saw something else, a knot of large birds in the darkness, their body heat registering white, hurtling across the distant valleys. She wondered how far away they were, and her mantle flashed an image before her eyes. Two hundred and twenty kilometers.

"Gallen, there are scouts flying this way, hundreds of them."

"I know," Gallen said. "The Inhuman is coming for you. It knows where we are, and because of the interference my mantle offered, it has guessed at our purpose."

"It could only have learned our location from the transmitter in your head," Maggie said, and she looked at Gallen sharply.

"I know," Gallen admitted. "The Inhuman sent a message to Zell'a Cree in his last moments, telling him to pull off my mantle so that the downloading could be finished. The Inhuman could only have sent that message if it were tracking us and knew that Zell'a Cree and I were together."

"Of course," Ceravanne whispered.

"Then if it knows where you are," Maggie said, "the Inhuman only has to follow you to find us."

Gallen looked about helplessly, threw up his hands. "Unless Maggie can remove the transmitter, or we can somehow block it, then you will have to leave me."

Gallen took Maggie's hand, looked steadily into her eyes, and touched it to the back of his head. "Here is where the Word burrowed into my skull. I can feel a small bump there. It only makes sense that the transmitter is still outside the skull; the Inhuman would not try to beam messages through bone. Perhaps the tail end of the Word is the transmitter."

Maggie had suspected this possibility before, but dared not admit it. The implications horrified and sickened her. She didn't want to have to pry this thing out of Gallen's head. "I know what you're going to ask, Gallen, and I can't do it. The Word has inserted itself into your brain. I can't just pull it out!"

An image flashed through Maggie's mind, a vision of neural wires slicing through the gray matter of Gallen's brain as she pulled.

"We have to try something," Gallen said. "I want you to try now to cut away anything outside the skull. And if that doesn't work, you must pry the Word out. I know it's dangerous, but it is the only way for me to remain with you. Unless you do this, I might as well be dead."

Maggie looked nervously to the south. "What of the scouts?"

"They will not make it here for several hours," Gallen said. "And we can hide from them tomorrow." When next he spoke, Gallen spoke not as himself, but as the Inhuman, and it was reflected in his demeanor. "For six thousand years, I've lived in this land. I can guide you to Moree like no others, except those infected by the Inhuman. But I cannot help you, unless you do this for me. And perhaps it will avail nothing."

Maggie looked to Ceravanne. "I don't think I can do this."

"I can, maybe," Ceravanne said. "I've mended festering wounds, and I'm handy with a knife. But I'm not sure what you'll require of me."

"Do you have any more Healing Earth?" Maggie asked.

"A pinch, perhaps, no more," Ceravanne said. "He can have a few drops of my blood."

Maggie wondered where to perform the surgery. It seemed ghastly to do it here in the stable, in the dim lamplight surrounding Fenorah's pale corpse, but it sheltered them from the chilly night air and from prying eyes. Maggie looked for some clean straw. Some of the horses nickered querulously as she pulled the hay from a crib and sprinkled it on the floor.

Ceravanne brought the lantern near, and Tallea brought her sharpest dagger from its sheath.

Ceravanne bit her lower lip, and her hands shook as she did the cutting, opening the back of Gallen's neck down to the blue-white bone. She pulled Gallen's hair gently, opening the flaps of severed skin so that she could see more clearly, and Maggie had to use a bandage from her pack to daub the blood away.

There was a small, perfectly circular hole in his skull, and two small wires dangled from what had once been the Word's hind feet. Maggie couldn't be sure what the wires were for, so she ran up to the wagon at the front of the inn and got her mantle of technology, then came back and looked closely at the wires. The sensors in her mantle magnified the image. From the Word's hind legs, tiny microfilaments, like veins, had grown out in a gray web, wrapping themselves around Gallen's skull. It was not a particularly powerful antenna for either receiving or transmitting information, but Gallen's skull acted as something of a dish.

"This is it," Maggie said. "This is the antenna. This is a more complex design than I'd imagined, but it's also easy to defeat—at least I think we can keep them from tracking us."

"Do it," Gallen said.

And to her own surprise, Maggie found that she was able to take the knife from Ceravanne. "It's too intricate to do this without a mantle," she explained. She severed the web in a circle, then dug out as much of the wiring as possible. She tried to clear her thoughts, concentrate only on doing the job. She watched for several seconds, to see if the web would grow back, but apparently this component of the nanotech weapon was too unsophisticated to regenerate. After thirty seconds, the wound so filled with blood that she could no longer see well.

Maggie blotted it away again with the bandage. "I'm done," she whispered.

"Try to pry the Word out," Gallen said.

"There's no need," Maggie argued, imagining how the webs of metallic neurons would slice through his brain if she pulled. "I've already cut off the antenna."

"I don't want it in me," Gallen shouted, his voice muffled as he yelled into the straw. "Cut it out! Pull it out partway, if you can, and then cut it in half."

Maggie found herself breathing hard, imagining the possibilities for infection in the wound, the possibilities of brain damage.

She touched the tail end of the Word with her knife, wondering if it *could* be pried out.

Suddenly, as if it had been burned, the Word lunged forward into Gallen's brain, and blood began gushing out from Gallen's brain cavity.

"Ah, God," Orick cried out in fear.

"What?" Gallen asked, moving a bit.

"Nothing," Maggie said, suddenly terrified, her knees going weak. "I'll close now."

Ceravanne held out her finger, and Maggie cut it, dropped a bit of Ceravanne's Immortal blood into the wound, and in moments the cut began to heal. Gallen lay quietly while Maggie washed the blood from the back of his neck. And when Gallen sat up, he replaced his mantle on his head and asked Maggie, "Did you get it out?"

"I couldn't get the Word out," Maggie said. "It dug itself in deeper. But I cut all of the connections to the antenna, and I dug out part of the wiring. I think the Word will be permanently disabled."

Gallen considered, got up and gazed off to the south. "I fear that my presence could be a danger to you even still. I will not guide you south, unless you all desire me to. But I warn you in any case that we may not be able to elude the Inhuman—a great race is afoot. I suspect that those marching hive cities have come searching for us, as have the scouts. Our enemies hunt us by land and air."

He looked back, into the faces of Orick, Tallea, and Ceravanne. "Will you have me?"

And Maggie looked into the face of Gallen, the Inhuman, and one by one, the others said yes, until at last Tallea said, "For now."

Twenty-four

Late that night after a brief and belated dinner at the inn at High Home, Ceravanne made arrangements with the innkeeper for Fenorah's body to be conveyed back to Battic, then Gallen loaded the group into the wagon and led the travelbeast downhill, under the blanketing fog.

Though it had good night vision, the beast could not see in such total darkness, so Gallen led it by hand. At dawn, he left the main road heading west by way of what appeared to be an old hay trail through some fields, but the deserted track held, and for many hours the wagon rolled through the lonely woods, passing only a few shacks that belonged to woodsmen.

And all through the morning, Maggie watched Gallen in horror, studying him for signs of change. They were everywhere—in the stealthy way that he walked, almost unnaturally quiet; in the way he sometimes tilted his head to catch a sound; the new way that he spoke. Twice, when they passed small clear pools, Gallen stopped to wash his hands, and he would sit and inspect them long afterward. He'd always been tidy, but never like this.

Maggie complained about it once under her breath, whispering, "What is he doing?"

And Ceravanne whispered in her ear, "The Faylan people have olfactory nerves on their hands. They wash themselves so. I think it is a habit from another life. He will forget about it, in time."

Because Gallen and Tallea feared Derrits in these woods, they made poor time, going little faster than a horse could pull, but the travelbeast was able to work all day at this pace. Twice they bogged down in lonely places and had to get off the wagon and push, and once they had to float the wagon across a broad river, but in the early afternoon they began climbing out of the wetlands to an ancient fortress on a small hill.

When they reached the hilltop, Gallen had them turn the wagon on its bottom and he removed a wheel so that it looked as if the wagon had been abandoned. "The scouts will be searching for us tonight," he said. "We don't want them to see anything suspicious." And Maggie saw by this ruse that this new Gallen was craftier than the old.

The fortress was small—a simple watchtower that looked out over the moors and woods, several crumbling outbuildings beside the walls.

Gallen let the travelbeast graze for a bit, then took it to an underground root cellar away from the main tower and penned it in for the night.

Maggie climbed the tower at dusk, and stood for a moment watching out, wishing that Gallen would come to be with her, come to put his arms around her. Doves had flown up to the tower's tiled roof, and were fluttering about the broken window. Maggie could not see the distant mountains, where High Home sat on the slopes, and she found it difficult to believe that any scouts would come so far in a single night to search for them. But Gallen seemed certain.

When Maggie went downstairs, Gallen and the others were milling about the courtyard. Tallea had found the dungeon, and she brought up a huge turd as long as her arm, poked on a stick, and held it out for Gallen to see. "Much Derrit poop," she said, "in dungeon."

Goose bumps rose on the back of Maggie's arms at the mention of Derrits, for even the Im giants had feared them, but Gallen seemed little concerned. "Fine, fine," he said. "We'll wet it down so that it looks and smells fresh, and put it in the tower and upper halls. The scouts will not be eager to search this place if they find it marked with Derrit spoor."

So Gallen set himself the task of carrying the loathsome stuff upstairs while the others went below and ate a cold dinner. Maggie could find no place where the odious, garlicky scent of the Derrits did not permeate. It was terribly dark in the dungeon, the only light coming from the open door leading upstairs, and so before they closed the doors, she rushed outside and picked a great armload of straw to use as bedding.

When Gallen finished his task of moving the Derrit poop, he came below, and sealed them in for the night, barring the door from the inside with a rusty iron pole.

They sat for a long time. The only light in the room came from Gallen's mask, a shimmering piece of starlight. Maggie did not find it comforting, for Gallen sat away from her, as if they were strangers.

Maggie found herself getting nervous, till Gallen began singing softly, song after song from their home on Tihrglas, until her heart nearly broke at the sweet memory. Everything here was getting out of control. Everything here was not as she'd imagined. And so she dreamed of the clean mountain rivers rushing under the lowering pines, the sky so blue that she could not quite hold it in her memory.

When the others had fallen asleep, Maggie crept to Gallen's side, held his hand, and looked up into his face.

"Gallen," she whispered. "I want to tell you I'm sorry."

"For what?" he said, not turning to look at her.

"I've, I've been thinking hard on it—and I'm pretty sure that I could have stopped the Inhuman from downloading its memories to you."

"How?" Gallen asked.

"If I'd cut the antenna sooner, yesterday morning perhaps, the Inhuman would not have known how to contact you. It never would have received a signal from the Word."

"Why didn't you do that, then?" Gallen said, his voice hard. He didn't turn to look at her.

"I—wasn't certain that I could get to the transmitter. I was hoping our mantles would block the Inhuman's transmissions. I didn't want to have to lay into you with that knife!"

"You wanted to spare me pain?" Gallen asked.

"Yes!" Maggie said, and she squeezed his hand.

Gallen smiled at her, barely turned in her direction. "Then you are apologizing for having a good heart?"

"I'm apologizing for being wrong," Maggie said. "For being weak."

"Apology accepted." Gallen turned to her then, and Maggie hoped that he would take her in his arms, but instead he held himself aloof, as if he were a stranger. "And your mistake may yet cause the downfall of the Inhuman," Gallen said. "Because I know its thoughts, its ways, we have a greater hope of defeating it. Now, go to sleep, and I will keep watch."

He reached out and patted her hand, as if she were a child. Maggie curled up on the straw and tried to sleep, disturbed by a steady drip, drip, drip of water falling into a corner from the sweaty walls.

Until at long last, she fell asleep for a while, then woke to a scratching noise. At first she thought it only a rodent gnawing on some old wood upstairs. But it came steadily, and she looked around. She could see little enough by the light of Gallen's mask, but soon she realized that while rolling around in her sleep, she had misjudged where the door was. What she had taken to be a far corner of the building was in fact the bolted door directly above them.

Maggie got up warily, wondered what to do. The insistent scratching was from something large. She went to Gallen, and pushed him gently in his sleep, praying that he would not waken with a shout.

To her relief, Gallen merely opened his eyes, took one look at Maggie, and sat listening for a moment.

Suddenly Gallen snarled, letting a low rumble escape his throat. It was a sound distinctly nonhuman, like some savage animal, and the noise frightened her. Then in a harsh voice he

shouted, "Ghisna, ghisna—siisum," and leapt up the stairs
and began fumbling with the bolt.

Something shrieked behind the door. There was the sound of
scurrying feet and flapping wings . . . followed by silence.

Ceravanne woke up, as did Orick and Tallea. "What's
wrong?" Ceravanne asked.

"A scout was here," Gallen whispered, "and it thinks it was
almost eaten by a tribe of Derrits. It will not be back tonight.
Quiet, now. Go back to sleep."

Maggie lay down again, but Gallen did not follow his own
advice. The last thing Maggie saw before she fell into a deep
slumber was Gallen's mask glowing in the dark as Gallen
watched the stairs, accompanied by the drip, drip, drip from
the seeping wall.

Just before dawn, Gallen roused the group and began preparing
to break camp. He went out and righted the wagon with Orick's
help, then harnessed the travelbeast.

They headed west again, and by midday they climbed up out
of the valley floor to an ancient stone highway, swept by the
wind. This road headed south once more, and it led through a
bleak grassy landscape where there was little shelter from
prying eyes. On it, their travelbeast raced like the wind, and
Gallen dared not slow down, though Tallea warned him
repeatedly to beware of Derrit traps.

During the day, Maggie asked Gallen how he'd been so
familiar with the old stone fortress, and he explained, "I played
there as a child. My mother went there daily, to take provisions
to my father, who was kept prisoner in the dungeon."

Maggie did not ask him more about who those memories had
belonged to, and Gallen offered no more explanation.

Shortly before dusk, Gallen pulled the wagon off the road,
then he flipped it and removed the wheel again, and led the
group up a narrow defile to a small cleft that went back twenty
meters into the rock. Scrub oak covered the opening so fully
that when they got inside, they could not see out. Nevertheless,
Gallen insisted on fortifying the entrance by stacking stones
around it.

As he stacked the rocks, Gallen said, "If I know of this place, then the servants of the Inhuman may recall it, too. I think it will be safe, but we must still keep watch!"

"To me, it seems more dangerous to stay here than to find somewhere else," Ceravanne warned him softly.

"Perhaps," Gallen said, "but last night I learned a lesson. I went to a place familiar to me, and the Inhuman searched that place. I hope not to repeat that experience. I've never actually visited this cavern in one of my former lives. Indeed, I was told of it only once, and sought it, but never found it. It wasn't until weeks later that I guessed where it might be. So my memories of this place are tenuous. I hope that the Inhuman's servants will not even consider searching for this old haunt."

They ate another cold dinner, and afterward Orick slept on guard near the entrance of the cave, while Gallen curled up next to him and finally took some rest.

Maggie wondered at this, for it had been two nights now since Gallen had held her, and she felt that her new husband was a stranger.

She tended the fire and sat with her arms wrapped around her knees for a long time, watching Gallen's sleeping form and thinking.

Ceravanne and Tallea had been talking softly together, and Tallea must have seen how Maggie watched Gallen. "Not worry," Tallea said. "He remembers love for you."

"Are you sure?" Maggie wondered aloud. She did not fear that Gallen would hear her. He was so tired, he was dead to the world.

"If not," Tallea said, "he would not try save us."

"She's right," Ceravanne offered. "It takes a great deal of willpower for someone to fight off the Inhuman's conditioning. The fact that he is working so hard is a sign of his commitment to you."

Maggie bit her lip, feeling that something was still terribly wrong. "Aye, he's fighting the Inhuman, but there's something amiss. He doesn't touch me. He doesn't kiss me. It's keeping his distance that he is."

Ceravanne frowned, and Maggie could see that this news

dismayed her. "Maggie, I think he loves you more than you give him credit for."

Something in the way that she said it, something in the way that her voice quavered, made Maggie curious. "Why do you say that?"

Ceravanne took a deep breath. "I have something I must confess: twice now, I've asked Gallen to give me his heart. I wanted him to give himself to me completely, just in case this happened. I wanted him to bond with me more strongly than he might with the Inhuman."

Maggie looked at the Tharrin and knew that Ceravanne was talking about more than just some mental bonding. The Tharrin was admitting that she had sought Gallen's complete love and devotion. She'd tried to seduce him. "But," Ceravanne continued, "Gallen has already given his heart to you. You're the reason he fights the Inhuman now. But if he isn't seeking you out, if he isn't touching you, you need to go to him. In his mind, he's been separated from you for a hundred lifetimes. The Dronon have tried to put an incredible amount of emotional distance between you. He needs to fall in love with you all over again. You need to remind him why he loved you in the first place."

Maggie bit her lip, looked around the cave desperately. Tears came to her eyes, and Tallea went to her side, put her hand on Maggie's shoulder.

"Why cry?" Tallea asked.

Maggie shook her head. "That's not Gallen anymore. That's not the man I married. He doesn't talk like Gallen, or move like him. He's six thousand years old." Maggie did not dare say what she was thinking. Ceravanne had more to offer Gallen than she did. Ceravanne was more beautiful than Maggie, and the lure of her pheromones could undermine a man's resolve. Ceravanne, like Gallen, had apparently lived for thousands of years. On the face of it, she was a better match for him, and something in Maggie made her wonder if Ceravanne hadn't tried to seduce him based upon such cold reasoning.

"Why did you do it?" Maggie said bitterly. "Why did you try to make Gallen love you if you knew that he already loved me?"

Ceravanne sat across the fire and licked her lips as she considered her response. "The first time it happened was when the Bock brought him to me. I didn't know then that he loved you."

"And the second time?"

She took a deep breath. "Was three nights ago."

Maggie considered the depth of the betrayal. She had a strong desire to pull a knife and gut the Tharrin right at the moment, but by telling Maggie of her betrayal, Ceravanne was also promising never to do it again. Still, a month earlier, the Lady Everynne had lured Gallen into her bed, and now Ceravanne was trying to do the same. Maggie wondered if all Tharrin were inherently untrustworthy that way. "Why did you do it?" Maggie asked. "Why do you Tharrin do this?"

Ceravanne was breathing hard, and she looked away, but she knew that she owed Maggie an answer. "I could tell you that it is because of Belorian, because Gallen looks like Belorian, and I love him still. It was dark, and I was frightened and lonely, as frightened and lonely as I have felt in five hundred years, and out of the goodness of his heart, Gallen was trying to comfort me. That was temptation enough for what I did.

"But . . ." Ceravanne gasped as if the truth were being physically wrung out of her. "If we Tharrin have a weakness, it is one that our human makers designed into us. Maggie, you know that we exude pheromones that attract you humans to us. You know that we are constantly aware of how we look, of a thousand tiny ways that our expressions and actions can manipulate you. But there is something else about us that you must know: as much as humans desire to serve us, we also desire to be served. I . . . crave devotion, as you crave air. I sometimes wish that I could be different, that I could be free of this, that I could be dead."

And suddenly, for Maggie it all made sense. The Tharrin had been formed to be leaders. They'd been given wisdom, beauty, an innate ability to sway others. But all of that would have been worthless if they didn't also, to some degree, crave power.

"We are our bodies," Ceravanne whispered. "We are all

imprisoned in a cage of flesh, doomed to sometimes think and act in ways we would prefer not to. You, I, Gallen, the Inhuman. Maggie, I hate myself for what I tried to do, and I am grateful to Gallen for resisting me. I won't let this happen again."

Maggie took her fists and rubbed her eyes with them. It was so late, and she was confused. She wanted to be angry, and it might have been that she was tired, or it might have had more to do with Ceravanne's ability to manipulate her, or it might have been that it was just the right thing to do. In any case, Maggie just shook her head. "All right, then," she said, and she went over to Gallen and lay beside her husband.

My husband, she thought. Mine. And I won't let any damned Tharrin or any damned Inhuman take him away from me.

She slept soundly that night, with no disturbing visitors. And such was Gallen's woodsmanship that for the next day, they saw no sign of pursuit. The only evidence that someone might live in this region came when they passed a small stream, and enormous footprints could be seen in the mud. Tallea was driving the team, and Orick sat beside her, but when Orick asked what made the tracks, she only urged the horses faster and said, "You don't want to know."

Maggie was sitting in the back of the wagon, and she'd been holding Gallen's hand, and she squeezed it as they passed the muddy tracks, and Gallen squeezed her hand back. He sat watching her for a bit as the wagon rolled away, and at last he bent forward and kissed her, experimentally, as if it were the first time.

On the evening of the third day out from High Home, Gallen left the ancient highway, taking the wagon up a narrow pass, beside ruins so ancient that no single building still stood.

For the first time, Ceravanne seemed uncertain of his direction. "Where are we going?" she asked. "Are you heading to Ophat? The Nigangi Pass is down below to the east."

"And it may be closed to us," Gallen said. "So we're heading to Ophat. I need to get some height, and from this peak, I should be able to see all of the way from here to Moree."

Thus he led them up an ever steeper trail, past ancient ruins above the tree line. Long the travelbeast climbed, until it was exhausted, foam dripping from its mouth. Often the road was ruined, and portions had dropped from the sides of the treacherous cliff to the chasms beneath.

Still, the road wound on, up through cold ruins where bitter winds blew among the rocks until at last they reached one sheltered niche between two arms of the mountain. There, some ancient hallways still stood, carved back under recesses of stone, a hundred meters in from the treacherous road. There was a great pillared hall, and beside each of its massive doors was a carved image of a somber giant in breastplates, carrying heavy spears in one hand, a gem in the other. Ancient cobblestones littered a broad courtyard, empty of all but the sparest dead grasses.

The stonework here was cracked and old, far older, Maggie guessed, than anything that she had seen before.

"The travelbeast can safely climb no higher," Gallen said, "and forage is scarce enough here as it is. You can camp inside the hallway, and may even build a small fire. No scouts will trouble you here tonight."

"Why is that?" Orick asked.

"We have been climbing for the past four days, and now we are at nearly three thousand meters on this peak. The scouts' wings give them little purchase in such thin air. Though they could walk up the road as we do, they are not likely to bother. Besides, we are on the far side of the mountain from where they will be searching."

So Gallen had them unload the wagon and let the travelbeast graze in the courtyard. Huge cisterns in the courtyard were full of water, though a green moss had built up all along the basins. Still it seemed drinkable.

Maggie went inside the ancient palace and found that some passages led to caves that delved deep under the mountain. Some Derrit dung littered the great hall, but it was old, dry dung that could have been there for years. Still, Gallen insisted on securing a defensible room, and he left Tallea in charge.

"I have much scouting to do on my own tonight," Gallen said

rather formally, "and I will be climbing the road higher. You should be all right."

"I'm coming with you," Maggie said.

"That isn't necessary," Gallen said, and he looked into her eyes with some relief, as if he'd wanted to beg her to come, but was somehow afraid that she wouldn't. "It will be bitter cold up on the mountaintop, and I'm not even sure if there's a shelter."

"I'm not going because it's necessary. I'm going because it's desirable," Maggie said. She took his arm in hers. "And I'll just have to trust you to keep me warm."

Before they left, Maggie kissed Orick on the snout, and Gallen patted his head, and then they were gone, heading out the doorway to the tower atop the mountain.

Something about the formality of their departure bothered Orick. It was as if they were newlyweds, scurrying off for their honeymoon. In a way, they were formally bidding the rest of the world goodbye. Orick felt a ponderous emptiness in his chest, for Gallen had been his closest friend, and now Orick felt somehow deserted. He went and curled up on the floor feeling empty and barren.

Ceravanne must have sensed his mood, for she came to him after a while, put her thin arms around him.

"Why do you think he did that, went off without me?" Orick asked.

"It may have been my influence," Ceravanne whispered. "I strengthened Maggie's bond to him when I let him touch my skin. The Inhuman tried to break that bond in him, but I think Maggie has reawakened it. It is a terrible thing to be alone when you become so deeply bonded. Gallen needs her now, as he needs water or air. And I suspect that she has needed him as badly all along. We should rejoice that they have each other."

Orick listened to the words, but found little comfort in them.

"And maybe it is also the fear of battle," Ceravanne said at last. "We are about to cross the Telgood Mountains, into the desert of Moree. None of us can be sure what our future holds. So he seeks to show his love for her, in case he dies."

Orick just grunted, and Ceravanne went back beside the fire.

A burning cold was seeping through the stone walls, though Orick hardly minded. But a minute later, Tallea came and knelt beside him.

"When I young, I live in crèche," Tallea whispered into his ear. "My sister slept with me, fought beside me, for many years. When grow, she go to marriage, I go to war. It hurt, when she slept with another."

Orick didn't answer, but Tallea went on. "Someday, you find bear woman to sleep with?" She said it half in comfort, half as question.

"No," Orick whispered. "Bear women don't love the way that human women do."

"Oh, very sad," Tallea said, and to Orick's surprise, she lay down beside him, curled up against his thick fur. And she just held him, like a friend, until he fell asleep.

For his part, Gallen took Maggie up an ancient stair, and on his back he carried firewood and some blankets. There, at the peak of the mountain, the memories newly downloaded in his head told him an ancient race with powerful vision had once built a tower to keep watch over the valleys below.

Indeed, he found the tower as legend said, though it was but a small, cylindrical shack carved from stone, stuck between a crevice in the rocks. Still, it contained two large beds carved into stone, and a dome-shaped fire chamber with a tiny chimney. Gallen built a good fire, and soon the room was surprisingly warm.

And there by the fire, wrapped in blankets, he made love to his wife and lay with her, holding her tenderly long after she fell asleep.

Once, just before she closed her eyes, she asked, "When the Inhuman finished downloading, and you came back to the stable at the inn, how long did it take you to decide to stay with us?"

"I decided when I saw how you feared me," he whispered honestly. "Until then I was unsure who I would keep allegiance with. But I could not stand to see you fear me."

"Oh," Maggie whispered, and she fell asleep, never guessing

what a truly difficult decision that had been for him to make. At times, the sea of voices, the memories, still threatened to overwhelm him. But always there seemed to be one bright corner in his mind where he could retreat, and in that place his memories were clear, and he could recall what the Dronon had done on his home world and on other worlds, and in this way he could bear witness against it.

And somehow, that helped. One by one, the voices in his head were going silent, like candle flames snuffed out under his finger. Over the past few days, his thoughts had begun to clear.

And yet he was afraid that somehow he would slip back into that dark place in his mind. He feared it, and he needed Maggie to help him remain strong.

So Gallen lay and thought for a long time, recalling the Dronon's atrocities, planning for the days ahead. He still had the Harvester to contend with, and if he guessed right, it was an ancient killing machine. So he let his mantle read out the files on its weaponry and defense systems.

Afterward, in the cold night, he wrapped his black robes around him, and took his mantle, and went out under the stars. It was bitter cold, and he softly spoke to his robe, asking it to reflect all heat back to his body.

He climbed to the top of the small tower, and there he sat upon a simple stone dais. And if anyone had seen him there, wrapped in dark robes, gazing out over the land, they would have thought him only to be an image carved in stone, so little did he move, for he closed his eyes and let his mantle gaze for him.

The sky was clear of clouds below him, and for a long while he sat, letting his sensors pick up sights and feed the magnified images to his mind. Letting the mantle scan radio frequencies, so that he could listen to the Inhuman's distant communications.

What he saw and heard disturbed him. Down in the Nigangi Pass, only forty kilometers to the west, three hive cities scoured the land, calling to one another, searching for him, and all along the valley floor he could see the scouts, flapping on swift wings as they fluttered from ruins, to cave, to crowded inn.

To the south, in the deserts of Moree, he spotted seventeen more of the hive cities, crawling like great spiders across the land, heading north to war through the desert. He could see the glowing lights of their plasma engines, red in the night, and could see tiny figures of men running about the upper war decks.

He'd never imagined that the Dronon had left such fearsome arsenals.

Yet far more disturbing than either of these were the armies. The whole south of Babel must have been coming northward, for warriors swarmed across the desert. He could see great armed encampments of giants in blood-red robes, sleeping in the open beside huge bonfires. And beyond that were tent cities of the blue-skinned Adare warriors, numbering in the hundreds of thousands. Vast armies of Tekkar marched through the night, running northward in their fluid gait, all swathed in black robes. And all of them were heading to the north and east, out to ports where they could cross the seas.

And their movements were stirring things up in the wilds. Twelve kilometers below, at the foot of the mountain, tribes of wild giant Derrits had gathered, apparently to defend themselves from the sudden encroachments of others. The giant Derrits were said to be solitary creatures, seldom traveling in more than small family groups. But Gallen spotted at least a hundred of the creatures in one great war band.

And down a curve of the mountain trail, a glowing figure walked. Gallen watched it, a scout with wings folded, scurrying up the road in small lunges, stopping every few meters to sniff. Indeed, as it studied the fresh wagon tracks, it seemed both hopeful and apprehensive. Gallen wondered why the creature had not spotted him—it was only six kilometers down the road—until he recalled that he'd asked his robe to reflect all of his body heat inward. Obviously, it cut down his infrared signature to the point that the scout could not detect him.

But most disturbing of all to Gallen was the great city of Moree, eight hundred kilometers distant. At such a great span, his mantle could make out little. Water vapors in the air, oxygen itself, formed a barrier.

Yet the images his mantle accumulated showed him one thing—five huge silver domes spread out equidistantly around the city. Gallen had seen such domes before, when he was on Fale, and so he recognized them.

The Inhuman was building starships.

Gallen sighed, and slipped from the tower, heading down to kill the scout.

Twenty-five

━━━━━◤

"I don't like it," Ceravanne said the next morning, in the great hall.

"The Tower Road is our best chance," Gallen urged, standing over the corpse of a dead scout. "The servants of the Inhuman have little knowledge of it. I remember it as a dark and dangerous track, a place of terror—one I would not willingly brave again. I was lost in the tunnels under the city of Indallian once, for many days—and so I think that the servants of the Inhuman will avoid the place. But you, Ceravanne, must have used the road. You were the queen of this land."

"That was five hundred years ago," Ceravanne said. "Even then, the road through the Hollow Hills was a maze. Few dared the tunnels without guides. And now, who knows what might live there? Derrits at the least would lurk in those caves, but many another folk are accustomed to the dark. What if the Tekkar have established an outpost? And even when the road lies aboveground, one must beware of wingmen. They've a strong taste for blood."

"Yet the valleys of Moree are awash with the armies of the Inhuman," Gallen said. "The word has gone out that a Lord

Protector seeks Moree. Scouts by the hundreds are scouring the land for us, and by our poor chance, great armies are moving through the night. We cannot go over the open roads. Already, one scout has found our wagon tracks. We must get through to Moree."

"And you think that it is better to face a hidden danger than a known one?"

"When the known danger is overwhelming, yes," Gallen said.

"I don't understand," Orick said. "What are you two arguing about?" Gallen had done a bit of scouting last night, and had decided to use an old trail, the Tower Road, to get closer to Moree. The rest of the group was willing to follow him blindly, but Ceravanne had blown up at the news.

She said, "The Tower Road is an old road that united Ophat with the underground city of Indallian, which lies west of here, under the Hollow Hills. From there, the road leads farther west, through the Telgood Mountains to the very edge of Moree itself."

"I don't understand," Orick said. "I thought we were already in Indallian. Is Indallian a city, or a country?"

"Both," Ceravanne said. "Long ago, there were many city-states in this part of the world, so the name of the Capitol was often the same as that of a country. We are already within the ancient borders of the land of Indallian, now Gallen wants to go through the city, under the Hollow Hills. But as Fenorah warned, the city is a perilous place, and has been for centuries. None go there nowadays."

Ceravanne looked about the room to the others. "We could take the Tower Road." She sighed. "But much of it lies underground—through forty kilometers of stone. You, Caldurian, what do you say?"

"Indallian is legend to me," Tallea said. "I not know if holds danger." Yet she feared it. Many races lived underground, and they could see in the dark. As aboveground, the most peaceful peoples tended to die out, while the fierce races thrived. And if Tallea had to fight underground, she knew she would be at a disadvantage. Indeed, her wounds were not all healed yet, though she found she could swing her sword.

"It is not a legend to me," Ceravanne said. "For eight thousand years, the city called to various peoples, and the Hollow Hills were carved with measureless tunnels. For long, it was but a peaceful city where folk of the underworld lived in harmony. Then the emeralds were discovered, and peoples flocked to the city in ever greater numbers. Even in its glory, when the city of Indallian was under my full sway, it was said that 'no man knows Indallian,' for no one could explore all of the many caverns in one lifetime. Indeed, there were rumors of strange and malevolent peoples inhabiting the far bounds of the realm even then.

"And I will be honest with you all," Ceravanne concluded, visibly shaking. "I fear that place."

"Still, three hundred years ago, I heard rumors," Gallen said, "that one could travel the Tower Road for over five hundred kilometers—from Ophat to White Reed. And that is a crucial stretch in our journey. And you must consider this— the Telgood Mountains form a formidable obstacle. No army could cross it on foot, not even an army of Tekkar, so the mountains themselves will form a wall to protect us."

"So that is why you brought us to this entrance," Ceravanne said, gazing away toward the back halls. "I suspected as much. Yet the road is dangerous. In many places aboveground, it will have crumbled away. And belowground, many of the caverns have fallen in, floors have collapsed into chambers beneath. There is good reason that no one has taken that track in ages. And when we do reach the city of Indallian, what will we do for light?"

Gallen reached into the pocket of his robe, pulled out a small crystal globe, and squeezed it. A brilliant white light shone from his gloved fingers.

"I see," Ceravanne breathed. "Technologies from other worlds. And you are determined to leave the travelbeast behind?"

"I am," Gallen said. "The closer we get to Moree, the more

impossible it becomes to travel openly, and the beast only marks us. Do you think you can guide us?"

"Perhaps." Ceravanne breathed deeply. "The road is easy enough to follow aboveground, and I know some paths below, though I am not certain they will be open."

And with that, they were off. Gallen went out to the travelbeast and whispered in its ear, pointing back north, and in a moment it nodded its shaggy head and raced down the mountain road.

Then they packed, and headed to a hallway where a statue of a giant stood guard beside a great stone door. Gallen pulled mightily on the handle, and cold air hit them, smelling of dampness and minerals. Ceravanne held up Gallen's glowing globe, and gazed down a stair that curved into the dark, and they began to descend, and to Tallea, the Tharrin looked as if she were a goddess, carrying a star in her hand.

"Wait," Gallen said, and his voice echoed through the corridors. He went back to the room, hoisted the dead scout on his back. "We'll leave it down below, where other scouts will not find it."

Then they began their descent. The stair went on and on, and Ceravanne led through the dark at almost a run. Their footsteps echoed off the stone. Tallea was acutely conscious of the noise they made, and she strained her ears for sound of pursuit.

Twice, during the long race down, they passed side tunnels of poor make that had been dug in more recent years, and from one of them they smelled the acrid stench of Derrit dung and cold ashes.

Beside that door, Gallen cast down the dead scout, leaving it as a meal for the beasts, and once again, as she had over the past several days, Tallea saw the craftiness in what he did. The Derrits would certainly prefer the carrion of a recent kill to hunting a party of armed men with bright lights and sharp swords.

The tunnel seemed endlessly long, and the cold of the rock seeped into her bones. Even as she ran, Tallea could not seem to warm enough to fight this cold.

In two hours they came out of the cavern under the mountain's shadow and found themselves on a broad road in the sunlight. Over the ages, stones had rolled down the hillside, so that in many places it would have been impassible by horse, but they were able to run and climb on foot.

Tallea's side ached from her recent wound, and though the sun warmed her a bit, she found that it didn't warm the wound. Instead, it burned like ice all along its length.

Still, they ran for hours, passing through more tunnels. Gallen took the lead, and twice he warned the others of Derrit traps—deep pits overlaid with a framework of twigs, then covered with hides and dust.

Tallea was glad for Gallen's sharp eyes, for she herself spent her time watching the skies for sign of wingmen, and secretly she felt relieved each time they were forced to make their way through a tunnel.

Thus, they spent the day running, and camped in a tunnel by dark. Tallea's wound throbbed through the night, and it heated up, as if it had become infected. She slept poorly, but was forced to run again at dawn.

That day, the road took a long, steady climb, higher into the bleak, gray mountains, so that the air was frigid, and they ran along a ridge that was incredibly steep and long. The mountain rose on their left like a wall, and dropped for five hundred meters below them. In places along the road, they found the splayed prints of mountain sheep, but no other sign of use.

That day they passed two ancient outposts, high stone citadels along Tower Road, and on one crenellated tower, twigs and leaves stuck out like a great nest, three meters across. Only a wingman could have carried such large sticks so far from the valley below.

Gallen called a halt, then crept up the crumbling stone stairs to the tower himself, with Tallea and Orick behind. The nest was old, the twigs whitened by age and rotted so that they could hold no weight, proving that the nest had been abandoned for years. But among the yellowed bones of sheep and deer was a human arm and skull, with tatters from a bloody wool tunic.

They climbed back down, hurried on their way, watching the

skies. Gallen rounded one long arm of the mountain ridge, then dropped to the ground, warning the others with a wave of his hand to stay back.

Tallea dropped and crawled forward, and together they looked over the bluff. A wild white river churned through a gorge far below, and pines climbed halfway up the mountains in a green haze.

Sweeping over the canyon in wide, lazy circles, a lone wingman hunted on leather wings. Tallea watched the creature. Its underbelly was pale blue in color, so that it was hard to spot from below, but its back was a mottled gray and green. If it had been sitting high in a tree, with its wings folded, it would have been hard to spot from the ground. But from above, while in flight, it was easily discernable.

"It's watching the valley," Gallen said, "hunting for deer or wolves. We're lucky that it's below us."

"Not much eat up here," Tallea agreed. The wingman would not bother hunting this high road through the barren, gray mountains. She watched the creature, and wondered. According to common wisdom, all of the races on Tremonthin had been adapted from human stock to live on other worlds. But of all the peoples in Babel, she found the wingmen to be the strangest. They did not look humanoid at all. The creature was large, perhaps ten meters from wing tip to wing tip—much larger than scouts. It had a broad tail that it used as a rudder as it flew, and fierce, razor-sharp hooks of a bloody red were attached to its wings. Its long flat head was filled with great teeth that Tallea could see even from this far distance, and its scaly hide was nearly proof against a blade. And it was said that the wingmen saw other peoples not as kin, but only as food. One could sometimes reason with a Derrit, but never with a wingman.

They watched the creature circling the valley. It did not move farther west or east, nor did it seem inclined to climb higher. "I think," Gallen whispered, "that it must have seen some prey down there in the trees. It's probably waiting for it to come back into the open. It could keep circling like this all day."

"Agreed," Tallea said.

"We'll keep low, crawl on our bellies if we must. We're only eight kilometers from the gate down into the city of Indallian."

Tallea looked ahead, feeling exultant. They had traveled far and fast in the past two days. The road snaked along the ridge, vertical cliffs above and below, following a U-shaped bend in the mountain. But Gallen was right—in the distance the road met with a great iron door in the rock, a door that stood closed.

"This foolish," Tallea said. "We don't even have bow."

"There is only one wingman," Gallen said, "not a flock. And I have my incendiary rifle."

Tallea had seen how much damage that weapon had caused on the ship, and she didn't doubt that it would send a wingman tumbling in flames.

"How many fire arrows have?" Tallea asked.

"Six," Gallen whispered. "And I may need to save two of those—one to slay the Harvester, one for the Inhuman."

Tallea nodded grimly. Only one wingman—as far as she could see. But there might be dozens more around the next ridge, out of sight, or others roosting in trees below. It was autumn, when the wingmen often flocked together to head south.

"What of door?" Tallea asked, nodding toward the iron door in the distance. "What if is locked?"

Gallen bit his lip and did not answer.

Tallea's wound was icy as it rubbed against the cold stone, and she felt deeply troubled. She recalled how the cold blade of the giant had pierced her aboard ship, and it almost felt to her as if the wound were alive, calling out for her demise.

She looked up the road ahead. The thin afternoon sun shone all along its length. There were few shadows thrown from rocks to hide in.

Gallen's robe had turned slate-gray, the color of the stones, and Tallea wished that all of them wore such robes to hide them.

"All right," she agreed. "We go on bellies."

Gallen signaled the others to come forward and drop low, and he crawled to the far edge of the road, inching along the stone wall.

The others followed. Tallea took up the rear guard, and the arduous journey began. The stones here had a peculiar, powdery scent, and they were cold and sharp, cutting into Tallea's hands and knees, and the coldness of the stone was peculiar. Tallea calculated by the angle of the suns that light had been shining on the road for hours, yet it had not warmed. Apparently, the cold in the rocks went too deep for that.

Orick took the journey easily enough, inching forward, his big rump in the air.

After two kilometers, Tallea began to notice blood on the trail. Maggie had cut her hand on sharp rocks. It was rumored that the wingmen could smell blood at great distances, but it was only a small amount. Still, Tallea felt uneasy.

Another kilometer down the road, Derrit spoor was on the ledge, the first Tallea had seen in nearly two days, and it was fresh.

Normally the sight would not have left her feeling so uncomfortable, but at the moment, Tallea was struggling to hug the rock wall as closely as possible, afraid that the wingman might spot them. She couldn't bear the thought of fighting a Derrit.

She could do nothing but crawl ahead. A croaking sound echoed up from the valley below, one wingman calling to another. Gallen waved his hand, called a stop. He inched forward to the edge of the cliff, and alarm became evident on his face.

He inched back, held up three fingers. Three wingmen now. Tallea looked up at Maggie's hand. Fresh blood was dripping from the deep wound in her palm. Tallea gestured at her, pointed to her nose and mouthed the words, "Smell your blood. They smell blood."

Maggie's face paled, and she clenched her other hand over the wound. Ceravanne brought out a small piece of white cloth from her pack, gave it to Maggie to use as a bandage.

In a moment, they were on their knees again, scurrying ever faster along the road. They made it past the bend in the road, almost five kilometers, when Gallen suddenly stopped. A lone wingman rose, riding the thermal updrafts from the valley below.

Tallea and the others froze, crouched against the stone wall, and the wingman rose on up. Like many animals, the wingman looked mostly for sign of movement, and at the moment, the creature was in full sunlight, while they were in shadows.

Tallea's heart pounded, and she tried to still her breathing, tried to stop the pounding, as the wingman flew along the ridge, then swept up over the mountain, sniffing loudly for the scent of blood.

Then Gallen was on his feet, motioning to them. "Run!"

Orick raced ahead of Gallen, running toward the door faster than any human could, while Maggie and Ceravanne hurried forward.

Tallea jumped up so quickly that one of her mending muscles must have ripped, for she felt a searing pain in her side. Still, she managed to run forward for nearly two minutes.

Suddenly Gallen shouted, turned toward Tallea and fired near her head. A searing ball of flame shot three meters over her, hotter than any oven, and a croaking scream sounded. She turned to see a wingman, mouth open, swooping toward her, the white flames from Gallen's rifle billowing in its mouth. The wingman crashed into the road not five meters behind her, bounced and flopped over the cliff.

They were nearly to the door. Tallea lurched forward, and saw more wingmen rising up from the valley floor, searching for the cause of the commotion. Five of them.

Gallen leapt over a smattering of fallen rocks, but Ceravanne tripped on one, fell onto others. Maggie grabbed her arm and nearly carried her, and Ceravanne was weeping from the pain.

Orick reached the iron door and stood looking at it.

Tallea felt a shadow, ducked and pulled her sword, swinging. A wingman was diving straight down from the precipice above, swooping over her, and it had extended the long red claw on its wing tip, hoping to snag her and sweep her off the road, over the bluff.

She twisted her sword inward, hoping to strike through flesh and bone instead of just claw. Her sword tip struck the scaly leather of its wing, and she was surprised at the fierce jolt, for it cut the beast but also tore the sword from her hand.

The wingman screamed in pain and swept past her, careening onto the road. Her sword clattered over the cliff, and Tallea drew her dagger, leapt past the wingman as it tried to get up.

She looked back, and the wingman screamed in anger, a roar that seemed to shake the very stone, and then it was after her, loping on clumsy feet, dragging its shattered wing.

Ahead of her, Gallen and Orick were at the iron door. They both pulled at its enormous handles to no avail. And then Maggie was with them, and Ceravanne, and they all stood in a tight knot.

A wingman swooped up from the valley in front of Tallea, trying to cut her off from the rest of the group, but she ducked under it, and suddenly all of them stood together outside the iron door.

Gallen held his incendiary rifle, looked back down the road. The wounded wingman was eight meters away, and when Gallen confronted it with his weapon, the wingman hissed and stopped.

"You don't want to die," Gallen shouted at the creature, aiming his weapon at it.

The wingman shrieked, raising its long neck into the air, teeth flashing. It watched Gallen with intelligent eyes, bright red, gleaming like rubies.

"Leave now, or die!" Gallen shouted.

The wingman watched him a second, its eyes filled with rage, then leapt over the side of the road, flapping clumsily toward the valley below.

"Who says you can't reason with a wingman?" Gallen asked, smiling toward Ceravanne. Then a huge stone fell and shattered at his feet.

Tallea looked up. A wingman was in the air, two hundred meters above them, and another swept over the ridge and dropped a large stone.

"Get under cover!" Gallen cried. And Tallea went to the door, pulled at it.

"It's locked!" Ceravanne said. "We need the key."

"But who would have locked it?" Maggie asked.

Tallea looked at the door. The lock was a mess of rust. Above the door was fancy scrollwork all along the lintel, images of twin suns rising above fields of wheat. At one time, gems might have adorned the centerpiece of each sun, but the gems had long ago been pried free.

Gallen studied the door for half a second. "Everyone grab the handles and pull," he said. "This lock can't hold us."

But despite their efforts, the door would not open.

"Watch out!" Ceravanne called, and she pushed Tallea backward. Tallea looked up, saw a wingman swooping toward them, a rock tumbling in the air, and she marveled to see such a deadly rain fall from such beautiful blue skies.

She dodged, and the stone hit the lintel of the door with a clang, then split and bounced to the ground. Rust drifted off the door in a thin sheet.

"Hey," Orick grumbled. "I'm not handy at pulling doors open, but I'm pretty good at knocking them down!"

The bear ran back to the ledge, then charged the door, slamming all of his weight against it.

The door creaked, and there was a snapping, and when Orick dizzily backed away from it, the door had cracked open a finger's width.

Three wingmen slid overhead, dropping stones in rapid succession, and Gallen stared up at them, raised his weapon as if trying to decide whether to use the last of his ammunition. Orick backed up and roared as he charged the door again.

The lock snapped, and one half of the door buckled under his weight. The bear climbed up onto all fours groggily and shook himself.

And then a wingman swept over the clifftop and shrieked, a long wail of alarm. Tallea was not certain, but she could almost distinguish words in that scream. Out above the valley, all of the remaining wingmen veered toward them and flapped their wings, gaining speed. They knew that this would be their last chance.

"Inside!" Gallen shouted, and several people ran for the door. But Gallen went to the edge of the road, his rifle in hand.

Tallea rushed up beside him. "Take my sword," he yelled, and she drew the weapon from his sheath. She felt it quivering in her hand, as if it were alive, and it emitted a soft and eager humming.

Tallea glanced back. Ceravanne and Maggie were already inside the iron door, but Orick was trying to squeeze his own bulk through the narrow passage, shoving mightily with his back feet, leaving claw marks in the stone.

Gallen fired at the four wingmen who flew forward in a loose formation, and it seemed that the sun blazed from his weapon. A fierce wall of heat struck Tallea's face, and the light burst out over the canyon sky, catching the foremost of the wingmen so that he tumbled downward in flames.

Two of them veered off, to avoid colliding with their dying kin, but the third came on.

Gallen fired once more, and the wingman tried to drop beneath his shot. The flames surged past the creature, but they had come too close. Even in passing, the heat was so great that it left a huge black smoking blemish on the creature's back.

The wingman screamed out in pain, diving toward the ribbon of blue river that shone in the forest far below.

Tallea looked back to the door. Orick was still trying to push through. Gallen shouted. "Get in!"

He raced to the door and charged into Orick, hitting him at full speed. Gallen bounced back, but Orick slid through the opening. Two more wingmen were sweeping from the ridge above, and Tallea ran to Gallen's side, leapt through the opening.

A huge stone hit the door and shattered, then Gallen leapt through.

The group sat inside the door for a moment, panting, looking at one another. Maggie's hand was bleeding, and Orick had lost a tuft of hair. Ceravanne may have suffered a sprained ankle, but Immortals healed so quickly that it would cause her no grief. A rock chip had struck Gallen in the chin, and he was bleeding.

Outside, the wingmen screamed in frustration, hurling rocks against the doors, but none dared land for the hunt.

Gallen sat panting for a moment, and Ceravanne held aloft the light globe. "Welcome to the city of Indallian," she said, and her voice was tight with emotion. "It has been long since I've given such a greeting."

Tallea looked up. The room flashed and reflected Ceravanne's light. They were in an incredibly large chamber, where gracefully carved stone rose high. In the distant past, the room had been painted cream or ivory, and stonework floral patterns had been painted in their own bright hues. High up, three magnificent silver chandeliers graced the ceiling, each with hundreds of sconces. Bright crystals at their base reflected back the light, throwing prismatic colors sparkling across the walls.

Beneath each chandelier was a high, arching passage that led deeper into the mountain.

The place smelled of dust and earth, and for once Tallea almost rejoiced at the cold, in spite of the tearing pain in her side, for at least they had escaped the wingmen. Yet there was more here than barren passages. Unlike the tunnels they had wandered before, this place still carried the faint scent of people, of ancient sweat and food, of tapestries moldering in distant halls.

"Hey," Orick said. "Are you certain that no one lives here?"

"Great is the lure of the city of Indallian," Ceravanne whispered. "I suppose that many people may live here yet. Miners may have ventured here in hopes of finding riches. . . . Other beings."

"That lock was rusted," Orick said, "but the door hasn't been closed hundreds of years. Thirty or fifty maybe."

"Then whoever closed the city is surely dead and gone," Maggie said hopefully.

"Do not be so certain," Ceravanne said. "Many peoples are fashioned to live long. Even a Derrit, with its thick hide, is likely to live three or four centuries."

"But would a Derrit be smart enough to lock a door?" Maggie asked.

"Don't be deceived," Ceravanne whispered. "Derrits are not dumb animals. They are foul, and live in their own filth, and they may eat you. But they are also clever and cunning. They were made to be workers on a brutal world, where conditions are harsh."

"But why would you make them that way?" Orick asked.

"I cannot speak for their makers, for the Derrits were formed long before I was born," Ceravanne said. "But I believe that it was not the creator's intent to form such foul beings. Often, peoples who have been created fail as a species. Their love for one another is too fragile. Their passions too untameable. Such peoples usually die out. But while the Derrits are a failure as a species, either unwilling or unable to lift their own kind by sharing their culture, they are successful as individuals."

"More than successful, I would say," Gallen put in. "For thousands of years, other peoples here in Babel have hunted them, trying to get rid of their kind. But it has proven damned near impossible to rid this world of them."

"So they're forced to live here in these lonely mountains?" Maggie asked.

"In the winter, when the snow comes on, they often move to lower valleys," Gallen said. "Where they sneak into barns and throttle sheep, or steal children from their beds."

"Let us speak no more about them," Ceravanne whispered.

"Yes," Gallen whispered. "They are unpleasant to think about."

Ceravanne raised the light toward the middle hallway, and began limping toward it. "Are you all right?" Gallen asked, taking her arm tenderly.

"Bloody, but unbowed," Ceravanne said, smiling. And Tallea followed them down into the darkness, holding her own aching gut. The pain was bad, but tolerable for a Caldurian.

Long they journeyed into the heart of the ancient city of Indallian, until Tallea felt certain that darkness must have fallen outside, but Ceravanne led them on. Several times they found corridors that were blocked by falling rubble, and once the floor had caved in beneath them to a deep shaft where great caverns had been excavated.

Ceravanne kept having to turn aside into new hallways, and

once she stopped and threw her hands up, crying, "This isn't the way." They had been traveling down a well-made corridor, but suddenly it turned into a crude cave, chiseled by rough hands. Ceravanne walked back a hundred meters, found a side passage that none of them had noticed, for it was purposely concealed behind a large stone slab. It took them in a new direction, and Ceravanne seemed less and less certain of this new path with each footstep.

Finally, she called a halt.

Tallea put down her pack, and the group sat wearily. They began eating a small dinner of apples and jerky. Their provisions were failing. In two or three more days, Tallea figured they would be down to scraps.

Ceravanne looked around the corridor worriedly, and Gallen whispered into her ear, "Perhaps we should scout ahead, while the others rest."

Ceravanne bit her lower lip, looked ahead down the passage. "Perhaps we should."

Maggie took two candles from her pack, lit them, and in moments Gallen and Ceravanne departed. Orick grumbled about the small dinner, and lay in a corner. Tallea went to him. "You can have my apple core," she offered.

"Ah, I've plenty of winter fat to eat," he muttered, but when she put the apple core under his nose, he gingerly took it in his teeth, gulped it down.

Tallea lay down beside him. She was falling asleep when Orick began muttering his nightly prayers. Cold from the stone seemed to be seeping into her wound, and Tallea lay wondering why the hosts of the Inhuman would remember this as a place of terror.

Tallea's muscles had been strengthening daily, and she stretched her arms in spite of her fresh wound, hoping that she would soon be ready to begin exercise. She considered sparring with Gallen, wished that her ribs would stand for it, but she was still too weak. Perhaps in a couple of days she would be ready.

She listened long, and realized that in the distance she could hear a sound like wind rushing through trees. But it could only have been water cascading through some underground chasm. For a while she thought of searching for the source of the sound, so that she could refill the water bags. But instead she lay still, thinking to do it in the morning, and fell asleep to the gurgling of water.

Hours later, when she wakened, Gallen and Ceravanne were just getting back. Ceravanne seemed greatly relieved, and when Tallea put her head up, Gallen explained. "We've been lost in a side corridor, but Ceravanne found the main road once again."

Tallea lay back down, and Gallen went to sleep beside Maggie while Ceravanne lay beside Tallea.

Tallea closed her eyes, and lay for a long while, but something felt wrong. She looked around, counted those sleeping nearby. Everyone was there, the candles were still flickering.

She sniffed, but could feel no strange air currents. And she held her breath. Aside from the soft snoring of Orick, there was no sound.

And then it hit her: no sound. She could not hear the rushing waters. Which meant that either the underground brook had subsided in a matter of hours, or else . . . someone had closed off a door, masking the sound.

Tallea loosened her knife in its sheath, and lay for the rest of the long night with her eyes open, perfectly still. Once, she thought she heard a distant thud, as if someone had stubbed a foot on the floor, but there was nothing else.

Still, when Gallen woke hours later, she whispered in his ear: "Take care. We may have visitors."

And as they quietly slipped away from their resting place, Tallea listened down each side corridor for the sound of running water.

For the next few hours they hurried along down passageways that were unimpeded, past storage rooms and old quarters where thousands of people had been housed. They were entering a section of Indallian that had been far more than the

mere service tunnels or mining camps found at the east
entrance. This was the full-fledged city, in its ancient glory,
and often they passed through huge chambers where sunlight
shone down through shafts in the ceiling upon vast reflecting
pools, or where wooden bedposts still sat in the musty ground,
petrified.

In these areas, where ancient shafts and fire holes littered
the ceiling, they had little need for Gallen's light, and
Ceravanne nearly ran through the halls, filled with a new
intensity. "This district was called Westfall," she said as they
passed through one great chamber where an underground river
rushed through a stone causeway, spilling out into the light.
"Children used to bathe here, laughing under the icy water."

And in the next chamber, vast brick ovens sat next to each
other. "Here the bakers worked night and day, cooking loaves
for the household."

And in the next great chamber, the tallest and grandest of
all, sunlight shone down through five holes in the roof, two at
one end of the hall, and three at the far end. There were long
reflecting pools under each light, and all along the great
chamber were statues of ancient warriors lining the central
hall—short, fat pikemen of the Poduni race; Tacian giants with
great hammers; the tall Boonta men with long spears and their
narrow shields, an army of warriors representing many nations.

And at the end of the hallway were two thrones. "And here,"
Ceravanne said nervously, "is where I ruled, beside my brave
Belorian."

She stopped, and looked away shyly. Above each throne was
a vast statue of marble that had once been overlaid with gold,
but the images had been defaced by thieves, all of the gold
chiseled away.

Maggie gasped, and rushed forward to the statues, as did
each of them. The statue on the right bore the image of
Ceravanne, as one would imagine she would look in a few years.
But the image on the left . . .

"Gallen?" Maggie called, and she looked back at Gallen,
horror and confusion on her face.

Ceravanne strode forward, clenching Gallen's glow globe so that the light shone from it fiercely, and she held it up to the statue.

The image was chipped and scarred. The hair had been cut shorter than Gallen's and the bearded face belonged to an older man. But there could be no mistake: the eyes, the chin, the nose, were all Gallen's.

"Belorian?" Maggie asked, still confused.

"When the Rodim slew him," Ceravanne said softly, "they destroyed his memories, so that he could never be reborn with those memories intact. But they did not obliterate his body. His genome was stored, so that his seed could be propagated, undefiled."

Tallea heard Gallen gasp. "You mean I'm— But how?"

"When the Dronon came, it was a dark time. Across the galaxy, the cry came out. 'We need more Lord Protectors.' And of all the Lord Protectors on our world, Belorian was judged the most worthy of cloning.

"And so, the Lady Semarritte sent technicians to our world, and they took what they needed. Seeds for the future, as they also harvested seeds from other worlds."

Ceravanne looked up at Gallen, and there were tears in her eyes. "I do not know your circumstances, but I can guess: you were born on a backward world, much like ours. Your mother and father had no other children, and it was voiced abroad that they were desperate."

"I never heard that," Gallen whispered.

"I did," Maggie countered. "My mother told me of it, when I was small."

"And so when you were born, no one worried that you did not look too much like your mother or father, for you were a gift from heaven. And you were a smart child, bright and resourceful, strong and fiercely independent," Ceravanne said. "That is the way it happens.

"In a time of peace, you would have become a trader, perhaps—fiercely competitive. But you were born during uneasy times.

"Gallen, it is no accident that you are a Lord Protector. Maggie told me how Veriasse found you only a few weeks ago, that he 'chanced' upon you in an inn. But though it is our good fortune that he found you, I suspect that little chance was involved. I suspect that he knew a seed had been planted in the town of Clere, so he sought for you in the town of your birth.

"And I am grateful that the Lady Everynne—when she learned the truth—sent you back to us, in the hour of our greatest need."

"I am a clone?" Gallen asked, and there was still disbelief in his blue eyes.

"Ah." Orick grunted, studying Gallen. "Now I see. The Bock never would tell us that Gallen was human!"

"He's not—quite," Ceravanne said. "Belorian was from a race of people called the Denars."

"The Denars?" Gallen asked.

"A race designed to be Lord Protectors," Ceravanne said. "The first race designed to be so. It is not by chance that your hands are quick or your mind is nimble. You were born with great gifts, and a desire to use them in the service of your fellow man."

Gallen folded his arms and looked up at the statue for a long minute. Then he spoke to Ceravanne, and his voice was husky with resentment and accusation. "You know these corridors. You brought me here on purpose, when you could have bypassed this chamber."

"All these past few days," Ceravanne said softly, "the memories the Inhuman gave you have been telling you what it wants you to become. I thought it best that you find out what you are."

"I think, rather, you are showing me what you want me to become." Gallen grunted as if it did not matter to him at all, and nodded. "Let's go, then."

And Ceravanne led them from the great hall, down some long corridors. They were near the borders of the city, and now they rushed for the east gate, but a few kilometers away.

Gallen looked back once, and his eyes were full of tears, and

Tallea pitied him for being a pawn in such a large game. He seemed to be running blindly, so she ran ahead of him, taking the lead in case there was danger.

They were jogging down a corridor, and entered a broad room when she smelled it—the garlicky scent of Derrits, thick as smoke.

She halted and turned, and there in the shadows, the great beasts were lying: three of them rose up on their knuckles and growled, each of them more than twice the height of a man.

"Run!" Gallen shouted, and he drew his sword. Tallea would have stood to fight beside him, but her sword was gone, and she had only a knife and her dueling trident—no weapons to pierce Derrit hide.

She rushed down the nearest passage, leading the way, with Ceravanne behind her. The Derrits lunged, their shadows dancing against the far wall. They had huge yellow eyes, and bones tied in their stringy gray hair clattered when they moved. The largest was an enormous male with dirty yellow skin and testicles as large as a stallion's. He wore a mail shirt, woven from bits of chain mail taken from a dozen human warriors, and he grabbed a massive door to use as a shield. In his other hand, he took an ancient halberd. He roared and charged, and Orick stood beside Gallen and rose on his hind legs. The two of them looked like children, hoping to withstand the monster.

And Tallea stopped and rushed to Gallen's side. Her Caldurian blood called her, and she could not leave friends in need.

Ceravanne and Maggie needed no urging to run, yet they did not go far—merely crossed the room, then stopped and turned. Ceravanne crushed the glow globe in her hand, squeezing it tighter and tighter, so that its light shone fiercely. Tallea admired the woman's bravery, for the Tharrin had no protection, and she held the light up only to aid the warriors.

The Derrits howled in pain, and raised their hands to shield their eyes, their pointed yellow teeth flashing. The huge male raised his shield, protecting his eyes. They were a shifting mass, acting as if they would charge, and Tallea dared not turn her back on them. She pulled her dagger and dueling trident, held one in each hand. They were small weapons, hardly big enough to do much damage, but she'd honed them as sharp as steel can be.

The male Derrit roared and surged forward, using his shield to slap Orick aside. The bear went flying like a doll, yelping in pain, and tumbled past Tallea. The male raised his halberd to strike, as if it were a hatchet, and Gallen danced in, struck the giant under the rib cage, and rolled away, his sword dripping blood.

The Derrit swung wide, slamming the halberd into the stone floor so hard that the weapon shattered. The Derrit raised his head and howled at the roof, never taking his amber eyes from Gallen, and swung his shield at Tallea. She ducked under its blow, felt the huge door whistle over her head, and knew that if she'd been hit, the blow would have shattered every bone in her body.

The Derrit howled again, and he must have spoken some command to the others, for the two smaller females rushed out from under his shadow. One of them lunged toward Orick, while the other tried to circle around Gallen, heading toward Ceravanne.

At the same time, the big male roared and leapt for Gallen, swinging the broken haft of the halberd like a club.

And in that moment, time seemed to stop. Tallea could see Orick on the floor, dazed, seconds from death at the teeth of a Derrit. Gallen was swinging madly, slashing open the snout of the big male as it lunged in to bite. The female on the far side of the room, rushing forward on her knuckles, headed toward Ceravanne and Maggie.

And in that moment, Tallea had to decide who she might save. Her little knife and trident were feeble weapons, but they were all she had. Ceravanne was on the far side of the room, and Tallea had served her poorly once before. Her heart was torn—Ceravanne or Orick? She could not make that choice. So she only prayed that she could fight swiftly enough to save them both.

The Derrit grabbed Orick in her claws and pulled him

forward with both arms, ready to sink her teeth into him. With a war cry, Tallea leapt onto her broad snout, sinking her trident into the giant's forehead to use as an anchor, then stabbed the big female in the eye—once, twice.

Blood gushed from the creature's torn eyelids, and the Derrit shoved Tallea away, knocking her across the room, and Tallea lost her trident, leaving it stuck in the monster's head.

There was a fierce tearing pain from the old wound in Tallea's side when she hit the floor, and she rolled to her knees.

Ceravanne began shouting, waving the light, and Tallea looked up, saw the other female Derrit hesitate not three meters from Ceravanne, pawing the air with one hand, shielding her eyes with the other. Ceravanne, though she lacked all skill in weaponry, also found it impossible to leave a friend in need.

Gallen had slashed the big male across the belly and one arm. The Derrit was a bloody mess, but still had some good fight in him. He was swinging his shield with both hands now. The Derrit's solitary lifestyle showed itself in the creature's poor fighting form.

The little female that Tallea had wounded began to shriek, and Tallea looked over in surprise to see Orick wrapped around her left leg. He was biting her, ripping her leg into shreds while she tried to pry him off and escape.

"Run!" Gallen said, looking right at Tallea. "Take Maggie to safety!"

Tallea got up, felt as if some ribs had snapped. She ran toward Ceravanne and Maggie, screaming a battle cry, and the female Derrit who'd cornered the women took an experimental grab at Ceravanne, her long yellow hands darting forward.

Tallea rushed up to the Derrit, grabbed a handful of hair near the Derrit's short tail, and drove her knife deeply into the Derrit's thigh, just below her left leg, trying to hit the femoral artery.

Tallea pulled her knife out, and though her blade had not made a deep cut, it was a painful one. The Derrit shrieked and lurched away.

The Derrit struggled to turn, hoping to throw Tallea off, but Tallea thrust the knife in again and again. The Derrit screamed in fear, released some acrid-smelling urine, then turned and fled, rushing toward Gallen's back.

Tallea could not hold the female Derrit from attack, but she clung to her, slowing her down for a moment. Tallea shouted for Gallen, then drove her blade deep into the back of the Derrit's knee, hoping to cripple her, and then Tallea lost her grasp on the monster and fell.

Tallea looked, and Gallen was swinging at the big male. With a mighty blow he leapt forward and slashed it across the forehead, seemingly unaware of the female rushing in behind, then suddenly he danced to the side, and swung a terrible blow at her leg.

The female crashed into the big male, knocking them both backward, and in that second Gallen rushed to Orick's aid, shouting to Tallea, "Flee!"

With a heavy heart Tallea ran, knowing it was the best thing to do. She lacked adequate weapons, and only Gallen was equipped to fight in that room. But few men survived an attack by a single Derrit, while Gallen and Orick had three to contend with.

Tallea found tears in her eyes, and recalled the teachings of her crèche masters: "A warrior cannot afford to weep in battle. It gives your foe the advantage." And so her masters had beat her, until she could hold back the tears. Yet the tears came now, for her friend Orick was battling without her, and Tallea knew that when this was over, she would have to weave a new rope belt for Orick, for her greatest bond now—beyond all her imaginings—was with the bear.

She passed by a room where wind blew in fiercely from a hole, a deathly chill, and Ceravanne was just behind Tallea, at the back of the group, holding aloft the light to ward off any more Derrits.

Their shadows danced madly upon the floor and the walls of the corridor, and then they ran into an open hallway, where suddenly the floor fell out from beneath Tallea.

There was a flash of darkness, and she found herself hurtling down—a rough hide and dirt falling all around her—then she landed with a jolt, and a searing pain shot through her back and arm.

For one brief moment she lay looking up, and Maggie shouted "My God!" and was staring down into the pit. It had to be a good five meters to the top, Tallea thought. Ceravanne called, "Are you all right?"

Tallea felt very confused. She could see the light above her, and her ears were ringing. She was breathing hard, panting, and a sweat had broken out on her forehead. She felt as if she'd landed on a rock, and it was digging into her back, but it hurt when she tried to move off it, and something held her in place. She tried to answer, but no words would come out.

"Are you all right?" Ceravanne repeated, and she held the light above her head so that she could see down into the pit.

"Derrit . . . Derrit trap," Tallea managed to say, and she felt lucky to say that much. She wanted to count her good fortune at being alive, but when Ceravanne's light shone on her, Tallea looked down at her own legs. A pointed stake as wide as her hand was poking up through her belly, and another pierced through the meat of her right arm. A third came through her leg just below the hip, but she could not feel it.

She could feel nothing below the waist. Her back was broken. She closed her eyes, listened. There was the roaring of Derrits in the far room, and it was getting closer. Gallen shouted something, and Orick roared in return, and Tallea's heart sang with joy at the sound. At least Orick will live, she realized, and she looked back up at the concerned faces of the women.

"Leave me," Tallea said, and her voice came out as a croak, barely audible above the yelling.

"Not yet," Ceravanne said, and she stood fast beside the pit.

There was more shrieking, more cries, and one final wailing roar. A few moments later Gallen and Orick came and looked down into the pit. Both of them were covered with blood, but little of it was their own.

"Three Derrits?" Tallea asked when she saw Gallen. "Perhaps a record."

Gallen's face was sad. Tallea felt light-headed, as if she were floating, and she almost thought she could float up to them, tell them that it was all right.

"What can we do for you?" Gallen asked, and Tallea tried to think of an answer.

"There must be something we can do for you," Maggie said, but even kind Ceravanne shook her head no.

"We're losing her," Maggie whispered.

"Save me!" Tallea found herself asking.

"There is nothing we can do," Orick said solemnly, and the bear had tears in his eyes. Tallea coughed, tried to speak.

"They say, in City of Life, Immortals with mantles can save people. Save me!"

And then Maggie's eyes opened, and Tallea realized that with all of his lore, even Gallen had not realized what she was asking.

"Not all mantles have this power," Ceravanne said.

"Of course," Maggie said. "We can download her memories into Gallen's mantle!"

"Yes, the rebirthing," Tallea pleaded.

Gallen held up the cloth woven of black rings, its glittering diadems shining in the light. "Can you catch it?"

Tallea nodded, and Gallen dropped the mantle onto her chest. Feebly, with her left hand, Tallea grasped the mantle and placed it on her forehead. Maggie called, "Command it to save you."

"Save me," Tallea begged. "Save me."

The silver rings sat cold upon her forehead, and she felt no different. She fell asleep for a moment, and she saw bright images: flashes of her childhood when she picnicked at a pond in carefree days. The time she first learned to hone a sword blade. A great meteor that she once observed streaking across the night sky for several minutes.

And then Gallen was beside her, stroking her head. He'd climbed down into the pit, though she had no idea how. He picked up the mantle, showed her a gem in the center where the mantle sat on his forehead, a gem that gleamed palest green with its own light.

"See this," Gallen said, pointing at the gem. "These are all of the memories that make you. All of your hopes and dreams. And I shall take a hair from your head, to remake you."

Tallea tried to thank him, but no words came from her mouth.

"Quiet now," he said, and he kissed her softly on the forehead. "The great wheel turns without you now for a while. Until you wake again."

She closed her eyes, and for a long time it was a struggle to breathe. She thought of one last thing she wanted to ask of the others, a gift she dearly wanted to give to Orick. But Gallen must have left her, for when she next opened her eyes, it was dark, and the stone floor beneath her was cold, so cold that it felt as if it were sucking all the heat from her.

Twenty-six

Though the remaining journey through the passageways of the city of Indallian took only a few hours, to Maggie it seemed to last forever. Gallen took the lead, watching for traps while Ceravanne told him which passages to take, and once more they heard the roaring of Derrits in distant recesses, but the company eluded them by slipping through passageways too small and narrow for the Derrits to negotiate.

Once, when they stopped to rest in an ancient hallway where dried and faded tapestries still hung on some walls, Gallen said, "I'd hoped we wouldn't find so many Derrits here. I saw a tribe of them in the Nigangi Pass. I think that the movements of armies has driven them here."

"With nothing but dirt to chew on for these past few weeks," Ceravanne said, "they'll be mad with hunger. How many did you see in Nigangi Pass?"

"Perhaps a hundred of them."

Ceravanne squinted her eyes, and her mouth opened in a little O of shock. "So many? Derrits only band like that in fear."

Yet Maggie had to wonder how many might be hereabout.

They'd fought off three Derrits and been chased by more. Perhaps Ceravanne was thinking along the same lines.

"We'll have to take care," Ceravanne whispered. "We may be the only food these Derrits see this winter—though they are known to feed on their own young, if necessary."

"What are you saying?" Orick asked.

"They'll hesitate to follow us into the sunlight," Ceravanne said, "but surely they will be hunting us tonight, and perhaps they will dog our trail for weeks to come. We can only hope that their band is smaller than the one Gallen saw in Nigangi."

"Right then, let's move out quietly," Gallen said, and Ceravanne held the glow globe aloft while Gallen led the way.

Thus it was that the group came out of the city of Indallian at sunset and found themselves on a long gray road. But they were still too close to the lairs of the Derrits, and Gallen kept them moving at a run over the long road for many hours, until the pack on Maggie's back felt as if it would burrow into her flesh, and her legs felt as massive and unyielding as stone.

At last, well past midnight, they could run no more. They came to an ancient guard tower dug into the mountain alongside the road, and prepared to make camp there. It was a good spot, out on a spur of a mountain ridge where they could see the road gouged into the cliff for four or five kilometers in each direction. The Derrits would not be able to come upon them unawares, so long as someone kept watch.

Maggie shrugged off her pack as soon as she got in the door of the guard room, then merely threw herself on the ground in exhaustion, glad to sleep on the rocks. She was almost blind with fatigue, still numbed with grief at Tallea's death.

But Gallen took her elbow and lifted her up. "Come," he whispered, "just a bit farther."

"No," Maggie whispered, but she was too tired to argue, so she let him guide her and the others to the back of the guard room, into a tiny shelter that had once been used as an armory. There, he got out the packs and began laying out blankets.

Maggie stood watching him stupidly for a moment, wondering why he bothered, and then said at last, "Wait, let me help."

"I can get it," Gallen said, spreading out the last blanket.

He began setting out the food and wine, and Maggie watched him and realized that for the past couple of days, whenever it was time to eat, Tallea had been quietly preparing the food. She'd taken that as her job, and now she was gone. It didn't seem fair that Tallea should be dead, while all of them walked around.

"Sit down and get some food in you," Gallen said. "You'll need your energy tomorrow."

"What if the Derrits come tonight?" Maggie said.

"I'll stand watch," Gallen whispered, looking up at her.

But she knew that he could not run all day and then stand watch all night. Indeed, he had dark circles under his eyes already, and Orick had been keeping more than his fair share of watches. And though Ceravanne was bright and intelligent, she was so small that Maggie feared the woman would be useless in battle.

Which meant that Maggie would need to take over some of Tallea's duties. Maggie felt the loss of Tallea as a sharp pain that sucked the air from her, and she realized that Tallea's death had given her an added responsibility. Tallea had saved them more than once. Maggie had felt secure with her solid presence on the ship as she guarded their door each night. And certainly Gallen would have been overwhelmed in battle with the Derrits and the wingmen had Tallea not come to his aid. Always, Maggie had imagined that Gallen and Orick could hold their own in any skirmish, but Gallen had never had to fight anything as big as a Derrit, or as swift as a Tekkar.

Maggie closed her eyes momentarily, and felt a slight disorientation, as if she were falling. And suddenly she found herself back in the hive city on Dronon, and ten thousand Dronon warriors surrounded her in the dark arena at the city's belly, their mouthfingers clicking as they chanted in unison. The air was heavy with the biting scent of their stomach acids, and only a dim red light of their glow globes in the high ceiling lit the room.

Gallen was battling a Dronon Lord Vanquisher who had spat his stomach acids into Gallen's face, so that Gallen stood with his flesh blistering, blinded as Veriasse had stood blinded in his final battle, while the Dronon Lord swooped overhead, slashing with his battle arms.

And in the dream, Gallen listened intently as the Dronon Lord made his approach, and he leapt incredibly high and kicked at the Lord Vanquisher one final time. Their bodies blurred together as they collided, and there was a spray of blood—both red and green—and Gallen tumbled back to the ground, the flesh ripped off half his face, to reveal a pale blue mask underneath. He was no longer breathing.

The Lord Vanquisher tumbled to the ground beyond him, wounded, the exoskeleton of his skull badly crushed, so that white ooze dripped from it. His left front cluster of eyes was shattered, and one of the sensor whips beneath his mouth had been snapped off. The Lord Vanquisher was almost dead, and he flapped his pee-colored wings experimentally, but was unable to lift his weight off the ground.

All around the room, the Dronon's voices were raised in a gentle roar of clacking, as if rocks were falling onto the metal floor, and the Lord Vanquisher turned toward Maggie and raised his serrated battle arms high for a killing blow, then began stalking toward her.

And Maggie looked up at him helplessly, feebly, knowing that she would die, just as surely as Gallen had executed the Dronon's weak and bloated Golden Queen after defeating her Lord Vanquisher.

And as the Lord Vanquisher came to destroy her, Maggie heard a voice whisper in the back of her mind, "This is what becomes of the Lords of the Swarm. Prepare."

Maggie's heart began hammering wildly, and she looked about, suddenly realized that she'd fallen asleep on her feet, and dreamed a dream that she knew she'd had on many nights before but that had been so terrible, she'd put it from her mind.

Perhaps her own feelings of inadequacy now brought it to the surface. Without Tallea to guard her, Maggie realized that the time had come for her to learn to fight for herself.

They ate a brief dinner, and Gallen urged Maggie to bed.

"You sleep," Maggie whispered. "I'll take the first watch."

"Are you certain?" Gallen said, eyeing her carefully.

"I feel better with some food in me. I'll thank you for the loan of your weapons though, and your mantle," Maggie said.

Gallen gave her his sword and incendiary rifle, then Maggie put on his mantle. "Are you sure?" he asked.

Maggie nodded. "I have to start sometime," she said and went into the large guard chamber where slits cut into the stone let her watch out into the darkness. The moons were out, but the road was deep in shadows, and Maggie wished that she could see better. Suddenly the whole scene lightened as Gallen's mantle complied with her wishes, and Maggie watched the snaking road. There was nothing alive out there except an owl that swooped silently down the length of the road, hunting for mice.

In moments, Maggie heard Gallen and Ceravanne settle down to rest, but Orick whined and barked, as bears will when they cry.

Maggie went back to check on him, and he was sitting up beside the door, shaking with the hurt. With the mantle on, she could see the tears in his eyes, and Maggie realized that Orick's feelings for Tallea had been stronger than she'd known, and no one had thought to try to comfort him.

"Are you thinking of Tallea?" Maggie whispered, and Orick nodded. Maggie patted his head, then petted him behind the ears. "She was a good one. We will all miss her."

"I know," Orick grumbled.

There was a rustling in the far corner as Ceravanne came awake, and sat up and looked over toward them, as did Gallen. "Do not be too hasty to grieve for Tallea," Ceravanne said from across the room. "Death is but a temporary state for many. She lived her life to the benefit of others, and she died to save us. The Immortals will be loath to let her perish."

"But she feels dead to me," Orick grumbled.

"Think of her as a friend who sleeps, but who will waken again."

"Aye, but when she wakes again, she wants to be a Roamer. She'll be different."

"I should think you wouldn't mind the differences," Ceravanne said. "She'll have fur, and she'll look more like you. You were becoming close friends. I should think that when she is a Roamer, you will be closer still."

"Och, she may resemble me," Orick said, "but I have to wonder what thoughts will lodge in her head. Certainly not human thoughts. And what will her heart feel? No, Tallea is gone forever."

Maggie patted his head. "By her own will she is gone," she whispered. "She died well, as she wanted. We should be happy for her in that. But I think she lived a sad life. She wanted others to depend on her, to own them and be owned—too much. It was a burden for her."

"So it's love you're accusing her of?" Orick said. "And I should be happy that she'll feel it no more?"

No one spoke for a long moment, and at last Gallen said softly, "I lived as a Roamer once. You are right to mourn for her, Orick. Roamers feel a certain closeness, but it is not love, and so Tallea now loses some of her humanity. Still, they can be happy. They revel in their own freedom, and their days pass quickly because they are unencumbered. She will learn to hunt for grass seeds on the plain, and squat beneath wide trees in a fireless camp, where she will have no care while she sings at the stars.

"And so, while you mourn her, take care not to mourn too long. This is the reward she has chosen, and if you had ever suffered under the emotional encumbrances of a Caldurian, perhaps you would feel that she has chosen wisely."

Orick thought for a long time, and his spirits seemed to lift a little. Maggie quickly kissed him on the snout, and when Orick said "You know, I'm at least as hungry as those Derrits," she knew that he was feeling better, but he was also reminding her of her duty.

She went back and watched the road, letting the others sleep through the long night. And as she waited, she clasped her hands and twisted, exercising her wrists as she often saw Gallen do, and she whispered of her need to Gallen's mantle, saying, "Teach me!"

And so during that night, she moved in the darkness,

exercising her body in new ways, swinging Gallen's sword as best she could while the mantle sent her visions of foes.

Only once that night did she spot a Derrit—a great brute of a male walking down a ridge on the far side of the canyon, carrying a greatsword in one hand, with a war hammer in the other.

Twenty-seven

Two hours before dawn, Gallen woke Orick with a kick. And Orick lay on the floor while Ceravanne packed, listening to the others talk in the main room of the guard shack. Maggie had chanced a small fire in the guard house and made a quick breakfast of cooked oats with cinnamon. It was their first hot meal in days, and to tell the truth, they would not have risked the smoke from a fire except that they had eaten all else. The cheeses were gone, as were the wine and corn, the plums and peaches. They were down to apples and oats, and they couldn't tell when they'd eat a cooked meal again. So it was the oats.

Orick had been living off his store of winter fat for days now, and he was beginning to feel a gnawing hunger that the others would soon share. Yet bears are tough, and Orick knew that the hunger that was a mere annoyance for him would quickly become dangerous for the others.

He was lying on the floor, thinking of these things, when Gallen came back and kicked him again. "Wake up, sleepy," Gallen said, laughing.

Orick felt as if he'd hardly slept at all, and he grumbled to Gallen, "Why must you rouse me so early? I'm dead tired."

"Better dead tired than merely dead," Gallen said, squatting beside Orick's ear. "We ran a good bit last night, but the next few kilometers of road are well exposed. Once dawn comes it won't be safe to travel that road for the wingmen, and we must make good time today. I fear the Derrits will be hunting us tonight."

"Och, I thought we left them all behind?" Orick grumbled.

"The Derrits and the wingmen own these mountains. The wingmen flocks are everywhere, and as for the Derrits, you saw how big they are. You saw their stride," Gallen warned. "They can run a hundred kilometers in a night without breaking a sweat, and they can track by scent as well as any wolf. We ran for six hours last night, but if a Derrit hunting pack gathers, they'll reach this spot in less than two."

"Do you think they'll come after us?"

"I think they'd have come for us last night, except that you and I made a good accounting against some of their number. But they won't be satisfied to eat the dead we left behind." Gallen leaned closer and whispered so that Maggie and Ceravanne wouldn't hear. "I told you once that this road is a place of terror for the Inhuman. They would not likely brave it this time of year. In the fall, Derrits do their hunting for the winter. They kill men and animals, and bury them in a cache to eat later. In one of my former lives, I was a soldier who hunted Derrits here. Thirty-two men were in my command, and a dozen Derrits fell upon us in an ambush, slaughtering them. They buried my men in a huge pit, piling the dirt upon them all. I was sorely wounded, and I was buried with them. I dug myself out of the grave after four days, and for the next week I dragged myself across this rocky road, trying to escape, until the Derrits came for me again. It was only by chance that they lost my scent, passed me as I hid in the night. The next day I was able to make it down into the river, float for hours in the icy water until the Derrits had no opportunity to catch my scent again. A fear of this place must burn in the memory of every Inhuman."

"So you think the Derrits will come for us? We only heard one other Derrit back there."

Gallen leaned close, watching through the open door as Ceravanne and Maggie hunched over the cooking fire. "I did not want to tell you, but twice I had Ceravanne turn aside into smaller hallways because my mantle smelled Derrits ahead. We heard one, but I smelled dozens. Believe me, we'll not get away from them this easily."

"Are you going to tell the women?" Orick asked.

"I think Ceravanne already knows the risk, but I do not want to frighten Maggie. What will come, will come, and perhaps our best efforts will avail us nothing. So now, my friend, if you will pick your shaggy carcass up off the floor, I think we should eat quickly, and then be running."

Orick obliged him, and in moments they were off, jogging on nearly empty stomachs through a maze of gray canyons, over the barren road. Their only light came from stars and moons, and just as the sky began to lighten, the road dipped precipitously, leading them deep into the gorge.

Before they could take the road down, Gallen stopped, and they stood panting while Gallen gazed far behind along the mountain slopes. A light snow dusted the tops of the peaks silver in the moonlight, and down near the bottoms were dark clots of pine forest running the slopes. But Gallen watched the gray middle slopes, almost featureless in the night, where the ancient road was bordered on one side by a precipice, on the other by walls of dark stone. The mountain chain here formed a huge S, so that though they had run perhaps forty kilometers since sunset, they were only fifteen kilometers as the wingman flies from the gates of the city, and with his mantle Gallen was able to see much of that road from this last bluff.

He stood for a long minute, then his breath caught in his chest, and his face became hard, impassive. Orick knew that look.

"What is it?" Ceravanne said, panting. "What do you see?"

Gallen looked up at the sky. It was growing light, a dimming of stars on the horizon. "They're after us," he said.

"How many in the hunting pack?" Ceravanne said, looking back up the trail.

"Twenty . . . or more." Gallen pulled out his incendiary

rifle, checked it. He had only two shots left, as they all well knew.

"So many?" Ceravanne asked in dismay. "We'd hardly make a meal for a dozen of them."

"They're hungry," Gallen said, slipping his rifle back into its holster. "Let's go. They'll have to hole up for the day in that guard shack. But they'll be after us again tonight."

He turned and sprinted down the road, into the depths of the gorge where the dark trunks of massive pine trees rose above them, and the road was overshadowed by vine maple and ironwood. On the slopes above, the world had seemed dead, sterile, but Orick was surprised that down here there was plenty of game—rabbits, squirrels, jays—things too small for the Derrits to bother with, all of them rustling through the detritus as they searched for their morning meals.

For that day they ran, scurrying from thicket to thicket like mice as Gallen watched for signs of wingmen.

So it was that near dusk, Gallen led them into the woods along the river. From high above, Orick had seen the river as nothing more than a silver ribbon in the canyon below, but down here he could see that it was more. Now, in the early fall, a cool flow rushed over boulders, flowed rippling across gravel bars. But all along the riverbank were great logs, cast up on the shores by the raging floods that tore down this canyon in winters past. Often, the river had gouged passageways through narrow chasms or left huge piles of flotsam. For nearly two hours after dark, the group made its way downstream through this mess. Then well after dark, under the light of the triple moons, Gallen led them all into the water, and they waded back upstream for several kilometers, often sloshing through pools that were chest-deep, until they passed the point where they'd first set foot off the road.

The water did not seem very cold to Orick, but all of his human friends complained of it, and Ceravanne often slipped on the mossy rocks.

When the women could wade no more, Orick let them sit astride his back, and carried them surefooted up to a tiny tributary creek that had become only a small flow of water. In the spring the creek must have been much larger, for it had eroded a deep and narrow gorge into the hillside.

"This will have to do for the night," Gallen whispered when they stopped at last, sheltered in a tiny nook. He pulled out the blankets from the packs, and they made a dismal camp behind a small tree.

Orick looked up and down through the gorge. He estimated that the walls were perhaps a hundred feet high here, and twelve feet wide. "I'm not very cozy with your strategy, Gallen," Orick whispered. "Sure, the Derrits could easily swagger through here two abreast."

"Aye," Gallen said, "that they could. But I'm hoping that they'll think we've headed downstream through the woods. The road takes us downstream, to the southeast, and I'm hoping they'll believe we've still gone that way. If they waste enough time hunting downstream, then we'll win through the night and they'll have to continue the hunt tomorrow. But even if we don't fool them, at the very least they'll have to split up and check the banks both upstream and down. That leaves us maybe five or ten to contend with at a time—not twenty."

"I thought the three we fought gave us more than ample exercise," Orick grumbled. "I really would prefer to leave these ones alone."

"Well, go to sleep," Gallen said, "and maybe you'll get your wish."

Orick tried to stay up the night, but in time he settled onto his paws. His heart was hammering heavy in his chest, and he was cold and hungry and miserable, but he thought of Tallea lying dead in the city of Indallian, naught but Derrit food, and though he missed his friend, he was glad to be alive.

"Gallen," Orick whispered, for both Maggie and Ceravanne had fallen asleep and were already snoring lightly.

"Aye?" Gallen asked.

"You've got Tallea's memories stored in your mantle, right?"

"Aye," Gallen said.

"Well," Orick wondered aloud, "how many people's memories can be stored in that thing?"

"Just one."

"And what would you do, I mean, if tonight a Derrit caught you? You couldn't save yourself the way you saved Tallea, could you?"

"Not without erasing her memories," Gallen said. "The memory crystal holds a lot, but I'm part of the Inhuman now, and I've probably got more memories than this one crystal can handle."

"So would you do it? Would you erase her memories to save yourself?"

Gallen thought for a moment. "The Inhuman in me would. Most of those people desperately want more life. They crave it. But the Gallen O'Day in me wouldn't do it."

Orick grunted. "I think that if you have to do it, you should. You should live for Maggie. Tallea would understand that, and she would forgive you."

"I'm not sure that I would forgive myself," Gallen whispered. "It's an unpleasant thing to have to consider. Go to sleep, now."

"No, you go to sleep," Orick said. "I'll take watch for a bit."

Orick lay watching quietly for a minute. Maggie had kept watch last night, so Orick was hoping to split it tonight with Gallen. Orick figured that the lad was worn to the nap, and he needed some time off, so tomorrow he considered taking watch with Maggie.

For a long time, he stared down the slope, and only the croaking of a lone tree frog kept him company.

Orick closed his eyes to rest them for a moment, and when next he woke, there was a fierce wind blowing down through the canyons. It did not buffet the small group much, sheltered as they were, but it was singing through the rocks and the trees.

He looked over at Gallen, who sat up awake and alert. "Any sign of them?" Orick asked, and Gallen looked over at him.

"I heard five or six of them walking upriver about an hour ago," Gallen said, "but the wind must have blown our scent away. Go back to sleep. It's nearly dawn."

Orick could not go back to sleep, since he felt so guilty about falling asleep during his watch, so he asked Gallen to catch some more shut-eye, then in an hour he woke them all. They ate a cold breakfast of the last of the apples.

"That was a good trick you gave them," Orick said after finishing his two apples. He eyed the cores that the others were eating as he talked. Without any more food to keep them going, he wanted to accentuate the positive. "You knew the wind would blow the scent away?"

"I hoped it would," Gallen admitted. "I've been through these canyons many times, and often at night the cold mountain air funnels down these slopes. It was a chance we had to take."

"Well," Orick said, "you've pulled us out for the day, but what about tonight?" He only hoped that Gallen had some kind of plan.

"That is a tough one," Gallen admitted.

"Farra Kuur?" Ceravanne asked, tossing Orick an apple core.

"Yes," Gallen said, "that is what I was hoping."

"It's a long stretch of road before us," Ceravanne considered. "We'll be hard-pressed to make it."

"Farra what?" Maggie asked.

"Farra Kuur," Gallen said. "A few kilometers south of here, the canyons narrow again, and down the road fifty or sixty kilometers, there was a fortress called Farra Kuur, virtually impenetrable. If we can make it there, and if the bridge is down after all these years, we should be able to hold the Derrits off for another night."

"If the bridge is down?" Orick said.

"Drawbridges," Gallen said. "Farra Kuur is burrowed into the spur of a mountain between two very steep chasms. Drawbridges were carved from great sheets of stone to span the gap, and the Makers created giant gears to raise and lower them."

"Certainly the bridges aren't in working order," Ceravanne said.

"They were three hundred years ago," Gallen said hopefully. "And the gears and chains were all well oiled back then. The Makers build for permanence. But even if the bridges aren't working now, so long as the bridges are down, we should make it into Farra Kuur. And once we're there . . . well, we'll see what I can do."

Orick didn't want to talk about the battle that would inevitably come tonight even if they made it to Farra Kuur, so he said, "Making it to this fortress of yours sounds like a fine idea, but it won't do us much good if we starve. You wouldn't happen to know where we might find some food around here?"

"Keep watch for mushrooms, berries, nuts," Gallen told him, "pick anything you find. We'll be running through the forest all day, and if we're lucky, maybe a young deer will impale itself on my sword," he joked.

"Are you sure that's wise, eating these strange berries?" Orick asked. He'd seen some small red berries the day before, but he'd been afraid to harvest any, not knowing if they were poisonous. And he didn't even want to chance the mushrooms he'd seen, for none were of varieties familiar to him.

"All mushrooms, berries, and fruits that you will find here on Tremonthin are edible—" Ceravanne said, "but one. The deathfruit grows on a bush low to the ground, and is dark purple, darker than a plum. It is to be eaten only by those who are sick or horribly injured, those who seek death."

Orick considered this good news, and they took off, climbing up the narrow gorge till they hit the road once again, and for most of the day, Orick foraged as he ran, eating a snail here, swallowing a few acorns there, nibbling a mushroom.

That day they ran among rounded hills beside where the river flowed, and once they stopped by the riverbank where the soil had a blue tinge so that Ceravanne could harvest some of the Healing Earth. They took off again, but shortly after that they lost the road altogether, for lush grasses and woods now covered the ancient road as if it had never been.

Still, Gallen kept a straight course, and on some high hills they would find themselves climbing over the remnants of a stone road that was worn and cracked, until well before noon they came to an ancient fortress that lay nearly all in ruins. One of its walls stood intact, rose to an incredible height of perhaps two hundred feet.

"Druin's Tower," Gallen called it, and he stood on the hill and studied the landmark wistfully, as did Ceravanne.

"Who was Druin?" Maggie asked.

Ceravanne answered, "Druin was a kindly scholar who united many people. He built this tower to study the stars, and he delved in forbidden technologies, hoping to carry the peoples of this land away with him to other worlds. But then he became old, and bitter, and turned away from peace, manufacturing weapons of war."

"I did not manufacture weapons," Gallen growled, gazing hard at Ceravanne, and it was as if another person spoke from his mouth. The memories the Inhuman had given Gallen were so strong, that for one moment, Druin spoke. "The Fengari workers turned against me, making cannons without my knowledge."

Ceravanne studied Gallen a moment. "The Immortals studied your memories most carefully, Druin. You were not guiltless in this affair."

"I was guiltless!" Gallen spat, and then he seemed to struggle for control and said heavily, in his own voice, "But that was long ago."

"The memories of the dead can be easily edited," Ceravanne said softly. "Druin's memories are in the archives at the City of Life. Someday you may see for yourself and learn the truth of it. Druin was a great man, a man of peace for most of his days, but his goodness died before he did."

"And if you read those memories and find that you have wronged him?" Gallen asked.

"We can review the records, and if he deserves a new life, then he will be granted one. But you must understand, Gallen, that he violated our strictest laws. Certain technologies are forbidden on this world, yet Druin sought them out. He may have been a well-meaning criminal, but he was a criminal nonetheless."

Gallen turned away from her, as if to lay the matter aside. The icy-gray river they'd been following flowed down below them through a green valley, where it joined an even broader muddy flow that came in from the north. For a moment, they sat and rested. There were no roads, no signs of homes or settlements. All of that was long gone. Gallen spotted some distant wingmen circling closer toward them, so they headed out for the shelter of the trees.

Orick could smell the garlicky scent of Derrits throughout most of the morning along the road, so he knew that they had gone ahead during the night. But an hour before noon they were climbing back up a long hill when the group passed an old mining tunnel carved into the stone cliff face alongside the road. There the odor of Derrits became so strong that even Maggie and Ceravanne could smell it.

The suns were shining bright and full, hidden only by the thinnest gauze of high clouds. Everyone crept quietly past the mine, and when they were well past, Gallen stopped and looked back toward it longingly.

"Give me the glow globe," Gallen said to Ceravanne.

"You aren't going in there?" Maggie hissed, grabbing Gallen's arm.

Gallen's face was pale, wooden. "They've got too much of a lead on us," he said. "I don't want them so close."

"What kind of plan do you have rolling around in that head of yours?" Maggie asked.

"I was thinking," Gallen answered, "that it would be interesting to see if they've posted a guard. Derrits normally don't, and I'm thinking I could kill two or three before any of them wake."

"No!" Maggie said. "It's not worth the risk!"

Gallen licked his lips. "The Derrits are not above eating their own kind. If I kill a couple, it leaves that much more food for the others to eat."

Ceravanne had fished the glow globe out of her pack, and she handed it to Gallen. "He's right," she said. "A well-fed Derrit is not as ferocious as a hungry one."

"Go ahead on up the road," Gallen said to Orick. "Derrits don't like the sun, but if they're angered, they might come out after us, and there's no sense being within arm's length if you don't have to."

"I'll come with you," Orick whispered.

"No, thank you." Gallen sighed. "With my cloak covering my scent, they won't smell me coming, and with my mantle, I can fight in the dark, so I won't alert them that way. I'd prefer to keep those advantages."

Orick's heart was sore to follow Gallen, but he knew it would not be wise, so he took the lesser course of action, and he hurried Maggie and Ceravanne up the road a couple of kilometers, where it turned around a wide bend, then had them hide in some bushes.

Gallen waited till they were set, then crept back to the huge entrance of the mine. It seemed he had hardly stepped in when they heard the bloodcurdling roar of Derrits.

Gallen staggered back out the door as if he'd been knocked backward, and he had his sword up in one hand, the glow globe blaring in the other. A huge yellow Derrit lunged through the narrow doorway after him, a stream of red blood at its throat, raking the air with its claws.

Gallen ducked beneath its grasp, slashed at its belly, then turned and ran. The Derrit careened around drunkenly for a second, then fell to the ground, and Gallen did not stop to watch it, for four other Derrits were lunging through the doors.

One of them stopped in the sunlight, raised his long snout skyward and roared his contempt, while three of the smaller Derrits gave chase to Gallen.

They were so swift, he could not hope to outrun them. Gallen sprinted for a hundred yards, pocketed his glow globe, then reached back and drew his incendiary rifle, whirled and fired.

A meteor of white plasma struck the first Derrit full in the face, and bits of plasma splashed backward, where they dropped and burned into the stone road and into the Derrits behind. The fire of it was bright as the sun, and even the Derrits inside the tunnel shrieked and grabbed their eyes, wailing like the damned.

The single shot managed to fry two of the Derrits and burn the leg of a third. Those monsters who were still alive stayed back in the mine.

Moments later, Gallen hurried up to Orick and the others, sweat dripping from his face, fresh blood spattered all across his robes. Behind him, the plasma fires from his rifle were still burning.

"They had a guard," Gallen said, shaking his head, stopping to catch his breath. He glanced back. "They sure don't like the incendiary rifle. Too bad we have only one shot left."

"Maybe this little display will have them thinking better about following our trail," Orick said hopefully.

Ceravanne shook her head. "Derrits are not easily dismayed, and they are a cunning people. They will try to outwit us."

Gallen merely grunted. "They will have to catch us first," he said and set off at a run.

That afternoon their trail took them through a land of broken hills, a wild land, with little game in it. They did see some rabbits from time to time, and once they saw three dark wolves fading away into the shadows under some trees.

Gallen and the women were wilting from lack of food and from the fast pace, so Orick made it his job to find something edible. Often that day, he imagined himself in Gallen's shoes, playing the hero. But he wasn't Gallen, he realized, and food is what they were lacking now.

While Gallen watched for wingmen and Derrits, Orick watched for mushrooms and pine cones, wild onions and berries. So it was that he managed to scrounge some snacks on the run, and near sunset, as he crossed a large stone bridge over the river, he smelled wild blackberries, and led the others upriver a hundred yards to a patch of berries that hung thick from the vines.

They picked what they could, stuffing as many berries as possible into their mouths, and when they set off again a few minutes later, it was with renewed vigor.

At dusk the road left the riverbanks and began to meander up through some dark hills, thick with scrub and the stone ruins of old buildings.

Gallen kept them running till well after dark. Clouds were blowing in, and it looked as if it would rain.

An hour after sundown, they topped a rise and found

themselves once again on a high canyon wall. Gallen called the others together for a council.

"If I guess right," he said, "the Derrits cannot be far behind us. We can either leave the road now and try to hide, or we can hope that the bridge is down at Farra Kuur, and try to fend them off there. Either plan may fail, so I ask you, which do you prefer?"

Orick looked down the cliff toward the river, then looked up at the sky. Their trail was still fresh, and the rains had not come yet, and might not come for hours. To run in hopes that the Derrits would lose their scent seemed foolhardy. Yet the path ahead was unknown. What if the bridge wasn't down, or what if it had been destroyed over the centuries? What if Derrits also lived in this fortress? There seemed to be no easy solution.

"The river here is not as wide as it was last night in the woods, and there are fewer places to hide," Ceravanne said. "You still have one shot for your rifle, and the Derrits will be loath to charge us so long as you wield that weapon. I think we should go ahead."

"I'm not sure," Orick grumbled. "How long could the bridges last at Farra Kuur before they weather away? At least if we leave the road now, we know what kind of a mess we've gotten ourselves into!"

Gallen looked at Maggie, who just shrugged.

"Farra Kuur, I vote, then," Gallen said. "Even if we get backed into a corner, the road behind us offers little room for the Derrits to maneuver. I think that up there, I might be able to hold them off until morning."

He nodded ahead, and Orick worried. Gallen had slept only lightly the night before. He was in no shape for battle. Still, Gallen had six thousand years of experience on this world, and Orick had but a few weeks. Orick had to bow to Gallen's wisdom.

They ran then. Blackberry vines crossed the road under their feet, attesting to the fact that even the game did not use this road as a trail, and as they ran, a burrow owl glided ahead before them, watching for any mice that they might disturb.

The moons were up enough so that they shed some wan light, and the four of them ran with their hearts, until at last they rounded a bend and saw a huge cliff face jutting out from the arm of the mountains, with broken towers crumbling along its rim, and all of the towers were riddled with dark holes that once had been windows. It was difficult at first to see much else, for the moonlight shone only on the upper towers, while the valley before them was in shadow, but the towers looked almost like living things, like giants tall and ready for battle, and Orick realized that indeed the whole face of the cliff was sculpted with their images. Four giants, their eyes hollowed out by age, their great beards hanging down to their belts, stood ready with huge axes in their hands, ever vigilant, ever ready for battle. Orick's eyes focused on those images.

As they ran, Gallen shouted in triumph, "The bridge is down! Hurry across!"

Behind them Orick heard the roar of Derrits.

Gallen spun about and shouted at Maggie, "Take the light. I'll hold them off!" He passed her the globe from his pocket.

Maggie squeezed the glow globe, and its bright white light flooded over the ridge. Then Ceravanne and Maggie rushed headlong, running faster than before, their stained cloaks flapping in the breeze, carrying a piece of the sun in their hand as they raced toward the dark tower.

Orick stayed beside Gallen. It was dark, with a thin blanket of clouds above, but not too dark for a bear to see by.

The Derrits were rushing uphill toward them in a disorganized pack, growling and hissing. They moved at a loping pace, sometimes lurching forward on their knuckles more than their feet, yet they moved at an incredible speed, so that a span of road that had taken Orick twenty minutes to cross took the giants only two. In the darkness, the Derrits' crude gait reminded Orick of nothing so much as that of an otter, with its head bobbing down and up as it ran. He counted seventeen of the brutes.

Yet when they were a hundred yards away, Gallen shouted at them. "Siisum, gasht! Gasht!"

The Derrits stopped, and stood gazing at Gallen and Orick. The ones in front would not move forward, but those in the back came inching up, shoving the others aside to get a look at the prey.

"Siisum s gasht! Ooongu s gasht!" Gallen shouted, and his voice was a snarling roar that mimicked that of the Derrits.

One of the Derrits called out to Gallen quizzically, a sound of grunts and snarls, yet Orick was sure that he heard words mingled in that growling.

"I told them to stop or die," Gallen said. "But their leader says that we are warriors of great power, and they want to eat us, to gain our power, so that even in our deaths our power will live on in them. He says that he will not be hungry for me, however, if I only give him you and a woman to eat."

Orick snarled and stood up on his hind feet. "Siisum a gasht!" he growled.

The Derrits lurched forward a step, as if angered, and Gallen fired his last shot into the pack. The plasma arced up into the night, then dropped in a spray. The whole side of the cliff lit up like noonday, and some of the Derrits screamed and toppled off the road in their haste to escape while others roared and lurched, trying to brush the flaming magma from them. In the light, their yellow hides were suddenly revealed, the white flashing of their fangs.

"Gasht!" Gallen roared, and he held his rifle up menacingly.

Those Derrits who could rushed backward down the hill at full speed, but four of the tribe were either killed outright by the blast, or were burning slowly, or had already toppled over the cliff.

Orick and Gallen turned and headed back toward Farra Kuur, and by the wavering light of the plasma fires, Orick could now see the great stone bridge spanning the chasm ahead, with its ancient guard posts still intact.

Orick started to hurry up the road, but Gallen whispered savagely, "Don't run! Don't let the Derrits see you run, or they'll know we're afraid, and they'll try to hunt us again."

And so they walked slowly up the road, and Orick felt as if a great weight had been lifted. With so many of the Derrits in flames, Gallen seemed confident that the others would not dare to attack again.

They could see the light up ahead, shining from within the walls of Farra Kuur on the far side of the bridge. Maggie and Ceravanne had gone deeper into the fortress, and the light shone from an archway far back along the northern wall.

As Orick approached the bridge, he could hear the sound of water rushing over rocks in the gorge below, could smell the faint vapors of water—and he caught a strange scent, something smoky and oily, a scent he recognized just barely. He was about to shout a warning, when suddenly a dark shadow detached from a corner and stood on the far side of the bridge, a man dressed in the dark, hooded robes of the Tekkar, which went down almost to his knees. And he wore tall black boots.

He held out a strange metallic device pointed at Gallen, and Gallen drew a startled breath at the sight of it. Orick could only guess that it was some type of gun, but it had an odd stock, one that required its user to hold the weapon forward with one hand on a trigger, the other on the stock.

"Well done, Lord Protector." The Tekkar's voice was soft, almost a hiss. In the dim light, Orick could see that the man's face was all a tattoo—of a pale yellow skull. "We've been waiting. You've saved us from an inconvenience with the Derrits, and for that, we owe you. Now, throw down your weapons, or we'll execute the women."

Orick's heart pounded in his chest, and he considered what to do. He wanted desperately to rush forward and tear off this man's limbs.

But the Tekkar nodded, and from the archway where the lights shone, seven more Tekkar came out in a tight knot, holding Ceravanne and Maggie. One of the Tekkar held a gun to Maggie's head.

Twenty-eight

Orick growled and paced back and forth, as if at any moment he would lunge ahead, and Maggie stood with the gun to her temple, her head cocked painfully to one side under the Tekkar's rough grip, unable to move. She remembered some of the basic kicks and punches that Gallen's mantle had taught her two nights before, but three of the Tekkar had her. She knew nothing that could help her now.

"Don't," Gallen warned Orick, to keep the bear from charging, and Maggie's heart went out to poor Orick. "Those are Dronon pulp pistols, made to pierce a Dronon's exoskeleton. You don't want to see what kind of damage they do."

Orick stood up on his hind legs and bawled, his claws raking the air, obviously confused. Maggie could see how much he wanted to save her, and she feared he would charge now to his own death.

"Please, Orick, stay back!" she called, and the bear roared loudly, got back down on all fours.

"Quite sensible," the Lord of the Tekkar hissed. "Now, Lord Protector, take off your mantle and throw it at my feet. Then drop your rifle belt, sword, and knives."

Gallen looked up once to the towering images of giants overhead, and he stood with eyes closed, as if meditating for a long moment, considering his chances if he should choose to fight, but at last he did not resist, simply threw his mantle down.

Maggie realized that the Tekkar couldn't know that Gallen's rifle was empty. If she fled now, the Tekkar might not chase her, since they wouldn't want to turn their backs on Gallen. She wondered if she could twist away, run through the dark tunnels of Farra Kuur to escape, but she knew that the Tekkar were terribly fast and Gallen had said that they could see in the dark, that to their eyes the heat from her own body glowed. She could not hope to escape them.

Gallen unbuckled his sword belt and knife sheaths, put them down on the ground, then kicked them forward with his foot and backed away. For one final second, Maggie almost hoped he would pull his sword and fight, but she knew that resistance would be futile. He was outgunned.

Gallen raised his hand out to the Tekkar's Lord, made a pulling gesture, as if summoning him, and Maggie recognized it as the same gesture he'd made days ago to Zell'a Cree. But the Tekkar ignored the Inhuman hand signal, kept their weapons trained on Gallen.

Only when Gallen had backed well away did the Tekkar Lord stride forward, watching Gallen as he carefully picked up the mantle.

Once he had it in hand, his men came to his side, and one held a Dronon pulp gun and kept Gallen and Orick covered while their Lord placed Gallen's mantle into the pocket of his robe.

The Tekkar Lord ordered Gallen to turn around, and two of his men went forward, pulled back Gallen's hands and began to bind him.

"What is this, my brothers?" Gallen said, addressing the Tekkar. "This isn't necessary. I was bringing the Tharrin to Moree—a goal that both she and the Harvester shared, though with different ends. I planned to deliver her into the Inhuman's hands."

And in the farthest recesses of her mind, Maggie worried that Gallen might be telling the Tekkar the truth. Perhaps in all of this journey he had been the unwitting accomplice of the Inhuman. At the very least, Maggie had felt his distance during the past week. The Inhuman had formed a barrier between them.

"And for bringing them here, I thank you," the Tekkar Lord answered Gallen.

When Gallen's bands were tight, one of the Tekkar reached up, pulled the hair back from Gallen's neck, and said, "My brothers, he does bear the mark of the Word!"

Ceravanne had the presence of mind to gasp and to look around in astonishment. "No!" she cried, as if horrified at the news. And because Ceravanne had been studying how to manipulate humans for nearly four thousand years, her performance carried a sense of conviction that few others could match.

All faces turned toward her, though the Tekkar Lord just glanced at her with a flicker of his eyes, but it gave time for Maggie and Orick to manage similar exclamations of horror and surprise.

The Tekkar Lord studied them, then addressed Gallen. "If you were delivering them to Moree, then why the subterfuge? You could have taken a more direct route."

Gallen looked up at him steadily. "I wanted to bring them in alone. It was to be my first and noblest act of service to the Inhuman. We all serve it in our own way, and I prefer to use deceit rather than force."

The Tekkar Lord reached into a pocket, pulled out a small ball. Maggie recognized it as a Dronon message pod. Like the Dronon weapons the Tekkar bore, it was an odd piece of work, an artifact that the Dronon must have left behind. The Tekkar hissed, "We have the Lord Protector and his company in custody at Farra Kuur. We are bringing four of them in. Request air transport for twelve to Moree."

He threw the ball in the air, and it flew with a hissing noise high up, heading southwest toward Moree. Maggie had seen the Dronon message pods before, even had some broken ones of her own, but she'd never seen a working model at such close range, and she longed to tear it apart to see how its miniature antigrav unit functioned.

"Perhaps you are indeed Inhuman," the Tekkar Lord said to Gallen, "and if so, we welcome you. But if you are Inhuman, then you will not fight your fetters, and you will rejoice with us as we introduce your friends to the mysteries of the Word."

He reached into his pocket, pulled out a small silver insect that struggled in his gloved hand. The Tekkar held it up, walked over to Ceravanne, and looked her in the eyes. Maggie could see from the way that his lips were gently parted, from the anxious breaths he took, that he enjoyed torturing others, but Ceravanne did not flinch away from him, did not let him see her fear, and thus denied him his pleasure.

"Hold!" Orick called out, still standing on the bridge. "You can't be doing that to her. This is the Swallow, come back to rebuild the Accord!" Obviously the bear hoped that his words would have some kind of influence on the Tekkar. Perhaps he even hoped that they would fall to their knees as the worthy Im giants had done.

But the Lord of the Tekkar only laughed at Orick. "Have you not heard? The Swallow is already in Moree, and she has gathered her armies. She is set to harvest this world, and the stars beyond."

He spread his hands, waving toward the stars shining above the fortress, above the dark canyon walls, then turned to Maggie.

"This one is for you, child," he whispered, and he dropped the Word into the hood of her cloak.

Maggie cried out, tried to struggle free of the Tekkar's grip, but two of them viciously twisted her arms up behind her back and held her wrists, forcing her to bow down on her knees into the dirt.

Gallen was still at the far side of the bridge, his hands tied behind his back, unable to do anything but watch. Orick could not come to her rescue with the Tekkar holding him at gunpoint.

Gallen stood watching, his face a carefully controlled mask, unable to do anything for the moment. There was no movement, only the sound of the tumbling waters in the chasm far below the stone bridge, breaking the silence.

Maggie grunted, breathing hard, and waited in cold terror for the Word to attack. In a moment, she felt a sharp stabbing pain at the base of her neck, then a rapid push as the Word burrowed under the skin at the base of her skull.

She cried out, and watched Gallen through tear-filled eyes. He was standing thirty meters away from her in the edge of the darkness, and she looked across at him as if across some great gulf, and she realized that she had been looking at him this way for days. Ever since the Word had infested his skull, he'd inhabited a place she could not quite reach.

And now I'm going there, Maggie realized, and it filled her with a new thrill of hope, mingled with fear. I will share the lives he has lived, feel what he has felt. And in the end, we will no more be strangers.

But only if I renounce the Word. And so Maggie conjured an image of the Dronon on Fale, and how they had tormented her, until the white hate boiling in the pit of her stomach burned away all fear, all pain.

She heard the sound of bones grinding in her skull, and she shrieked, "Gallen!" And suddenly, the world was turning, and Maggie felt herself dropping forward into the dust.

When Maggie woke, she lay for a long moment, her eyes opened to slits, and her first thought was to wonder if she were dead.

The room was dark but for a small fire, and Maggie recalled lives past, in bodies where she could see more keenly, smell through the palms of her hands, hear the rustling footsteps of mice through stone walls. In comparison, this body seemed sluggish, its senses dulled. She remembered her sense of power living as a Djudjanit under the ocean and swimming as fast as any fish, and recalled as Entreak d'Suluuth flying on hot summer thermals for days, never needing rest, and so she felt weak now in comparison. And this was the Inhuman's first message to her, that because of her humanity, she was inferior.

She thought for a moment of times spent gazing placidly at

campfires, of passionate loves lost and won over the course of a hundred lifetimes, of battles and defeat, and she saw how whole lives were often colored by emotional themes, recurring cycles of anger or despair or hopeful delusions. People were too often cramped by their own inadequacies, or made pawns in the larger affairs of men. Maggie thought back on her lives and saw them as a painter's palette of colors, each with its own distinctive hue and texture.

And the experience made her feel rich, and buoyant and wise and old beyond the counting of years. And this was the Inhuman's second message to her. Be grateful for what I have given you.

The lives and customs and thoughts and ideals of a hundred different people roiled around in her brain, and Maggie had learned much from the Inhuman. It was as if before there had been only a night sky, and now a vast and yawning galaxy of stars suddenly burned before her.

Almost without exception, the lives the Dronon had shown her were lived by people of passion, people who loved life and wanted to continue indefinitely, and now Maggie saw how truly precious a gift it was, and she wanted to live over and over again, each time experiencing a new form. And in her mind, the Inhuman whispered, Follow me, and I will give you endless life.

And she recalled the hundred lives lived and wasted, and felt how each of those people had seen their own deaths as unfair. And the Inhuman whispered, The Tharrin-led humans are your enemies.

But as she cast back into her new memories, she also recalled thousands of nonhuman people who had been granted the rebirth. So she reconsidered the lives she had led, and recalled from each person something of the unbridled passions that might have kept them from being reborn. For Entreak d'Suluuth it may have been his contempt for the "wingless," for another it had been complacency, for another greed.

So Maggie felt unsure as to whether the human lords had misjudged these people. Perhaps the human lords had been right to let them pass away, forgotten. And the Inhuman within her cringed at such thoughts, tried to get her to consider other arguments.

Then Maggie recalled her own captivity under the hands of the Dronon, and her rage began to burn in her. A wave of confusion washed over her as the Inhuman sought to take control of her, but Maggie focused on her own memories. And she saw without a doubt that the information she'd been given was tainted, an emotional argument designed for the naïve and inexperienced. Her own experiences with the Dronon precluded any possibility of being drawn into their cause, and her resolve to destroy the Inhuman had not weakened. Indeed, the Inhuman's Word had not been able to have the slightest effect in changing her view of the world, and she marveled at how Gallen had been so strongly influenced by the Word.

It seemed almost a defect in his character to have become so misguided, but she recalled Ceravanne's warning that some people found it easier to fight the Inhuman's Word. Indeed, the Bock had not even feared that Orick could be infected. So Maggie wondered if it were some biological difference in her that let her defeat the programming so easily.

She opened her eyes to slits and looked around. She was lying on the floor in a large room—the same room that the Tekkar had hustled Maggie and Ceravanne into when they first entered Farra Kuur. The room may have once been an inn. It was large enough for one—twenty meters on one side, thirty long, with a huge hearth on the far wall and a couple of entryways that might have led to kitchens or sleeping chambers. Maggie's head was pillowed by the packs that Gallen, Maggie, and Ceravanne had carried.

In the far corner of the room, two Tekkar had built a fire in an ancient stone oven, and they were cooking some fry bread and beans seasoned with desert spices. The scent made Maggie hungry.

Her legs and arms were not bound, which suggested that the Tekkar believed that she would be converted when she woke— or perhaps they thought only that she would pose no threat.

Maggie looked around for the others. Two Tekkar had Gallen and Orick sitting in one corner, guns trained on them. The other Tekkar did not speak much, and then only in whispers, but they moved about the room as if in a dance, each performing his own task—cooking, packing, guarding—and Maggie noticed something odd about them: the Tekkar had set themselves up around the room so that none were really close to the others. They did not congregate. Instead, they moved about the room evenly, almost gracefully, but always chose their path so that they maximized one another's body space. It was a distinctly nonhuman behavior.

In another corner, Ceravanne sat, hands bound in front of her. Orick was at her side, both of them under heavy guard. Maggie was surprised that they had not yet been infected by the Word.

The Tekkar Lord had Gallen's mantle in his hands, and he turned it over and over, studying it. Finally, after a minute, he put it on his own head, and smiled at his men. He stood for a moment, breathing deeply, and said, "Ah, now *I* am a Lord Protector."

Maggie knew that she had to get the mantle back. It was too powerful a tool to leave in the hands of a servant of the Inhuman. She got up, stretched, and smiled warmly at the Tekkar. Their leader saw her and hurried over, the memory crystals of Gallen's mantle glinting under his hood.

Maggie waved toward Ceravanne, her voice expressing confusion. "Have we no Word for our sister, or for the bear?"

The Tekkar Lord gazed into her eyes, and his own purple eyes looked like black holes in his dark skin. "None," he hissed, his voice whispery, as is often the case with those who have keen ears. "An aircar will be here soon. Perhaps more will be provided."

Maggie looked about the room, still wondering what to do. "I . . . want to serve the Inhuman," she said. "But I don't know how."

The Tekkar nodded graciously. "The lives you have lived— they train you in the use of technology and weapons, strategy and history. All that remains is for you to be assigned to a unit."

Maggie considered. She had the lives of forty-one men and

women who'd gone to war—swordsmen and bowmen, tacticians, scouts, squires, kings, and supplymen. Merchants who understood the economics of war, a Dronon technician and worker from the City of Life.

She hadn't considered before, but she was prepared for just about any situation that the future could throw at her, and she also realized that much of what she'd learned was designed to help accommodate other nonhuman species. The passionless Wydeem would learn about lust and the desire to build. The gentle and shy Foglarens would learn how to be confident in open spaces and understand the thrill of battle. The Roamers would learn of trade and economics.

"Yes," Maggie whispered for the first time. "I see what you mean. May I be in your command for now?"

"Of course," the Tekkar hissed. "It is always an honor to work with a kitten whose eyes have just opened."

Maggie gave him her hand, let the Tekkar help her rise. She nodded toward the food. "May I? We haven't eaten well in days."

"Of course," the Lord said. "But you will need to hurry. The transport will be here soon."

Maggie made up a plate, and the Tekkar Lord knelt beside her, watching her every move. Maggie nodded toward Ceravanne. "I almost envy them."

"Why?" the Tekkar asked.

"Because soon they will hear the voice of the Inhuman, and they will feel what I felt upon awakening. That first moment of being alive."

"Yesss," the Lord hissed, obviously pleased.

Maggie sat eating, wondering what she might be able to do to help the others break free. Probably nothing. She noticed the furtive glances the Tekkar gave her. They were watching her closely now, and had not yet offered her a weapon. She knew that they wouldn't offer her one until she had been safely delivered to Moree.

She had just finished her plate, when the building began to rumble and vibrate as the gravity waves of a Dronon flier bounced against it.

"The transport is here," the Tekkar Lord said, and his men began picking up their packs. They had great mounds of food and blankets, and most of the men had to fill their arms.

The Tekkar Lord himself was about to grab his pack, but instead ordered one of his men to do it and took both of the Dronon pulp guns, waved Gallen and Orick forward, and they went out into the night.

On the stone bridge outside Farra Kuur, a lone flier had set down. It was a large military job, an oblong blue disk with rows of windows. One of its doors swung upward automatically on landing. It was large enough to carry twenty men, and its forward weapon array held twin plasma cannons and several smart missile mounts. No one had come with the flier, so obviously it was piloted by an AI. Maggie was not wearing her mantle, but she knew upon looking at the flier that this was a completely new machine, not more than a week old and designed for use by men, not some artifact left by the Dronon.

So the Inhuman was building its own arsenal.

The Tekkar carried their bundles and went ahead, stopped to look down the road. The Derrits had come back to retrieve their dead. The whole pack of them were gathered out in the darkness far down the road, growling low and snarling.

But they seemed disinclined to charge up the road with the military transport and a squad of Tekkar there.

Gallen, Orick, Maggie, and Ceravanne were herded behind by the Tekkar Lord, waving his gun. He'd put the spare in his belt.

Just as Maggie got to the main gate of Farra Kuur and stood under its black stone arch, Gallen stopped and looked back at the Tekkar Lord.

"Veriasse, kill them now!" he whispered.

The Tekkar Lord's eyes suddenly rolled back in his head, and he leapt sideways and fired the Dronon pulp pistol in a frenzy. It made burping noises as it fired, and Maggie looked to see a Tekkar take a hit to the head, opening a hole. The whole side of his face exploded outward, the shattered bones of his skull stretching the skin incredibly taut, and then his skull seemed to shrink in on itself, and he crumpled to the road.

Another Tekkar took a body hit, and the left side of his chest ripped away as the shell of the pulp gun exploded, spattering blood and bits of bone and lung all across the transport.

One of the Tekkar managed to pull a knife and fling it at his Lord, but it was a hasty throw, and the Tekkar Lord simply dodged aside, then finished shooting down his own men.

And then he pulled the spare gun from his belt and dropped both weapons, and merely stood. Maggie watched him in confusion, wondering if the Lord were changing sides. Down the mountain, the Derrits began to roar quizzically, as if trying to decide whether to charge.

"Quickly!" Gallen shouted. "Cut us free! There is no telling how long the mantle will be able to control him!"

Maggie grabbed the fallen knife from the road, went to Gallen and cut his bonds, then did the same for Ceravanne. Before Maggie could finish with Ceravanne, Gallen went to the Tekkar Lord, pulled the man's knife, and plunged it into his heart.

The Tekkar dropped with a sigh, and Gallen grabbed the pulp pistols and his mantle. In moments he had hurried to the flier, and they began throwing in the packs that the Tekkar had carried, then leapt in and closed the doors just as the Derrits charged up the road.

"Vehicle, rise eighty yards and hold position!" Maggie commanded the flier's AI.

The flier rose up in the air and hovered.

"I don't understand," Orick grumbled. "What happened?"

Gallen had already put his mantle back on, and he whispered, "Not any man can wield the power of a Lord Protector's mantle. The mantle is a living machine, and it partakes of the desires and intents of its makers, and of those who use it. And like a Guide, it has some measure of control over its wearer. Most of the time, it gives me free rein to do as I please, but I have felt it tugging at my limbs, using me in battle as much as I use it. So when the Tekkar asked me to surrender it, I asked my mantle if it could protect me. It said that it could not serve an evil man. It warned me that it might be able to battle the Tekkar, once one of them put it on. I knew that the Tekkar would covet the thing, and eventually one would try to claim it, so I had only to wait my chance."

Maggie looked out the window at the dead Tekkar strewn across the road. She recalled how the Tekkar Lord had innocuously obtained both the guns. She realized that Gallen's mantle had been prodding him even then.

Maggie had understood that her mantle was designed for a special purpose, and that its abilities and memory were all aimed at fulfilling its own desires and objectives. She had felt her own mantle tugging at her mind, filling her with curiosity when she'd studied Dronon technology, but she hadn't quite grasped how symbiotic the relationship between man and mantle might be—until now. And Maggie realized that she would need to begin studying mantles more explicitly, learning more of their creation, abilities, and desires.

Down on the road, the Derrits fell upon the bodies of the dead Tekkar, grabbing them and scurrying away. Food for their babies, Maggie thought.

"Where to now?" Maggie said.

Gallen looked at her quizzically, the green running lights of the flier soft on his face, and she smiled. "I'm not Inhuman, if that's what you're wondering, Gallen O'Day!"

"I didn't imagine you would be," Gallen said. "But one can never tell." After a moment of thought, he said, "We've got air transport, and we've got food. We might as well fly to Moree."

"Surely we can't just fly into the city," Ceravanne said. "They'll be waiting for us."

"We can land nearby," Gallen said. "Close, but not too close."

Ceravanne closed her eyes, thinking. "I'm not sure, but I believe I know just the place."

Twenty-nine

———

"Where should we go?" Maggie asked again, staring hard at Ceravanne, but Ceravanne was still thinking, unsure if hers was the right course.

"If I judge right," Ceravanne said, "we cannot just go straight into Moree in this vehicle. We will have to set down outside the city. Is that right?"

Gallen nodded curtly.

"And I have seen the Dronon aircars streak across the sky like meteors," Ceravanne said, "so that a journey of a thousand kilometers takes but an hour."

"More like six minutes in this car," Maggie said.

"We need rest and food before we go into Moree, and a place of safety," Ceravanne continued. "Could we go back to Northland for one day, to the Vale of the Bock on Starbourne Mountain?"

Maggie and Orick both dropped their jaws. They had been struggling so hard to reach Moree that both of them thought only in terms of that small goal, and so they had imagined landing as close as possible to that place.

"It might not be a bad idea," Maggie said. "When this aircar doesn't return on schedule, the Tekkar at Moree are going to become suspicious. They'll close the gates tight, and start looking for us. It wouldn't be a bad idea to stay away for a while."

Gallen stared out the window, considering. "But every moment we waste only allows the Inhuman's agents to get stronger. They've already got the Dronon hive cities, and now they are building armed and armored air transports. I think we should go in immediately."

"It is hours till dawn," Ceravanne said. "The Tekkar are awake, but most of them will be sleeping by morning. We should wait to infiltrate the city by daylight."

Gallen nodded in acquiescence, and Maggie told the aircar to take them to Northland, to Starbourne Mountain. The aircar did not know the coordinates, so Ceravanne gave it an approximation, and the transport rose in the air and swept away. Ceravanne looked out her window and saw the small campfires and lights of villages down in the cities below, and she watched the clouds, like floating sheets of ice on a swollen winter river, sliding away beneath her. She had never been in an aircar before. Though the thing sounded noisy from the outside, there was absolute quiet within the vehicle, and this seemed somehow wondrous to her.

Gallen sighed, then said, "With all of their military buildup, I don't understand why the hosts of the Inhuman haven't attacked Northland yet."

"Perhaps they are afraid that Northland is stronger than they know," Ceravanne said. "In the City of Life, we have long allowed our guards to carry weapons that are restricted elsewhere on the planet, and our resistance fighters became expert at using those weapons on the Dronon, and at sabotaging the Dronon walking hive cities."

"Even with that," Gallen said, raising a brow, "I suspect that the Inhuman has amassed enough weaponry to wipe out your people. Something else is holding it back."

There was a long moment of silence, and at last Ceravanne said, "Could it be compassion?"

Gallen studied her a moment, wondering. "Why would you say that?"

Ceravanne shrugged a little. "It was something the Tekkar said when Orick told him that I was the Swallow. He said that the Swallow had already returned to Moree, and had gathered her armies."

Gallen whispered, "And she was set to harvest the stars?"

Ceravanne nodded. Gallen had been so convinced that the Harvester was a machine that for a moment he did not understand what she was trying to imply.

"Could it be that the Dronon have set up an imposter?" Maggie asked Ceravanne. "Someone who could take advantage of your reputation."

Gallen blurted out, "Why would they bother, when they could have the real thing? They would only need to clone Ceravanne and fill her with the Inhuman's memories—and they'd have their Harvester." He spoke the thought as quickly as it came to him. And finally, she saw that Gallen understood.

Orick gasped, and Maggie looked crestfallen as together they saw the simplicity of it. Ceravanne turned away, for she could not face them.

Gallen looked into Ceravanne's eyes and said more gently, perhaps only realizing the truth now, "And that is why you insisted on coming with us, isn't it? You knew that the Harvester is not a machine. You came to face your darker self?"

Ceravanne hesitated to speak, and Maggie shook her head in denial. "Certainly the Dronon couldn't turn a Tharrin—even with the Inhuman's conditioning. It wasn't able to turn me!"

Ceravanne wondered, as she had wondered on countless nights, just how susceptible she herself might be to the Inhuman's persuasion. The Inhuman had come after her again and again with such persistence, and always she'd managed to kill herself to avoid being taken. But she had not been able to defend her dead body. The Dronon had had countless opportunities to recover her genome, create a clone, and fill it with whatever thoughts or memories they desired.

Ceravanne looked into Maggie's dark eyes. The young woman

had been losing weight due to the rigors of their journey, and for the first time Ceravanne really noticed how this was wearing at her. "I have never wanted to talk to you about these things until now," Ceravanne said. "I didn't want to betray how much I knew of the Inhuman, nor did I want to betray my plans on how to deal with it once we reach Moree. You see, there was always the possibility that one of you could be turned. But now Orick and I are the only ones who have not received the Inhuman's Word, and Maggie, you and Gallen will need to continue my battle without me, should I die."

Ceravanne looked deep into Maggie's eyes, took a deep breath, and said, "Maggie, you are wrong if you think we Tharrin can withstand the Inhuman's Word. The sad truth is that the Inhuman's Word, as a weapon, has proven to be more effective against my people than any others. It was designed to persuade us to join the Dronon's cause. It is almost by accident that the Inhuman has also worked so well against the Tekkar and other races."

"Oh, Ceravanne," Maggie said, and she crossed the hull of the ship, took Ceravanne in her arms, and for one sweet moment, Ceravanne wept and let Maggie embrace her.

"We are our bodies," Ceravanne whispered close to Maggie's ear. "You see, the Tharrin were made to serve mankind, and men, by their very nature, are predispositioned to serve us in return. The Dronon knew that if they could control us, we Tharrin might hold the key to controlling mankind. None of us can escape what we are. And in some cases, we cannot escape what we feel, what we must do."

Ceravanne wiped her eyes, leaned back, and looked at Maggie. "The Inhuman argues for greater compassion, and to the Tharrin its arguments seem persuasive, for the Tharrin have always sought to rule with compassion above all else. And so the Dronon use our most basic needs to undermine us. But the Inhuman's Word does more to us than that—it seeks to manipulate its victims subconsciously. It convinces them that only by surrendering their individual freedom can they hope to serve mankind with total compassion—"

Gallen and Maggie both said at once, "By best serving the

state, we best serve mankind." They looked into each other's eyes, recognizing that the idea they'd spoken had not been their own, but had been planted in them by the Inhuman.

"Exactly," Ceravanne said. "But of course when the state becomes supreme, it inevitably becomes corrupt, catering to some undefinable mass rather than to the individual. By trying to serve everyone, ultimately it serves no one well. You've seen how ruthless the Tekkar are, yet even they believe that their ruthlessness toward others is in fact a compassionate service to the state.

"The Dronon do not care about this flaw in their system, for they are hopelessly enthralled by their Golden Queen, and they have no ideals beyond serving her. But we Tharrin agonize over the problem. We are trained to consistently review our actions so that we leave humans as much individual ability to make choices as they desire—"

"But you can never leave us totally free," Maggie said. "You always have the desire to manipulate us. I've seen it in the way that you treat Gallen."

"I was wrong to try to control him," Ceravanne said. "If I had not felt that my own world was at stake, I would not have done it. I . . . was so afraid, that I was not thinking well. What I did was contemptible. Please forgive me."

Maggie watched her, and though her expression showed only compassion, there was a hardness in her eyes. She might forgive Ceravanne, but she no longer trusted her completely, and she would not forget what Ceravanne had done.

"Sometimes I wonder," Maggie said. "How do I know you are not trying to manipulate me now?"

Ceravanne studied Maggie and considered how she might best address this question. She could have said something to placate the woman, but she did not want to frost the hard facts with sweet-tasting half-truths. "I am trying to manipulate you, of course," Ceravanne said. "I have shown you my world's need, and I have asked you to enlist with me and risk your lives in my cause. But I have not tried to deceive you about the dangers involved. I ask you to come willingly.

"But of course," Ceravanne continued, "on the larger scale

we must also consider your biological needs, your inborn desire to serve your fellow man. That is what motivates you now. And in fact, Maggie, I suspect that whether I am a Tharrin or not makes little difference at the moment. If I were a Derrit leading you on this quest, you would still follow me, despite my odor and ungainly appearance.

"But as to the larger question as to whether you are free, of course we cannot lead men who are totally free, because none of us is free of the basic human desires that define what we are. So, ultimately, none of us are free, and all must share responsibility for our group acts.

"Perhaps only if you were a Tharrin could you understand completely how dependent we are upon one another—and how much responsibility a leader has for the group: if I call a man into battle, and we win, I must always wonder if I've done the right thing, if my enemies deserved death. But if we lose the fight, and the man I've called into battle dies, then I have to wonder if I'm responsible." Ceravanne took Maggie's hand and squeezed it. Maggie sat down beside her on the soft, green bench. "I can ask myself, Did the man die because our enemies were too strong? Did the man die because he was too weak or too unprepared? Or did the man die because I failed to resolve the conflict peacefully long before that?

"It may be that in any given defeat, I am totally at fault. It may be that the man died because of all my failures. And so when we resort to battle, we Tharrin always count ourselves as having lost the conflict, for we are ill-prepared to tolerate such guilt.

"For this reason, we prefer never to resolve conflicts through violence. Often we accept the responsibilities of leadership only so long as they do not lead into battle.

"This resolve is so strong that when my people here on Tremonthin saw what the Inhuman could do, most of my brothers and sisters removed the records of their genome and their memories from the City of Life, then destroyed themselves outright in order to avoid capture. We had to avoid becoming pawns in the Dronon's game."

Orick had been sitting quietly on the floor, resting, but he perked his head up, raised his nose questioningly in the air. "But you said earlier that the Dronon had *killed* your people?"

"I've never said 'killed.' They *destroyed* my people," Ceravanne corrected. "Those that they did convert became . . . monsters, creatures that we Tharrin find reprehensible. And so they were no longer Tharrin. And by forcing upon us this conflict, others of my people were forced to seek oblivion. I did not lie when I said they destroyed us."

"How many Tharrin are under the Inhuman's domination?" Gallen said.

"The Resistance killed the others. As for the Harvester—I am still not even certain that she is Tharrin," Ceravanne said, "though I have greatly suspected that my sister is there. . . . But if they do have my clone, it is just one."

Gallen's focus turned inward for a moment, and he rocked in his seat. The flier was equipped with benches with thick green cushions that were very comfortable, and he leaned back casually and said, "When we first met, you suspected that you wanted me to kill your dark sister?"

Ceravanne nodded. She knew that to their eyes, she still looked very much like a child of fourteen. She'd thought that by keeping a younger body, it might afford her some protection, provide something of a disguise. Adults in power tended to discount youths. And yet she had also felt the need to try to attract Gallen sexually. "I knew when we met that you might have to fight off the influence of the Inhuman, and that you might be forced to kill my dark twin. I wanted your commitment for those things only."

She did not admit that she wanted him because she'd known immediately that he was the clone of her beloved Belorian, and that she was in love with the image of the man she remembered, and that she hoped that Gallen might become that man still. Perhaps both he and Maggie might recall her reasons, but Ceravanne spared reminding them of this sad fact. She spared reminding them most of all because as she looked at Gallen, saw how faithful he'd remained to Maggie, he reminded her more than ever of Belorian. Indeed, he had been reborn both in body and spirit, but had given himself to another, and

Ceravanne could not seek his affection in good conscience, though the pain of being so close to him tore at her heart. And so she was resolved that she would leave them gracefully, with a lie.

"So," Gallen said, "Maggie and I have tasted the persuasions of the Inhuman, but you, Ceravanne, still seem to know our enemy better than either of us can. What is the Harvester's next step?"

"I'm not certain. I cannot guess what memories my clone might have, and those memories could turn her on paths that I might not anticipate," Ceravanne said. "But I fear that she may have all of my memories, along with those of the Inhuman. But even if she doesn't, as the Bock were fond of reminding me, we are our bodies. I know what she feels. I may know how she thinks. And so I imagine myself in her place. . . . If I were the Harvester, I would try to minimize the amount of force needed for the operation. I would seek converts, not corpses."

"And how would you do that?" Gallen asked.

"I would seek to indoctrinate every man and woman on the planet by supplying them with the Word. If a person remains neutral after indoctrination, I would accept this. But if they actively tried to fight after their indoctrination, I would do nothing . . . just let the Tekkar handle it, as—to my shame—I let my people handle the Rodim ages ago. And all of the evidence leads me to believe that this is precisely the path that the Harvester is taking."

"So you don't believe the Harvester will go to war?" Gallen asked.

"I can only guess," Ceravanne said. "And I imagine not. Yet we in Northland can't not prepare for that eventuality."

The deep voice of the ship's AI sounded—"Approaching destination"—and Ceravanne herself was forced to go to the front and describe how to reach the Vale of the Bock.

The aircar settled down then in a valley at the foot of the mountains, and Ceravanne looked out the windows. Snow was on the ground on the mountain peaks, silver in the moonlight. And in the Vale of the Bock, a single teardrop-shaped pool also glowed silver, its water unrippled. It gave off only a thin mist, which was odd, for at this time of year the hot springs here often fogged the cold air. Which suggested that it was an unusually warm evening, almost summer weather.

All around the pool, the Bock stood with arms raised, looking for all the world like twisted stumps. On a gentle hill above the vale, a temple made of white stone glowed yellow in the night because of the fires burning at the twin beacons beside each temple door. The gentle Riallna devotees who tended the Bock were already locked in for the night. Yet Ceravanne was concerned that the air transport landing so near the temple would frighten the Riallna, so she decided to let them know that it was she who had come.

She ran out into the evening air, using Gallen's glow globe for light, and hurried up to the temple, knocked at the door. In a moment, to Ceravanne's surprise, a Riallna devotee actually opened her door just a crack and peeked out, terrified. The devotee was a plump woman of middle age for her species, a woman named Alna, and Ceravanne had known her for a hundred years.

"Do not be afraid," Ceravanne whispered. "I've been to Moree, and we captured an aircar. I've come back tonight to speak to the Bock. We will sleep in our car, and leave in the morning."

The dear Alna gazed out at her in surprise, unconcerned about the possibility that Ceravanne might be Inhuman. "You'll do no such thing. You'll have a good dinner and some music by the fire, and sleep with us tonight," and then she opened the door wide and gave Ceravanne a hug.

"Oh, thank you," Ceravanne said.

"But first," Alna said, reconsidering, "I think that you and your friends should bathe, while we fix your dinner." The tone of her voice clearly let Ceravanne know that a bath was not optional, it was required.

Ceravanne went back into the main cabin of the transport and found Gallen and Maggie searching through the food stores.

Ceravanne said, "I've been informed by the priestess of the temple that if we would like a nice dinner and warm bed tonight, we need only to take a bath and wash out our clothes. The night is warm, and the pools here are heated by hot springs, which is why the Bock winter in this valley. Would anyone care to join me?"

It had been so long since they'd had a chance to bathe in anything but an icy river, that Ceravanne was not surprised when the others eagerly came out and enjoyed the luxury together, swimming naked in the moonlight. Orick the bear began slapping water at Ceravanne, and she splashed him back, and soon they were chasing one another around the pool and having a great time.

Afterward, they returned to the transport to get their packs, and in the darkness, Gallen said, "Ceravanne, when we first met, you asked me not to question you about your plans. You asked me to simply trust you, and till now I have. But we'll be going into Moree tomorrow. I came with the idea of destroying the Inhuman, dismantling the artificial intelligence that drives it. But you obviously hope to reclaim the Harvester. Is that your plan?"

"If I can reason with her," Ceravanne said, "yes, I think I can reclaim her. But there is much more that I hope to do."

Ceravanne went to her pack. It was a small pack made of brown leather, and she'd carried it a long way without anyone becoming suspicious of its contents. It held but one change of dirty clothes and a comb, and in all these past weeks, she had never given the others a clue as to what else might be inside it.

She pulled out a small but heavy parcel wrapped in fine leather and laid it out on the floor, then began to unfold it. The thin golden chains that formed it tinkled as she worked, and the memory crystals woven into it glittered like diamonds. When it was all laid out on the floor, the huge mantle looked like the treasure of some ancient king. "This is what the Inhuman looks like," Ceravanne said. "This is an exact replica. Over the past two years, we gleaned information from all of the technicians who worked on it. In the City of Life, our technicians are not well versed in making such things, and so it was a great task. But we were able to learn whose lives are stored within the Inhuman, and so we went to our archives and retrieved those lives, whole and unedited, and placed them in this mantle. We could not get them all, for the Dronon were careless, and so some of those people's memories were lost forever. And in those cases, we replaced the lost crystals with new ones, showing the lives of those who *were* successful in obtaining rebirth.

"And our technicians created a program that will nullify the subliminal teachings that the Inhuman tries to plant in its victims."

"You mean you are going to fight the Inhuman's indoctrination?" Maggie asked, for like Gallen, she had assumed that the destruction of the Inhuman was their ultimate goal.

"We will do what we can," Ceravanne said. "If we can only destroy the Inhuman, burn it forever, then much will have been accomplished. But I fear that if that were to happen, our world would continue in civil war. You've seen the weapons that the Dronon left: if it comes to war, this world will yet be destroyed. But even that is better than letting the Inhuman's influence spread to the stars.

"Better still, the Council of Immortals in the City of Life hopes to diminish its influence. We hope to combat it on its own terms, counter its lies by telling the truth."

"But," Orick growled, "you'll be little better than they are. You'll have your own Word burrowing into Maggie's skull!"

Ceravanne shook her head violently. "I do not understand a great deal about how this technology works," she said. "But I know this: everyone who has ever been affected by the Word already has a built-in receiver, and this mantle can send to the Inhuman's frequencies. But our mantle isn't fully operational. If it were, we could send our message out now and be done with it."

"What more do you need?" Maggie asked. "Maybe my mantle can help you make it?"

"We need the *key* to the Inhuman," Ceravanne said. "When a Word burrows into its victim, it sends a coded message telling the Inhuman to begin sending information. The memories are then sent, but they are only readable by the Word that requested them."

"So this 'key' contains an encryption program?" Maggie

asked. She sounded so much like one of the technicians in the City of Life that her question startled Ceravanne.

"Yes, that is what the technicians called it."

"And they couldn't just break the encryption program?"

Ceravanne shook her head. "The key was made by the Dronon, using their own technologies. Our people cannot duplicate it. But I do know that if you take the key off the mantle, the Inhuman will cease to function, for the key also bears the power source for the memory crystals on the mantle."

"And so in the most favorable scenario," Gallen said, "you would capture this key intact. Is that what you imagine?"

Ceravanne nodded. "If I can speak to the Harvester, I hope she will give it to me. If not, you may have to kill her and take the Inhuman's key."

Gallen rubbed his chin thoughtfully. Perhaps he had imagined rushing into a room, killing everyone and everything there, considering that the job would be finished. But Ceravanne had come to see that it could not be done so easily. She had imagined that the journey into Moree itself would be an easy walk, with only minor elements of intrigue—not a constant mad dash for her life. And now she saw that stealing the key to the Inhuman would be no small feat. Obviously, by the way that Maggie and Gallen furrowed their brows, they were thinking along the same lines.

Gallen got up, paced in the darkness, gazed off south toward Moree. The windows in the aircar showed only the mountains. He rubbed his hands together as if to warm them with the friction. "Moree is a hive worse than the city of Indallian, and its keepers are more fearsome than any tribe of Derrits. Do we even have an idea where to find the Harvester in that maze?"

Ceravanne went to her pack again. "Traders have been to Moree often enough, and some of them have been to the old king's throne room. It is well defended, and we believe that the Harvester is there. I have some intelligence on the place." She brought out a large map on thick gray paper. It showed three routes into the city, and from each route it displayed the number of doorways and chambers to the Harvester's throne room.

Gallen studied it for a moment, and his brow furrowed in dismay. Much of the map consisted of blank spaces, unknowable regions of the city that could easily house warriors. But what the map *did* show was that with each route, there were several guarded entrances, fortified gates. The Tekkar were a fierce race, created for a harsh world where survival seemed improbable, and their inborn need for a strong defense showed in the design of their city. It made for an impossible journey through the warrens of the Tekkar.

Thirty

That evening, Gallen was relieved to find that instead of another sleepless night sitting among cold stones, he was able to enjoy the company of the Riallna in their temple at the Vale of the Bock.

The Riallna devotees were all women, with cream-colored complexions and hair that was long and as soft and golden brown as corn silk, and though he knew that they were each hundreds of years old, they looked as if they were only handsome women of middle years. Their lives were simple and peaceful, and in their own way they were as devoted to making the world a place of beauty as any of the Makers.

On the outside, the temple seemed to be only a large blockish building of ivory-colored stone with a row of four fluted-stone columns that rose in front to form a large porch. It was a variation on a theme common in this rainy region, and it was a simple design, and graceful.

But inside, the temple was a masterpiece of functionality and comfort. The walls were covered over in some gold cloth and decorated with large wooden panels of ash, carved with delicate scenes of the suns rising over mountain fields.

On the main floor, low beds were laid out on rich carpets around a central fireplace that was shaped into a tall cone, with perhaps a dozen small holes near the bottom so that heat and light could escape the fire, while the smoke would be drawn up the chimney.

Various oil lamps burned around the room, keeping the place bright inside, but the soft wine-colored sofas and the forest-green carpets muted the brightness, creating a lighting that reminded Gallen of a forest glen at dusk, rampant with earth tones.

Evidence that the Riallna had a strong sense of smell was also abundant. Gallen noted a cleanness, a freshness to the room that had seldom been duplicated among other cultures. The scents of lightly seasoned foods were evident, but no harsh perfumes, and perhaps it was the scent more than anything else that gave the room a sense of wide spaces, an openness that size alone did not account for.

In moments, the Riallna began serving them silently, bringing in warm water to wash with first, followed by plates heaping with food. Some of the priestesses played flutes and cymbals at the far side of the great hall, so that the music of woodwinds floated dreamily through the air, and Ceravanne's friend Alna sat quietly with them, anticipating their needs, willing to let them steer the conversation in any direction they desired.

After a while, it became evident that the priestesses were seeking to serve their every whim, to give themselves completely in a manner that Gallen had seldom seen, even among the many lives the Inhuman had shown him, and he was pleased by the effect. He knew that this night, he was free to do whatever he pleased—whether it be to eat, sleep, listen to others, or talk quietly, and he realized suddenly how shallow the Inhuman's training had been.

Among the lives that he'd been shown, none of the peoples he'd met had been as generous as the Riallna. Instead, they'd often been grasping and outright selfish. Perhaps not overtly so, but it ran like a strong current beneath all of their actions. Even the best of the people he recalled had been . . . unconcerned about anyone beyond their own kin.

And as Gallen considered where he most would like to be this night—home in Tihrglas listening to some old hand playing the violin, or among the Suluuth listening to the piping song of the winged people, or on the plains singing at the stars with the Roamers, he realized that he was most content to be here.

Almost effortlessly, he fell asleep beside Maggie upon one of the couches, unaware of when the music ended.

Shortly after dawn, Gallen woke to the sounds of women cooking. Orick was asleep on one couch, lying on his back, his paws in the air. Maggie slept beside Gallen, and he gently disentangled himself from her arms. Ceravanne was no place to be seen, and Gallen imagined that she might be out bathing in the pool again.

He got up, wanting to plan for the day's coming battle, so headed out to the transport.

The suns were just rising in a soft violet haze over the mountains, and down the slope below the temple, the Bock had gathered near the pool, where they were dipping their feet into the pool's edge.

Ceravanne was sitting down with them, dressed in a clean green tunic that one of the priestesses must have given her. She was talking energetically to the same Bock that Gallen had met before, though something odd was happening. When they'd first met a few weeks before, the Bock had been a dark green in color, but now the color of its skin was tinted with a grayish-brown, like the stalk of a plant that is dying. Gallen walked toward them.

The Bock spoke back to Ceravanne, slowly, in dreamy tones, telling her, "Too late, too late for me to come now. Winter is upon us . . . task falls to you!"

Gallen stopped beside them for a moment, looked up at the green man, with his knobby joints, his long fingers splayed up toward the sun.

"Is everything all right?" Gallen asked Ceravanne.

She looked up at him. "The Bock are not awake yet. They have trouble this time of year. When the sun rises a bit more, and the blood warms in his veins, he will understand me more."

"Can't . . . can't go," the Bock said dreamily, the voice of an old man, long senile.

"I'll leave you two, then," Gallen said. He went to the transport, got Ceravanne's map out for further study, laid it out on the floor, trying to imagine alternate routes into the Tekkar warren that might exist somewhere in the gray unknown spaces the map did not show.

In a few minutes, Maggie came to join him. "The Riallna are making breakfast for us," she whispered, kneeling behind him. "I told them we'd be there in a while." She too was wearing her mantle and a new green tunic, and she knelt over the map just behind him to his right. Gallen inhaled her clean scent, tasted her exotic perfumes from Fale, and was very conscious of the way her left breast pressed against his arm. He felt somehow old. I should be rutting with her, celebrating with her, instead of making plans for war, he considered, but he put the stray thought from his mind.

Maggie stroked him quickly up the spine with the back of her hand—an act that made the nerves tingle all along his body. It was an odd caress, one that the Worren women used to good effect in their lovemaking. They were a lusty people and Gallen smiled at some of his memories.

"I love it when you smile at private little dirty jokes like that," Maggie said. She put both hands on his shoulders, knelt behind him, and nibbled his ear. "You know, darlin'," she said in her rich brogue, "I know more tricks than any madam in Baille Sean. In fact, I'll bet the Inhuman taught me more than the whole lot of them know together."

Gallen licked his lips, considered what it would mean to have someone with the memories of an Inhuman as a lover. "Then I'd say our time here has been well spent for that, if for nothing else."

Maggie giggled and twisted him down to the floor, then straddled him, commanded the car's AI to close and lock the security door to the transport, then she smiled at Gallen and wiggled enticingly. "It would be a shame if we disturbed the others with all of our moaning and yelling, now wouldn't it?"

Gallen nodded, and Maggie bent over and kissed him, and her breasts brushed against his chest. She just knelt there for a moment staring into his eyes, and then she began to untie his tunic slowly, sometimes reaching up to stroke his face or to snatch a kiss in gestures that he recalled from dozens of lovers over a hundred lifetimes. And yet being with her was better than being with any of the others, for Gallen saw that she knew all of the women he had ever loved, and with her gestures, she showed that she was willing to become all of them, to give what each had given before.

Gallen reached up and began to untie the strings on the front of her tunic, but Maggie shook her head, did it herself, and pulled off her clothes.

For the next half hour, Maggie led him on a tour of wonderland, and what they shared was as pure and beautiful as any moment he ever remembered. Somewhere in the lovemaking, he recalled some of the things he'd learned about women over the past six thousand years, and he began to give as good as he'd gotten, so that at the height of her excitement Maggie actually let out a jubilant shout of "Thank God and Gallen O'Day!" though when he teased her about it later, she denied recalling that she'd ever said it.

When they finished, Gallen held her for a long time, just lying on the cushions of the benches, and realized that for the first time in weeks he'd been able to completely forget about the Inhuman, about the world, and just enjoy the one woman he loved.

For a long time, he said nothing, till the suns began to shine higher through their window, and then Maggie said, "I was meaning to ask, what did you come in here for, anyway?"

"I was studying the map of Moree," Gallen said, "trying to figure out how to get in, but I don't see any easy path."

Maggie smiled at him. "That's because you're looking at the wrong map." She looked up toward the ceiling, to the crystal-web in the cryotank above the doorway. "Car, can you see the map Gallen has here spread out on the floor?"

"Yes," the car's AI said.

"Show us a holo of the aerial view of Moree, as it was last night, and superimpose your image over the map."

A holoimage appeared on the floor, an image of hills and trees in perfect miniature. Gallen sat up, and his feet sank into the landscape just below the knees, and he felt like a giant towering over the earth. The land around Moree was a yellow desert, with but one thin river flowing through it. Gallen could see individual Russian olive and juniper trees clumped among the rocks, and along the river was a veritable sea of cattails. By looking close, he could see the smoke holes from chimneys carved in rocks, along with the rare entrances where the Tekkar let in light to their world. Much of the land above the warrens was dedicated to farms that were carefully tended at night.

The starport facilities spread out on three sides of Moree, with five separate ships, like silver globes, set equidistantly around the city.

Crouching to the north, south, and west of Moree were three Dronon walking fortresses, like huge black crabs guarding the carrion from which they would make a meal.

South of Moree were parked seven aircars, lozenge-shaped vehicles like the one they were in. "Wait a minute," Gallen said, pondering the image. "Car, is this the total number of air vehicles that have been created?"

"Yes," the car said.

Gallen looked closely at the holograph. The airfield at Moree was only lightly guarded by a handful of men—and they were best positioned for a ground assault.

"Do you see what I see?" Gallen asked Maggie. She looked at him craftily, and Gallen suspected that she did. "The Tekkar are ready to fend off a ground assault, but they're not prepared to fight off an air attack."

"Of course not," Maggie said. "These are the first aircars they've ever owned, and they know that Northland has no air power. So they haven't even considered how to best defend them. The servants of the Inhuman are relying on techniques and tactics they've learned over the past six thousand years—not the tactics your mantle knows."

Gallen considered, questioned his mantle about the best way to assault the city from this transport. The other military fliers at Moree were parked too close to one another—a single rocket could blow them all into vapor. And the walking fortresses would not be able to defend the airfield from a smart missile fired a hundred kilometers away.

He considered shooting at the fortresses too, but shook his head. His memories from Tkintit, a Dronon technician, warned him that those walking fortresses were so heavily armored that he couldn't make much of a dent in them, and they had enough fire power to devastate his little transport. But Maggie pointed out that the whole reason the starships were spaced so far out from the city was to avoid damage to metropolitan areas in case the combustible liquids stored in the exterior radiation shields leaked out and caught fire. In space the liquids cooled to below their freezing point, and there was no danger of the shields exploding on impact with a meteor. But so long as they were down here in the atmosphere, those starships were just fancy bombs, and one of Gallen's rockets could light a fuse that would blow the nearest hive fortress off its feet, and Gallen suddenly saw some interesting ways to wreak havoc on the Tekkar. Four missiles was all he had—one for the airfield, one for each of three starships.

"You know," Gallen said, "if we convinced the Tekkar that our purpose in attacking was to destroy their technological buildup, it could form a decent diversion, allowing us to land near the Harvester's throne room."

By studying the map he realized that in all likelihood, a single rocky hillside hid the chambers where the Harvester lived. The hill was nestled deep in the heart of the city, and from the air it looked rather innocuous. But if the maps were right, then somewhere on the hill's northern slope, a huge chamber had been hollowed out. Gallen imagined that if they could blow a hole in that room, they could drop themselves right into the middle of the city. But after a few moments, he shook his head in dismay. "I'm not sure. This vehicle has enough firepower to knock out the airfield and probably even take out a couple of spaceships, but I might not have enough rockets to blow a hole into those chambers."

Maggie shook her head, and her mantle jangled. "You're still thinking like some backward hick. What is it that makes our aircar fly?"

"The fusion reactor?" he said.

"No," Maggie answered, "that's the power source. The car flies on waves of directed antigravity."

Gallen looked at her, and his mantle began to hint to him what she planned, but he did not have a technician's mantle, with its own arcane wisdom, so he let her explain it. "Most of the time the antigrav generator gives off weak pulses, but I can vary those—creating phased wavelengths if I want to. And I guarantee that none of these subterranean hives here on Tremonthin were built to withstand the stresses I could put on them! If I fly over this subterranean city, spiking out harmonic frequencies—well, these Tekkar will be surprised at how quickly their stone walls can get pounded into sand."

Gallen looked up into Maggie's eyes. "Do you know how many people you're talking about killing? There may be a half million or more Tekkar in that city."

Maggie leaned back, and her hair fell behind her shoulders, accentuating the impassive lines of her face. "Gallen, when we talked to Ceravanne, you must have noticed that she has no idea how to run a war. She wants to go to Moree and 'talk to' the Harvester, for God's sake! Well, that's not how *we're* going to do it. The Dronon brought technology here to use as a weapon, and the Inhuman is tearing these people apart. I think we should cram these weapons down their throats and let them know just how monstrous a war can be."

"We're talking about killing innocent women and children," Gallen said. And he surprised himself by saying "we're," for he knew that he had to consider it.

Maggie shrugged. "So hit them where they least expect it. Play on the Harvester's weaknesses, and on the Inhuman's inexperience. We can't afford to be nice. We can't afford to fight cleanly. I keep . . . I keep thinking about something my uncle Thomas told me just before we left Tihrglas. When he came into the inn, he planned to move in and use me badly. He lay on one of the beds in my inn, wearing his dirty boots, and he said something like, 'If you ever have to play the villain in someone's life, play your part well. Savor it. It's one of the greatest joys in living.' He hinted that you should stab the fellow in the back, and twist the knife with glee.

"Well, the Inhuman tried its best to make our last two weeks on this planet a living hell, and I for one don't think we should pull our punches. When you see the Harvester, Gallen O'Day, I'll not have you making any nice kissy faces at her just because she's Ceravanne's clone. If you don't blow her head off, I will!"

Gallen stared at her in wonder. "Jesus, you Flynns are a bad-tempered lot! It's a wonder the priests don't catch on and drown the lot of you when you're born!" Gallen leaned back, and his mantle was already considering the approach it would use when they attacked. He could trace the battle lines in his imagination.

He considered the carnage they would wreak on Moree, wondered about alternatives. Maggie was right. Her diabolical ideas did have the virtue of offering them the best chance at success, but Gallen couldn't bring himself to seriously consider such a plan. In some ways, he realized, Maggie was tougher than he was. She'd been the one who first put her life on the line when battling the Dronon, and now she was willing to wage a full-fledged war with the Tekkar.

He looked back down at the holographic image hovering over the floor, his legs rising like giant tree trunks from the land. But the image of the land transposed over Ceravanne's map gave him an idea.

Thirty-one

That morning, after Gallen and Maggie announced their battle plans, Ceravanne took Gallen aside and argued against his method long and vigorously. Neither she nor the Bock could countenance the kind of attack he proposed. They were standing in the Vale of the Bock, beside the hot pools, which shone emerald in the morning light. It was a bright day, and fair here, and it seemed to Maggie somehow odd to be talking of such things in the bright sunlight. Around Maggie, Gallen, Ceravanne, and Orick, dozens of the Bock had gathered, and they stood nearly motionless in the morning sun, their hands upraised as if they were some strange priests gathered in convocation, offering up their prayers to Tremonthin's double suns. But Ceravanne's favorite Bock stood beside Gallen and Ceravanne, as if to referee the dispute.

"Remember, Gallen," Ceravanne warned him, her voice shaking from emotion, "I want no violence, if we can avoid it. Not all of those infected by the Inhuman are evil. Like you, they are people, just people who were infected—by something they did not understand and something they lacked the ability to fight!"

Ceravanne's eyes blazed, and Maggie was surprised, for she'd never seen a Tharrin show anger.

"But if we fail here today, this world may not get another chance at freedom."

"And I would rather lose my freedom than destroy one innocent life!" Ceravanne argued. She looked like only a young girl, with her pale green eyes blazing and her platinum-blond hair. For the first time since they met, Maggie sensed that Ceravanne was losing control, speaking openly of her deepest feelings.

"But you cannot make that choice for others," Gallen shouted. "I won't let you! I've already modified my plans so that I spare as many of the Tekkar as I feel safe in doing. If that does not gratify you, then I will leave you displeased! Perhaps I should take your mantle and fight this battle without you!"

"No, please!" Ceravanne said, and her voice faltered, as if she'd considered the possibility that Gallen would go into battle without her. She begged, "I must come. Don't deny me that. I've already seen all of my own people destroyed in this conflict. And far too many people of other races have been maimed or slaughtered. If I can save only one life, then it will be worth it. I've convinced the Bock to come with us. He too may offer some help."

Gallen's voice became softer. "Your Tharrin compassion does you merit, but it also is your greatest weakness. I wish you would stay out of this."

"This world is my home," Ceravanne said, and she knelt forward a little, almost as if bowing to Gallen, pleading. "I must serve it as I can. There are children in the Tekkar's warrens. Innocents. Be gentle with them. Please, let me speak to the Harvester. Perhaps between us we can resolve this."

Maggie watched Gallen, and though both she and Gallen had known that Ceravanne would argue for this, and both of them had agreed that they should leave her behind, such was the quality of Ceravanne's voice, her ability to persuade, that Maggie suddenly found herself unable to argue against the woman. Indeed, to have done so would have been cruel.

Maggie knew that it was only a combination of pheromones,

body language, and the use of voice that made them give in. And perhaps it was their own desires that Ceravanne was working on. But as Ceravanne leaned forward, looking like little more than a child herself, the sunlight falling on her golden hair, her words seemed to weave a powerful spell, so powerful that Gallen's voice was stopped almost in mid-sentence. And suddenly Maggie saw why Ceravanne had been admired for millennia on this world. She'd helped bring peace to warring races for thousands of years, and such was the power of her presence that Maggie felt almost compelled to throw down the Dronon pulp gun she'd stowed in her waistband.

Ceravanne took Gallen's hand. "Do you not think that the Harvester argues for peace against the Tekkar, even as I sue for peace with you now? Why else do you think they have not attacked Northland yet? We see now that they could easily take it," Ceravanne said. And Maggie knew that it must be true. Ceravanne's other self was suing for peace two thousand kilometers away. "Once we reach her throne room, there will be no need for weapons or battle. The Harvester will not let her people hurt you, if she sees me and the Bock in your retinue. That much, I feel confident, I can promise you."

"Ceravanne is right," the Bock urged in his slow voice, the brown-tinged leaves at his crown rustling in the morning wind. "She has experience with many races, even the Tekkar. I do not hesitate to put my own life in her hands."

Gallen studied the Bock, his face still set and implacable. "All right, then," he said. "I will give you a moment with the Harvester—no more. If you do not succeed in persuading her, I will kill her."

Ceravanne closed her eyes gratefully, and sighed. She took Gallen's hand and kissed it. "I—thank you," she said, too overcome with gratitude to speak more, and Maggie wondered then if perhaps they had not given in too easily.

After they had discussed their plans once again, they saw the Riallna come down from the hill, bearing a breakfast of cheeses and fresh rolls filled with fruit.

They spread the food out into a circle and ate, watching one another in the morning light, and Maggie's heart was full.

And Orick the bear ate his rolls with fruit, licking the jam from his upper lips so that his tongue almost wrapped around his snout.

Gallen and Maggie silently held hands as they ate, sharing secret glances. The Bock gathered down at the banks of the pool and stood with their toes stretching out into the water, while the Riallna washed their feet with a paste of nutrients.

And so it was that as they finished eating, a few meadowlarks began to sing, and Orick began to speak slowly. Maggie had always known that Orick wanted to be a priest, and she had imagined him as an ascetic, perhaps some monastic brother living in the woods. She'd never thought him to be one with any missionary tendencies, but he spoke softly to Ceravanne then of the things that were in his heart.

"You know," he told her, "it hasn't escaped my notice that you don't have any proper churches here."

"The Riallna have their temples, the Bock have their woods," Ceravanne said. "And others build places to worship."

"But what of Catholic churches?" Orick asked. "What of Christianity?"

"What is that?" Ceravanne asked. And Maggie suspected that because she respected the bear and saw him as a friend, she asked kindly, as if she were truly interested.

"I've had a mind to tell you about it," Orick said, and then he told her of a young man named Jesus who, like her, sued for peace among mankind thousands of years ago, then gave his life for others. Orick told her how Jesus had died, betrayed by a friend, and how on the night before his death, he had broken bread and blessed wine, asking his disciples to always do this act in remembrance of his sacrifice.

Then, to Maggie's surprise, the bear said, "Normally, I don't have proper authority from the Church to do these things, but I think that they must be done. Today we go into Moree." And with that apology he began singing the words to the Sacrament, and he took some rolls and passed them around, and Gallen fetched a skin of wine, and each of them took it.

Orick then gave a brief prayer, asking God to bless them on

their journey and deliver them from harm, and Maggie felt the solemnity of the occasion.

After the sacrament they each made final preparations for the battle. Gallen checked his weapons, while the Bock stood gazing at the sky. Ceravanne laid her pack on the grass. She reached into it, put on a gray silk cloak with a deep hood. Then she unwrapped her mantle and put it on her head, its golden ringlets falling down her shoulders. Last of all, she pulled up the hood to her robe, to conceal her mantle.

Maggie saw that Orick was shaken, pacing nervously, but Ceravanne rumpled the coarse black hair on the back of his neck, and whispered, "Now, let us go, but not in haste, and not in fear. If we go to our deaths, remember that it is but a brief sleep."

Those words held no comfort for Gallen, Orick, or Maggie. Though Maggie had a mantle herself, it could not save her, and Gallen already had Tallea's memories stored in his own mantle. And Orick looked resigned. Though he had his faith to sustain him, Maggie knew he hungered for love and a life of peace, yet the road to any greater reward led down this dark path.

And suddenly Ceravanne caught her breath as she realized that what she had meant as a comforting word was only a cruel reminder to the others, since none had their memories recorded, none of them could be reborn, as Ceravanne could.

Orick growled lightly, and bounded forward to the aircar, followed by Ceravanne, the Bock, Gallen, and Maggie.

Maggie went to the cockpit, did a manual system's check, and as she did so, Gallen came in behind her, and she slid back up out of the pilot's seat, into his arms. They held each other for a long time. Gallen kissed her, brushing her forehead with his lips, and she leaned into him. "Promise me," he whispered fervently, "that once you drop me off, you'll get the transport away quickly. I don't want you sitting there, a target for the Dronon's walking fortresses."

"I may be brave, but I'm not stupid." Maggie smiled up at him sweetly. "And you promise me—come back alive?"

"I guarantee, I plan to grow old with you," Gallen whispered. Then they kissed so long and tenderly that Maggie was sure that the others must be getting impatient. Gallen was slow to leave, to close the bulkhead door behind him.

Maggie strapped herself into the pilot's seat and had her mantle silently radio the ship's AI, link intelligence with it so that the ship would know her commands before she could articulate them.

Their flight time would be short, a swift hop at low altitudes over the ocean, with the ship's antidetection equipment operating at full capacity. Once they reached the Telgood Mountains, the ship's intelligent missiles would fire, taking out their primary targets, if those were still available, or taking the secondary or tertiary targets that Maggie had already chosen.

And so they slipped quietly over the ocean for the next few minutes as Maggie's mantle displayed the view ahead. The sky was clear until they reached the coasts of Babel, and there a thin line of dark clouds showed on the horizon, an approaching thunderstorm.

"Buckle in back there and prepare for rapid descent," Maggie called to the others.

The aircar dropped low and screamed over the hills and valleys just above treetop at mach 9. The clouds and rain obscured her vision out the windows, so Maggie relied completely on the head-up holo that her mantle displayed. The holo showed the Telgoods looming ahead, a line of bony white teeth, and Maggie fired her smart missiles, then opened her eyes and looked out the front windows to verify that they left. The missiles streaked ahead of her on antigrav, leaving a flash as the air around them became superheated.

The aircar whirled, dove through some narrow canyons, and the AI fired a burst on the incendiary cannons, blasting a lone wingman from its path.

And suddenly the aircar seemed to leap in the air as it cleared a mountain, then lurched as it plummeted toward Moree.

"Four targets hit, three destroyed—" the AI flashed a message on her screen as soon as the ship had visuals. The head-up holo displayed the scene—three of the five dome-shaped spaceships going up in mushroom clouds. A fourth had been hit, but had not exploded. Maggie looked out the windows through a heavy rain, saw the trunk of fiery mushroom cloud begin billowing up as she passed, an incredible inferno. They were diving right through the periphery of its flames.

Two Dronon walking fortresses had taken fire from the explosions. One was flying apart, huge metallic chunks spewing out in odd angles as its munitions blew. The other had flames boiling out its cargo hold and was trying to retreat from the white inferno that had once been a starship. The Dronon walking fortress left a trail of flames and burning debris as it crawled away, looking for all the world like some great black spider in its death throes.

A smart missile was coming in from directly ahead, launched from one of the intact walking fortresses ten kilometers to the south, and Maggie almost subconsciously fired both plasma cannons, detonating the missile in midair so that a brilliant flash blinded her for a moment.

Their aircar was still dropping toward ground—toward the perpendicular rocky cliff face where the Harvester's chambers should be—when the AI flashed a message in red letters through the head-up holodisplay, "Permission to abort mission?"

Maggie looked about desperately at the scene below, wondering why the AI would ask that, wondering why one of her missiles hadn't taken out the Tekkar's airfield instead of a starship, its secondary target. She looked toward the dun-colored fields below and saw the reason: none of the Tekkar's military transports were on the field. They'd all been moved.

"No!" Maggie shouted in frustration, but her AI took that as a rejection of permission to abort, and in half a second they slammed to the ground, and her aircar began sending pulsed bursts of antigravity through the substrata.

Maggie looked out the windows, shouted, "Gallen, the airfield was clear! The Tekkar must have their transports out searching for us!"

But Gallen was already clearing the hold, with Orick,

Ceravanne, and the Bock all following. Maggie silently willed her mantle to radio the message from mantle to mantle, and she looked around.

"Message received," Gallen said through his mantle. "But we can't stop now. Do what you can, then get out of here!"

Maggie wondered what to do. She couldn't leave Gallen stranded here in Moree, but certainly the Tekkar airships, with a capability for mach 10 speeds, would be here in seconds. Even if they were out a hundred kilometers away, they could be here in thirty seconds.

Maggie bit her lip, studied her surroundings. For the moment, her ship was partly hidden under the rock cliff face to her south. To the north and east, the mushroom clouds from the exploding starships were growing redder and redder as their caps of smoke and flame rose higher into the thunderheads. Static discharges caused by the explosion were suddenly setting off a series of lightning blasts that spanned the sky. The door to the shuttle hummed shut, and almost unconsciously Maggie realized that a huge hole had opened in the cliff face to her south. From inside the aircar, with the exterior sounds shielded, she heard and felt nothing as tons of rock slid down the face of the cliff, leaving a gaping hole.

Gallen, Ceravanne, and the others were running over the ground, and now that the hole was opened, the transport's AI began emitting a cloud of Black Fog, a harmless aerial dye that blocked nearly all light.

At this moment, Maggie was supposed to move the hovercar, begin circling on a path around the Harvester's subterannean throne room, collapsing the tunnels leading to the room so that the Harvester and the Inhuman would be sealed off from aid, and from any avenues of escape.

Maggie swung the hovercar forward in a long arc, covered a kilometer in a matter of seconds, and watched as her aircar's antigravity collapsed the tunnels ahead, leaving furrowed ruins.

Tunnels fell in and chambers opened in a regular pattern. Maggie had made nearly half the circle when an alarm sounded. Her AI flashed an image of two approaching aircraft, smart missiles blurring toward her.

Maggie had no missiles left to fire back, and it was too late to escape.

Orick was running up the hill behind Ceravanne and the Bock, with Gallen in the lead. A gritty rain hammered his snout, and red pillars of fire blazed across the countryside. All around them the ground had collapsed in pockets as tunnels and chambers caved in. In those places, Orick could see slabs of broken stone protruding from the ground. In many places across these fields, there were fires coming up out of the horrific rents, and dust rising from the earth. Armageddon. It looked like some vision of Armageddon.

Orick had seen that much of the damage was already done before their transport even landed—apparently the explosive power of the starships had been more than the architects of this city could have planned for.

Orick was running full tilt when suddenly the ground at his feet began to give way, and he lunged forward just as a tunnel collapsed beneath. In front of him a hundred yards there was a sound of splitting rock, and almost all of the face of the cliff just before the group began sliding down, as if it had been a sandcastle dashed apart by a child's foot.

The sounds of the splitting rock, the roaring infernos of the distant mushroom clouds, the blasts of lightning, the cries of people, the shaking of the earth—all rose together in an incredible tumult, and for one breathless moment Orick stopped to watch in the distance as one of the starships—a gigantic globe nearly half a mile across—lifted from the ground without any visible means of propulsion, heading upward for the safety of the stars.

Gallen stopped for a moment, and Orick could feel the ground weaving and bucking beneath his feet. The movement bothered the humans and the Bock more than it did Orick, and they stood balancing precariously.

Where the rock wall had collapsed, they could see at least

six levels of rooms that had been in that part of the Tekkar's city. At the highest level was a tall chamber, with forty-foot ceilings. The Harvester's throne room. But to reach it they would have to climb the wall of broken rubble that lay before them, scaling the stones.

"That way!" Gallen shouted, pointing out a path over the rocks.

The whole world smelled of fire and smoke and broken stone.

Orick was vaguely aware of Tekkar running through those apartments, of wounded people crying out, but suddenly a wall of Black Fog swept over them as Maggie released their camouflage. And then they were swallowed by utter darkness.

Ceravanne pulled the glow globe from her pocket, and even its brilliant white light would not let them see more than five yards ahead.

The aircar made a deep thrumming, grinding noise as it swung around to the southeast.

Gallen called to the others, telling them to form a group as they climbed. He was merely waiting for the ground to stop shaking, for rocks to quit sliding from the cliff wall above, and Orick hoped that as Maggie moved the aircar, it would become safer for them to begin running again.

And suddenly Orick heard the whine of rockets accelerating toward them, off toward the aircar. The rockets slammed into the car with a pinging noise, and a huge explosion lifted them all from their feet.

Orick looked toward the aircar for any sign of a flash or burning. But in the inky darkness, Orick could see nothing but a brief lightening of the darkness, and then bits of metal and rock and ash began to rain down upon them.

"Maggie!" Orick cried, and Gallen stood watching the empty space, a look of utter desolation on his face. "Maggie!" Orick called again, and he began to run toward the car.

"Stop!" Gallen shouted at Orick's back, and when Orick turned to look at his face, Gallen turned away. "She's gone," he said. "She's gone, and there's nothing we can do."

For one brief moment, it looked as if Gallen would crumple under his own weight. It looked as if some invisible support had been kicked out from beneath him, and he dropped partway to one knee. But then he lifted himself and began scrambling up the rocks. Orick heard Gallen sniff, saw him wipe at his eyes with his sleeve. Then Gallen pulled his Dronon pulp gun, and his robes suddenly used their chameleon abilities to turn jet-black, to match the darkness.

Somehow, Orick found that he was unprepared for this. He'd imagined that if anyone would die in this battle, it would have been frail Ceravanne or the Bock or that maybe even Gallen would take on more than he could handle—but not Maggie.

"Gallen?" Orick cried at his back.

"She's gone," Gallen shouted, and he leapt forward to a boulder, then another, running up over the broken field of rubble without thought of stones still tumbling and crashing from the face of the cliff. Ceravanne ran behind him, calling for him to slow down, holding the light aloft, but she soon lost him in the dark.

And so she stopped and waited for the Bock and Orick to catch up. With his mantle, Gallen could see in the full darkness better than any man, and within seconds there was no sound of him.

Orick stopped beside Ceravanne, and the Bock made his way slowly over the rocks. Ceravanne nodded up toward where Gallen had run, and she muttered, "He's in a foul mood. Can you track him for us?"

Orick grumbled, "Not with those damned robes on. They mask his scent. I can't smell him."

Ceravanne sighed in disgust. "Then we'll track him by the corpses he leaves behind."

They began scrambling up over the fallen rocks from the cliff, and it seemed to take minutes upon minutes to get anywhere. As they passed beneath the cliff, they could still hear boulders and scree falling through the darkness around them, but they did not see the dropping stones. By now, between the thunderheads, the Black Fog, and the deep shadows of the Tekkar's city, the air around them was darker than any night.

And as they rushed through the rooms, Orick smelled blood

ahead. The rooms were like nothing he had imagined: they had a peculiar fluid form to them, and the walls were covered with some white plaster. Orick could almost sense the sleek lines of some living creature, and he realized that the walls reminded him of nothing more than bones, as if they were in some vast hollowed-out bones.

There were torches lying about here and there, bodies crushed under falling rocks, tapestries sitting in heaps on the floor, wide silver washing or drinking vessels. And along the walls were thousands of small clay pots with long stems. Many had fallen over, and lay broken, with bits of ash and bone spilling out.

"What's this?" Orick called as they ran.

Ceravanne said, "The dead. It is said that the kings of Moree were protected by the spirits of their dead." And Orick saw that it was still true, more so than ever, for the Inhuman also relied upon those who had died for protection.

The group passed a Tekkar servant woman whose head was horribly crushed, part of her cheek ripped away, and she cried out from a swollen mouth, grasped the fur on Orick's leg, begging aid. Orick looked into her deep purple eyes as he passed, saw how they were not focused, and knew that she would die whether he helped her or not.

They reached some smoothly undulating stairs with golden handholds fastened to the wall, each shaped like the head of a dog.

They rushed up several flights, climbing over debris, and Orick saw Gallen's tracks in the dirt.

A moment later, they reached a landing and found the body of a Tekkar guard, his chest blown apart. And from up ahead there came shouting, followed by the burp of gunfire and the explosion of shells.

"This way," Ceravanne cried, leaping over the corpse, and she redoubled her speed as she chased the sound of battle.

And Orick suddenly realized that Gallen was doing it all without him, that Gallen had rushed ahead and was avenging Maggie by killing the Harvester and the Inhuman. Always in the past, he had been left behind. He'd let Gallen fight the great battles and get the glory, and never had he minded.

But over the past days, he'd lost three friends. Grits had been left behind, and Tallea was now food for the Derrits, and Maggie had just been blown apart, and Orick decided that he'd rather be damned in hell than let Gallen take all the vengeance this time.

They reached a huge set of double doors, twenty feet tall and ten feet wide, made of thick wooden planks with great brass rings to pull on. The doors were already opened just wide enough for a thin man to squeeze through.

Lying at the foot of the doors were eleven or twelve Tekkar, sprawled in a bloody heap. Orick leapt up and grabbed a brass ring in his teeth, then pulled back the door, swung it wider.

Ceravanne held up the glow globe, and peered inside. There was a great chamber, sixty feet long, with ceilings forty feet high. The dim red lights scavenged from a Dronon hive city glowed at the far end, and beneath the lights on a broad-backed throne of gold sat a small woman, her shoulders hunched, a golden mantle cascading over her shoulders.

Gallen himself was kneeling before the throne, his mantle spread before him on the floor, his Dronon pulp pistol discarded at his side. Orick's heart skipped a beat. Gallen had come all this way to protect them, to fight for them, and now Orick saw him kneeling, helpless before the Harvester. The heavy scent of the Harvester's pheromones filled the room, sweet and cloying.

For her part, the Harvester seemed to be staring into Gallen's face, and she looked up as Ceravanne and Orick entered, her sad green eyes gazing at them, so much like Ceravanne's eyes.

All along the walls were doorways, and at each doorway stood a Tekkar guard, draped in black robes that were longer than the norm, holding a sword pointed down toward the floor. Four guards lay sprawled upon the carpet just inside the door, where Gallen had killed them.

The Harvester reached out toward them, made a pulling

gesture, as the Inhuman's agents often did when greeting one another, and said softly, "I've been waiting for you."

The room's lights shone over her platinum hair, sparkled in her pale green eyes. Ceravanne looked at herself, the Harvester.

The Harvester glanced about at Gallen and the others in confusion. "It took only four of you to cause so much destruction?"

Ceravanne nodded, and her heart pounded in her chest. She looked to both sides. The air in here was still heavy with the scent of the explosive charges from the Dronon pulp gun, but there was a mustier smell of things long dead. As Ceravanne scanned the room, she recognized the source. What she had first thought to be Tekkar guards lining the walls were in fact the dead, mummified remains of Tekkar, their bodies dried, their faces painted over with some preservative lacquer. Gallen had already killed the living guards, yet he knelt before the Harvester's throne, unmoving, and Ceravanne's heart pounded within her.

"What are you doing?" Orick growled at Gallen. But Gallen did not move, did not answer.

"You have damaged him," the Harvester said, and she reached down and removed Gallen's mantle. "Someone tried to remove his Word, but enough of it is still intact. He is Inhuman still, and here in Moree, he cannot harm me."

Ceravanne looked at Gallen in horror, saw that he was breathing heavily. He grunted, a faint cry, and Ceravanne realized that he was only holding still with a great struggle. The Inhuman held him.

"Who is he?" the Harvester asked, looking at Gallen's face.

"Don't you know?" Ceravanne asked. "He is Belorian."

"No," the Harvester said angrily. "Belorian is dead. His memories are lost."

"Yet his genome lives," Ceravanne said. "You know that much. And this one was reborn on a world like ours. He is Belorian in all but name."

The Harvester looked at him thoughtfully. "I shall keep him, then, as my own."

There was an electricity between the two women, almost sizzling. For long years, Ceravanne had wondered if even she could be subverted by the Inhuman, and now she saw the proof of it. If this woman remembered Belorian, then she could not be some empty-headed clone created by the Dronon. This had to be Ceravanne's older self, the woman who'd been lost a year ago. Ceravanne, with all her memories intact. Here was a Tharrin who proposed to rule a world of slaves, who claimed that she would keep Gallen as her personal pet, and yet Ceravanne wondered. Ceravanne and the Harvester were of the same flesh. How could they take such divergent paths? Though Ceravanne often felt the tug, the desire to manipulate others to her own ends, she had rejected that path a million times. It seemed to Ceravanne that at the very core of their being, there must be some commonality, some shred of decency that they still shared.

"We share much," Ceravanne said, "but we do not share a belief that we can own others. I have come to reclaim you, my sister-self. I suspected that you could not be lost among the Tekkar. Even taken as a slave, you would soon make yourself queen."

"There is nothing here to reclaim," the Harvester whispered vehemently. "I am Inhuman now."

"A lover of war?" Ceravanne whispered. "Then why have not the Tekkar already been unleashed on Northland? Instead you send spies, carrying copies of the Word. It is a frail weapon indeed, for one who professes not to value life. No, you lead a peaceful war, a beneficent war, and you tame the dogs that serve you.

"Even now, I suspect that you have guards ready to do your bidding. Have them cut us down, if you can. But I know that you can't. No matter what the Inhuman has taught you, no matter how it has sought to turn you, we still share something." Ceravanne pointed to her heart.

Silently, two Tekkar swordsmen walked out from behind the throne, confirming Ceravanne's suspicions that there were more guards in the room.

"You sneer when you speak of my converts," the Harvester said. "I can hear your ill-conceived judgments in your voice."

"It is unnatural for a Tharrin to take slaves," Ceravanne said.

"The humans created us to be their slaves," the Harvester spat. "Loving masters, wise stewards, beloved lords—or so they call us. But we were made to serve. We are their drudges."

Is that what the Inhuman had taught her, Ceravanne wondered, contempt for mankind? "They love us, and we love them in return," Ceravanne said. "Is that slavery, or something greater? We—you and I—have always *given* ourselves to them freely."

"And what have they given you in return?" the Harvester spat.

"Their love, their companionship." Ceravanne gestured toward Gallen and the others. "I came in the name of the Swallow, and three people gave their lives that I might make this journey in safety. What greater love could I ask of them? What less could I give in return?"

"Judgment!" the Harvester said. "Control! For ages you have sought to bring peace to this land. For generations you sought to bring the peoples of Babel together in harmony! And you failed! You failed with the Rodim, and for centuries have felt the worms of guilt eating at your soul. You have sought to bring about peace and happiness among mankind, but how can there be peace when there is no self-control? The Immortal Lords in the City of Life created the Rodim. They created the Tekkar. They created the Derrits and the Andwe and the Fyyrdoken— all without wisdom, always knowing the misery that such creatures would cause. For millennia they have set evils loose upon the world, ignoring your counsel *if* they ever deigned to seek it. You know that they are but ignorant children when compared to you. You would not give a child a surgeon's knife to play with, but you have given mankind their liberty, knowing that with their liberty they would create the instruments of their own destruction. But in one year, I've accomplished more for the cause of peace than you ever did."

"But at what price?" Ceravanne said weakly. "You enslave

millions to control a few. You hobble mankind so that a few evil people cannot run free. Is it worth it?"

"Yes!" the Harvester shouted. "Worth it and more! There will be generations born in peace, people who never know discontent or suffering!"

Ceravanne listened to those words, and they cut her to the soul. Oh, how she had yearned to bring about such a change. For centuries the temptation had gnawed at her, to grasp control and put an end to as much human misery as possible. It did little good for the humans to create Tharrin leaders, and then continue their barbaric ways, killing one another and squabbling over soil as if nothing had changed. But the Tharrin hoped to lead men into some golden era of peace, not sit in judgment on them as if they were children.

And yet, and yet, Ceravanne knew that to seize control, even in the attempt to bring greater peace to mankind, would be to destroy the very people she most loved.

She gestured toward Gallen and the Bock. "You feign hardness and anger, but I know you. I have brought you the two men you have loved most in your life—Belorian and the Bock. Men whom you love, but men who love freedom more than they value their own lives. They've come to stop you. If you still love them, if you seek to strip from them their humanity, then be merciful to them. Give them the death they would prefer, rather than the slavery you offer! I say once again—cut us down and be done with it!"

The Harvester began shaking, and her gaze turned deeply inward, as if she were fighting some mighty battle. Her mouth opened, as if against her will, and she made a fist, pointed her finger at the Bock as if to speak the command for her guards to slay him, and lowered her eyes.

"It's her mantle!" Orick shouted. "It's controlling her! Take it!"

Gallen raised his head, and he was shaking mightily, his muscles spasming.

Ceravanne imagined the net of tiny wires in the woman's head, like those she had seen in Gallen. The Inhuman might be broadcasting the Harvester's every thought, every action, until she was no more than a puppet, moved at its whim. But if that were true, then all of them would be dead by now. And so she realized that the Inhuman was unable to control its subjects fully. It struggled to hold both Gallen and the Harvester at once.

Orick bounded forward.

"No!" the Harvester shouted, and a Tekkar guard obediently leapt to intercept the bear.

Gallen snatched his pulp gun, shot the Tekkar as he rushed past, and the bullet popped under his right eye. His skull cracked and expanded outward for a moment like a burgeoning wine bag, and shards of bone ruptured the skin. His eyes flew out, and smoke issued from the holes. His upper teeth broke off unevenly, spitting out to the floor. White shards of skull cut through skin, and blood spattered Ceravanne's face.

The Tekkar guard crumpled in ruin, and Ceravanne screamed in horror at the sight. Time seemed to slow.

Gallen cried out, and the gun fell from his hand as the Inhuman regained control. Suddenly Gallen dropped back to one knee.

Orick stopped halfway to the Harvester's throne as the second guard rushed forward, swinging his sword in complex arcs.

The Harvester merely stood, watching them all, and Ceravanne studied her every tiny gesture, every seemingly unconscious movement of the eyes. The Harvester had not cried out at the horrible sight of her guard, crumpling in ruin. The image of it had struck Ceravanne to the very core, but the Harvester was merely watching. And suddenly Ceravanne felt very uneasy. She had come here imagining that she and the Harvester were one, single organisms that had branched out on different paths. But now she wondered just how far they might have diverged. The Harvester stood rigid, trembling, but the murder of a man before her eyes had not seemed to cause her undue discomfort.

Ceravanne knew that the Inhuman planted memories from the lives of warriors in its victims, but now she wondered what that would be like, wondered how the horror of committing such atrocities would leave their mark on the Harvester.

In ages past, Ceravanne had turned her back on the Rodim, let their kind be slaughtered, removed from the face of the earth. It had not been a sin of commission. She had killed no one herself, had never even seen a Rodim die. But she forced herself to remain silent as the slaughter began. It had taken all of her will, sapped her strength, left her unable to sleep for thousands of nights afterward. She could not imagine ever committing a crime more horrible than what she had done.

But the Harvester stood before her, and she bore memories of war, of her own hands bathed in another's blood. Somehow, Ceravanne had imagined that the Harvester would be able to disassociate herself from such memories, to recognize that she had never committed such atrocities.

But Ceravanne knew better than that. The peoples of Babel had been created because of the Tharrin's inaction, their unwillingness to control mankind. If the Tharrin asserted more control, they could end this madness. Human misery was the gauge of Tharrin inadequacy.

And so Ceravanne felt the stain of blood upon her, the stain of blood for every man who had ever died under the sword, the guilt of every good man who was forced to kill in order to defend himself. The stain was always there. Ceravanne could feel her conscience whispering to her, though she tried to block it from her mind.

But how much more horrible would it be to have the Inhuman show her true waste and destruction, to live through the horrors of becoming a killer, to suffer the atrocities committed by others? How could Ceravanne bear it, if the Inhuman were to show her the misery her people suffered? How could the Harvester even bear to stand, to breathe, to speak while under the weight of such guilt. It was not the lies that the Inhuman told that so much bothered Ceravanne, it was the threat of all the damning truths. How could anyone bear it?

Indeed, the Harvester only stood gazing at the room, and the muscles at her mouth twitched. She drew weak, rapid breaths, and her eyes gazed around in bewilderment.

The Harvester was struggling for control, struggling against the Inhuman.

Gallen climbed to his feet, turned and looked at Ceravanne. His eyes had rolled back in his head, and slowly, as if fighting a great battle with himself, he whispered, "Leave us!"

"Gallen?" Orick said, gazing deep into his eyes. "Are you in there?"

Gallen said nothing intelligible, but his voice gurgled. And Ceravanne looked at Gallen's mantle on the floor, realized that his mantle was still fighting, trying to block the Inhuman's signals, just as Gallen was still struggling against it.

Ceravanne stepped forward. The Tekkar guard swung his sword menacingly, still blocking the path, and though the guard would not let Orick pass, Ceravanne suspected that she herself might have a better chance of reaching the Harvester.

Ceravanne crossed the room, pulled back her hood, and the Tekkar stood looking at her in her splendor. She hesitated for a moment, waiting for her scent to fill the air around her, so that her powerful pheromones would have time to work on the Tekkar. By nature, Ceravanne was aware of subtle forms of manipulation. Tone of voice, gestures, scent—all worked together to create a mood.

The Tekkar stopped swinging his sword, considering, and Ceravanne watched his purple eyes. There was a hint of widening, as if the Tekkar were surprised by her lack of fear, but his eyes did not stare beyond her, losing their focus, as so often happens when one is planning to kill. Ceravanne held her hands together and hunched her shoulders, making herself seem smaller. It was a pose that spoke at once of unconscious authority and vulnerability. Her beauty and scent confused the Tekkar with a sensual aura. Ceravanne had called mortal enemies together and got them forging alliances within minutes, yet even after thousands of years of experience, she could not be sure that her persuasive powers would work on the Tekkar.

"Let me pass," Ceravanne said softly, as if reminding him that she had the perfect right to command. "I will not harm you, and I do not believe you wish to harm me. There has been too much violence already."

The Tekkar's lips parted and he looked back to the Harvester in confusion, and in that moment of hesitation, Ceravanne crossed the room, stood at Gallen's side, rested her hand on his shoulder, and looked up into the face of the Harvester. There was sweat running down the woman's forehead, and she held her jaw clenched, trembling.

"Fight it," Ceravanne whispered vehemently to both Gallen and the Harvester. "Fight with your whole souls."

Ceravanne stepped toward her, and the Harvester reached for the knife on her hip.

"Please, not one more life!" the Bock said, holding its arms high. "I beg of the Ceravanne who once was, do not let this Inhuman force you into taking one more life!"

The Harvester stood, and beads of sweat began dotting her forehead. "I can't . . . stop it. I can't hold . . . it!"

Ceravanne pulled back her hood, exposing her own mantle. "Yes you can, for a moment, at great cost. And in that moment, you are free. I've spoken with those technicians who designed the Inhuman," she whispered. "The memories it shows you are flawed, and all of its conclusions are lies. You are not responsible for the sum of human misery. I've come to bring you truth. Put on this mantle, and let it teach you peace. It will free you."

She began walking slowly toward the Harvester, who looked toward the exits. Ceravanne feared that she would jump and flee down one of those corridors. The Tekkar guard moved uneasily, as if to intercept Ceravanne, and the Bock hurried toward the throne.

The Harvester raised her hands, as if to ward Ceravanne away. "No," she whispered. "Leave now! I do not want to hurt you!"

"And I do not want to hurt you," Ceravanne said softly, all feigned vocal tones aside. The Harvester would know if she lied.

The Tekkar guard moved to intercept the Bock, and the Harvester cried, "Stop him!" The Bock stopped beside Orick, unable to advance farther.

The Harvester pulled her dagger from her hip sheath, and its shining curved blade gleamed wickedly. Ceravanne recalled how deeply it had bit into her in the past, the cold poison at its tip. "I have killed myself before," Harvester whispered.

"Yes, to avoid being infected by the Inhuman," Ceravanne answered sadly, realizing that her sister-self was planning suicide. "The Swallow has returned to her ancient land of Indallian. She came to bring peace and unite her people. But you're infected by that which we both fear. If this is all you can do to save us, then do what you must. I forgive you."

And Ceravanne saw the pain on the Harvester's face as her muscles worked against her. She marveled at the Harvester's struggle for control, for few could hope to fight the domination of a machine designed to manipulate the human will, and Ceravanne knew that the Harvester must have been fighting the Inhuman's control for months.

"Forgive me and die," the Harvester said, and she leapt at Ceravanne. In that brief instant, Ceravanne saw her mistake.

The Tharrin compunction against taking a human life was nearly unbreakable, but it did not extend to self, and the Harvester viewed Ceravanne as self. And in that instant, Ceravanne saw that the Harvester was relinquishing control. She could not have moved so swiftly otherwise. Indeed, for that brief moment, she was the Inhuman.

And a sudden shocking urge welled up inside Ceravanne. For one moment, she wished the Harvester dead. She wanted to hide the ugliness of what she had become from the world. Expunge it. Make it as if it had never been. While humans feared most the death of the body, Ceravanne feared more for the death of her soul, and she wanted now to unmake the thing she had become.

"No!" the Bock shouted, rushing toward them.

Ceravanne grasped the Harvester's hand as her knife plunged downward. And for a moment they struggled, fighting for control of the knife. The Harvester's face was a mask of determination and rage, the face of a stranger. Ceravanne turned and kicked at the older woman's legs, trying to unbalance her, and very nearly succeeded in driving the knife into the Harvester's neck.

The Harvester cried out for aid, and her guard spun and

rushed toward her. Ceravanne saw Orick leap in behind the guard, catch the Tekkar's rear leg in his teeth, and shake the man vigorously. With a mighty heave of his neck, Orick threw the Tekkar against the near wall, and bones snapped.

The Bock lunged forward past Orick, trying to throw himself between the women. With his long fingers, he grabbed for the knife as it arced toward Ceravanne a second time, reaching up. The knife pierced his hand, driving deeply along the outside of his palm. Bright blood spattered over his arm, and he backed away from the Harvester.

"She's . . . innocent! You're both innocent!" the Bock cried.

The Harvester stared at the Bock, eyes wide, and staggered backward, running from her deed.

Ceravanne stood, watching the doomed Bock collapse at her feet. "Ah," he muttered courageously, making a show as if the wound were a scratch, backing away. "I . . ." Confusion crossed his face, and he sat down heavily, his many knees buckling. "What?"

"I've killed you," the Harvester cried, as if the words were torn from her throat.

Ceravanne felt her heart pounding fiercely in her chest, but she couldn't breathe. She fell to her knees beside the Bock, hoping to comfort him.

Her eyes filled with tears, and the Bock looked up at her incredulous. "How? No, it's a small wound!"

"With the juice of deathfruit in it," the Harvester whispered.

The Bock fell back, gasping, and looked up.

And in that second, the Harvester dropped her knife to the floor. Ceravanne stood there stunned, holding the Bock, as the Harvester cried out from the core of her soul, and the cry seemed to echo from some recess in Ceravanne's mind. It was a scream that was unlike anything she had ever heard—almost bestial.

The Bock looked up, and his brown eyes did not focus. He stared blindly at the ceiling. "Wha . . . gulls crying?" Ceravanne knelt, her heart pounding, blinded by tears. The Bock looked up and said, "Ah, the cry of a child as it dies into an adult."

Then his voice rattled, and he went still.

The ground twisted beneath her, and Ceravanne fell forward, still weeping.

Ceravanne had come hoping to find common ground with the Harvester. She'd known that somewhere, despite the Inhuman's manipulations, its distortions and outright lies, there had to be some core, some essential, unchanging element, that would remain the same in them.

And as the Bock died, the one man both Ceravanne and the Harvester had loved most in this life, the Harvester was touched deep in her soul, in a place where the Inhuman could not enter.

The Harvester crawled on her knees toward the Bock. Then Ceravanne grabbed the mantle of the Inhuman, pulled off the gold clip that her technicians had told her would be its key, and laid the Inhuman over the Bock's face like a burial shroud.

Suddenly freed from the Inhuman's influence, Gallen leapt up, came to Ceravanne's side and held her a moment. Ceravanne was trying to snap the key onto a corner of her own mantle, but her hands were shaking too badly. So Gallen took the key from her hands.

From one of the side doors, Ceravanne could hear shouting as several of the Tekkar tried to clear rubble, gain entrance to the great hall.

"Quickly, put the key on my mantle," Ceravanne whispered, "if you love truth, if you seek rest."

Gallen took Ceravanne's mantle from her, placed its golden net over his own head. Then he sat down, arms wrapped around his knees, snapped the key onto the mantle's golden rings, and lived another hundred lifetimes.

For nearly two hours, Ceravanne sat with Orick.

The Bock's body cooled, and Ceravanne cleaned it up, weeping softly. She could not keep from touching him, and for a long hour after the body was cleaned, Orick nuzzled her, pressing his nose under her arm.

Orick could not believe how badly the day had gone. Gallen had not been able to fight the Inhuman, and Maggie was dead.

Both Ceravanne and the Harvester had lost the man they loved, and the city of Moree was in ruins. Orick had hoped for much better, and it left a great gaping hole in his heart, to see all the pain that others would have to endure.

He kept looking over at Gallen, who sat with his arms wrapped about his knees, his forehead bowed to one knee, with the great golden mantle draped over his head and shoulders, wearing a look as if he were some philosopher, exhausted from profound thought. And in a way, Orick feared that. The teaching machines on Fale had changed him some. The Inhuman had sought to rip away his free will. And now, he would waken and be something new.

Everyone Orick loved most was being taken from him.

He had begun to fear that terrible light that was growing in Gallen's pale eyes. Now he felt it keenest. A few short weeks ago, Gallen had been little more than a boy who had to cope with his incredible talent for battle and his desire to set the world right. Now, he was growing into something new, something unpredictable.

So Orick sat and thought, trying to comfort Ceravanne. Orick remembered that when the Lady Everynne had connected with the omni-mind, she'd wakened after the initial shock, and she'd become something powerful—a goddess, with nearly unlimited knowledge. In his own smaller way, Orick knew, Gallen was doing the same, step by step. The light was steadily growing in his eyes, and Orick could see what he was becoming, could see how he was leaving ordinary men behind, leaving Orick behind.

When Ceravanne's tears had eased some, Orick asked gently, "When Gallen wakes, how will he be changed? What will he become?"

"The demons inside him should never bother him again," Ceravanne whispered. "We didn't alter the memories much, just restored the true versions, so that Gallen may see upon reflection our judges were not harsh. When Gallen wakes, everyone will know that I've returned to make peace among the peoples. Some may resent me for it. Some may still hold allegiance to the Inhuman, but we've removed the hidden thought structures that the Inhuman inserted into its hosts. People will be free to make up their own minds."

Ceravanne sat, her arms wrapped around her Bock.

"And what of those who do resent you?" Orick asked. "What if some of the Tekkar try to kill you?"

"I suspect that they will," Ceravanne said. "I've been killed before, but always I've been reborn. Still, such actions anger the faithful. The Rodim were destroyed as a people for such acts. The Tekkar know what will happen to them if they are too harsh."

Orick licked Ceravanne's hand, and together they waited for the awakening.

Thirty-two

In the recesses of his mind, Gallen lived through the days of Druin after the fall of Indallian. He rode his huge war-horse through the forests in his youth, and suffered the pangs of lost loves, he fought many battles and learned to crave blood as much as he craved the wider world. He united many people, before he was crippled by a spear in the back.

As an old man, he became frustrated in his designs. Many admired him as a man of learning, for he could do little more than lie in his bed and study. He became devoted to the welfare of his people, yet he dreamed of walking again, of visiting the stars.

He learned to hate the walls of his bedchamber, and so he sent messengers to the City of Life and hired travelers from other worlds to come and be his tutors. He began acquiring metals to build his starships, and studied the designs.

When word reached him that the Immortals planned to stop him, he built cannons to guard his city, and great were the battles waged against him, until in ruin he was forced to put aside his weapons.

In old age, his men took him to the City of Life, and there

sought the rebirth. And the judges found him unworthy. Still, they took pity on him, and gave him back his legs, sending him away. He took his gift, but turned and cursed his judges.

Thus Druin wandered far, and never visited his realm again.

So it went, life after life, Gallen saw the portion of meanness in character that the Dronon had chosen to hide.

And then Ceravanne's mantle showed Gallen other lives, the lives lived by some of those who had won the rebirth—Tottenan the Wise, from the race of the Atonkin, who felt no desire to dominate other peoples. He spent his days buying old swords and melting the steel to be used in building nails.

And Gallen recalled the life of Zemette, a shipbuilder of weak mind but great heart, a man who somehow understood by nature how to be happy, who used all of his money to buy slaves from the southlands, so that he could set them free.

And Gallen lived the life of Thrennen Ka, a Derrit who sought to teach farming to her own people.

Over and over, the lives came to him, and he was shown an equal portion of the divine and the damned. And while the Dronon whispered to him that all men were equal, and therefore should serve their new Dronon overlords, Gallen saw that all men were given time to make of themselves what they would, and that while some became vile, and others merely consumed, always there were a few who earnestly strove to make the world better for all, and such people were rewarded in the City of Life.

And thus Ceravanne's mantle sought to make Gallen a wiser man, full of hope and experience, and then it left him.

When Gallen finally woke, raising his head so that Ceravanne's mantle jingled, Orick came to his side. There was a noise reverberating through the darkened hive, and the shadows jangled to the querulous notes of people waking to a new world in wonder.

And when the Harvester woke, Ceravanne hungered for a private conference with her sister. So they sat close together and held one another and cried. Gallen sat listening to the women talk.

"I've killed with my own hands," the Harvester whispered, almost a wail. "I need cleansing. Can you feel it?"

"Five hundred years will not suffice," Ceravanne agreed, not concealing the worry in her voice. "I would come with you, aid you if I could. But one of us must stay here. The Swallow must return as promised, and bring peace with her."

"I know that you still hurt for the Rodim," the Harvester said. "Your healing is not complete. How can we bring peace, when we feel none ourselves?"

Ceravanne opened her mouth, but spoke no answer for a moment. "We are our bodies," she whispered at last. "Neither of us can escape our guilt. And both of us must seek to establish peace in our turns. You go to Northland, to the Vale of the Bock." Ceravanne went to her pack, fumbled out a small seed. She held the unborn Bock up with evident care, as if it were a great treasure. "Plant this in the Vale. And there you can find peace for both of us."

The Harvester took the seed, held it up in wonder, then grabbed Ceravanne, hugged her fiercely, and whispered, "Thank you. Thank you. Look for me again in summer, in some distant year, when both our hearts are lighter. A Bock will come with me."

They held each other, crying softly for a moment, and Gallen petted Orick's head, stroking it softly. There were cries in the land again, the sound of Tekkar awakening, and Gallen was looking off into the distance, into the shadows of the corner of the room. He did not mention Maggie's name, though his heart was heavy for her.

Then the main door to the throne room squeaked on its hinges, and Gallen glanced over, expecting to see some Tekkar.

Maggie poked her head into the room.

"Maggie!" Orick shouted, bounding toward her. "I thought you got killed."

Orick reached her, sat on all fours and licked her hands, wanting to jump up and hug her, but knowing she would fall over if he did. She bent forward and kissed his forehead. "Very nearly, but the AI ejected me before the car blew."

She stood looking at Gallen across the room, and neither one of them spoke or moved for several long seconds.

"I was afraid for you," Gallen said at last.

"I love you, too," Maggie said, her lower lip trembling, and they rushed into each other's arms.

He was surprised how, even now, her touch could be electric. He kissed her, looked deep into her face, and was surprised at what he saw. There was a peace in her eyes that had never been a part of Maggie Flynn before, a new clarity and softness.

The hallways leading to the Harvester's chamber had begun to fill with people, and Gallen could hear them talking reverently, saying, "The Swallow, yes, she's in here." They stood outside the doors, afraid to come in, until Ceravanne rose to greet them.

They slept that night under the bright stars of Tremonthin, with the Tekkar camped around them. The people knew the Swallow from ancient memories downloaded into their skulls, and they showed her great reverence. The Tekkar vied for the honor to become her protectors, and chefs brought her their finest meals.

Maggie looked about, and it was hard to miss the adulation shining in the eyes of the people. But all of it was for Ceravanne. Gallen, Maggie, and Orick were all but strangers in the city, people who were obvious friends to the Swallow, nothing more.

The Harvester had dressed in black robes and a hood to hide her face, and she went out into the darkness beside the river, and for long she stood alone in the moonlight.

And so at last when Maggie and Gallen staggered off to sleep in a thicket, Maggie listened to the sounds of the night, and for the first time on this world, she slept unafraid.

In the morning, they had a short funeral where they buried the Bock beside a small river. And because the Swallow herself came to the funeral, everyone from the city of Moree turned out.

Ceravanne spoke his eulogies, praising the Bock so that everyone within listening range felt as if they'd lost something important without ever knowing exactly what it was.

An engraver carved a large stone from the river's bank for the Bock, showing a treelike figure with his hands raised toward the suns, and they left it over the gravesite, beside the road, where folks would reckon it a significant landmark in the city for a thousand years.

Ceravanne offered to send Gallen and Maggie back to Northland in a flyer, but after a brief conference, they all decided that they were in no hurry. The Dronon would be hunting for Gallen and Maggie across the worlds, and Tremonthin seemed as good a place to hide as any.

Orick voiced the suspicion that both Maggie and Gallen were loath to leave because they shared so many memories of this land, and Maggie thought back through the lives she'd lived here, and did not deny it.

And so Ceravanne gave them a fine cart and a pair of horses, and Gallen, Maggie, and Orick prepared to head to Northland with the Harvester.

They were in no hurry, but Maggie found that there was a great weight upon her. She needed to go north, to the City of Life, to petition the Immortals in Tallea's behalf, seeking her rebirth.

Ceravanne came to give her final farewell to them before they departed. She thanked them profusely for their help, and wished them good fortune. She gave them many gifts from the hands of the people of the city—warm blankets for their journey, good food and clothes, a bag of coins.

She wept as she hugged them goodbye, and then she was hustled off into the city by her Tekkar guardians, all dressed in their black robes, their faces hooded from sunlight.

They walked away in a tight knot, almost as if Ceravanne were a prisoner rather than a dignitary, and something about it gave Maggie the chills.

And in the afternoon sunlight, Maggie watched them heading back to the dark catacombs of Moree, leaving Maggie, Gallen, Orick, and the Harvester to make their own way back across the seas to Northland, and whatever destinations might lie beyond.

In the bright sunlight, Maggie watched Ceravanne waving goodbye from up a slope, a streak of lightning in her blue dress, with her platinum hair, all against the dark lines of the hills of Moree, and Maggie felt a profound sense of distress. Though Ceravanne's mantle had perhaps tamed the hosts of the Inhuman, Ceravanne herself was staying among the Tekkar, men who by their very nature were little more than monsters.

Maggie looked up at Gallen in frustration. "Why is she staying with them?" she asked in dismay. "That's no proper reward for her labor."

"She is staying with them because she must dismantle the armaments in Moree, tear down the starports," the Harvester said softly. "She is going back with them, because governing them will be her greatest challenge. And if she is to rule this land in peace, she must first get them under her sway."

"But . . . but Maggie's right," Orick grumbled. "She's lost! A lifetime of work is all she has before her. What kind of reward is that?"

"Perhaps by your human perspective she has lost," the Harvester whispered from beneath her dark hood, so that her soft words seemed to hang in the cool air about her face. "But Ceravanne is not human. She desires to serve, and now she has won that opportunity."

And you have lost yours, Maggie realized, studying the hooded woman.

Now Maggie saw what was really troubling her. Ceravanne had won only a new kind of captivity, just as Maggie and Gallen had. By defeating the Lords of the Swarm, she and Gallen had sought to win freedom, but all they had won was a responsibility that was too great to bear. She looked into Gallen's face, and by his troubled look, she knew he was thinking the same.

Even now, the Lords of the Dronon Swarms were hunting for Gallen and Maggie, and perhaps might soon be searching this planet. But Tremonthin was a big planet, easy to hide in.

So they headed home at a leisurely pace, while the fall grew steadily colder. A week later, when they crossed the Telgoods in their travels north, there was snow on the peaks, and a bitter nip in the air.

All during their journey home, they found peace in the land, and a new sense of brotherhood among the people of Babel. Where before they had received distrustful stares when they drove through a town, now they found merchants smiling and alehouses full of people who laughed and were quick to joke or sing or tell some outlandish story.

Indeed, Maggie found herself falling more and more deeply in love with the land, and one night, when she and Gallen had snuggled in a cozy bed at an inn, and a fire was burning in their hearth, she asked him as she had once before, "Gallen, if we ever escape the Dronon completely, would you want to live here?"

"We've already lived in Babel for more than seven thousand years," he whispered, and she saw that strange new peace in his eyes. "It's my home. Yes, I could live here ten thousand more."

And Maggie curled tighter against him, and felt that one thing at least had been settled. Now, if only she could figure a way to escape those damned Dronon. But she feared that she would never be rid of the threat, not until they'd killed her.

And on their journey, though Maggie and Gallen continued to fall more and more deeply in love, and Maggie found greater contentment, she worried for Orick. In all of their travels, they had not found a single bear who could speak. Oh, on the trip home they once saw a bear walking along a lightly forested ridge in the wilderness, but when Orick called out to it, the creature growled stupidly and ran away, for it was only a simple animal, without Orick's genetic upgrades.

A month later, when they reached the city of Queekusaw on the ocean shores, the whole land was blanketed in white, and snow was pounding the land. They left Babel on a slow freighter in the afternoon, on dark and wild seas, and Maggie watched the gray city fade behind a blanket of soft white.

They had a rough sea voyage, and Maggie took sick, vomiting

every day. Five days later she was glad to be in Northland, where muddy roads were the greatest inconvenience a traveler had to contend with.

When they landed, they bought a new wagon, and that night, as they headed north, Orick, who had been very quiet for several days, came to Gallen and Maggie.

"Once we get to the City of Life and petition the judges there to give Tallea the rebirth, what is your heart set to do?"

"I don't know," Gallen said honestly. "Everynne has warned us that the Lords of the Swarms are searching for us, so no place is safe. And some of the servants of the Inhuman escaped in that starship during the battle at Moree. They might tell the Dronon where we are—if Thomas doesn't. For a while, anyway, we'll have to keep moving, search for safer worlds. Why do you ask?"

"Well," Orick growled, plainly very troubled. "You've been a good friend to me, Gallen. But I'm starting to wonder. I'm thinking maybe I should go home, to my own kind."

"But Orick," Maggie whispered, "I'm not sure there are more bears like you."

Orick sniffed, and Maggie petted his snout, rubbed the thick black fur behind his ears. It was a cruel thing to have to say to him, but Maggie knew that Orick was terribly lonely, and she knew that the she-bears in Tihrglas would never give him the companionship he deserved.

"Still," Orick grumbled, "I need to go back home."

"Then I will take you there, my best and dearest friend," Gallen said, and Gallen took the huge bear by the ears and kissed his forehead.

It was a long and lonely drive northward. The seasickness didn't seem to leave Maggie for several days after they landed, yet soon things got back to normal and they arrived in the City of Life near mid-winter. It was a vast city, with great bubbles rising up at the spaceport on its edge. Tall white buildings with lofty spires gleamed against the mountains. A wide and deep river poured through the city, and white snow geese swam, mirrored in its black waters.

There, the group checked into an inn more like something they would find on Fale, a stately building with fountains at its feet, with vast clean rooms and a beautifully constructed hearth where the fire was already laid.

Maggie said goodbye to the Harvester, who had kept her distance and never really become a close friend all during this trip. "Perhaps I will see you sometime," the Harvester said, surprising Maggie with the sentiment.

"Where will you go now?" Maggie asked.

The Harvester pointed east to the mountains. "I have friends in the Vale of the Bock. Ceravanne gave me a seed from my friend, so that at least he will bear offspring, though he will never be reborn. I will raise his child as if it too were my son."

"Then may you find peace," Maggie said, and she gave the woman a hug, then the Harvester drove off alone in the wagon toward the snow-covered mountains.

Straightaway, Maggie, Gallen, and Orick took Tallea's hair sample along with the gem of memories from Gallen's mantle and sought out the Hall of Rebirth—a vast building made of crystal that held more than three hundred thousand workers. There, they presented the items to the judges, along with their petition for her rebirth.

Because of the unseasonable weather, there were few travelers in the city, and three judges, an ageless man and two women, each dressed in white and wearing the platinum mantles of their profession, said they would be able to consider the petition that very evening.

"You can come back in the morning, and hear our decision," one of the judges said.

"Fine," Orick grumbled. "But I'll be waiting out on the steps to hear your word tonight, if you don't mind. I'll come in just when I see that you're closing your doors."

The judges glanced at one another, as if considering the propriety of this inconvenience, and Maggie went back to the inn with Gallen for a bit.

At sunset they returned to the Hall of Rebirth and found Orick waiting. A light snow had begun to fall again, powdering the streets, and the weather seemed only cool. Orick, with his thick pelt, didn't fret about the weather, but after a bit, Maggie found herself stamping her feet, trying to keep them warm.

After an hour, one of the judges came running from the building in his thin white gown, came and took Maggie by the hand, then bent low and put one hand on Orick's shoulder. "Why did you not tell us who you were?" the judge said.

"Would it have made a difference in our petition?" Gallen asked.

"No," the judge said, "but at the very least, I would not have had you standing out here in the snow. Twice these past two weeks, the vanquishers from the Seventh Swarm came to search the city for you. Apparently, the Dronon are scouring the worlds for news of you. Right now, they've headed farther south, to a warmer clime. Still, I expect that they will return. You are in grave danger!"

"We know that they're hunting us," Orick grumbled, "and we're getting damned tired of it! Now, what about Tallea?"

"We have reviewed her memories, and I am happy to report that she will be reborn."

"How soon?" Gallen asked. "We don't want to leave the city without saying goodbye."

"Just as I am equally sure that she will want you to wait for her," the judge said. "Still, she poses a problem for us. She seeks a new body, one that will have to be modified to meet her desires, and then we will have to force-grow it in the vats for a week."

"Yes," Maggie said, "she wanted to be a Roamer."

"How soon?" Orick urged the man.

The judge breathed heavily. "Eight days, maybe ten. I will have the technicians begin within the hour, but it cannot be hurried any faster."

Maggie knew from her mantle that, indeed, the judge was offering to perform a near-miracle. "Thank you," she whispered, hugging him briefly. "Now, you had better get back inside before you freeze."

"Tell me where you are staying," the judge whispered. "I

have friends who were in the resistance. They will know best how to help you stay hidden."

Gallen told him where to find them, and then they headed back toward the inn. They had not gone two blocks before two burly gentlemen in dark cloaks stepped out of a doorway, their warm breath making a cloud of fog around their faces. One of them whispered, "We're friends."

He walked up ahead, taking point, and looked at each cross street, then waved them along. Maggie had felt secure for weeks, but her guardians' behavior unnerved her. For the next four kilometers, they found themselves under such guard, and when they reached the hotel, no less than a dozen such men could be seen loafing at the street corners, watching from roofs.

When they got to their room, Gallen took off his cold winter cloak and hung it in the closet. "It sounds as if we're hotter on this world than we'd anticipated," Gallen said, trying to sound nonchalant.

He went and looked out the window, to the lights burning in the buildings, the snow falling, and Orick went and stood looking out with him.

"Eight days. Eight days from today is Christmas day here on this world, you know," Orick said. "I figured it up on their calendar."

"No one here will be celebrating it," Gallen said. "There are no Catholics here."

"I will be celebrating it," Orick muttered.

"We all will," Maggie said. "That is the day that Tallea is reborn . . . if we're lucky."

"Ah, that would be grand," Gallen said. "But don't get your hopes up."

And so, that following week they spent some time searching for gifts for one another in the shops of the City of Life. The shops carried no fantastic goods, like the near-magical items one might find on Fale. Instead, there were only good woolen coats dyed with bright colors, shoes that would last. Fine cheeses from all corners of the world.

On Christmas eve, in the kitchens at the inn, Maggie cooked

a ham and made rolls and Christmas pies all filled with red cherries and topped with white sugared cream. It was a huge feast, fit for a bear, and by the end of it, Orick's snout was plastered with jam and cream.

Early on Christmas day, they exchanged gifts. Gallen got fine new scabbards for his knives from Orick, and Maggie and Gallen had scrounged together to find Orick a handsome new leather-covered copy of the Bible, for Orick had been obliged, in his haste to escape Tihrglas, to leave his Bible at home.

"Where did you get this?" Orick exclaimed, and Gallen said, "I told you that there were no Catholics on this world. I didn't say that it completely lacked Christians."

"But Ceravanne had never heard of them," Orick said. "How is it she never heard of them?"

"We found the Bible at the spaceport," Maggie finally said, unwilling to keep the bear in suspense. "Travelers from many far worlds come through there. One of them had sold it to a man who trades in . . . curiosities."

Orick and Gallen then gave Maggie their gifts—a light perfume of exotic flavor, and a green silk nightgown. Both of them were fine, indeed.

When they were done, Orick asked, "All right, Maggie, don't keep us hanging at your elbow. What did you get for Gallen?"

"Oh, nothing much," she said honestly. "It's a small gift."

She presented him with a little package wrapped in bright red paper with a white bow.

He opened it. Inside was a pair of booties and a receiving blanket. Orick looked up, his eyes wide with surprise.

"I got sick on the ocean, all right," Maggie said, "but I never did really stop feeling queasy. I checked with the doctors here. It will be a boy."

Gallen grinned, and looked away wistfully. "No blood kin left," he whispered, "so you'll make your own."

"I will," Maggie said, "with your help. And I'll have a dozen of them if I want."

Gallen grabbed her and kissed her roughly, and Orick smiled and left them alone.

It was a pleasant day, with cold suns rising up through the

clouds, and a sky filled with streams of light. Later that day, Orick sat Gallen and Maggie down and read to them from his new Bible about the birth of Jesus in ancient Jerusalem, with King Herod seeking the lives of infants, and angels announcing the birth of the King of Heaven.

That afternoon, there came an insistent pounding at the door. Maggie answered it, and one of the guards stood outside. "You'll want to be leaving the city tonight," he said softly. "The Dronon are back."

"We can't leave yet," Maggie begged. "We're waiting for a friend to get out of the rebirthing vats."

"I checked on it," the guard said. "They're taking her out early. Her body will be a little younger than she wanted, but they're downloading her memories now."

"We can be there right away," Maggie said. She didn't need to tell Gallen and Orick the news. Both of them were already racing around the spacious room, grabbing clothes to pack.

This will have to be a hasty farewell, Maggie realized, and she fretted for Tallea, a young girl who would be traveling alone through the winter, heading south.

In a matter of minutes, they were hurrying through the dark streets. A chill wind had picked up, and it blew frozen snow through the air. Clouds were moving in from the south, a horrendous dark storm.

They reached the great halls, which were closed for the night, just as the snow began to fall. One of the judges had come out to meet them. He was appropriately dressed in a long gray cloak and a sagging peaked hat with a broad brim.

"There you are!" he called as he saw them running up the broad stone steps from the street. "Your friend is reborn, and she awaits you!"

He waved up toward a darkened doorway, and Maggie saw movement behind the thick glass. The door opened a crack, and something hairy moved in the darkness.

Maggie had expected to see a young woman covered with the soft reddish-brown fur of the Roamers, as she remembered them from previous lives. But this creature was more heavily furred than she'd imagined, and its pelt was far darker.

Tallea lowered to all fours, and Maggie heard Orick gulp in astonishment.

"She's a bear!" Gallen said.

"Yes," the judge said. "When we read her memories, we found that at the last moments of her life, she had a change of heart. So we made her the body she desired."

The young black bear was small, and appeared to be only about a year old. She walked down the steps carefully, as if unsure of herself.

But when she was within twenty meters, she suddenly hunkered down and ran toward them at great speed, hit Orick full tilt and knocked the bigger bear over on his side. He grunted, and she jumped up on him playfully, and bit his ear. "Orick! Orick!" she shouted. "Being a bear is great! Why, you're strong as an ox and all dressed in leather!"

"Well, I've never minded it," Orick grunted, not quite sure what to think.

Tallea hugged his neck, wrapping her paws around him, and licked his face. He licked her back shyly, and Tallea growled in his ear, her voice husky with desire, "Ah, Orick, you and I will have a grand time. That is, if you'll have me?"

The little she-bear looked up at him with big brown eyes, and Orick glanced at Maggie and Gallen imploringly, as if they would tell him what to say.

"Do it," Maggie said.

"She's not like the she-bears on your world," the judge told Orick. "She loves you as fiercely as any Caldurian can, and she will stay by your side always."

Orick got up on all fours, then very gently, very passionately, licked the young she-bear's muzzle with his long tongue, softly at first, then more fiercely, and Maggie found herself vaguely disturbed at how sensual a bear's tongue could be.

And after the bears exchanged long, sweet kisses, the guard came through the dark and stood at the foot of the steps. "The Dronon are coming," he urged. "We must hurry away."

"Where are we going?" Tallea asked.

"I don't know," Orick said, though Maggie was sure that Gallen had told him the name of the world. But for the moment, that information seemed to be driven from his mind. Orick just stared at the young she-bear.

"To new worlds, and safety, I hope," Gallen said, and he took Maggie's hand. They hurried down the broad steps and into the streets.

The new falling snow swirled around them in the darkness, and covered their tracks. Within moments, no one would ever have guessed that they had passed along that road.

TOR
BOOKS The Best in Science Fiction

LIEGE-KILLER • Christopher Hinz
"*Liege-Killer* is a genuine page-turner, beautifully written and exciting from start to finish....Don't miss it."—*Locus*

HARVEST OF STARS • Poul Anderson
"A true masterpiece. An important work—not just of science fiction but of contemporary literature. Visionary and beautifully written, elegaic and transcendent, *Harvest of Stars* is the brightest star in Poul Anderson's constellation."
—Keith Ferrell, editor, *Omni*

FIREDANCE • Steven Barnes
SF adventure in 21st century California—by the co-author of *Beowulf's Children*.

ASH OCK • Christopher Hinz
"A well-handled science fiction thriller."—*Kirkus Reviews*

CALDÉ OF THE LONG SUN • Gene Wolfe
The third volume in the critically-acclaimed Book of the Long Sun.
"Dazzling."—*The New York Times*

OF TANGIBLE GHOSTS • L.E. Modesitt, Jr.
Ingenious alternate universe SF from the author of the *Recluce* fantasy series.

THE SHATTERED SPHERE • Roger MacBride Allen
The second book of the Hunted Earth continues the thrilling story that began in *The Ring of Charon*, a daringly original hard science fiction novel.

THE PRICE OF THE STARS • Debra Doyle and
James D. Macdonald
Book One of the Mageworlds—the breakneck SF epic of the most brawling family in the human galaxy!

TOR
BOOKS The Best in Science Fiction

MOTHER OF STORMS • John Barnes
From one of the hottest new names in SF: a shattering epic of global catastrophe, virtual reality, and human courage, in the manner of *Lucifer's Hammer, Neuromancer,* and *The Forge of God.*

THE GOLDEN QUEEN • Dave Wolverton
A heroic band of humans sets out to save the galaxy from alien invaders by the bestselling author of *Star Wars: The Courtship of Princess Leia.*

TROUBLE AND HER FRIENDS • Melissa Scott
Lambda Award-winning cyberpunk SF adventure that the *Philadelphia Inquirer* called "provocative, well-written and thoroughly entertaining."

THE GATHERING FLAME • Debra Doyle and
James D. Macdonald
The Domina of Entibor obeys no law save her own.

WILDLIFE • James Patrick Kelly
"A brilliant evocation of future possibilities that establishes Kelly as a leading shaper of the genre."—*Booklist*

THE VOICES OF HEAVEN • Frederik Pohl
"A solid and engaging read from one of the genre's surest hands."—*Kirkus Reviews*

MOVING MARS • Greg Bear
The Nebula Award-winning novel of war between Earth and its colonists on Mars.

NEPTUNE CROSSING • Jeffrey A. Carver
"A roaring, cross-the-solar-system adventure of the first water."—Jack McDevitt